3

6

A Place To Call Home

A Place To Call Home

JUNE FRANCIS

First published in Great Britain in 2004 by
Allison & Busby Limited
Bon Marche Centre
241-251 Ferndale Road
Brixton, London SW9 8BJ
http://www.allisonandbusby.com

A catalogue record for this book is available from the British Library

ISBN 0 7490 8375 1

Printed and bound by
Creative Print + Design, Ebbw Vale

JUNE FRANCIS was born in Blackpool and moved to Liverpool at an early age. She started writing in her forties producing articles for *My Weekly* and has since gone on to have seventeen novels published. Married with three grown-up sons she enjoys fell-walking, local history and swimming.

Part One

1

Greta Peters dragged the key on the string through the letterbox with cold stiff fingers and unlocked the door. She stepped inside, glad to be out of the freezing fog. Scarcely any daylight filtered through the fanlight that was grimy with dust. Silence greeted her and she experienced a familiar sense of loss. She hated this house. Since the deaths of her younger brother and sister from measles and her mother from pneumonia, it no longer felt like home.

It was miserable coming into an empty, cold house when in the past, at the end of a school day, there were those she loved to greet her. A pan of scouse would be on the fire or a hotpot in the oven, and smiling eyes would welcome her and a loving voice would ask how her day had been.

Greta walked slowly up the lobby, hoping she would feel better once she put a match to the making of the fire her father had set before they left the house that morning. She pushed open the kitchen door and froze. The gaslight was on and there was a fire already burning in the black leaded grate. Her spirits lifted and, crazily, she thought that the past three months had been just a bad dream as she inhaled the delicious smell of fried bread and egg. Her stomach rumbled because she had eaten little that day.

'Mam! Alf! Amy! Are you there?' she whispered, and rushed into the back kitchen but it was empty. She dumped the shopping on the drop-leafed table and slumped over it. Her grief was like a weight in her chest and she wanted to cry but she had told herself that she had to be brave for her dad. She had sensed from the beginning that if she had given way to tears then he would have broken down, too, and neither of them could have coped with that.

Greta straightened and walked like a zombie back into the kitchen and went over to the fire. She rubbed her numb fingers and held them out to the blaze, staring hypnotically into the fire's flaming heart. Could her dad have lit the fire? No! It was too early for him to be home yet, especially with the fog. Unless he had been allowed home early because of the weather but if that was so, then where was he? She experienced a feeling of dread. Dear God, please don't let him have done something terrible! Fear caused her legs to lose their strength and she had to reach out and cling to the mantle-shelf. She took several deep breaths and closed her eyes and, in that moment of silence, heard footsteps overhead.

'Dad!'

Her fear evaporated and she left the kitchen and began to climb the stairs. A sudden blood-curdling yowl caused her to stumble in the darkness and she would have fallen if she hadn't clutched the banister rail. What the hell was that? 'Dad! Dad, are you there?' She rushed up the rest of the stairs and along the landing to the front bedroom.

Light showed beneath the door and filtered through the crack round its edge. The door was not quite shut and she pushed it open wider. Instantly, she saw that the curtains were drawn and that the room looked empty. Her heart was hammering from her dash upstairs and she felt dizzy. For a moment she could only wonder whether her dad, Harry Peters, had gone off his head and was playing some kind of game of hide and seek with her. But no, what was she thinking, he wouldn't be so cruel. Then she noticed that the chocolate box, in which her mother had kept old letters, photographs and other precious knick-knacks was open and its contents spilled out on the blue and white cotton bedspread.

What was that doing there? Greta stepped towards the bed and, as she did so, out of the corner of her eye, glimpsed a youth standing behind the door. She whirled round and for one heart-stopping moment they stared at each other.

Skinny and of medium height, he wore a jacket and trousers that had seen better days. His shabby tweed cap was pushed to the back of his head, so that it rested precariously on his tousled, nut brown hair. His face seemed all bones and angles. He opened his mouth as if to speak and that blood curdling yowl she'd heard earlier was repeated. Then the light went out.

Blinded by the sudden darkness she screamed and then felt him brush past her. The bedroom door slammed and she heard his feet stumbling along the landing and then thundering down the stairs. She half-expected him to fall and thought it would blinking serve him right, frightening the life out of her like that. She heard the front door slam and breathed a sigh of relief.

Now her eyes were accustomed to the darkness, she opened the door and, feeling for the banister rails with her left hand, walked along the landing. Then out of the blue came that yowl again and all courage and common sense deserted her.

She fled down the stairs, through the kitchen and down the yard in the fog. She unbolted the door and darted down the entry to her maternal grandmother's back yard door, but it was locked. She hammered on the wood. 'Gran, are you there?' she shouted, but to no avail.

Greta hesitated before trying the Millers' place next door to her gran's. Mrs Miller was crippled and would not be best pleased to have to come down the yard and let her in, especially in this weather. It would be OK if her daughter, Rene, was home. She had known Greta's mother, Sally, most of her life and, until a fortnight ago, Greta and Harry had seen a fair amount of her. Then suddenly Rene had stopped coming round to their place and helping out.

Greta sighed. It looked like she was going to have to go down the entry and round to her gran's front door and let herself into the house with the key on the string. She just hoped to God that nobody was lying in wait for her.

She jogged along the entry, her hand brushing the walls and doors on her right. Then she spotted the gas lamp on the backyard wall of the end house, signalling that she was approaching the wider, shorter entry that ran between the two streets. Here she slowed, her breath wheezing in her chest, knowing she didn't have far to go.

Soon she was touching garden fences and counting steps, worried about missing her gran's house in the fog. At last she reached it and hurried up the front step. She checked that she had the right number and only then did she wonder whether her gran would be pleased to see her. What if she had not answered the backyard door because she was in bed with her live-in fella? Should she knock first? Sometimes it was a real embarrassment having Cissie Hardcastle for a gran.

Shivering with cold, the girl lifted the knocker and banged it hard. Nothing happened. She tried again and still there was no sound of footsteps hurrying down the lobby to let her in. Perhaps her gran really wasn't in. Greta delayed no longer. She would freeze if she didn't get indoors soon. She fumbled through the letter box for the key on the string but it was not there! What had happened to it? Dismayed, Greta slumped against the door. Then, to her relief, she heard the sound of footsteps coming down the street and shot to her feet.

Rene Miller peered through the fog which hung, like a heavy blanket, over Liverpool that February evening in 1939, not only muffling sound but also distorting landmarks. She could hear someone calling and, despite her sore feet, she hurried, thinking something might have happened to her mother. Then she recognised the voice.

'Is that you, Greta?' she called.

'Yes!' answered the girl. 'And I need you! I don't want to go back into our house on my own! There was someone in there. He lit the fire and fried himself an egg … the cheeky thing! But then after I heard our front door slam, I heard him again, so either he didn't leave or-or he-he was a g-ghost!'

'A ghost!' exclaimed Rene in her husky voice.

'A ghost!' echoed the girl, as she swam into Rene's vision.

Greta was a slender figure in a well-worn, navy blue winter coat that had once belonged to her mother. On her head she wore a hand-knitted red hat, its plaited ties fastened in a bow beneath her chin, and two, thick, dark plaits of hair dangled down over the slight swell of her breasts. She was shivering as she stood on the foot high wall that fronted the wooden fence on which she was leaning. She gazed up at Rene from worried hazel eyes that seemed huge in her thin, sallow face.

'I presume you didn't get an answer at your gran's?' said Rene.

'No! And I couldn't find the key on the string either.'

'Perhaps it broke off or she's taken it away. There was a big argument going on in there last night and it sounded like things were getting thrown about. Eventually we heard Cecil shouting something and then the front door slammed.'

Greta's eyes widened. 'You think he's left?'

'Sounded like it. It all went quiet after that.' Rene hoped last night's row was the last in the string of arguments that had gone on since Christmas. Perhaps now Cecil had gone her mother, Vera, would sleep nights and not be rousing Rene from her bed to make her cup of tea or get out the po.

Greta looked relieved. 'Mam would have been glad. Although, do you think she'll get another? I remember hearing Mam and Dad talking, saying they hadn't minded so much when she lived with

14

Marty because they'd been together years but since he died she's just gone from bad to worse.'

'It was like a blow to her when Marty died,' said Rene in a low voice. 'I think she's been lonely. Anyway, never mind your gran right now … what was it you were saying about a youth and a terrible yowling noise?'

'Oh yes!' Greta heaved an enormous sigh. 'I heard this horrible yowling sound like a soul in torment! Three times I heard it … the final time after the door had slammed and I thought he'd gone … but-but perhaps that was a trick and he's still in the house. I don't want to be a nuisance, Rene, but I would appreciate it if you'd come back with me,' she added earnestly.

Rene was tired after her walk from the dried goods and wine importers and distributors in the city centre where she worked as an invoice clerk. She would have a meal to make when she got in. Her mother's rheumatism had worsened since Rene's father had died, and if it was not for Wilf, the lodger, and the neighbours, Rene would never have managed to hold on to her full time job. Once she arrived home, her mother expected Rene to wait on her hand and foot. She would hit the roof if she knew her daughter was contemplating going round to the Peters' house. It was Vera who was responsible for Rene no longer helping them out. She still felt angry and wretched when she thought about the vile words her mother had said about her and Harry.

Greta reached out and touched her arm. 'I've been thinking and I don't think that youth could really have been a ghost. A ghost can't light a fire, can it? An-And it wouldn't fry an egg either, w-would it?'

'Probably not!' Rene smiled, thinking about the film she and Wilf had taken her mother to see on Saturday evening. It had been a real effort to get her there but Vera loved a good horror and she had been quite pleasant afterwards, so it had been worthwhile. 'More likely it was just your plain, common burglar. D'you know if he got away with anything?'

Greta shook her head. 'No! But Mam's memory box was on the bed … I saw that first … then I spotted him and he opened his mouth an-and yowled … an-and then as if by magic the light went out and he slipped out of the room.'

'I see,' said Rene softly, wondering if the girl was making the whole thing up to get her round to the house. She knew how badly the deaths in the family had affected Greta and Harry. She had been deeply saddened herself. She had been Amy's godmother and watched both of the children who had died grow from babies. Rene also had a strong feeling that perhaps Sally might not have succumbed to pneumonia if her younger children had survived.

'I swear it wasn't my imagination, although since Mam and the kids have gone, it's really … spooky in our house and … ' Her voice faltered.

'I know,' said Rene, squeezing Greta's hand. 'I'll come with you and we'll get this sorted out.'

Rene gripped her handbag tightly in her other hand, thinking she could use it as a weapon if she had to. If there really had been a youth in the house that was worrying. Since the Depression there were thousands of desperate people out there.

They hurried down the street and turned into the entry. Almost immediately Rene's foot slipped on the wet cobbles. 'Be careful here,' she warned.

'I hate the fog,' said Greta, clutching at Rene. 'It makes things even more scary.'

Rene did not argue with that and understood when Greta kept giving her hand little squeezes. It was somehow comforting. As they came to the next entry, Rene said, 'You said … your mother's memory box. Was there anything of value in there?'

'Nothing worth money,' replied Greta. 'I mean if there was, I'm sure Mam would have hocked it when Dad was out of work a few winters ago. Although, she did hang on to a couple of things against … a-a real …rainy day.' Greta swallowed noisily.

Rene hugged the girl against her, remembering so many difficult times, not only for the Peters, but also for herself and her mother. The year Harry Peters had been out of work, her father had died after years of suffering from the wounds he had received in the Great War. The burden of keeping the household going had fallen completely on Rene's shoulders and life would have been even more difficult if Wilf Murphy, retired seaman, had not turned up on their doorstep looking for rooms. He had lodged with them ever since.

They came to the Peters' door, which stood ajar. Greta bit her lip. 'I must have forgotten to shut it in the rush to get away.'

'It doesn't matter now,' said Rene, and urged the girl inside the yard.

They hurried past the outside lavatory and the small lean-to where in happier days Harry had spent time making toys for his children for Christmas. A lump rose in Rene's throat but she forced it down and pushed open the back kitchen door. Immediately the smell of fried bread and egg filled her nostrils and she realised how hungry she was, but food was going to have to wait. She stood a moment listening, but could only hear the sound of their breathing, so she led the way through into the kitchen.

Except for the glow of the fire, the room was still in darkness. 'Let's have a light on things,' said Rene. 'Where are the matches?'

'On the shelf next to the fireplace but we need a penny for the meter and I'm all out of pennies,' said Greta.

'I think I can spare you a penny,' said Rene with a smile.

'Thanks! I'm sure the light will chase the ghosts away,' said Greta brightly.

There are ghosts here, thought Rene, but they don't go bump in the night in the accepted sense. Even so they needed to be laid to rest, but that was easier said than done. Her heart ached as she remembered the love and laughter that had once filled this house. She removed her gloves and rammed them into her coat pockets. Then she reached for her handbag and rummaged for her purse. She took out a penny, and after dropping her handbag on a chair, she headed for the parlour. Greta was close on her heels.

Despite the darkness, Rene found the meter cupboard with no trouble. She crouched in front of it and discovered the door was ajar. Had the youth broken into the meter? Any sympathy she might have felt for him disappeared but then a growl from the depths of the cupboard caused her to rethink that idea and she fell back on her haunches, her pulses racing.

'What is it?' demanded Greta, kneeling beside her.

Rene gave no answer but leaned forward and cautiously reached into the cupboard again. A hiss, a meow, and a stinging pain as claws raked the back of her hand. 'Hell, and bloo – ming hell!' she exclaimed, clutching her hand and bringing it up to her mouth to lick where it hurt. 'I think this is your ghost! There's a cat in here!'

Greta was silent a moment before saying slowly, 'I wonder if it's that moggy that's been hanging round our back door! Dad told me I wasn't to encourage it because you know what he's like when he's round cats. What's it doing in the gas cupboard?'

'Whatever it's doing, it can't stay here,' said Rene, taking a handkerchief from her pocket and wrapping it round her injured hand. Then in a soothing voice, she said, 'Come on, Mog, behave yourself, so we can have a light on things.' She hummed *Rock a-bye-baby, on the treetops* as her fingers edged towards the meter slot. A rumbling growl accompanied her movements, but it was not until the coin dropped into the metal box inside the meter, that the cat lashed out again and this time Rene was too swift for it and escaped injury.

She got to her feet and hurried out of the parlour and into the kitchen. As she lit the gaslight, she thought a shadowy figure flittered across the far wall and could have sworn that she heard the gentle whisper of voices. She shuddered. Dear God! No wonder Greta had the spooks!

She replaced the matches on the shelf, then took the shovel from the bucket of coal next to the fireplace and heaped coal onto the fire. How could Harry stand this place? It wasn't a home anymore, just somewhere for him and his daughter to rest at the end of the day. If only her mother was less dependant and possessive, in time she could have helped make this a home once more. What must Harry have thought when she had stopped coming round without a word of explanation? Not that he had said a word to encourage her to defy her mother, not one word that might have hinted that he needed her. Yet before then, despite the bleakness of his expression, she had sensed that he found some comfort in her presence in the house as she had helped Greta with the washing and ironing and preparation of meals.

Rene sighed. Having to refrain from helping Harry and Greta, she had often wished Cissie Hardcastle's nature was more maternal. Rene did not doubt that Cissie grieved for her daughter and her grandchildren in her own way, but she did not show it. She and Harry might have drawn some comfort from each other if they had been the sort to unburden themselves on other people. Rene thought about the derogatory things her mother had said about Cissie's husband upping sticks and vanishing well before the Great War and the manner of things she had done to keep her head above water and support her children. She had had little thanks for it from her two sons, who had gone to fight in the Great War. Both had survived, one marrying a girl from the south of England and never bothering to get in touch again. The other, having suffered from shell-shock, had moved to the comparative peace of the Welsh mountains, leaving Cissie and Sally to fend for themselves. Rene often pondered on the different ways women left without their menfolk managed to survive.

'Well?' demanded Greta.

Rene spun round. The girl stood in the doorway, her narrow shoulders hunched, her arms crossed over her breasts, hugging herself.

'Well what?' asked Rene.

'What are we going to do about the moggy?'

Rene smiled and reached for the matches. 'Let's have a look at her.' She touched Greta's cheek as she passed. It was cold. 'Five minutes, then you get in front of that fire, kid,' she said firmly.

It took less time than that for the scrawny tabby cat and her four mewling kittens to be revealed. 'Aren't they tiny?' marvelled Greta, reaching out a hand.

'Don't!' warned Rene, grabbing the girl's wrist and dragging her away from the cupboard.

At that moment footsteps sounded in the street. Greta turned her face up to Rene's and her hazel eyes widened. 'Dad! Blinking heck! He's not going to like this! What are we going to do?'

Rene could only think to shut the cupboard door and get out of the parlour. Although Harry was bound to have noticed the light was on when he came up the step, he was not to know there was a cat in the cupboard just yet. She stretched up and turned off the gaslight, before thrusting Greta out of the room and into the lobby, nervous at the thought of facing him.

The front door opened and Rene stared at the man who stood in the entrance. At thirty-six, he was two years her senior and at five foot, ten inches, their eyes met almost on a level. She was tall for a woman, standing five feet eight inches in her stocking feet, and built on generous lines, with long legs and a large bosom. From childhood she had been teased about her height and people had, more often than not, judged her older than her years.

'Rene?' he said, peering at her through the darkness. 'I didn't expect to see you round here again. What are you doing?' His voice sounded lifeless.

She swallowed, trying to ease the tightness in her throat. 'Someone was in the house and Greta came looking for help,' she rasped.

'What d'you mean … someone? A burglar? Is that why you were in the parlour? Has the meter been robbed?'

Rene was glad that she had startled him into life. Harry would have gone in there if she had not stopped him by grabbing his arm. Immediately she was aware of the swell of muscle beneath the damp fabric, as well as the acrid smell of cement and brick dust.

'Don't, Harry! I put a penny in there and it didn't sound empty … and I'd better tell you now … there's a cat with kittens in the cupboard.'

He turned towards his daughter. 'What did I tell you about not encouraging that cat?' His tone was sharp.

'I didn't!' she insisted, slipping a hand through Rene's arm. 'It must have got in when the youth got in.'

'Get rid of it!' croaked Harry. 'Then you can tell me about this youth!' He freed himself from Rene's grasp and, closing the front door, strode up the lobby and into the kitchen.

Rene and Greta peered at one another through the dimness of the unlit lobby. 'I knew he'd say that!' said the girl sadly. 'A cat would have made this place feel more homely but there it is. You-you won't have the kittens drowned, will you, Rene?'

Rene did not want the kittens but she knew that she could not let them be drowned. 'Of course not,' she said firmly. Then she followed Harry into the kitchen.

He had taken off his gaberdine mackintosh, revealing building-dust covered brown corduroy trousers and a grey shirt beneath a fair-isle patterned pullover. He dropped the coat over the back of a fireside chair and, removing a tweed cap, slung it at the hook on the back of the door. He ran a work-roughened hand through curling black hair and stared at her, his expression grim. 'Why the hell couldn't she go bothering her grandmother instead of you? You shouldn't be here! Our problems aren't yours. You have enough on your hands with your mother.'

'You're telling me something I already know, but that doesn't mean I don't want to help you,' said Rene, her green eyes concerned. She folded her arms across her breasts and leaned against the wall next to the door. 'Besides, Greta did go to Mrs Hardcastle's but couldn't get an answer and the key on the string wasn't there. Mrs Hardcastle had a helluva row with Cecil last night. From the way the house shook when he slammed the front door, he's probably gone for good.'

Instantly Harry's expression changed. 'You're sure?'

'Mam and me could hear almost every word. He accused her of being too wrapped up in herself and being no fun anymore. He wanted her to go dancing with him but she said there was nothing doing. That he was a selfish swine! Hadn't she lost her daughter and two of her grandchildren! Also, that she had her part-time job to go to. He hated her having that job. I can't see him coming back.'

Harry sighed, 'I bloody hope not! I could never see what she saw in him.' He rested an arm along the mantelpiece, and drummed his fingers on the cream painted wood. 'Thanks for telling me,' he muttered, then after a moment's hesitation, added, 'This youth … did he take anything? Do you know?'

She shrugged. 'As far as I know he fried himself an egg and some bread and turned over Sally's memory box.'

He raised his eyebrows. 'Bloody cheek! He wouldn't have found much in there. Only … ' He paused, swallowed, and his dark brows hooded his eyes so that she could not read his expression. 'Only memories.' His voice was hoarse. 'But if he was frying eggs and bread then he's someone down on his bloody luck, so I'm not going to get myself worked up about it.'

'He might have thought there was jewellery in the box,' said Rene.

He made a noise in his throat. 'The only jewellery Sally had was her wedding ring and that brooch Mrs Armstrong, whom she was in service to, gave her. I have that hidden somewhere else. I suppose I should get rid of the box, only …'

'You didn't have the heart,' she finished for him.

He took a deep breath. 'Have you been home? Does your mother know you're here?'

'No!'

'Then you'd best be going.' He didn't look at her. 'She'll work herself up into a state thinking you're out in the fog.'

'I don't plan on enlightening her that I've been somewhere else.'

'Too right! You don't want her knowing you've been here.' He looked into the fire.

She murmured a goodnight, wondering why he should say that, and left.

It was only when Rene reached her front door that she realised that she had left her handbag behind. Fortunately the Millers' key was on its string, enabling neighbours to pop in and out to see if her mother needed any help. Vera could be very sweet to people when they served her purpose. Rene was about to enter the house when a voice said, 'Is that you, Wilf?'

'Not unless I've grown a moustache and shrunk four inches,' said Rene, turning to her next door neighbour. 'What d'you want him for, Mrs Hardcastle?'

Wilf was a quiet man, who had never married. He had been a ship's chippy, who, just like Harry, could turn his hands to most things and would do anything for most people. Yet he was forever making excuses not to do jobs for the next door neighbour. Rene guessed he was terrified of what Cissie Hardcastle might do to him if she was ever to get her hands on him.

'Very funny! Yer should be on the stage at the *Empire*.' The fag dangling from Cissie's painted lips jiggled as she spoke. 'I need a chair fixin'! I suppose I'll have to go round to Harry's. Isn't this fog bleedin' awful? It doesn't do me chest any good but I've got to get to work. I can't let people down and the customers like to see me behind the bar.' She patted her peroxide blonde hair, which was fashioned in sausage curls.

Rene almost laughed out loud. Cissie's sixtieth birthday must have come and gone years ago. It didn't take much of a mathematician to work that out. She was mutton dressed as lamb and had provided the neighbours with plenty of entertainment in her time.

'Greta knocked on your back door earlier but got no answer.'

Cissie scowled. 'I need me beauty sleep with working evenings at the pub … and then, you must have heard the row! I've thrown my fella out, yer know?' She drew on her cigarette, choked and burst out coughing.

'Is that how it was?'

'Aye!' gasped Cissie, her eyes watering.

'Want me to bang you on the back?' offered Rene.

Cissie shook her head, and managed to stop coughing. She wafted smoke in Rene's direction with podgy, nicotine stained fingers. 'I'm fine,' she wheezed.

'That's alright then. Greta found a burglar in the house, so I went round there with her.'

'A burglar! What kind of burglar?'

Rene smiled faintly. 'A young one who cooked himself egg and fried bread. It doesn't look like he's stolen anything else at the moment.' She hesitated before adding, 'Do me a favour, Mrs Hardcastle, don't say anything about my having been round there to anyone. I-I don't want to worry Mother with her being the way she is.'

Cissie looked at her knowingly and tapped her nose. 'Your secret's safe with me, girl. I know Vera better than you do, believe me!'

Rene stared at her with a fixed smile. 'Well, you've known her a long time, I know that. I'm going in. Don't go exposing too much flesh, Mrs Hardcastle. You don't want to catch a chill,' she said seriously. "Tarrah!' She slipped inside and closed the door.

'You're bleedin' hardfaced, you are!' shouted Cissie.

Rene was startled by the words but realised she must have said something that had offended her moody neighbour. She stuck her tongue out at the door and then hurried up the darkened lobby, calling 'I'm home!' She unbuttoned her coat on the move, stuffing her hat in a pocket before hanging her coat on a hook among several on a piece of wood nailed to the wall at the foot of the stairs.

As she entered the kitchen, her mother looked up. The lines of her bony face were dragged down and her mouth was a thin straight line. 'You're late, madam! I thought you might have left early with the fog.'

'No, Mother! Did one of the neighbours get the liver as I asked?'

Vera pursed her lips. 'Liver! You know I hate offal! Mrs Woods got us a rabbit and even skinned it for us and put it in the pan with some carrot, onion and rice. Can't you smell it?'

Rene sniffed. 'Come to think of it … I can! That was kind of her. But rabbit, Mother! Liver would have been cheaper.'

Vera sniffed. 'I don't know what you do with our money. I'm not well. I need good food to keep my strength up.'

Our money! thought Rene indignantly. She went over to the black leaded grate and taking the pan of stew from the hob, she placed it on the fire. Her mother paid nothing into the kitty. If Rene's father had died on the battlefield then she would have received a teensy pension from the government. As it was, she didn't and she resented that. Rene's mother hadn't always been such a moaner and so critical of everything her daughter did. Rene put it down to the pain she suffered with the rheumatism. If only that hadn't developed the way it had, then her mother would have been able to get some kind of part time work after she was widowed: cleaning, washing or ironing. 'I take it that Wilf hasn't arrived home yet?' said Rene.

'Does it look like he's home?' muttered Vera, lowering her eyes to the newspaper on her lap.

'He could be in his room. Ready for your rabbit stew in five minutes?'

'What d'you think I've been waiting for all these hours? I don't know why you can't get a job nearer home, then you could nip in at lunchtime and see how I am,' said Vera querulously.

'You mean go back to being a shop girl or work in the laundry or a factory? I worked hard at night school to get my typing qualifications so I could get office work as Dad wanted.' Rene moved over to the sideboard and took two bowls out of the cupboard and placed them on the table next to the window, that overlooked the back yard. She sat down and eased off her shoes. 'I like where I work. It's interesting.' She also liked the office being within walking distance of Church Street and not too far from the Pierhead. During the long summer evenings, there was nothing Rene enjoyed more than going down to the Mersey and watching the ships go by before having to make her way home. There was little opportunity for her to do what she wanted in her time off.

'As you've grown older you've got selfish, that's what you have,' moaned Vera. 'One of these days you'll come in from work and find me like a tree in winter with its branches all twisted and sticking out, unable to move.'

'You should try and keep on the move, Mother, you're 57 not 87!' Rene held her stocking feet out to the fire to thaw her frozen toes.

'You'll get chilblains like that.'

Rene let the words go over her head. 'Miss Birkett said knitting is good for helping prevent the fingers from stiffening up.'

Vera said moodily, 'It's alright for her to talk. She's got the shop and only herself to think about. Anyway I don't want to talk about Miss Snooty. I thought I heard raised voices outside. Was it Cissie Hardcastle you were talking to?'

24

Rene chuckled. 'She told me she'd thrown Cecil out.'

'He walked out on her more like!' Vera sniffed, a satisfied expression on her face.

'She thought I was Wilf and wanted him to go in there and fix a broken chair.'

'She's got a nerve!' Vera sat up straight and the newspaper fell onto the rag rug in front of the fire. 'She'd expect him to do it buckshee ... would choose to forget he's only got his old age pension and his savings. Mind you, knowing her she'd think of another way to pay him. Have his trousers off and be giving him it in no time, I bet.'

Rene was as shocked by the crudeness of her mother's comment as she had been by the words she had shouted at her after returning from Harry's house one evening. *You're a frustrated old maid, prepared to give him what he's missing because you've had a pash on him for years. All the neighbours are talking about you. So you've got to stop going round there, my girl!* Rene had wanted to tell her mother to wash her mouth out with soap but had been so stunned and hurt that she had been speechless.

Rene picked up a ladle and dipped it into the stew. 'You could be wrong about Cissie Hardcastle. It could be that she'll turn over a new leaf now Cecil's gone.'

Vera's eyes narrowed as she looked at her daughter. 'Leopards don't change their spots.'

Rene returned her stare and said politely, 'Are you having your stew on a tray on your knee or d'you want me to help you to the table?'

'I'll have it at the table ... and I'll manage without your help, madam!' Vera pushed herself up from the chair, which had an extra cushion, enabling her to get to her feet more easily. 'Pass me my stick!' she ordered.

Rene picked up the stick, leaning against the chair, and handed it to her. Then, ignoring her mother, she went and sat at the table and picked up her spoon. Once seated at the table Vera said, 'So what's been going on at your place today?'

'One of the wine cellars is being turned into an air raid shelter,' murmured Rene.

Vera's black button eyes widened in dismay. 'Your boss must think there really is going to be a war.'

'He's just being prepared. Better that than leaving things too late if it was to come to a fight with Germany. You mustn't worry, Mother!'

'Easy for you to say that, girl. You were too young to remember what the last war was like.' Vera chomped on her lower lip.

Rene didn't bother arguing with her but actually she remembered quite a lot. She could recall the sense of horror and misery that seemed in the very air she breathed, the women with pale, drawn, grief-stricken faces, shop windows being smashed, food shortages ... and never would she forget her dad coming home a different man from the one she had known. His arrival had filled her with confusion and fear ... the compassion had come later. It had taken a couple of years for them to be able to talk and feel comfortable with each other again. Together they had attended the Remembrance Day services that were held at the newly built cenotaph in Lime Street. Paying his respects to his dead comrades had somehow helped him to cope with his guilt for still being alive.

'I haven't forgotten what it did to my father,' said Rene firmly, filling two teacups. 'And all the women, like Miss Birkett, who never got to marry because they lost boyfriends and fiancés.'

'She never had to struggle,' sneered Vera, holding her spoon awkwardly between swollen, crooked fingers. 'And men can be more trouble than they're worth. You mark my words, madam! You're better off without a husband as long as you can earn your own living.'

'So you keep saying ... but we couldn't manage half so well without Wilf being here,' said Rene, an edge to her voice. She had never spoken to her mother of the offer of marriage she had received that she had turned down, believing not only that her duty lay in looking after her mother, but also that there was only one man that she had ever felt passionate about and that was Harry, whom Sally had met first and laid claim to.

Vera looked vexed. 'A lodger's not the same. Now shut up and let me eat in peace.'

Rene was glad to do just that. She had not forgotten that she had left her handbag at Harry's and was wondering what excuse she could give to get out of the house and go and collect it. Probably best to wait until Wilf came in, then she could slip out the back way and her mother would think she had just gone to the lavatory. The thought of seeing Harry again so soon caused a frisson of excitement to tremble down her spine.

'I reckon the Civil War in Spain's as good as over since the Italians stepped in and helped Franco capture Barcelona last month,' said Vera loudly, startling her daughter out of her reverie. 'Once that happens everything'll calm down in Europe.'

Rene did not argue but thought that Mussolini was another one of them fascists like Hitler and she didn't trust either of them as far as she could throw them. Thankfully, before Vera could get into her stride, there was a sound at the door and Wilf entered the kitchen.

His grey moustache drooped due to the damp but his lined, weathered face wore a cheerful expression. Rene stood up and relieved him of his seaman's greatcoat and hustled him over to the fire. He was the grandfather she had never had and she was very fond of him. 'I couldn't see a hand in front of me face down at the Pierhead,' he said.

'One of these days you'll fall in a dock and we won't see *you* again,' said Vera, waving a fork at him. 'You'd be best staying here some days, Wilf. I can't understand you, at your age, wanting to be down there every day.'

Rene and Wilf exchanged looks and he winked at her. 'Keeps me on the go, girl,' he said.

Vera said something that Rene did not catch because she was no longer listening. Instead she was dishing up Wilf's stew. As soon as he sat down and began talking to Vera, Rene slipped out of the kitchen and went down the yard. As she crossed the entry, Rene could hear the mournful sound of a ship's foghorn on the Mersey, and hoped the weather would clear by tomorrow.

She was about to press down the latch on Harry's yard door when it opened from the other side and Cissie appeared. She was carrying a large cardboard box and on one arm hung two handbags. She looked red in the face and started when she saw Rene. 'I know what you're doing here, but yer almost bleedin' frightened me to death appearing suddenly like that.'

'Sorry!' Rene smiled. 'I see you've my handbag.'

'I've got something else for yer ennal. He bleedin' forced them on me, his chest wheezing and sneezing his head off.'

Rene realised what was in the cardboard box. She had forgotten about the cat and its kittens. 'Poor Harry!'

'Never mind poor bleedin' Harry! Warrabout me? I've got work to go to right now. I can't be seein' to finding a home for a bleedin' cat and its kittens ... but at least ... ' She stopped abruptly, and surprised Rene with a beaming smile. 'I've got some news for yer. It's gonna surprise the life out of yer.'

'What's that?' said Rene cautiously, wondering whether Cissie'd already found another fancy man.

'I've asked them to come and live with me.'

'Who?'

'Harry and me granddaughter, of course!'

Rene could only stare.

'Well, say somethin'!'

'You mean you and Harry living under the same roof? Will it work?'

Cissie's smile evaporated and she sniffed. 'And why shouldn't it? It's the perfect answer! I can't afford to live by meself and that bleedin' house is getting him down. Even I can sense that. The only bloody thing wrong is that he's like Cecil and wants me to give up me job. I told him I could have a fire and a hot meal ready for Greta and him when they come in without doing that.'

'So you could,' agreed Rene, amused. 'Did he accept that?'

'He said we could see how it worked out.'

'Makes sense. Is there anything I can do to help?'

Cissie gazed at her across the top of the box and her face brightened. 'I think yer really mean that. Here yer are, girl ... take this!' She shoved the box at Rene, who clutched it frantically as it threatened to slip to the ground. The old woman chuckled and placed Rene's handbag on top of the box. 'Thanks, girl. See yer around.'

'But ...!' cried Rene, clinging to the box as it lurched in her arms, scrabbling and mewing coming from its interior.

'Tatty bye,' called Cissie, and disappeared into the fog.

Exasperated, Rene stared after her but she knew there was only one thing to do and that was to take the tabby and its offspring home with her. At least their presence would provide her mother with company and some entertainment. Cats were creatures Vera had voiced a liking for ... although, after their last one, Ginger, had died, she had vowed to have no more. Rene did not doubt that after an initial moan her mother would relent and make them welcome. As for where they had come from, Rene would tell Vera that she had found them in a box by the bin.

2

Rene drew back the curtain in her mother's bedroom, letting the morning light flood in. Only a few days ago, gales had caused the Crosby lightship to snap its mooring and be cast adrift in the Mersey but today, the first Sunday in March, felt like spring. She peered down into the street and spotted Harry and Greta standing in the middle of the road, talking to Miss Birkett who lived just across the way from the Millers. Rene's eyes lingered on the black hair that curled in the nape of Harry's neck and felt an urge to rush out and ruffle those curls. Crackers! She was going crackers. He did not want her, he'd been mad about Sally. Still, maybe she should go down later and ask if he needed any help. Surely if they were to be neighbours, he'd appreciate a touch of neighbourliness?

'What are yer staring at? Is it Harry Peters and his girl moving in next door?' asked Vera suspiciously.

Rene groaned inwardly. 'How did you guess, Mother?'

'I'm psychic. Will yer come away from there!' she called.

Rebelliously, Rene stayed where she was. 'They've a fine day for the move.'

'Aye! But we don't want him seeing you nosing,' muttered Vera.

'He's not looking up here. They're talking to Miss Birkett.'

'I wonder what about.'

Rene shrugged. 'Perhaps she's welcoming them to the street. She'll be one of the first to be glad that Cissie's got family living with her.'

'He'll stop her gallop that's for sure. But will you come away,' said Vera fretfully. 'I'm waiting for you to tie me shoelaces.'

Reluctantly, Rene moved away from the window, thinking about her dream last night. It could have been a scene from a Hollywood film with Harry playing the role generally taken by Douglas Fairbanks Jnr or Cary Grant. Remnants of how she had felt still clung and words sang in her head about birds and bees, educated fleas and falling in love. A blush warmed her cheeks and, absent-mindedly, she sat down beside her mother on the bed.

'Expecting me to get me foot up there, are you?' said Vera sarcastically. 'On your knees, madam!' She dropped her voice to a whisper. 'Wilf's still in his bedroom and I need to go to the lav so get a move on!'

'Sorry, Mother.' Rene sank to her knees and fastened the brown shoelaces. Then she helped Vera to her feet and opened the bedroom door. They managed to get to the bottom of the stairs without any mishap. Once in the back kitchen, she handed Vera her walking stick, and opened the back door for her and helped her down the step into the yard, before returning upstairs to fetch her mother's breakfast tray.

Rene took the opportunity to glance out of the window again and saw that Harry and Greta were still talking to Miss Birkett. She hurried downstairs and went out the front, glad that she had not lingered in bed but had given herself plenty of time to wash and put on her Sunday best that morning. This consisted of a green V-necked hand-knitted sweater and a brown skirt that came just below the knee, which she'd bought from *C & A Mode* in the January sales. Trembling slightly with a mixture of excitement and nerves, she walked down the step, just in time to see Miss Birkett striding up the street, her Bible and prayer book under her arm. Harry and Greta were heading for Cissie's front door.

Rene smiled. 'Hi, Harry! Hi, Greta! You all finished or would you like some help?'

Harry's vivid blue eyes met hers and, for a moment, she'd have sworn he was pleased to see her, but then it was as if a shutter came down. When he spoke, his voice was gruff, 'No thanks! We're nearly done.'

Disappointed but still determined, Rene murmured, 'Cup of tea? Moving must be thirsty work.'

He hesitated. 'Sorry! I've still some things to do that only I can see to. Anyway, you must be busy what with your mother and Wilf, and Sunday dinner to get ready.'

'How right you are! Never a dull moment in our house!' she said brightly, and with an ache inside that felt like a weight, she made to go indoors, only to be stopped on the threshold by a question from Greta. 'How are the kittens?'

Rene whirled round and smiled. 'Why don't you come and look when you're not so busy helping your dad?'

Greta looked at Harry, wrinkled her pert nose, and said hopefully, 'Can I?'

A faint smile lit his eyes. 'OK! Go now but don't take forever and don't get hairs on you. I need your help in sorting what to keep of your mam's bits and pieces.' He vanished indoors.

Greta hurried to catch up with Rene and burst into speech immediately. 'I didn't think the move would be so hard on him. He's had a face on him for days like a week of wet Sundays. He's been almost as bad as just after Mam died.'

'It's a big step leaving the house where he took your mam as a bride,' said Rene. 'How do you feel about living with your gran?'

Greta shrugged. 'I wasn't asked. Dad told me it would be better for me … that there were things that only an older woman could help me with. I suppose it's something that he hasn't thought about marrying again just to provide me with a new mother. That's what a girl in school's dad did and she and her new mother hate each other.'

'It's a difficult age, thirteen,' said Rene, leading the way into the kitchen.

Greta squared her shoulders and tilted her chin. 'I'll be fourteen in October! In six months I'll be leaving school and getting a job.'

Rene smiled. 'Then make the most of your days of freedom before starting work.'

Greta's expression was incredulous. 'What freedom? You can tell it's years since you were at school. I can't wait to leave and be a better help to Dad. I've already got a little Saturday job. Miss Birkett asked me would I like to do her messages while she's in the shop.'

'Great!' said Rene, thinking, so that was what the conversation had been about in the street. Good for Miss Birkett!

There was no sign of Vera in the kitchen, so Rene left Greta kneeling on the floor beside the cut down cardboard box with mother cat and kittens inside and went outside. She found her mother leaning against the lavatory door, one hand resting on her walking stick. 'Did you hear them?' she asked, her eyes dark with malicious excitement.

'Hear what?' asked Rene.

Immediately a youthful voice provided the answer. 'Will yer bloody let me go, mister? I haven't taken nuthin'! There's little I'd give yer tuppence for on that handcart!'

'Nobody's asking your opinion, lad! What I want to know is what you're doing up this jigger? I haven't seen your face around here before.'

'That's Harry,' whispered Vera.

Rene rolled her eyes. She folded her arms and rested a shoulder against the wall and listened.

'Know everybody in the neighbourhood, do yer?' said the other voice.

'Less of the bloody cheek! You either explain to me what you're up to or you can say your piece to the bobby,' said Harry, sounding grim.

At that moment Greta came out into the yard. 'Was that Dad's voice I heard?' she asked.

Rene nodded and, with a sparkle in her eye, said, 'Shall we have a look?' And without waiting for the girl's answer, she opened the gate and stepped into the entry. Greta followed but Vera hung back, holding the door open by leaning against it. They weren't the only ones drawn by the voices. Several of their neighbours had come out of their yards to see what was going on.

A handcart loaded with odd bits and pieces from Harry and Greta's house, including a flowered vase, a golliwog, a wooden box twice the size of a shoebox, and Sally's chocolate box of memories, blocked the passage a few feet away. Harry stood at one end of the cart, holding a youth aloft by the lapels of a tweed jacket that was frayed at elbows and cuffs. As he struggled, he appeared in danger of losing his trousers, which were held up by a length of rope. With one hand, he was helping to keep them in place while with the other he was attempting to loosen Harry's grip on his collar. His face was narrow with high cheekbones and his expression was tight with anger.

Greta stared at him and then gasped, 'That's him!' She shot out an arm and pointed a finger. 'He was the one in your bedroom, Dad! He must be daft to come back here. What's he after?'

Harry's frown deepened and he hoisted the youth over to where Greta was standing. 'Are you sure, luv? Have a good look at him!'

Greta peered into his face and the youth drew back his head. 'I've never seen her before in me life!' he muttered.

'You're a liar!' said Greta fiercely. 'I only saw you for a few moments but I haven't forgotten what you look like. You frightened the life out of me.'

The youth's lips curled in a smile of derision. 'You didn't half scream but it wasn't me that made that yowling.'

'You're admitting you were there, though, now, are you?' she said robustly.

The young man said warily, 'I let myself in with the key on the string that's hardly breaking and entering.' He glanced at Harry. 'Now how about putting me down? The air's a bit rarefied up here.'

'Smart Alec, aren't you?' said Harry, heaving the lad up several more inches and bringing the edges of his jacket closer together and squeezing.

'You're choking me,' he gasped.

Rene took pity on him. 'Let him down, Harry! What's the point of scaring him to death if all he took was an egg and some bread? Unless ... has he actually taken anything from the cart?'

'I haven't stolen anything!' wheezed the youth.

'Only because I caught you hovering before you had a chance to pinch anything,' said Harry. Even so, he loosened his grip and the lad slid to the ground, but he didn't get the chance to escape because the man grabbed him by the back of his jacket. 'I haven't finished with you yet. I'm going to have a word with your father. Where d'you live?'

'My dad's dead!' The youth lowered his eyes and scuffed at an empty cigarette carton with the toe of his boot.

'Are you an orphan?' asked Rene.

The lad's head came up swiftly and there was a flush on his cheeks. 'I was no bloody orphan when I was put in the orphanage. I've a mother and sisters!' he said, a bitter note in his voice.

Harry cuffed him across the head. 'Watch your language!'

'Tell us where you live!' demanded Greta, moving closer, her skirts swaying, her head thrust forward like a snake ready to strike. 'If you haven't done anything really wicked, you've nothing to worry about.'

He glowered at her. 'I've heard others say that and I believed them but it turned out that they were lying.'

'I'm not a liar,' said Greta indignantly.

'Take him to the bobby,' shouted one of the neighbours.

'No!' cried Rene, involuntarily taking a step towards the youth.

Harry glanced at her. 'Don't interfere, Rene. We can't let him off scot-free. He needs to learn the difference between right and wrong.'

'I know the difference between right and wrong,' said the youth

33

hotly. 'I also know a person's innocent until proven guilty. So how about giving me the benefit of the doubt … sir?'

'Sir?' Greta looked him up and down. 'Polished, aren't we? And I notice … you're putting the voice on … gone all posh.'

'I'd say polite is the word,' said the youth, flushing.

'The police could have him on a charge of vagrancy,' said Vera, breaking into the conversation and tapping her stick on the ground. 'A night in the cells'll be good for him.'

Several people nodded, and as if it had been decided, a woman said that she had a joint to put in the oven so was going in. A man muttered something about getting back to feeding his pigeons. Within minutes only Rene, Vera, Greta, Harry and the youth remained.

The latter's gaze rested on Rene. 'I don't want a night in the cells. I bet none of you has ever had to stay where you don't want to be. You're just like the rest, think you know what's best for other people.'

Rene wondered who *the rest* were. Perhaps he had once had a father who beat him and so had run away from home? Maybe he was a thief and had spent time in a borstal. Or could he be one of the many adolescents who couldn't find work and so had taken to the road? Yet he'd said he had family. It was difficult to know what to do with him without knowing all the facts. One thing was obvious: he had gone hungry lately, there was barely any spare flesh on him. 'What are you going to do, Harry?' she asked. 'I remember you saying that you weren't bothered about an egg and some bread.'

He frowned. 'That's before he tried to steal from the cart. If he gets a short, sharp shock then he mightn't end up in Walton gaol. I'm going to take him to the police station and see if he's known. If he's not, then I won't press charges and they'll let him off with a warning.'

The youth looked dismayed. 'But that's not fair! You didn't catch me in possession of anything. You've got no evidence.'

Harry whistled through his teeth. 'You seem to know a blinkin' lot about the law, lad! Now I'm having no more messing about … and if you've got any sense you'll come quietly.' He glanced at his daughter. 'Wheel the cart into the yard and go through what's there. Decide what you want to keep and get rid of the rest. You can tell your gran where I've gone.'

'Hang on!' said the youth, and he looked quite desperate. 'Should you be letting her decide what to throw away? I know something about old things, vases … ornaments … letters. Even toys can be valuable. I mean my dad had a letter from Kitchener, himself. You'd be surprised what some things can be worth.'

Harry stared at him and then surprised Greta and Rene by laughing. 'Changed your tune now, have you? I'll give you something, lad, you're good at delaying tactics but it's not going to work with me.' And without further ado, he dragged the youth, still protesting, down the entry.

Greta turned to Rene. 'What d'you make of him?'

Vera answered for her. 'I think Harry's right. Our Rene's got a soft heart but the lad needs a good fright to help him stick to the straight and narrow.'

Greta bit her lip. 'I know he frightened me but he didn't hurt me. I suppose you and Dad are right, he can't be entering other people's homes and doing what he wants.' She turned to Rene. 'Thanks for letting me see the kittens but I'd better do what Dad says now. See you around.'

Greta took hold of the handles, lifted the cart and, with some difficulty, managed to manoeuvre it through the doorway and into the yard. She set the cart down and began to root through the items her father had placed inside it. The golliwog had been Amy's and Greta had been unable to part with it after her death. Her mother had picked it up at a jumble sale and it had shared the girls' double bed for years. Was now the time to get rid of it? She was no longer a child, she'd started growing up when her brother and sister had died. She took a deep breath. It would have to go. If she washed it then perhaps the pawnbroker in Breck Road would give her a couple of pennies for it.

She put it to one side and picked up one of a pair of ugly pug dog ornaments which, for some reason Greta could never comprehend, her mother had loved; the other had been broken when the girl had been dusting them one day. She could almost hear her mother's high pitched scream of horror and feel the slap she had administered. She had said that the pair together was worth something. Greta frowned. Could that youth be as knowledgeable as he claimed? She placed the ornament aside and picked up the dark oak wooden box. This she would definitely keep as it contained all her mother's sewing things; cottons, bodkins, needles, pins and hooks for pulling rags through sacking to make rugs.

Next she took up the chocolate box, remembering her mother fingering the different items; a baby's shoe, a dried flower, ribbons and buttons. She would linger over a postcard from Cape Town and reread letters. Greta could picture her mother's blonde head bent, a smile toying about her mouth. The girl blinked back tears and decided that it would be wrong to get rid of items that her mother had thought so much of. Perhaps when she had time she would read the letters herself. Next she picked up the flowered vase and inspected it. She turned it upside down and scrutinised the mark on its base. This had been a gift from Sally's employer when she had left to get married.

'Warra yer doin' with that?'

Greta glanced at her grandmother, who was standing by the back kitchen door, holding a cushion in one hand and a cigarette in the other. 'It was nearly stolen, Gran. That boy, who broke into our house, was rummaging through Mam's things out in the entry.'

Cissie's eyes widened. 'I wonder what he was after!'

'Mam always said the vase was worth something and wouldn't part with it even when we were hard up. She pawned it once but wouldn't rest until she could redeem it.'

'Waste of money,' said Cissie, placing the well-worn cushion on the back kitchen step and lowered herself onto it. She took a long drag on her fag. 'Real sentimental was our Sal but no commonsense. Yer don't hang on to things for sentiment when yer kids are hungry. It's probably only worth a couple of coppers.'

Greta turned on her fiercely. 'We never starved! Mam felt deeply about people and places.'

Cissie's eyes widened. 'Don't get yerself in a twist, girl! I knew me own daughter. Sal did her best for all of yer by her lights, although she got a bit hoity-toity at times after she went into service. Don't ask me why, when all she did was wait hand and foot on those who thought themselves better than us. Surprisingly, her mistress turned to her when she was in trouble. Now have yer finished there? Because if you have, I'd like yer to peel the veggies for me. I won't have yer slackin' thinkin' I'm gonna be carryin' yer around now yer've moved in with me.'

'No, Gran,' said Greta. 'I haven't quite finished here but I won't be long.' There were only two other things on the cart that were worth keeping and they were the two china chamber pots decorated with deep red roses. She told her grandmother that she would be back for them and stepped past her and into the back kitchen.

The smell of roasting mutton filled the kitchen and her rumbling stomach reminded her that she hadn't eaten since seven that morning and it was almost midday. She hurried upstairs to the small bedroom at the back of the house. It was almost identical to the one her brother had occupied in her previous home, and smaller than the bedroom she had shared with her sister. From its sash window she could see not only her grandmother's backyard but that of the Millers', too.

She moved away from the window and gazed about her. Harry had whitewashed the walls because the room had been empty for some time and he wanted to make sure there were no bugs around. He had sold the double bed Greta and Amy had once shared, and bought a new mattress for her brother's single bedstead, which now belonged to Greta. She had her own second-hand chest of drawers, but no wardrobe or rail to hang her few dresses and winter coat. They would have to go over the foot of the bed until her father could rig something up.

She placed the vase on the chest of drawers and, after hesitating a moment, put the golliwog on the bed and the sewing and memory boxes beneath it. She could only hope that she and her father and grandmother would get on living together. At least there were no ghosts here. She went downstairs to fetch the chamber pots, and after that set about peeling the veggies for Sunday dinner.

'So how did you get on at the police station, Dad?' Greta looked across the table at Harry as he helped himself to mint sauce.

'Got away from me, didn't he? Like a blinking eel he was and wriggled free.' His expression was bland. 'Then ran hell for leather and was out of sight before I could catch up with him.'

Greta stared at him suspiciously. 'So you didn't bother going to the police station?'

'Oh, I went.' Harry lifted his head and his expression was serious. 'I thought they should know that he's on the loose.'

Cissie's eyes went from one to the other. 'Yous talking about that youth, who was after pinchin' our Sal's things?'

Harry nodded, and said loudly, 'A young down-and-out, Mrs Hardcastle.'

'I'm not deaf!' sniffed Cissie, taking a pinch of salt from the dish and sprinkling it over her food. 'So who was he?'

'No idea!'

'He didn't get away with anything?'

'I didn't give him a chance to get away with anything,' said Harry.

'I didn't tell you before, Gran,' said Greta. 'But you know what he had the cheek to say … that he wasn't a burglar because he used the key on the string to let himself in … said it wasn't the same as breaking and entering.'

'Ha!' said Cissie and pointed a knife at her. 'I've always had me doubts about making me key available to every Tom, Dick and Harry.'

Father and daughter exchanged looks but refrained from commenting.

'I know what yous two are thinking and yer wrong. I'm more choosy than yer realise.' Cissie stuffed a forkful of meat in her mouth. She chewed thoughtfully before saying, 'Our Sal never understood but then I didn't expect her to. She never got over her father leaving us … always blamed me.'

Silence.

Greta did not know what to say except *Was it your fault, Gran?* But what a question to ask! Her gran might be utterly offended and that wouldn't be a good start to the three of them living together.

The silence seemed to stretch and it was Cissie who broke it. 'So, Harry, d'yer think we'll see the lad around here again?' she asked.

Harry shook his head. 'He's had a fright. If he's got any commonsense at all he'll stay away.'

Greta thought that he hadn't stayed away the first time and she had a feeling that they hadn't seen the last of him.

'So where d'yer think you're going? Yer haven't washed the dishes yet.' Cissie thrust out a leg and blocked her granddaughter's way.

Greta only just managed to prevent herself from falling over by grabbing the arm of the sofa. 'Do you mind, Gran? I could have broken something. One of these days I'll catch your foot as I fall and you'll be sorry, because it won't half hurt your bunions!'

The old woman sat up and reached for the packet of Woodbines on the occasional table nearby. 'And you'd be sorry if that were to happen, because I'd not only hit the roof but you'd have all the housework and cooking to do. Now fill me cup again, there's a luv. I'm dead parched this morning.'

'It'd do you good, Gran, to do it yourself,' said Greta firmly. 'We've been here a fortnight now and I've yet to see you make a cup of tea for me or Dad.'

Cissie made no sign of having heard her, was too busy lighting a fag. It wasn't until she'd inhaled deeply several times that she flashed a honeyed smile at her granddaughter. 'What's the point of yer moving in here, queen, if yer not going to make me life easier?'

Greta almost dropped the teapot. 'I thought part of the reason we moved in was so that we could help each other. I didn't think I was signing on to be your skivvy!'

Cissie chuckled. 'You will have yer little joke! And don't forget me two sugars ... and stir it well.'

You can blinking stir it yourself, thought Greta, placing the cup down with such force on its saucer that the tea spilt over.

'Watch what yer doin'!' Cissie raised her hand but the girl dodged out of the way and made for the door.

'I'll tell me dad if you try that again,' she said, and walked out.

'I never touched yer. Come back and mop it up and I'll give yer a penny for sweets.'

'I'm late, Gran!' called Greta.

She paused on the front step to button up her coat, knowing that she would not say anything to Harry about her grandmother. Living with her was not all bad. More often than not she was there waiting for her when she arrived home from school with a welcoming fire in the grate and something hot to eat. She was a fair cook was her grandmother, even though the food was sometimes a strange mixture that had your taste buds wondering what was coming next. Besides, Harry had enough on his mind as his job was finishing next week.

Greta fastened the ties on her hat, watching a toddler kick a flattened tin can along the gutter. She was reminded of her brother at that age and her vision blurred as tears filled her eyes. Why did Alf have to die? She remembered Harry taking him to Goodison to watch Everton. He had been a chirpy little soul and loved not only kicking a ball about but dancing along with Amy to the music on the wireless. She and her mother used to laugh and laugh, watching the pair of them cavorting about, her brother pulling faces at them. A sob rose in her throat but she forced it down and wiped her damp eyes with one of the bobbles on the ties of her hat.

Slowly she walked to the bottom of the step, her gaze taking in some girls with a skipping rope. One of them looked her way and said, 'Wanna join in, Gret? We thought we'd play *Old Soldiers Never Die!*'

Since her mother's death, Greta had little time to play. She was gratified to be asked and sorry that she had to turn them down. 'Love to, but I've Miss Birkett's messages to do. Perhaps another time.'

She walked to the bottom of the street and hurried along Whitefield Road to a draper's shop. Above its window a sign said BIRKETT'S DRAPERS – CHILDREN'S AND BABYWEAR A SPECIALITY. She pushed open the door and a bell jangled overhead.

Miss Birkett glanced up and smiled. 'Just a moment, Greta,' she said, her voice as precise as her appearance.

Greta watched as the woman wrapped a dazzling white satin frock in tissue paper, and presumed that it was for the girl who stood with her mother this side of the counter. She guessed that the frock was for a Confirmation Service.

Greta's gaze wandered about the shop, taking in a compartmentalised wall filled with hanks of knitting wool in more colours than a rainbow. A rack of skirts, dresses and blouses stood in a corner, and on the wall behind Miss Birkett were wooden and glass cabinets, containing trays of underwear, socks and stockings, babies' bibs, rubber pants and fluffy white nappies. A wave of sadness swept over Greta, as she was reminded again of Alf and Amy, and the times she had come in here with her mother.

'Are you alright, dear?'

'Yes!' Greta blinked at Miss Birkett who, having finished serving the customer, was now slipping a hanger inside one of the discarded white frocks heaped on the counter. The woman's intelligent, sympathetic eyes gazed into hers and Greta thought, she knows what I'm thinking! She remembered Miss Birkett had suffered, recalling her gran telling her that this woman's hair had turned white overnight after receiving the news that her fiancé had been killed on the Somme.

'Perhaps after you've done my messages you can have a cup of tea and a bun with me. That is, of course, if your grandmother doesn't need you?' Miss Birkett's eyes were twinkling.

Greta smiled. 'She's forever saying she needs me but I've done my chores for today. I've brushed the rug and hung it on the line. I've washed the lino in the kitchen and scrubbed the step. I made her tea and toast and took it to her … yet she still wants more.'

'Enough said, dear,' interrupted Miss Birkett in a gentle voice. 'Your grandmother hasn't had an easy life. However tempting … we mustn't criticise her.' Miss Birkett disappeared beneath the counter, reappearing a minute later with a wicker basket and an oilskin shopping bag. 'The list and money are in the bag.'

Greta thanked her. 'I'll be as quick as I can.'

'There's no rush. I've more things on the list today so it might take you two journeys. Perhaps you can take the shopping to the house and wait for me there.' Miss Birkett fumbled in the pocket of her black skirt and handed a key to her.

Greta thanked her and, once outside the shop, opened the folded slip of paper. She gazed in surprised dismay at the length of the shopping list. Could Miss Birkett be throwing a party? She placed the note and money in her coat pocket and set off down Whitefield Road.

There was a queue at the grocer's but Greta spotted a girl from her class and they whiled away the time talking about what they'd like to do during the Easter holidays, which were still weeks away.

'But that's only if war isn't declared first,' said the girl, a quiver of excitement in her voice. 'Dad said if that happens we'll be evacuated.' Greta gasped, but before she could say anything, the girl spoke again. 'And have yer heard that there's going to be a trial blackout on both sides of the Mersey?'

Greta's heart sank. 'I hadn't heard anything and I know Gran has done nothing about blackout curtains.'

The girl smirked. 'She's going to have to! If there's a war …'

Greta wanted to tell her to shut up about a war. What if they wanted her dad to go and fight? She couldn't bear the thought of being parted from him. 'When is this blackout?'

'Saturday the thirtieth to Sunday the thirty-first of March,' said the girl.

Greta knew that she would need to tell Harry as soon as she saw him that evening. She bit her lip, worried about that word *evacuation*. She was glad when the girl's turn came to be served and she was left in peace.

The shop assistant was vocal about the items Miss Birkett had on the list. 'Stocking up, is she, in case there's a war? Don't blame her. When it comes there'll be rationing sooner or later.'

Heads turned and a customer fixed Greta with a stare and said loudly, 'It's alright for those who can afford to spend out on extras.'

'It's not my money,' said Greta indignantly and, hunching a shoulder, turned her back on the woman, wishing that she, too, could afford to buy the provisions the shop assistant was placing in the basket. There were tins of salmon and peaches, a couple of packets of Rowntree's cocoa, several jars of meat paste, two tins of butter beans, three of peas and several of evaporated milk. Then came the dried goods; currants were measured out on the brass scales, and packets of tea and sugar were all added to Greta's load.

Then she was off to the bacon and dairy counter, where she held her breath as the man sliced bacon and boiled ham so swiftly that he appeared to be in danger of slicing his fingers off. Butter was weighed and slapped into shape with two wooden paddles, and was joined in the oilskin bag a few minutes later, by half a pound of crumbly Lancashire cheese.

Weighed down, Greta hurried to Miss Birkett's house and deposited the first lot of shopping before doing the next lot. It was well past one o'clock when she arrived back at the house, where Miss Birkett was waiting for her, the shop being closed for lunch.

'You're a good girl,' she said, smiling as she took the basket. 'You remembered the buns?' Greta nodded. 'Well, one is for you to take with you.'

'I thought I was having it here with you,' said Greta, disappointed.

Miss Birkett hesitated. 'I'd have enjoyed your company. But, as I walked up the street, I noticed a young man knocking on your grandmother's door. I couldn't resist peeking from behind the parlour curtains when I got in. She'd opened the door to him by then and they were talking … must have talked for a good ten minutes before she invited him in. I thought you just might want to go home straightaway and find out who he is. Maybe he's a long lost cousin!' She handed a bun and a shilling to Greta.

Greta murmured a word of thanks, her pale brow creased in thought. She didn't know of any long lost cousins, although she supposed it was possible there were some on her Mam's side of the family. Harry had no living relatives. His three elder brothers had been killed in the Great War. 'I'll go and see,' she said, 'and I'll come round to the shop later and let you know who he is.'

Miss Birkett saw her out and Greta ran across the road. Lifting the knocker, she hammered on her grandmother's door.

3

'What's wrong with the key on the string?'

Greta glanced at Rene who was standing at the foot of the step, a green and white floral scarf over her hair. 'Gran and Dad said it had to go! They aren't taking any risks after that boy broke in. Miss Birkett told me she saw a young man knocking here and Gran invited him in. I'm dead curious to see who it is.' She turned and banged the knocker again.

Rene, also curious, dumped her loaded shopping bags on her own tiled step. Her neighbour had never had young men visiting her. The door opened to reveal Cissie wearing a navy blue skirt and red jumper that stretched tightly over her enormous bosom. Her stockings were wrinkled at the ankles and she wore slippers. She must have been in the process of removing her metal curlers because half of her head was still covered in that armour while the other half looked like hairy fat sausages. She held the poker and looked put out. 'What the hell's the racket about? Yer'd think the bleedin' house was on fire.'

'I heard you had a visitor, Gran, and I wanted to see who it was,' explained Greta, attempting to push her way in.

Cissie's expression changed and she said grimly, 'Miss Birkett tell yer, did she? Well, yer never gonna guess in a month of Sundays who it is. He came as a surprise to me I'll tell yer that!'

'He's not a long lost member of the family, is he, Mrs Hardcastle?' called Rene.

Cissie's face twisted in a parody of a smile. 'That'll be the day!' She fastened a hand on her granddaughter's shoulder and yanked her into the lobby before slamming the door.

'Gran, d'you have to slam the door on Rene like that?' whispered Greta.

'Yer didn't expect me to leave it open for every Tom, Dick and Harry to come in, did yer?' Cissie said, looking surprised.

'No, but ...'

'Never mind Rene right now, girl, I thought you wanted to run an eye over me guest.'

'I do! Who is he?' Greta followed her grandmother up the lobby, her heels clicking on the linoleum.

'Name's Alexander Armstrong so he says! The name mightn't be familiar to you but it is to me. Not that I recognised the lad because I only ever saw him twice, once when he was a babby and the second time when he was five … but he has his story off pat. So I thought I'd take a chance and invite him in. I've the poker and I'm big enough to sit on him and squash him if he tries any funny business.' She pushed open the kitchen door and waved her granddaughter inside.

Greta stepped forward and then stopped abruptly, staring at the youth as he rose from the green moquette armchair that had come from the house in the next street. He was looking a lot smarter than the last time she had seen him. Dressed in navy trousers, jumper and jacket, his nut brown hair slicked down. 'You!' she gasped.

'Yes, it's me,' he said, a rueful expression in his grey eyes. 'I-I thought I'd best come and explain before I disappear for a while.'

'Disappear? Where to? A borstal?' she retorted.

A tide of scarlet ran along his cheekbones. 'I suppose you've got a good reason to think that, but I never meant to frighten you and thieving doesn't come easy to me. If I'd been surer of my welcome, I'd have told you and Mr Peters the truth straightaway.'

'The truth! What's that?' She walked over to him and peered into his face.

Before he could answer Cissie said, 'He claims to be the son of that Mr and Mrs Armstrong our Sal worked for when she was in service in Crosby. The family fell on hard times after that Wall Street crashed and the son was sent away to an orphanage in the Lake District when he was just eight years old! His mother was in a right state after his father supposedly topped himself, and came to our Sal for help.'

Greta was astounded. 'Is this true?'

Alex's face was pale as if all the blood had drained from it. 'Do you think I'd make up a story like that?' There was a hint of anger in his voice.

'No, but … is it because of Mam you came to our house?'

'Yes! I was only a toddler when your mother left to get married but she used to visit regularly and take me and my younger sisters out to the park and down by the river. She was there after my father died and my uncles came.' Alex's hands curled into fists at his sides. 'I was hustled away the next morning to the orphanage. I couldn't understand it. Anyhow, your mother found out where I was and wrote to me every Christmas and birthday. I wrote back to her when I could. It got that way that I almost forgot what she looked like but I appreciated her never forgetting me.'

'What happened to your mother and sisters?' asked Greta, enthralled by the story.

Before he could answer, Cissie interrupted, 'I can see you believe him, girl, and I must admit I do because his tale seems to hang together. So why don't the pair of yer sit down and we'll have a cup of tea.' She bustled over to the fireplace, and took the kettle from the hob as they both seated themselves at the table.

'I don't know what happened to them,' said Alex, resting his elbows on the table and looking across at Greta. 'Your mother only ever told me that they were in good health. She never answered my questions about where they were.'

Greta was puzzled. 'I wonder why?'

He shrugged. 'I gave up asking myself that question years ago.'

'You were filled with anger, probably,' said Cissie, putting milk into cups. 'I know how it feels to be deserted.' She nodded knowingly.

'So how come you're here now?' asked Greta.

'Last Christmas there was no card, so I wondered if something had happened to her.'

'So you came all the way from the Lake District to find out why Mam hadn't sent you a Christmas card?' Greta shook her dark head slowly, her expression incredulous. 'What took you? It's months ago.'

He looked taken aback. 'I'd been given a job on a farm. I was determined to make a go of it but living in with the family ... it wasn't the happiest of places and I was paid buttons. So I decided to leave and see if I could find my own family.' He paused, looking slightly embarrassed, pleating the green chenille table covering with restless, slender fingers.

'You thought Mam might be able to help you find them?' said Greta, feeling dreamlike. The story reminded her of a film, yet Alex couldn't be making it up because her gran had vouched for its truth.

'Yes!'

'You think she was in touch with your mother still?'

46

'I don't know. But if your mother kept in touch with me, then perhaps she did so with my mother or sisters.'

'You mean you believe your mother might have written to Mam but not to you, her own son!' Greta was shocked.

He was silent, gazing down at his hands.

'That's exactly what he is saying,' said Cissie sharply, filling the cups with steaming tea. 'And he could never write to her... and why? Because she withheld her whereabouts from him. It's lousy to wake up one morning and discover the person yer loved has betrayed yer. I'm starting to realise that me and this lad could be kindred spirits, girl!'

Alex smiled. 'Thanks, Mrs Hardcastle. I appreciate that.'

Greta's gaze went from one to the other. She had never heard her grandmother speak of her feelings when her husband had left. Nor how she felt about her sons. For the very first time, Greta wanted to know about her grandmother's past life. Her mother had never spoken about her brothers or her father. Only once had Greta asked about them and then her mother had told her that part of her life was a closed book.

'Wake up, girl! Here's yer tea!' Cissie nudged the cup and saucer closer to Greta.

'Ta, Gran!' Greta took a sip of tea and then remembered the bun Miss Birkett had given her. She looked across the table at Alexander and taking the bun out of the paper bag, said, 'Want half?'

His grey eyes lit up. 'If it's a peace offering, thanks.'

She flushed. 'Think of it like that if you want.' She stood up, took a knife from the drawer in the sideboard and cut the bun exactly in half on the paper bag and held it out to him.

'I won't say that'll spoil yer dinner,' said Cissie, with a faint smile. 'But I'm gonna have to go off to work soon, I'm putting in a couple of extra hours, so yer'll have to cook something for yerself, girl, and Alexander, if he wants anything.'

'Don't worry about me, Mrs Hardcastle. You've been kind enough to me already by listening and I appreciate that,' he said, his expression warm.

The old woman blushed. 'Gerraway with yer, lad. Our Sal wouldn't have bothered keeping in touch with yer if she hadn't thought it was the right thing to do.' She moved over to the mirror and began to remove the rest of her curlers.

Greta bit into her half of bun and was suddenly uncertain whether they were right to trust to his telling the truth. He certainly knew how to twist her grandmother around his finger. 'So have you any idea where your mother and sister are?' Even to her ears her voice was slightly aggressive.

'No! I came here looking for your mother, only to find she had passed away!' His eyes challenged her. 'Remember?'

Greta sighed, remembering the expression in her mother's eyes after Alf and Amy had died. Her throat felt suddenly tight and she put the bun down and reached for the cup of tea. She took several gulps of it before she managed to say, 'Did you guess she was dead when you went upstairs and raided through her things?'

He hesitated and then nodded. 'No fire, no dinner in the oven at four on a foggy freezing afternoon. Your mother would have been at home, ready with a welcome if she was alive.' Greta's eyes filled with tears. He stretched out a hand and tentatively touched hers. 'Sorry! I didn't mean to upset you.'

She tried to smile, shook her head and wiped her eyes with the back of her hand. Then she took a deep breath. 'So you lit the fire and fried an egg and some bread, and went looking for anything that might help you find them, such as … letters?'

He nodded. 'I didn't get the chance to read any of them because I heard you come in and then that first yowl. I nearly … ' He paused. 'Anyway, you know what happened next. You came into to the bedroom and found me.'

'Why didn't you say all this then?'

'The light went out, you screamed and I panicked.' He put the last of the bun in his mouth.

'So when Dad caught you in the entry, you'd come back for the letters?'

'Yes! I should have told him then but my story sounds so far-fetched I didn't think he'd believe me. I felt like a bandit in one of those Westerns about to be lynched by the mob with me protesting my innocence and them not believing a word I said.' He pulled another face and a lock of brown hair fell onto his forehead. It made him look more attractive.

Greta understood exactly what he meant. 'So what changed your mind about telling us the truth?'

Before he could answer Cissie broke in on their conversation.

'I'm going now, queen.' She stood with her coat and hat on, one hand resting on Alexander's shoulder and her face powdered and rouged, her lips heavily caked in red. 'You take care, lad! Have a good trip!'

'Thanks, Mrs Hardcastle!' He smiled up at her.

'Ta-tah for now, lad,' she said, and left.

There was a silence for several moments after she had gone. Alexander drained his cup and placing it on the saucer, said, 'When I let myself into your other house, I only had a couple of pennies to my name. I hitched here from Keswick. I thought I'd easily manage to find a job in Liverpool. Well, you won't know yet because you're too young ... but jobs aren't easy to find if you haven't got a reference or someone to speak for you.'

Greta folded her arms across her chest and said tartly, 'I'll be fourteen in October! I'll be looking for work then and I know already how tough it is out there.'

He grinned. 'Keep your hair on, I didn't mean to offend you.'

She said stiffly, 'OK! I believe you. So what did you do after you managed to escape from my dad?'

'I didn't! He took me to the nearest vicarage, which amazed me. He told the vicar I was on my uppers and needed help finding a job.'

She gazed at him in amazement. 'Dad did that! Golly! I thought he didn't believe in God.'

He scratched his ear and his smile widened. 'Well, if he does or not, he did the right thing. The vicar spoke to someone who spoke to someone else and I've a job as a deck boy on the SS Arcadian Star. She's berthed at Brocklebank dock, out Bootle way. I'm sailing tonight for South America.'

'What about finding your family?'

He sighed and scratched his ear again. 'I thought you might let me have a look at one of the letters.' He glanced at the clock. 'Although, I haven't got much time.'

'I'll get them,' she said immediately, feeling a stir of excitement and hurried upstairs. She took the old chocolate box with its picture of red, yellow and pink roses on its top from beneath the bed and blew off a light layer of dust and opened it. She hadn't had time to read the letters as she had promised herself and, after hearing what Alexander had to say, she would like to see what they said, too. She did have a quick peek to see if any of them were from a Mrs

Armstrong, and saw that more than half of them were. Should she hand all of them over to him?

Greta was still undecided when she entered the kitchen. But as soon as she saw the expression on his face as she placed the envelopes, tied up with yellow ribbon, on the table, she was moved to do what she considered the right thing.

'You take them,' she said, shoving them towards him. 'You can read them while you're at sea.'

He stared at her and a muscle in his throat convulsed as he gripped the envelopes. 'That's real generous of you. Thanks!' He got to his feet. 'I'll have to be going. I was given an advance on my wages to buy a few things that I need to go to sea.'

'I'll see you out then.' She walked with him to the front door, thinking that he was not going away empty-handed. 'You will come back and let us know how you get on? I mean I'm sure Gran'll want to see you again,' she added hastily. 'You two being kindred spirits.'

'I'd be glad to. Thanks again for these.' He patted his pocket before lifting a hand in farewell, then he strode off down the street.

Greta experienced a sense of anticlimax after he had gone. He had brought a bit of excitement into her life and now everything felt flat. If the letters told him of his mother's and sisters' whereabouts and they were reunited, would she ever see him again? She questioned why he wanted to find his mother when she had allowed him to be placed in an orphanage. She felt certain that if her mother had been in the same position she would never have parted with her son. Of course, it was terrible for Alex's mother to have lost her husband and income but Greta was convinced Sally would have worked her socks off to keep her family altogether. Perhaps she shouldn't have given the letters to him after all!

She grimaced, then remembering her grandmother was not going to be there to prepare their evening meal, she placed strips of breast of lamb in the blackened pan and set about preparing the vegetables. Suddenly it occurred to her that her father might know all about the Armstrongs. Should she ask him when he came home from work?

But when Harry entered the house at four o'clock that afternoon with a tight expression on his face, and having dumped his haversack of tools on the floor by the door, announced that he'd been paid off the job, Greta knew that now was not the right time to

50

mention the Armstrongs. When Cissie returned, Greta whispered not to mention Alexander to Harry.

Cissie nodded. 'I agree with yer, queen, I'll keep me gob shut. Let's pray that it won't be long before he hears of another job.'

It was a quiet, tense weekend.

Greta entered the kitchen the following Monday evening and found her grandmother setting the table and her father reading the *Echo*.

'What's in the paper tonight?' she asked.

'Nothing good!' he rasped, not looking up. 'Hitler's troops have marched into the capital of Moravia and Liverpool Corpy are asking for more ARP personnel. They want each district to provide its own air raid services and each group of streets its own personnel.'

'Air raids,' said Greta, and shivered. 'I suppose you know, Dad, there's going to be a blackout over Merseyside in a fortnight. We need to get some curtains.'

He said softly, 'Speaking to me now, are you, luv? You've been that quiet the last couple of nights I thought I'd offended you.'

Her eyes widened. 'Of course, you haven't, Dad! I just thought you might be glad of a bit of peace.'

He smiled. 'You saying I've been acting like a bear with a sore head?'

'I know you're worried, Dad,' she said, promptly pulling out a dining chair and perching on it sideways so that she faced him, one slender arm resting on the back of the chair. 'I didn't want to bother you with something that isn't important, compared to you being out of work.'

His dark brows knitted and he folded the newspaper and pushed it down the side of the cushion. 'What is it?'

'The name Alexander Armstrong mean anything to you?'

His expression was blank.

Cissie rolled her eyes at her granddaughter and took the sizzling frying pan from the fire. 'Speak up, Gran,' said Greta.

Harry looked at Cissie. 'So you're in on this, too, are you?'

'He's that lad our Sal used to write to. She looked after him when he was a baby. You can't have forgotten that she worked for a family called Armstrong? Didn't the name come up a short while ago?'

'Most likely! But I don't remember our Greta knowing the name and she certainly never met the boy.'

'I have, Dad! And so have you,' said Greta.

There was a short silence that was broken by Harry saying, 'Out with it, luv! You've got that expression on your face I remember your mother wearing. You have been keeping secrets from me, haven't you?'

She shook her head. 'Only one, Dad, and only since Saturday. He was here and you would have recognised him without knowing who he was.'

'You're not making sense, girl!'

'He's the lad who broke into the other house,' said Cissie, forking out sausages. 'He came looking for our Sal. He's had a bad time of it stuck in an orphanage. I'm sure you know some of the story. Our Sal must have mentioned it to you.'

Harry's face registered incredulity. 'That lad was the Armstrong boy! What did he want of Sally and why didn't he tell me who he was?'

With part of her mind Greta noticed that Harry had managed to speak her mother's name without tripping over it. 'He didn't think you'd believe him. And by the way, Dad, you lied to us! He didn't escape you, he ...'

'He told you that, did he?' Harry sighed. 'So much for me having secrets. So what did he come back for?'

'He wants to find his family,' said Cissie. 'He had hoped to find out where they were from our Sal. He found the letters upstairs but didn't have time to look at them. So Greta gave them to him to read while he's at sea.'

'You gave Sally's letters to him!' Harry frowned.

'I thought they were his by right, Dad! What use were they to us?' asked Greta.

'I agree,' said Cissie.

'And he's got a job on the *SS Arcadian Star*, Dad,' added Greta.

'Good for him! But ...' Harry rubbed his forehead. 'You asked me about the Armstrongs. I know hardly anything except that your mam thought a lot of that woman, not that she spoke much about her after the husband died, but I know she always got a letter from her at Christmas. Except last Christmas ... the letter came earlier ... October or November. I know nothing more. Now let's get the food your gran's putting out while it's hot.'

Greta wondered what it was her mother had seen in Mrs

Armstrong. There must have been something good. That meant Greta was mistaken thinking about her the way she did, and could only hope that there would be something in the letters she had given to Alexander that would be of help to him.

The next morning Rene met Greta on the way out of Ridgeway's Dairy with a jug of milk clutched against her. 'Can't stop,' said the girl, not pausing. 'I'm late up with Dad not working, and I haven't had my breakfast. I've got to get a move on or I'll be locked out of school."

'Wait!' said Rene, stopping her with a hand. 'I haven't seen you the whole weekend ... who was your visitor?'

'He was our burglar from the next street ... the one Dad caught in the entry!'

'You're joking!'

'Nope! Tell you more next time I see you!' Greta hurried away.

Rene climbed the step into the dairy in a mood of frustration and concern. Poor Harry out of work! Did he know about the burglar? What was Cissie thinking of inviting him into the house? Had he tricked his way in? Could he have stolen anything? Should she warn her mother?

Rene had her jug filled with milk and then walked home to find her mother, sitting at the table across from Wilf, reading the *Daily Mirror* that he had brought in earlier. Rene placed the milk jug on the table.

'There's going to be rationing. You're going to have to think more how you're going to feed me. How about getting some chicks?' said Vera, her expression shrewd. 'I'd still be able to have an egg for breakfast, but we'd have to watch the cats with them.'

Rene glanced at Wilf. He nodded, 'I'll see what I can do.'

Vera nodded too. 'That's right, you'll get them and look after them, won't you, Wilf?'

He agreed, looking pleased with the idea.

'And we must remember there's going to be a blackout soon. We'll need curtains,' said Vera, frowning at her daughter. 'You'll have to see to that.' A little shudder ran through her. 'Bombs falling on Liverpool, I don't want to believe it. Like I don't want to believe that soldiers are going to march off to Europe again.' Her voice quickened and rose an octave. 'And they're expecting women to join up this time, too! You won't go, will you, Rene?' She reached out and clutched her daughter's arm. 'You'd like to, I'm sure, but you can't go and leave me!'

'Don't be daft! I've no intention of leaving you, Mother! I'm sure in the circumstances they'll allow me to stay home.' Rene freed herself with difficulty. It might have been fun joining the forces but she knew her duty and there were other activities she could get involved in. 'What about us joining the WVS? They'll teach us useful things to do when… if … war comes.'

Vera sighed with relief and managed a watery smile. 'There'll be little I can do with my rheumaticky fingers and poor old feet but I suppose I could knit socks for the forces.'

'It would help stop your fingers from stiffening up completely,' said Rene, as she sat down and reached for the cereal packet. Remembering her meeting with Greta, she decided that now was not the time to warn her mother that there was a burglar about.

A couple of evenings later Rene saw Greta coming out of the newsagent's and quickly caught up with her.

'Hello, Greta! You OK?'

'Fine. I hear you're getting some chicks.' Greta placed the newspaper under her arm.

Rene smiled. 'Who told you that?'

'Wilf told Dad. Dad asked if you were going to get a cockerel when the chicks grow into hens. You'll have to if you want more hens for more eggs or for Christmas dinner.'

Rene grimaced. 'I hadn't thought of that … but perhaps one of the chicks'll grow into a cockerel.'

'One thing's for sure, it'll get us up mornings.'

The two of them parted at the bottom of their respective steps and went indoors. It wasn't until she was cooking the tea that Rene realised she had forgotten to ask about the burglar. Ah well, if he had been a danger to them, Greta would have told her so. She was still curious about his being invited into next door, though, but finding out why was something that would have to wait. She had plenty of other things on her mind that had to be done straightaway.

That week Rene bought blackout material and made curtains for all the windows. Doing the sewing was murder on the eyes but when it was finished and the curtains hung, Rene was aware of a sense of relief. She stood on the pavement in the dark the Friday evening before the trial blackout, relieved to see not one chink of light showed through them.

'Something interesting up there?' said Harry.

His voice startled her and a hand went to her breast as her eyes searched for him. He was standing in the doorway. 'I didn't notice you!' she called. Considering they had lived next door to one another for almost a month now she had seen little of him.

'Sorry!' He stepped down from the lobby and strolled towards her, hands in pockets. He came alongside her and looked up at their two houses.

Rene was very conscious of his nearness and her heart quickened its beat but she told herself to keep her eyes off him and act casual. There was no future in getting excited just because they were being neighbourly at last. He was still mourning Sally and she had her duty to her mother. 'Ugly things, blackout curtains,' she murmured. 'Give me a nice floral print or gold damask any day.'

'I remember Sally telling me about the pair of you getting dressed up in curtains once.'

Rene remembered it too, and smiled at the memory. She said in a dreamy voice, 'It was the first of May and we didn't have anything else that we could think of to dress up in. I remember we paraded all the way to Lime Street with an empty jam tin with a slit in the lid and several dried peas inside, so it rattled, and sounded like people already thought us good enough to give money to.'

'Up until last year she still remembered the taste of the ice cream you all bought with the money you made.' There was a tremor in his voice as he recalled the conversation. Sally had been making a headdress from a length of net curtain for Amy at the time. For once his wife had opened up and talked about what her life had been like before her father had disappeared, painting those days in rainbow colours. It wasn't until she was dying that she had told him about her father's letters and their meetings. Harry had been devastated, having always believed that they had no secrets from each other.

'Happy memories,' said Rene softly.

He could only nod and for a moment was unable to speak. This time last year, despite money being short, he had felt fulfilled, his aim to take care of his family. He had been content with his life and secure in Sally's love, believing that they had no secrets from each other. There were still times when he dreamed of her being in bed beside him. He would wake and reach out for her, his whole body throbbing with his need for her, only to embrace the chilling emptiness that spoke of his loss.

'Are you OK, Harry?' Rene placed her hand on his shoulder.

He cleared his throat, saw the concern in her eyes and forced a smile. 'Greta mentioned curtains to me but I chose to forget about them.'

'You're going to have to get some. Surely you can get financial help to buy them from the Corpy if you're out of work?'

Shame flooded through Harry. He had already pawned Sally's brooch. It had been a difficult thing to do, regarding it, as he did, as Greta's inheritance from her mother, but he was desperately short of money and they could not live on Cissie's wages and the dole alone. His black eyebrows rose and his expression was austere. 'Don't tell me what I can and can't do!' he said stiffly.

She flushed at the anger in his voice and withdrew her hand. 'Don't be so proud! There'll be planes overhead tomorrow night, checking for any lights!'

'I know that ... and I know they're going to blow up a building in South Chester Street in town ... and that there'll be fires and other explosions ... but we'll be in our beds, so we won't be showing a light.'

'But you'll need blackout curtains if war comes.'

'I'll worry about that when it happens,' he said in a voice that said, *I don't want to talk about this anymore.*

Rene nodded, letting the subject drop. She hugged herself. It was getting cold, but she didn't want to go indoors yet. 'How are you and Mrs Hardcastle getting on together?'

A faint smile relaxed his lean, craggy face. 'She's a better cook than I gave her credit for in the past ... and she and Greta seem to be rubbing along OK.'

'Greta told me you had a visit from your burglar.'

She caught the gleam of his teeth in the lamplight. 'Tell you he came looking for Sally, did she?'

Rene started. 'Sally?'

'She didn't tell you that?' He sounded surprised.

'To be frank, Harry, she told me hardly anything and I was dying of curiosity.' She smiled.

He laughed. 'That wasn't smart of her! I would have thought

you'd have been the one person she should ask… you and Sally having been such friends.'

'Ask what? Honestly, Harry, it's almost as frustrating talking to you as to her!' A small laugh escaped her. 'What's this about? What's that lad got to do with Sally?'

'Give me a chance! He's the son of that family Sally was in service to … the Armstrongs. You'd know more about them than I would.'

For a moment she was speechless, then a memory came vividly to mind. Sally had come to her in tears. Apparently Mr Armstrong was dead. Sally was married to Harry by then and no longer living in at the family's house in Crosby on the outskirts of Liverpool, but Mrs Armstrong had written to her, asking if she could help her out with the children for a few hours a week. She'd had to sack all her staff and the family had moved to a smaller house, but she couldn't cope with the children on her own and Sally had always been wonderful with children. The day Sally had come to Rene in tears, Mr Armstrong had apparently been having stomach pains and had lost weight since losing most of his money in the aftermath of the Wall Street crash. He had told his wife that he had nervous debility and had been taking pills bought from a herbalist, since he had no faith in doctors. His death had come quite suddenly and was caused by an overdose of the pills, so there had been an inquest.

Sally had asked Rene to go along with her as she was likely to be called on as a witness. The room had been crowded. It was the only time that Rene had set eyes on Mrs Armstrong, and she already had preconceived ideas about the woman, being of the opinion she had used Sally for her own gain. But when she saw her, she had pitied her. If ever a woman was near breakdown, it was Mrs Armstrong. Yet, just like Sally, she had managed to put up a good show and had stood up to the questioning extremely well. But when the death had been declared accidental, the relief on both the maid's and mistress's faces had been palpable.

Harry shook her shoulder. 'You've gone off in a trance. A penny for them!' Rene stared at him, transfixed, and for a moment forgot everything else but being close to him. He shook her again. 'Rene, what is it?'

She cleared her throat and drew away from him, remembering what she had been thinking. 'What does the boy want?'

'To find his mother and sisters. Apparently he was put in an orphanage and hasn't seen or heard from them. Did Sally ever mention Mrs Armstrong to you?'

'They kept in touch?'

He nodded. 'There's a bundle of letters. Greta gave them to him to read while he's at sea … but who's to say that he'll find what he's looking for.'

She nodded and her brow creased in thought. 'I've a feeling an uncle had something to do with the lad being placed in an orphanage. Mrs Armstrong had a brother so it was probably him who took charge of things. I do seem to remember that the girls were put with an uncle and an aunt. Perhaps he thought a boy would be too much work for his wife. Unfair, but there are people who believe girls are much easier to handle than boys.'

'As a father of a girl of nearly fourteen I'd dispute that it's true,' he said dryly.

'But you've her gran to help you!' She put a hand to her mouth, her eyes wide with mock horror. 'I can't believe I just said that of Cissie Hardcastle.'

He said seriously, 'Aye! She's not as bad as she's painted … but she's not going to live forever … that cough of hers worries me. If anything were to happen to us both where would that leave Greta? How would she cope on her own? I want her safe.'

Rene's heart lurched. 'What d'you think is going to happen to you? You weren't thinking of joining the army? I mean you're thirty six.'

'You saying I'm past the post?'

Before she could answer Greta called from the doorway. 'Your cocoa's ready, Dad. Come and get it while it's hot.'

'OK! I'm coming now,' called Harry. He smiled at Rene. 'Perhaps it's best you don't answer my question. I'll tell Greta what you said about Mrs Armstrong. Goodnight, luv.'

'Goodnight, Harry.' She watched him go into the house, warmed by his use of the word *luv* to her; although she knew it didn't mean what she'd have liked it to. Still, they were friends and on that thought she went indoors.

The evening of the blackout was misty and, for a while, Rene lay awake, thinking of next door not having any blackout curtains. She could hear planes overhead and wondered if any lights were showing on Merseyside. On Monday evening Rene read in the *Echo* that the blackout had been declared a success but, because of the weather conditions, it was decided a repeat performance would probably be necessary.

4

The days started to draw out and Miss Birkett, having learnt that Harry was out of a job, asked him to turn his hand to repainting the sign over her shop and whitewashing the backyards to the house and shop.

The Easter weekend in April brought sunny skies. Greta, Harry and Cissie joined the crowds waiting at the landing stage to take the ferry to New Brighton. They could have almost forgotten the possibility of war as they tried to relax. Cissie sat on a towel, reading *The Red Letter* magazine for women, Harry strolled along the water's edge, and Greta sunbathed, eyeing up the youths on the beach. That morning there had been an announcement on the wireless that Parliament was recalled due to Italy's march into Albania and the effect that would have on Greece and Yugoslavia.

The following day there were fierce attacks from the German press, accusing England of frightening small nations like Greece, Yugoslavia, Rumania and Turkey into believing they were in danger of being invaded. 'But they are in danger, aren't they, Dad?' said Greta, placing a bowl of porridge on the table in front of him. She had to repeat the question twice because her father didn't appear to have heard her.

'I think so ...' Harry hesitated before adding, 'That's why I've joined the Civil Defence. I'll feel happier being trained to know what to do if the air raids come, rather than just sitting in a shelter twiddling my thumbs.'

The news was a relief to Greta. She had worried that with the job situation the way it was, he might after all go and join the army. But that was not her only worry. 'There's talk, Dad, of whole schools being evacuated if it's war. It would be a waste of time me going, Dad. I'm not a little girl, anymore,' she said urgently. 'In a few months I'll be looking for a job.'

'She's right,' said Cissie, her jowls wobbling as she nodded her head. 'We'll need her here. I'm not leaving me home for Hitler or anybody else!'

Harry's expression was a mixture of amusement and exasperation.

'You'd be safer in Wales or Lancashire, the pair of you. It's not going to be any fun when the bombs start falling.'

'We've seen the newsreels, Dad,' said Greta, her teeth crunching into a slice of toast. 'Besides, what's the point of shelters being built if everybody leaves the city?'

Harry picked up his spoon. 'Now you're being daft! But we'll wait and see what happens when it comes.'

Shortly after he spoke those words, all men of twenty and twenty-one were called up. On the evening of May Day, Greta sat in the cinema with her grandmother, watching a newsreel showing Hitler sitting on a golden throne reviewing thousands of troops on his birthday parade. In the newspaper the next day, it was reported that Goebbels had told Germany's young people that they were immune to international hysteria, protected by what was probably the greatest army in the world.

His words made Greta's blood run cold. The world was a frightening place and she wondered how a war would affect Alexander when it came. It was a while since she had given him the letters and in the first few weeks she hadn't expected to hear from him, and she still hoped he would write sooner or later. But as a month passed, then five weeks, six weeks, she began to believe that he wasn't going to get in touch with them again, and felt really disappointed.

She was scrubbing the step one Saturday morning in the middle of May, planning on doing the Millers' step as soon as she had finished theirs, when the postman stopped next to her. It was such an unusual event that she stared at him. The only person who had ever received post in their family had been her mother. 'Can I help you?' she asked.

'You Miss Greta Peters?'

'Yes!' She felt a stir of excitement.

'Postcard for you.'

She dropped the scrubbing brush in the soapy water and quickly wiped her hands on the pinafore, that had been her mother's, before taking it from him. 'Thanks!' She gazed at the small black and white photographs and the words in a foreign language. *Buenos Aires* were two of them. She turned the card over, knowing that *Buenos Aires* was in South America, so was already expecting to read Alexander's name on the back. She wasn't disappointed, although he had signed himself Alex.

The writing was small and cramped into the space allowed for a message.

Dear Greta,

I'd hoped to be back in Liverpool before now but didn't expect the ship to be stuck on a sandbank up the Rio Parana for several weeks after leaving Fray Bentos' factory. Nor did I expect us to go on to Columbo after leaving Buenos Aires to deliver a cargo of rice!

The letters are all from my mother and explain some things and give me a lead. It's really frustrating that I can't get back home and get on with the search. Not sure when I'll see you. Perhaps you should keep your eye on the Arrivals and Departures in the Echo's Shipping News for SS. Arcadian Star. *You could come and meet me. Hope you, your gran and dad are well,*

Yours sincerely, Alex Armstrong.

Greta read the words again, smiled and placed the card in the front pouch in the pinafore. She wrung out the floor cloth and began to wipe the tiles and sing *What Shall We Do With The Drunken Sailor?* Harry and Cissie were out, so she would have to wait to give them the good news.

When Harry arrived home he had some good news himself. He had been given a job helping construct outdoor air raid shelters. So all told, Greta felt happier than she had for a while.

Just as their Majesties, King George and Queen Elizabeth, took ship for Canada, the summer fashions arrived in the shops. In T. J. Hughes a check stroller coat could be had for fifteen shillings, and six shilling and eleven pence could buy a floral patterned frock in art silk with puffed sleeves, a fitted waist and the new swing skirt. Rene bought one and showed it off to her mother and Greta, who had come in to see the kittens. Vera reminded them both that the day might come when clothes would be rationed, as well as food. But Rene hadn't bought the frock with that in mind but to cheer herself up. She was still dreaming of Harry, sensual dreams that brought a blush to her cheeks and made her realise just how hopelessly in love with him she was.

A few days later Merseyside had its next air raid practice; this time Greta and her grandmother had blackout curtains up at all the windows. The girl stayed awake listening to the drone of the planes overhead, and wondering what her father was doing, out with the Civil Defence. She hoped that he wasn't in any danger.

Harry arrived back at the house Sunday morning, and was about to put his key in the lock when the Millers' door opened and Rene stepped out, carrying the milk jug. He was tired and dirty but exhilarated after the night's events. Yet at the sight of her, a different kind of thrill ran through him. Her appearance was bandbox fresh and her curves looked luscious in the clinging fabric of the dress she was wearing. He only just prevented his jaw from dropping to manage a smile. 'Morning, Rene!'

'Morning, Harry!' She could not have been more delighted to see him. 'How did things go last night?'

'Great! Ready for bed, though, now.'

Their eyes met and held.

'I know what you mean!' She moistened her lips, remembering her dream and had to swallow hastily before adding, 'You must be exhausted after being up all night.'

'You can say that again. I'll probably go out like a light.'

'Well, sweet dreams!' She tore her gaze from his and hurried down the step.

For a moment Harry stared after her, his heart thumping, and then he thrust the key savagely into the lock and went indoors. He did not say anything about his previous night's work to Cissie and Greta and, as soon as he'd washed and had something to eat, went straight to bed to dream of Rene lying in his arms. When he woke, he lay there wracked with guilt for lusting after Sally's best friend so soon after his wife's death.

Greta did not forget what Alex had said about scanning the local paper for the arrival of the *SS Arcadian Star*. But weeks passed with no mention of the ship. Then the first evening she did not scan the arrivals and departures, she arrived home, from the pictures with her grandmother, to find Harry talking to Wilf on the front step. The two men looked up and there was the slightest of frowns on Harry's face. 'What are you two talking about at this time of night? Secrets?' teased Cissie.

Wilf smiled tentatively. 'What secrets could we have? Unless you think that knowing that the last of the kittens have been taken by their new owners to good homes would be useful to Hitler?'

Cissie chuckled. 'I believe yer've made a joke, Wilf. Although, I'm not convinced yer were talking about kittens.'

'No,' said Harry. 'We were talking about young Armstrong. I know our Greta's been watching out for his ship docking for ages. Well, it's there in tonight's *Echo*. It's due to dock at Brocklebank tomorrow morning. What d'you say, lass, if the pair of us go and meet him? It'll be first thing in the morning so we'll make an early start.'

Greta couldn't have been more pleased by the suggestion and knew she would probably lie awake, thinking of the coming reunion with Alex.

Greta dogged Harry's heels as he strode along the dock road, his unbuttoned tweed jacket flapping like a ship's sail with a rising wind. Beneath the jacket, he wore a collarless blue shirt that was open at the neck, revealing a patch of white singlet. She didn't know why he was in such a hurry but she was having a job keeping pace with him. Since she hadn't given any thought to why he wasn't working that morning, having spent too much time planning what to wear and getting ready. The trouble was, she didn't have anything she'd call decent. Nothing grown up! Her clothes were all kid's stuff. This morning she hadn't bothered with a coat but was wearing a navy blue cardigan over a blue and yellow floral frock in last year's style. She couldn't wait until she left school and got a job, so she could buy some decent clothes, especially if this different kind of job her father had said he was working on now was permanent and brought in better money than the last one.

Despite it not yet being nine o'clock on a fine July Saturday morning, the cobbled dock road was busy. The clatter of hooves and the ring of metal rimmed cartwheels, the noise of engines and the shouts of men, almost drowned out the rattle of a train as it drew into the Brocklebank Station. They reached the gateway and the gateman came out of his box.

He was just about to ask them what they wanted, when there was a commotion inside. 'What's going on?' asked Harry.

The gateman made no answer but hurried into the dockyard. Harry pushed his flat cap back, freeing a head of curling black hair. The muscles of his face were taut and his wide-set blue eyes wore a determined expression. 'You stay here, Greta,' he ordered. 'I'll go and find out.' He followed in the man's wake.

The last thing Greta wanted to do was stay where she was but supposed that she had better appear to do as she was told ... at least for a couple of minutes or so. She wondered what the fuss was about. Had there been an explosion? Only the other week the IRA had planted bombs in two pillar boxes, a couple of miles from where they lived. Or was it possible that German saboteurs were behind it? She could stand the suspense no longer and sidled through the gateway.

To her left, timber was piled up in a yard that led to a slipway into the water. Ahead she could see ships at loading berths and her father going up the gangway of one of them. The gateman was shouting up to a youth on the deck. The next minute, the gateman came running towards Greta. Hastily she got out of the way and watched him head for his box and go inside. She saw him pick up a telephone. Obviously something had gone wrong aboard the ship that Harry had boarded. She prayed that Alex's vessel was not involved.

She headed towards the ship and saw that it was called the *Baroness*. There was no one else near it, although the dockers unloading the other ship, surely Alex's, were gazing in the direction of the *Baroness* and gesticulating and talking excitedly.

She waited, gazing up at the ship and then suddenly the youth appeared on deck again and came down the gangway. It was only as he made to run past her, and she asked him what was happening, that he gasped, 'Pipe burst down in the steam room! Can't stop! Big trouble!' and she realised it was Alex. She stared at him, her pulse racing. He had filled out, his clothes were wringing wet and his sunburnt face was running with sweat and speckled with what looked like coal dust.

She ran alongside him. 'Alex, it's me, Greta! Is anyone hurt?'

'Yes!' He stared at her and recognition showed in his eyes. ' Hi, Greta! Can't stop! The shore gang from Brown's engineering yard was getting up steam. Several have been scalded. The screams were terrible! You shouldn't be here.'

'You told me to come and meet you!' she countered. 'Dad came too. He remembered Mam writing to you and knows that your mother wrote to her.'

'Blinking hell! I never expected him to come with you.' Alex looked gratified but then said, 'I'm going to have to leave you. Some of the blokes are in a right mess and we'll need more than one ambulance.' He tore off in the direction of the dock gate.

Greta stopped, seeing no point in following him and turned and walked back to the *Baroness*. The thought of scalding hot steam sounded terrible. She remembered getting a tiny slap off her Gran once when she was younger for getting too close to a hot kettle that she had placed on the hearth. It had really hurt. Cissie had gently rubbed butter on her painful scorched skin, and told her not to go near steaming kettles again.

Greta became aware of screams and there was such a depth of pain in the sound that she felt cold all over. She gazed towards the deck of the ship and saw Harry staggering under the weight of a man, half-carrying him. Someone else on deck took the injured man from him and Harry vanished out of sight again. There were other men on deck and one was pushing a wheelbarrow but, only as he approached the top of the gangway did she notice the man in it was not moving and, with a sick feeling, she wondered if he was dead. She chewed on the inside of her lip, praying that her father and any other men below would be safe.

Several men and youths dressed in overalls joined her in her wait, gazing up at the ship, murmuring amongst themselves. Then came the clanging of bells and she glanced over her shoulder and saw two ambulances heading their way. Rear doors opened and stretchers were taken out and carried aboard. Alex reappeared with the gatekeeper and a policeman. He came and stood next to Greta as the injured were brought down the gangway. She heard the hiss of his breath and caught a brief glimpse of one man's face that was covered in a mass of blisters. Her stomach heaved and she turned away. She could not bear to look at the rest of the men and kept her eyes lowered, her heart pounding as she wondered what was happening to her father.

The clanging of bells as the ambulances sped away caused her to look up and her gaze caught Alex's. If her face was the colour of his, then she must look like she'd seen a ghost. 'I hope I never see a sight like that again,' he said hoarsely.

She nodded, trembling, so glad he hadn't been hurt, wishing her father would appear. Suddenly, he and a sailor were on deck, supporting one of the injured men. She felt her chest swell with pride, thinking that if she was ever to marry, it would have to be someone really special to match up to her dad.

The stretcher bearers went aboard. Harry came down the gangway, walking jerkily behind them as they carried the injured man to another ambulance. Harry's face was sweaty and his eyes were red-rimmed. She could hear him taking deep gulps of air.

She darted towards him. 'Are you OK, Dad?'

He blinked and nodded. She thought he didn't look it and put her arm round his waist and told him to lean on her. 'You're coming home with me.'

'Here, let me help you, Mr Peters.' Alex made to take his arm but one of the ambulance men put a hand on Harry's shoulder, and said, 'He's not going anywhere until he's been to the hospital and the doctor's run an eye over him. Step away, you young'uns and I'll get him into the ambulance.'

Greta said firmly, 'He's my dad! I'm coming with him.'

'No, girl, you can't. It'd be too much of a tight squeeze,' said the man. 'Besides it's not the place for you.'

She would have argued with him if Harry had not said, 'Leave it, luv. You and Alex make your way home and I'll see you later.' He climbed into the back of the vehicle with the ambulance man and the doors were shut. Greta gnawed on her lip, staring after the ambulance as it drove away.

'He'll be fine,' said Alex, taking a handkerchief from his pocket and wiping his face.

She sighed. 'I hope you're right. Where will they take him, d'you think?'

'Bootle Hospital. It's only about ten minutes away, if that.' He hesitated. 'I have a problem with your dad's suggestion.'

She glanced at him and thought how his frame and face had filled out. It suited him. 'What is it?'

'I wasn't intending going straight to your house. Truthfully, I wasn't certain you would turn up but I decided to hang around for a bit in case you did. The rest of the crew headed for Liverpool or home, but I was going to make for Stanley Road after tidying myself up.' He took a letter from a trouser pocket.

Her expression brightened. 'You mean you know where your mother and sisters are?'

'Not exactly. But this is the last letter my mother sent to yours. Perhaps you'd like to read it?'

Greta took it from him and saw that it was dated November 1938 and noted the address.

Dear Sally,

I am writing this ahead of my usual Christmas letter because I have such exciting news for you. I am to marry again. A charming man, who has his own shop selling bicycles. I cannot believe my good fortune. He is much older than me with four grown up children, who, fortunately, are all married with their own homes. As you can imagine everything is in confusion here, what with dress fittings for the wedding and honeymoon, and arrangements to make about what to do with my bits and pieces that I can't take with me. I will write to you again soon and tell you all about the wedding and my new home. He lives in a flat over the shop. It is quite large, big enough for two anyway.

With all fond wishes for a happy Christmas to you and your family. Yours in a rush, Abigail Armstrong.

P.S. I have sent word asking if my dear girls may attend the wedding but I have little hope that their uncle will allow it. He will say that it will unsettle them.

Greta lifted her eyes and met Alex's grey ones. 'Rene said your uncle took the girls. It sounds like he doesn't allow your mother to have much to do with them.' She returned the letter to him.

There was a deep scowl on Alex's face as he folded the sheet of paper. 'I presume it's Mum's brother, David. He and his wife have a couple of girls of their own. I've a feeling he handles Mum's finances, giving her a small allowance to live on. I remember Dad saying she was hopeless with money. Probably the lack of it was the reason I was sent to the orphanage. There's no mention of why in the letters … although she hints at being forbidden to have any contact with me.'

Greta almost said, *She could have still made contact.*

'I know what you're thinking,' said Alex fiercely. 'That if she cared, she could have still visited me or written … but I could tell from the letters that it took her all her time to look after herself. She's not like your gran! She wouldn't know where to start coping on her own and looking after us when we were kids.'

'But won't things be different now she's married someone else?'

'I hope so! That's why I've got to find her.' He pocketed the letter and ran a hand through his damp hair. 'I don't expect her to be at the flat in Stanley Road but I'm hoping to be given a forwarding address.'

Greta was so interested in his concerns that she almost forgot about her father on his way to Bootle Hospital. Even so, she told herself that there was nothing she could do for him and felt certain he would not mind her going with Alex before heading home.

'Can I come with you?' she asked.

A slow smile lighted his face. 'I was hoping you'd say that. I think you're almost as eager as I am to find my family.'

She could hardly admit that wasn't true and it was Alex himself who interested her, so said, 'You know a bit of Gran's story. I've family I've never met and I suppose I am curious. So I can understand how you feel.'

Alex said, 'Come on then! Let's get cracking.' He started towards the dock gates and Greta quickly followed him.

It took them more than half an hour to find the address on the letter as they had to walk most of the way. The pair of them stood, leaning against the railings of the North Park on the far limits of Bootle, gazing at a three storey house on the opposite side of the road.

'So are you going to go over and knock then?' said Greta. 'We've been standing here for five minutes just looking at it.'

Alex frowned. 'Don't exaggerate! Two at the most.' He took his mother's letter from his pocket and checked the number of the house and flat again, although there was no need. He had them off by heart, but now he was within a breath of discovering where she was he felt sick with apprehension. What if he was a big disappointment to her and she felt ashamed of him?

'Let's go then!' said Greta, nudging his elbow. 'It amazes me that someone like you, who thought nothing of breaking into our house and cooking yourself something to eat, should be taking their time going over there.'

'You aren't half pushy for your age,' muttered Alex, putting the letter away. He took a deep breath, glanced right and then left and crossed the road. Greta was close on his heels, hoping whoever came to the door would have the answer they wanted.

The door was opened by an old woman dressed in a pink flannelette nightgown, and with a paper crown on her lank grey hair. She beamed at them. 'You carol singers?' Before they could answer in the negative, she added, 'Give us a burst of *Away in a Manger* then?' She cupped her hand over her right ear.

Greta almost laughed. 'It's not Christmas,' she said unsteadily.

Alex cleared his throat. 'We're looking for my mother. She used to live here. Mrs Abigail Armstrong?'

She screwed up her wrinkled face. 'I don't know that carol … don't recognise the words.'

Greta giggled. Alex tried to ignore her and repeated loudly, 'I'm looking for my mother, she used to live in 3b.'

'You want a wee! Well, don't tell me, young man! There's lavatories in the park. Go over there!' The old woman made to shut the door.

Quickly Alex jammed it open with his foot. 'I'm looking for my mother!' he yelled. 'She lived on the second floor.'

'There's no need to shout. I'm not deaf.' The woman shook her head and the crown fell off. 'You young people, none of you know how to speak properly.'

Convulsed with laughter, Greta had to turn her face away.

'My mother's name was Abigail Armstrong,' enunciated Alex carefully, whilst struggling to cling on to his patience.

'Armstrong, Armstrong!' The woman sucked in her breath and looked toothless, then she exhaled. 'Hang on! I'll ask me old man!' She was in the act of closing the door when it was wrenched out of her hand.

'Mother, what are you doing answering the door in your nightie? What will people think of you?' chided a dark haired younger woman in a pinny. She gazed at Alex and Greta. 'What is it you two want? I could hear one of you shouting from upstairs.'

A relieved Alex told her.

The woman looked astonished. 'Holy Mary, Mother of God! Who'd have believed you really existed. She was always going on about how well you were doing at Merchant Taylors' in Crosby, where you were a boarder. I never believed her because, although she said she had private income, more often than not she didn't seem to have two pennies to rub together. She did a moonlight flit and there's no way she'd leave a forwarding address in those circumstances, is there?'

Alex's heart sank as he stared at her, dumbstruck. His mother had made up stories of him being at one of the most prestigious public schools in Crosby. He could imagine what she would think when she discovered he was only a deck boy! He glanced at Greta and immediately her expression sobered. She pulled on his arm, 'Let's go!'

The woman nodded. 'I'd do exactly that if I was you and quick! I don't collect the rents but Mr Brown, who does, is in the back. Your mam owed for two months, got away with getting into debt because she spoke nice and charmed him. He might expect you to pay it.'

At that moment a voice called, 'Who's that at the door, Mrs Cheetham? Someone interested in the top flat?'

'That's him,' whispered the woman. She placed a hand on Alex's chest and pushed hard. 'Go on! Scram!'

5

Cissie stared at Harry's reflection in the mirror above the fireplace as she dug two matching tortoiseshell combs into her bleached hair, which she had piled up on top of her head. 'Yer a bloody fool! Don't yer know that most heroes end up dead,' she chided. 'Did yer bother to think that yer could have made Greta an orphan?'

Harry did not lift his head from his perusal of the cartoon strip of *Jane* in the *Daily Mirror*. 'I wasn't in any danger. I'm not stupid, Mrs Hardcastle.'

'I can back him up,' said Alex, who was seated at the table, eating a bacon butty that Greta had made for him. 'It was just uncomfortable because of the heat and the damp ... and upsetting seeing the state of the men who'd got the full force of the escaping steam.'

'She's proud of him really,' said Greta, putting an arm around Cissie's ample waist and hugging her. 'Isn't that right, Gran?'

'If yer say so. Now get out me way, girl! Yer slowing me down!' She nudged her granddaughter with her hip.

Harry lowered the newspaper. 'Why are you getting all dolled up? I thought you said you weren't going into work 'til this evening.'

A thick layer of face powder did little to conceal Cissie's wrinkles, she had black pencilled over her greying eyebrows, as well as having applied lipstick. 'I'm going to see an old friend.' Cissie bent to check the seams of her stockings were straight.

Harry glanced at his daughter and winked. 'You're putting on your face to see another woman?'

'As it happens it's a fella! We were sweethearts before I met Mr Hardcastle and he swept me off me feet ... not that any good came of that. So be warned, Greta,' she glanced at her granddaughter, 'don't be fooled like I was but get to know a bloke first before yer decide to tie the knot. Mr Hardcastle waltzed into my life, dressed like a waiter, and I fell for him. He could tell a tale and sweet-talked me into marriage before I had time to get me bearings.' She switched her gaze to Harry. 'As it happens, Mr Nosey, me ol' sweetheart's wife's just died. I saw it in the *Births, Marriages and Deaths* in the *Echo* last week, so I wrote him a little letter and he wrote back.'

'Isn't that romantic, Greta, luv? Doesn't it make your heart glad to think your gran might have found true love again after all these years,' said Harry.

Greta chuckled and Alex smiled faintly.

Cissie looked at Harry suspiciously. 'Are you taking the mickey?'

'As if I would.' He gave his attention to the *Mirror* again.

'I deserve some happiness,' said Cissie, reaching for the russet hat perched on top of a fruit bowl that contained several hairgrips, a handful of buttons, a cotton reel with a needle stuck in it and a pair of gloves. She gazed at her reflection and placed the hat at a jaunty angle, then fluffed up the bottom of her hair with the back of a hand. A satisfied smile lit up her face. 'There, I think I'll do.' She picked up her gloves and handbag and made for the door into the lobby.

'You behave yourself now,' said Harry. The old woman made a noise somewhere between a snort and a giggle, performed a backward kick with her left leg and disappeared down the lobby.

Greta closed the door behind her. 'He might be desperate and lonely enough to want another wife to replace the one he's just lost, Dad.'

'She's not free as far as we know.' Harry's eyelids drooped and he stifled a yawn, thinking that the last thing he needed was for Cissie's long-lost husband to arrive on the scene.

Greta had forgotten her grandparents were still married but then that hadn't stopped Cissie living with a man in the past. It was as if she had no shame about living in sin. Still, it was no use worrying about it now. She was late for her Saturday job and might have to do some of Miss Birkett's shopping after lunch. She lifted her cardigan from the back of a chair. 'I'm going to have to go. Dad, you'll look after Alex?'

Alex swallowed the last mouthful of bacon and bread and gazed at her. 'You don't have to worry about me, Greta. I've been paid off the *Arcadian Star*, and should have picked up my gear and brought it away with me. I thought I'd go and get it and then find myself a bed at the Sailors' Home.'

Harry folded the newspaper. 'No need for you to pay out for a bed there, lad. If you don't mind sleeping on the sofa in the parlour, you can stay here. For just a shilling a day you can have breakfast and a hot meal in the evening thrown in.'

Alex's face showed a mixture of surprise and pleasure. 'Thanks, Mr Peters, I really appreciate the offer.'

'You're welcome, isn't that right, Greta?' He glanced at his daughter, who was standing in the doorway.

'Fine by me, Dad, and I'm sure Gran'll say the same.' She smiled at Alex. 'Tarrah! See you later!'

It took Greta some time to do all Miss Birkett's shopping and she had lunch with her in between, telling her all about her morning.

'If Alex's mother has done a flit, Greta dear,' said Miss Birkett, spooning coffee into cups, 'it seems possible that she might have spun a few fairy stories for your mother in her last letter.'

Greta put down her ham sandwich and stared at her. 'You mean she mightn't have been getting married at all? There mightn't be a widower with a bicycle shop?'

'I could be wrong! But why disappear without paying the rent if she had a man of substance, who was going to marry her?' Miss Birkett's pale blue eyes wore a troubled expression.

'Maybe with having to fork out for her trousseau she ran short of money and didn't want him to know that she wasn't a good manager,' said Greta, picking up her sandwich again and biting into it.

'Could be,' said Miss Birkett, stirring sugar into her coffee. 'But remember she also lied about Alex's whereabouts. Sadly, whatever is the truth we are not in possession of it, so we can only surmise the facts.'

That was all too true, thought Greta, feeling sorry for Alex.

By the time Greta returned to the house she found it empty. She wondered how long it would take Alex to collect his gear and get back home. She remembered how down in the dumps he had been on the way home. Perhaps the same thing had occurred to him as it had to Miss Birkett, but at least he could comfort himself with the thought that his mother had not forgotten about him. Greta still had mixed feelings about Mrs Armstrong despite Alex's defence of her.

Although it was a warm day, Greta relit the fire and set about peeling vegetables for the stew that evening. She thought about Alex staying under the same roof. It would be lovely having him around as long as he didn't try to boss her about. She sighed, remembering his comment about her being pushy for a girl her age. He wasn't that much older than her. If he had been two years old when her mam had left to get married, that would make him about sixteen. Maybe he'd like to go to the pictures one night in the week.

He would probably enjoy seeing a film after being away at sea so long.

She wondered what he would do next about finding his mother and sisters. He had never said how old his sisters were or mentioned their names. What would they have thought when separated from him? Surely they'd have been upset? She placed the stew in the oven, made herself a cup of tea and went out to the front with the drink and *Red Letter* magazine, to enjoy the sunshine and wait for Alex's return.

Vera was sitting in a chair on the step, obviously struggling to turn a heel on a khaki sock, whilst Rene was emptying a small, steaming heap of horse manure onto the soil at the base of a rose bush in the centre of the tiny garden.

'You must have been quick to get that,' said Greta, watching her.

Rene's eyes twinkled. 'As it happens I was cleaning the windows when the coal lorry went up the street. I wasted no time when the horse dropped its load and raced Mrs Woods for it.' Rene straightened, easing her back.

Greta glanced in Vera's direction and decided she didn't want Rene's mother knowing her business, so she lowered her voice. 'I've got something to tell you!'

Rene looked down at her. 'Something exciting by the look on your face.'

'It is … but sad, as well. Me and Dad went to meet Alex's ship and when we got to the dockyard we found there'd been an accident. Something to do with a steam pipe bursting and-and you should have seen some of the men's faces.' Greta shuddered.

'Alex wasn't hurt?' said Rene.

'No! It wasn't his ship but he went down into the bowels of the other one and so did Dad. He helped to bring a couple of the men up and Dad ended up having to go to hospital.'

Rene's face blanched and she dropped the shovel. 'Harry was hurt?'

Greta rolled her eyes. 'His breathing was all over the place! So while he went off in the ambulance, Alex and I went to see if we could find his mother's whereabouts.'

'Never mind that now … is Harry OK?'

Greta nodded her head vigorously. 'He's been home and gone out again so he must be OK.'

Rene smiled her relief. 'Of course, he must. So did you find Alex's mother?'

Greta heaved a sigh and then shook her head. 'She'd done a flit but we already knew she probably wouldn't be there because in her last letter she wrote that she was getting married to a man with a bicycle shop.'

'Lucky her!' said Rene, bending to pick up the shovel.

Vera called, 'Who's lucky? What's all the whispering about? Doesn't Greta know it's rude to whisper in company? I heard Harry's name mentioned. Are you planning to do something with him, Rene?' There was suspicion in her voice.

'Chance would be a fine thing!' said Rene, facing Vera. 'I think you're going deaf, Mother.'

Vera's face flushed with fury and she dropped her knitting on the step. 'Don't tell me I'm going deaf! Now pick that sock up for me! You're going to have to turn the heel. I can't be arsed with the bloody thing! Be arsed, be arsed!' she yelled, startling not only the cat that was cleaning itself on the pavement but Greta, Rene and the neighbours.

A shocked Greta stared at her, never having heard Vera lose her temper and swear before. She swallowed an embarrassed giggle. Then watched as Rene picked up the knitting and Vera swiped her across the head with her clawed hand. 'That'll teach you to give cheek to me!' she said savagely.

Greta was even more shocked and willed Rene not to stand for such behaviour, but she just stood there looking stunned. Greta could not keep silent. 'You shouldn't have done that, Mrs Miller! Rene's a good daughter to you. What I was telling her is none of your business!'

Vera's face went puce and she looked as if about to explode. 'Get off my step!' she spluttered. 'I don't want you here! There's been no peace since you and your father moved in next door.'

'That's a lie!' said Greta, losing her temper, oblivious to those of the neighbours who had been gossiping five minutes ago but now had fallen silent. 'But I'm going! I don't want to stay on your stupid step. I feel sorry for Rene being your daughter, you old crow!' She flounced away, picked up her cup and magazine from the lobby, and went indoors, slamming the door behind her.

'That girl! I'll speak to her father,' said Vera, her body shaking with rage.

76

Rene felt sick with a mixture of red hot emotions. She was aware they were being watched by several pairs of eyes and overheard by children, playing a game of rounders, who had stopped to listen. She felt deeply humiliated, and so angry she wanted to smack her mother across the face. Instead, she picked up the ball of wool, which had unravelled, and took the knitting inside, knowing that she needed to calm down before attempting to assist her mother indoors.

Greta felt gloriously alive. Was this how St George had felt when he had slain the dragon? Perhaps Mrs Miller would think twice before treating and speaking to Rene the way she had again. She should appreciate her daughter more. It was because of her that Rene was not married. Greta felt certain there were plenty of fellas who'd have proposed to Rene. She was such a lovely person, helpful and caring.

It was lousy for Mrs Miller, of course, being crippled, but Greta remembered overhearing her own mother saying that Mrs Miller had been a right cow to her husband, who'd been in a bad way after the Great War, so perhaps she was being punished and serve her right.

Later, Greta went out to buy an *Echo* from the newsagent's round the corner. She was reading the report of the accident in the newspaper when she literally bumped into Rene. 'Sorry!' said Greta.

'I should think so, too! I'm still trying to unruffle Mother's feathers and get her down from the roof,' said Rene severely.

Greta hung her head and sighed in mock contrition. 'Sorry again! That's a good joke about the feathers and the roof, by the way.'

'It was no joke! Mother was that mad with the pair of us that she got up out of her chair and zoomed up the lobby to tell me exactly what she thought of you. She's going to have a word with your dad about you.'

'Oh dearie me,' said Greta, putting on a squeaky voice. 'He'll tie me to the yard arm and give me ten lashes.'

Rene's eyes twinkled. 'You are naughty! Anyway, what's so interesting that you can't wait to get home to read it?'

Greta thrust the newspaper at her and stabbed the article with a forefinger. 'It's in the paper about the accident.'

Rene read *Four Men Killed And Two Injured in Engine Room Explosion*. There was a full report about the incident and it mentioned

Harry's bravery and that of an unemployed stoker and a deck boy from another ship, who had been quickly on the scene.

'Where is Harry?' Rene's eyes glowed as she rustled the newspaper. 'It isn't every day I discover I'm living next door to a hero.'

Greta beamed at her. 'My dad a superhero! He's not back yet and neither is Alex. Gran's been home and gone to work. I didn't get a chance to tell you earlier, but Alex's staying with us while he's got shore leave.' Greta reached for her *Echo*. 'I'd let you have this but I want to cut out the article and pin it on the wall.'

'I'll buy my own copy. Wilf's bound to be interested,' said Rene. 'Besides I want to read it out to Mother. It's about time she appreciated Harry's good qualities.' She paused, jingling some coins in her skirt pocket, her rosy face thoughtful. 'About Alex's uncle ... I got to thinking and I'm sure Sally pointed out whereabouts he lived when we went out for the day. You were just a toddler. I was working in a shop at the time and it must have been a Wednesday afternoon because that was my half day off. It was near one of the stations on the Liverpool to Southport line.'

'Which one?' asked Greta, excitedly.

'It was after Seaforth.' Rene sighed. 'Sorry, I can't be of more help.'

'Better than nothing,' Greta reassured her swiftly. 'I'll tell Alex what you said when he gets in. Bye! See you soon!'

She walked slowly home with two things on her mind. Would Alex want to take a trip to Southport on the train ...and what was Harry going to say if Mrs Miller moaned to him about Greta calling her an old crow? He would hate the woman having cause to complain, even if he sympathised with his daughter and Rene. Perhaps he would feel he had to punish her for what she'd said? It would be the first time ever if he did. Punishment had been left to her mam, who had known just where to slap the once to get her message over. Greta decided that it might pay her to tell her father what she'd done. If nothing else he'd be prepared when Mrs Miller put in her complaint.

But before Greta saw Harry, Alex arrived back at the house. He was wearing a clean shirt, open at the neck, and navy blue trousers with a knife edge crease to them. On his back he carried a rucksack that had a tin plate and mug tied with string to one of the straps. His face looked like it had been scrubbed and his hair appeared still damp. Greta felt unexpectedly shy faced with this Alex. He seemed much more mature, somehow.

'What is it?' he asked, a quizzical expression in his eyes. 'Have I still some coal dust on my face?'

'No!' she answered hastily. 'I was just thinking how different you look to when I first saw you.'

'I am different thanks to your dad … and you!' There was an note in his voice that made her feel warm inside and she remembered her mother saying good deeds bring their own rewards.

She felt at ease with him once more and showed him to the parlour, where she had placed a clean blanket and a pillow. There was also a faint smell of gas from the meter in the cupboard. 'You can open the window if the smell bothers you,' she said.

'It's nothing to some of the smells I've come across since I went to sea.' He dumped his rucksack on the sofa and eased his shoulders.

'Did you like being at sea?'

He shrugged. 'It wasn't too bad once I got used to it. It's no fun in a storm when you're stuck up in the crow's nest on watch.' His eyes held a faraway expression. 'When you've stared out over the sea for a couple of hours you start imagining you can see things.'

'What things? Sea monsters!'

He grinned. 'You mean like Moby Dick?'

'Who's he?'

'He's not a he but a huge whale that figures in a book.'

'A true story?'

'I don't know about that.'

'What about places? Buenos Aires … was that fun?'

He nodded. 'There was some festival on so there was dancing in the street.'

Greta's eyes sparkled. 'You lucky duck! Did you dance?'

'I had a go.' He looked slightly embarrassed.

'What kind of dancing was it? Did you do the Tango?'

He laughed. 'I'm no Rudolph Valentino! But there were some girls who tried to teach me and a couple of the other deck crew the Samba. Then we had a go at the Conga.'

She perched on the arm of the sofa. 'My dad had me doing the Conga at the Coronation … that was at the street party. I was only a kid then but it was fun. Nobody had much money but all the mams and dads managed to put some food on the table. We were happy then. Since Mam died …' She stopped abruptly.

'Go on!' urged Alex, resting an elbow on the corner of the mantelpiece. 'I don't remember ever being at a party where there were mums and dads.'

Greta shook her head and moved away from him over to the bay window. After a few moments Alex followed her and unlocked the sash and pushed up the bottom window. The blackout curtains fluttered in the warm breeze that blew in.

'I'm not sure whether to carry on with my search,' said Alex sombrely.

She shot him a startled glance. 'You feel like you've come up against a brick wall?'

He shook his head. 'If Mum was telling the truth then there's the clue of the bicycle shop. No! It's what she said to that woman about me that really bothers me. She must have had such plans for me and …' He stopped abruptly and gazed out of the window.

Greta noted the misery on his face and forgot her own reservations about his quest to find his family. 'And what?' she demanded. 'Are you thinking that you're going to be a disappointment to her?'

He shrugged. 'Something like that.'

She seized his arm and shook it. 'Then think again! Any mother in her right mind would be made up to have a son like you.'

He smiled grimly down at her. 'Nice of you to forget my breaking into your house but then you're the forgiving sort … and besides, you weren't brought up to expect too much from life, especially when it comes to this world's goods. In my mum's case things were different. Even when things were almost as bad as they could be, Mum still hung on to the conviction that everything would work out. She certainly stopped us kids worrying for a while … until everything fell apart. Dad died and I found myself torn from my family to live amongst strangers miles away. Don't want to bore you with anymore.'

Greta was unable to speak, could almost feel that small boy's pain and loneliness. She took a deep breath. 'We all try to hold on to our dreams. Your mother was no different from lots of others. You mustn't give up.'

He was silent.

Well, she wasn't going to say anymore, decided Greta, making a move towards the door. 'How about some grub?'

Alex followed her out and into the kitchen. Greta put on the wireless to kill any awkward silences. The easily recognisable music of a palm court orchestra flowed into the room. Immediately she fiddled with the knobs until something more to her taste came on the air. *'We're in the money ...'* sang a tenor.

She hummed the tune as she opened the oven and took out a casserole. She heaped food on to a plate and placed it on the table. Alex thanked her and sat down. She picked up the *Echo,* folded it so that it was easier to read and placed it against the sugar basin. She pointed out the article to him. 'It's all about the accident. I've got other news for you, too. I don't know if you want to know it now or how much help it'll be, but Rene thinks your uncle lives close to the Southport line after Seaforth.' She sat down opposite him and watched him eat. She found it intensely satisfying to see people enjoy her cooking.

Alex did not respond immediately but forked tender beef into his mouth. After a few minutes, he murmured, 'It could be several places then. The trouble is we seldom visited Uncle David's house. More often than not he came to ours. I can't even remember what he did for a living. Although, strangely enough I've just remembered Dad's brother, Uncle George, was a solicitor but we saw hardly anything of him.'

'So what are you going to do?' said Greta, thinking the search could still grind to a halt with so little to go on.

Alex did not get a chance to answer because at that moment Harry walked in. He looked exhausted and appeared covered in more building dust than usual. Immediately, she filled his mug with tea and handed it to him. 'You look like you need this, Dad. What have you been up to?'

'Thanks, luv, I'm parched!' His eyes creased at the corners as he smiled. He took a couple of gulps and then placed the cup on the table. 'I'll have to get this jacket off. I'm roasting!' As he tried to remove his jacket, Greta could tell from the tightening of his lips and the flaring of his nostrils, that he was in discomfort. She went over and tugged gently on first one sleeve and then the other, removed his cap, and hung both on a nail on the back of the door to the coal cellar. Then she went over to the sink and placed the plug in the hole of the shallow brown sink and turned on the tap. 'Why all this special attention?' he asked, smiling faintly.

She faced him. 'I'm in trouble, Dad.'

He stared at her, and moistened his lips. 'What kind of trouble?'

'Mrs Miller!'

For a moment Greta thought her father was going to collapse on the floor but then he began to laugh weakly. 'You gave me a fright then, girl!' He ran a hand over his face, his fingers rasping a day's growth of beard. Then after rolling up his sleeves, he reached for the block of green washing soap. 'What have you done?'

Greta began to explain. She thought he didn't appear to be listening as he washed his face, neck, arms and hands but then suddenly he interrupted her. 'She said that about Rene and me?' he said wrathfully. 'That woman's got a one track mind.'

'Rene said, *Chance would be a fine thing!*'

His eyes glinted. 'She's right there! That woman hardly gives her a minute. So what did Mrs Miller say to that … and what did you do that was so terrible?'

Greta told him and she could see that he was doing his best not to smile. When she finished, he said sternly, 'You go and say sorry.'

Greta groaned. 'She's going to love that, Dad.'

He nodded. 'You got pleasure from calling her an old crow, didn't you? So it's her turn now. Off you go!'

'Yes, but … '

He shooed her out of the back kitchen with the towel.

Greta saw that the Millers' front door was open. Wilf was sitting on the threshold, his lips pursed. He had his sleeves rolled up and was polishing a small engraved brass tray with a soft cloth. She knew the tray had come from India. Wilf had a collection of brasses from different corners of the Empire. She remembered him saying he found few things more soothing than giving his brasses a good rub. He had added with a wink that he never gave up hope of a genie appearing and granting him three wishes.

'Is Mrs Miller in?' she asked.

Without looking up, Wilf said, 'You thinking she might have flown off on her broomstick?'

Greta said gravely, 'I didn't call her a witch.'

'Naw, luv, yer didn't! It's what I call her meself, sometimes. Yer can do hell and all for her and she's still not grateful.'

'Then why stay?'

He put down his duster and stroked his moustache, his eyes narrowed against the rays of the sun. 'Got used to the place and I'm too old to go looking for another berth. Besides, Rene's life would be more cat and dog without me.'

Greta nodded. 'Can I get past?'

Wilf got to his feet, his knee joints creaking. Greta stepped up into the lobby. Taking a deep breath she knocked on the open door and called, 'Rene! Mrs Miller! It's me Greta! Can I come in?'

The kitchen door opened and the cat shot out, skidded on the lino and then did a quick turn and whizzed towards Greta. She watched it spring onto the step and then she turned and saw Rene standing at the foot of the stairs, outside the kitchen door.

'Has she heard there's free fish at the chippy or something?' joked Greta. 'I've come to say sorry to your mam.'

Rene's face showed a ghost of a smile. 'Now's not the right time,' she whispered. 'The cat got one of the chicks and Mother's spitting nails because I didn't notice the evidence and she put her foot on the remains. I only just managed to save us both from landing flat on our backs. She said she's severely damaged hers and has taken to her bed.'

'I'll go then,' whispered Greta. 'You'll tell her I came to say sorry?'

Rene nodded.

Greta left the house almost as fast as the cat had done, jubilant that she had managed to get away without actually having to say that word *Sorry!* to Vera Miller.

She found Harry reading the *Echo* and Alex poring over a Bartholomew's Pocket and Atlas Guide to Liverpool and its environs. 'Seen what they say about you, Dad?' she said as she put on the kettle. 'Think there's a chance of you getting a medal?'

He shrugged. 'I want no medal, luv. I didn't do anything that merited it. What gets up my nose is that I doubt there'll even be compensation for the injured men or for the families of those who've died,' he said with a hint of anger. 'It's something the unions are fighting for but the employers want to carry on putting the responsibility for safety in the hands of the workers.'

'One of the men who died left a wife and two daughters, name of Cox,' said Alex, closing the book of maps. 'I wonder how the hell they're going to manage. I notice it gives their addresses.'

Harry's craggy face quivered. 'God only knows how they're feeling.' His voice was uneven. 'I haven't been able to get the men's faces out of my head.'

'Me neither,' said Alex in a low voice.

Harry stood up. 'I think I'll go and write letters sending our condolences,' he said huskily. 'Depending on the day and the time of the funerals perhaps I'll go and pay my respects.'

As Greta watched him leave the kitchen, his shoulders drooping, she felt a lump in her throat, remembering that shortly they would be coming up to the anniversary of Alf and Amy's deaths. She felt like crying and had to avert her face in case Alex noticed the tears in her eyes.

The following evening, Rene was kneeling on a sheet of cardboard in the tiny front garden. She looked up as she heard Harry's footsteps, her fingers relaxed on the kitchen fork she was using to dig up weeds. She could not afford proper gardening tools. Her mother was still tucked up in bed with a hot water bottle and a library book.

'So you're a hero, Harry!' She smiled, even as she tried not to think of his performance in her latest dream.

'I'm nothing of the sort,' he said, but it was uplifting to know that Rene thought so. He hesitated before crossing to her step. 'Is your mother OK now Greta's said sorry?'

'Greta didn't tell you?'

'Tell me what? I've had that accident and those poor families who've lost a father and breadwinner on my mind.'

Rene's green eyes were immediately concerned. 'It was a terrible thing to happen. All that scalding steam! How those poor men must have suffered!'

Harry nodded and cleared his throat. 'I've written a few words of sympathy and I'm just going along to pop the notes through the families' doors. I don't want to intrude but it can help knowing someone else is thinking about you when you've got troubles.'

Rene squared her shoulder and blurted out, 'I'm glad you realise that, Harry, it was how I felt when I popped round to yours after Sally passed away. I never intended being a nuisance or to set the tongues wagging.'

'You were never a nuisance,' he said hastily. 'I'm sorry if I gave you that impression. You were a real help. It was your mother who made me see that I hadn't to be selfish and use you. At least I think that was what she was trying to say to me.'

Rene's eyes widened and she scrambled to her feet. 'She said that to you! She told me that the tongues were wagging, putting two and two together and working things out.' Her fingers tightened on the fork. 'I don't want to soil my lips with the things she said.'

Harry was angry and he smoothed back his curly hair with a rough hand. 'What the hell's she at? She must know the kind of people we are.'

'Of course she does!' whispered Rene, glancing up at her mother's bedroom window. Then she looked at Harry. 'She's a selfish woman! Always has been, I suppose, but I never questioned her behaviour. Since her rheumatism's got worse, she's in pain and she's terrified of being completely helpless. I can only think that's the reason for her cruelty and possessiveness. Even now, when I hardly speak to you she thinks that I'm making plans to see you.'

Harry said grimly, 'Greta told me that you said, *Chance would be a fine thing.*'

Rene blushed and then suddenly she laughed. 'Your Greta! She did my heart good the way she leapt to my defence.'

Her laughter and words brought a smile to his face. 'I just hope her mouth doesn't get her into real trouble one day.'

'If it does, fate will probably take a hand and rescue her. Did she tell you about Mother slipping on a chick?'

'No! Poor chick.'

Rene giggled. 'It was already dead. But Mother's in bed now, suffering from a bad back. I know I shouldn't laugh but it does mean I'm getting the chance of a nice bit of peace out here.'

With warmth in his eyes and voice, Harry said, 'You deserve it, luv. It's a pity you don't get more chances to relax and do what you want to do.'

'Yes, that would be lovely, but you don't get much chance to take the weight off your shoulders, either, Harry. Wouldn't it be great to be free of all responsibility for a while? Just think what we could do.'

There was silence as they stared at each other hungrily. Then Harry said with a catch in his throat, 'I'd best get going or I won't be back until midnight. See you around, Rene, and don't work too hard.'

She watched him walk away and told herself that she mustn't read too much into the look in his eyes but she was in no mood to garden anymore. So she sat on the step, watching the children who were still playing out, some whipping tops into frenzies. She imagined being young and carefree, remembered games of *Catch the Girl, Kiss the Girl* and imagined being kissed by the young Harry. If she had met him first, instead of Sally, would it have made a difference?

Sally had been desperate to have a man in her life as soon as possible. Strange, considering she and her mother had been deserted by Mr Hardcastle and his sons. But maybe that was why Sally had grabbed Harry, having recognised a good'un when she saw him. There was a yearning inside Rene that refused to go away.

'Hello, girl! Making the best of the warm evening, are yer?'

Rene didn't need to look up to know who it was. 'Looks like it. How are you, Mrs Hardcastle?'

'Can't complain.' Cissie lit a cigarette and rested a plump shoulder against the door jamb. 'Did Greta tell you I've been to see an old flame today?'

'No!' Rene looked up at her in surprise. 'But then it has been a strange kind of weekend.'

'You can say that again! What with Harry doing his hero act and young Alex turning up. I take it you know about his looking for his mother and sisters?' She cocked an eye in Rene's direction. 'An unnatural mother in my opinion! I could have put my lot into a Home if I wanted but I was in one meself for a while, so I wasn't going to subject my kids to what I suffered. I said that to our Sal and maybe that's why the lad was put away but not the girls. Although, you can't always trust men wherever you are.' Her voice trailed off and she stubbed out her cigarette and went indoors without even a good night.

Rene wondered what had happened to Cissie in that Home but guessed she would never find out and decided to call it a day, too.

A few hours later Harry arrived back. 'What took yer so long, Dad?' asked Greta, looking up from the game of cards she was playing with Alex. 'I was about to send out a search party.'

Harry hung up his jacket and sank thankfully into the chair opposite Cissie. 'Where've yer bin?' she asked.

'Greta didn't tell you?' He scrubbed his chin with his fist and yawned.

'Tell me what?'

'I went to post a few notes of sympathy. I ended up getting caught in the act in Great Mersey Street. Mrs Cox asked me in. I said I didn't want to intrude but she insisted on making me a cup of tea. It was hard to get away.' Harry thought about the woman and her two daughters, who had plied him with so many cups of tea that he'd felt awash with it. She had shown amazing self-control but he had suspected that tears weren't far away. One of her daughters had shown no such restraint, had obviously loved her father very much and been sent out of the room with her sister because she couldn't control her grief. He had wanted to rail at God on their behalf ... that's if he'd believed in a deity ... instead he had promised that he would do his best to be at the funeral. It would help to take his mind off that exchange with Rene earlier. He had sensed undercurrents that had belied their sensible behaviour. He needed to put some distance between them or, one day, he would be tempted to grab her and kiss her ... and that'd give the neighbours a field day.

6

Edith Cox smoothed her skirt over rounded hips and then adjusted the collar of the jacket. The black gabardine costume fitted snugly and did wonders for her figure. She tried to look miserable but couldn't and instead smiled at her reflection in the sideboard mirror. She tucked a newly touched up strand of blonde hair into place beneath the narrow rim of the black felt hat and carefully unpinned the veil and let it fall over her face. She looked the part now and reckoned she could fool anyone into believing that she was a grieving widow.

Her mourning weeds were the first new clothes she had spent out on in a long time. Thank God, Rodney had kept up with his life insurance payments. Although, he had been tight-fisted at times, unlike Mr Lawrence Macauley, the brother of Mrs May Dunn, her employer when she had been in service. He had been so good looking and generous with presents that she would have done and forgiven him anything, and had, but she had probably done the right thing in leaving when she did although, she still had her regrets.

She thought of her husband crying poverty when she asked for money for new clothes for herself or the girls. Although he never did without his baccy or his pint at the Heriot Arms, where he was a regular for the last couple of hours every evening. Not that he ever got falling down drunk. In fact the only time she had known him worse for drink had been the evening she had taken advantage of him. She doubted he had ever suspected that she had tricked him into marriage. The last few years, though, it had been difficult to believe that he had once been passionate about her.

At the beginning of their marriage, she had certainly been grateful towards him and determined to be a good wife, but such ambition had lasted only a few years and she had grown bored with him. Perhaps she hadn't disguised her feelings enough and that's why he had become so mean in their latter years together.

Money! She had always had to worry about it. Fortunately both her girls were in work, although they only earned buttons. Joyce, her elder daughter, was a trainee machinist at Brown's ship repairers down Sandhills Lane, not far from Huskisson Dock, and Winnie, her younger daughter, worked at Jacob's biscuit factory. Edith would have liked more for her girls but life hadn't worked out the way she wanted. Her spinster sisters had died just when she had thought she could rely on them to help her out.

Always headstrong, she had been the youngest in the family, believing she could make life go her way. She had been a starry-eyed innocent when Lawrence said he was mad about her and would marry her if she got into trouble. Well, he had lied but that had not really surprised her. It was his widowed sister who had all the money.

Still, thinking about those far off days was not going to get her anywhere. She had to look to the future and find a job. For a moment panic seized her. She was thirty-nine and the only thing she knew was how to keep house. She had loved the one where she had been in service. It had been conveniently situated near the railway station one stop up from Crosby, which meant she could be in Liverpool in no time. So many rooms in the house and such lovely furniture and beautiful crockery, ornaments and pictures. Unlike this dump!

She gazed about the small room with its yellowing cream walls, adorned only with a mirror and a couple of plaster plaques, one of a thatched cottage and another of a black and white collie. The shabby sideboard, sofa and fireside chairs had belonged to Rodney's father, who had rented the house before him.

How she would love to return to that house near Hall Road, but she would not be a servant again, having her every action controlled by other people, getting her hands filthy, cleaning out fires and polishing brass and silver, as well as a dozen and a half other piddling jobs. At least when Rodney had been at work, her hours had been her own to fill and as soon as Winnie had been old enough she had passed the really dirty jobs over to her, but she would have to find some kind of work now or they would go hungry.

Edith clasped her hands tightly together and tapped her knuckles against her teeth. Keep calm, keep calm! The insurance would tide them over the next few weeks, although she had spent more on the funeral than was sensible. That was because she had wanted to impress the neighbours by giving Rodney a good send off. In her ignorance, she had believed there would be compensation for the accident but the other families were of the opinion that the bosses would worm their way out of paying them anything.

Dear God, Rodney had looked terrible, like someone out of a horror film. She shuddered, and wished she had not seen him like that. The memory would be with her for the rest of her days.

Her thoughts were disturbed by Joyce entering the kitchen, a sparkle in her eyes. 'Mum, the hearse is here and it's pulled by two black horses. It's really fancy! And you should see the carriage we'll be going in. If it wasn't all black and shiny brass, it could pass for Cinderella's coach like we saw in the pantomime the other year.'

Edith pulled herself together. She was proud of this daughter. A blue-eyed blonde with a heart shaped face, a straight nose and a cupid bow mouth, Joyce had inherited her parents' good looks. 'Good!' she said firmly. 'We want the best for your father, don't we?'

'Yes. Gosh, Mum, you look smart.'

Edith smiled, knowing she could always depend on Joyce to say the right thing. With a finger and thumb, she removed a long blonde hair from the girl's shoulder. 'You look smart, too. Black suits you. Do you like the pleating on the bodice?'

'Yeah!' Joyce glanced at her reflection in the mirror. 'But it would have been nicer with a bit of lace to pretty it up. I know it had to be all black so I'm not complaining, Mum.'

'Yes, Joyce, not yeah … sound your words properly. Perhaps in a few months time we could add some lace.' Edith stroked her daughter's silky hair. 'But now we've got to get through this funeral without any of us breaking down, so fetch your sister. She's been down that yard for ages. Tell her no more tears. Your father would expect no displays of emotion. You know how he hated it when the pair of you cried during weepies. I'll go and speak to the undertaker.'

She had refused to have Rodney's body brought home, not wanting either of her daughters to see his face and get even more upset. She knew that hadn't pleased some of the neighbours, who had known Rodney for donkey years and had expected to pay their respects here in this house, but she hadn't allowed them over the threshold.

Joyce paused in the doorway, a hand on the doorjamb. 'I'll tell Winnie what you said, Mam, but you know how she hates being told to do things by me.'

Edith frowned. 'You tell her that she'll make me angry if she doesn't pull herself together and get in here.'

'OK.'

Joyce went down the yard to the lavatory near the bottom. The door was slightly ajar and she peered through the gap. Winnie was sitting on the wooden seat, her face miserable, her button nose pink, and her eyes swollen and red. Short tendrils of brown hair clung damply to her plump face.

'Mam said you're to stop crying or she'll belt you one,' called Joyce through the gap.

'Get lost!' said Winnie, and leaning forward pulled the door towards her, scraping Joyce's cheek as she did so.

'You bitch!' Joyce's hand went to her face. 'It's what she said, not me! That wasn't fair! You don't want to be upsetting Mum. You know her temper. I'm sad, too, but us being miserable isn't going to bring Dad back.'

'He shouldn't have died!' Winnie's voice cracked. She rose from the lavatory seat and smoothed the skirt of the black frock, which, although fashioned in the same style as her sister's, was too tight under the arms and looked stretched across her breasts. She was fourteen and hated her body, wishing she could be a child again. Her father had been so much nicer to her when she was a young girl. She had danced for him in the kitchen, pretending to be a fairy or a dandelion clock, imagining she was as light as air and could fly. Then she had developed a bosom and her hips and stomach had swelled, and she just knew there was no sense in pretending she was anything other than the heavy lump of dough that a boy up the street had called her.

She opened the door and gazed at her older sister, who was sixteen with an enviable thirty-six, twenty-four, thirty-six inch figure. 'It's all right for you,' she said sullenly. 'You're Mum's favourite!'

'If you tried harder to please her and were less miserable then she wouldn't have it in for you so much,' said Joyce, her expression bored. 'We're all going to have to pull together if we're to get by.'

'But it'll be me that'll be given all the lousy jobs in this house if Mum goes and gets a job. You'll get the easy ones!' The thought of the unfairness of the treatment her mother meted out to her made Winnie so angry that she reached out, grabbed a handful of her sister's blonde hair and pulled hard.

Joyce screamed and slapped her sister's arm. Then she pushed her so that she fell backwards onto the lavatory seat. Winnie jarred her elbow on the lead pipe that ran up the wall behind the toilet and yelped.

'What the hell do you think the pair of you are doing?'

Neither of them had heard their mother's footsteps and both jumped visibly. Edith's face was tight with annoyance. She grabbed Joyce's arm and pulled her out of the way and then seized Winnie's shoulder and heaved her up and out of the lavatory. She slapped her across the face. 'Now no more nonsense!' she said coldly. 'Into the house and get your hat on! It's time to go.'

'It's not fair!' wailed Winnie, a hand to her scarlet cheek. 'Why did you hit me and not her?'

'Because you're moping about feeling sorry for yourself. Now come on!' Edith marched up the yard. The sooner she got this funeral over with, the better she would be able to decide their future.

As Edith entered St Aidan's church, she was gratified to see that her efforts to put on a good show had not been wasted. She had expected the church to be full as the deaths of her husband and the other men had roused a lot of sympathy for their families. She had received several letters of condolence, one from a man who had been among the rescuers. He had actually called at the house. Having still been in shock, she had had a rather awkward, yet soothing, conversation with him. She'd appreciated his call and, in fact, had not wanted to let him go. He was the first man to really attract her since Lawrence. His black hair and blue eyes were an unusual combination and, being recently widowed himself, he proved a sympathetic listener. He'd even promised to try and come to the funeral. Would he be there?

As Edith followed the coffin, to the strains of Bach on the organ and flanked on either side by her daughters, she was conscious of heads turning. A lot of the people she knew, at least to say hello to on the street, but when she saw *him*, pent up breath escaped her. He wasn't what one would call exactly handsome but his craggy face was terribly attractive and she remembered he had good teeth. Rodney's had been false and didn't fit properly and would make peculiar clicking noises when least expected.

In an attempt to ignore Winnie's weeping, Edith thought about Harry Peters for the rest of the service. When it was over, she stood at the church door, shaking hands with people and thanking them for coming and supporting her and her girls in this their darkest hour. In such a way *he* could not leave without having to speak to her.

'Thank you for coming, Mr Peters.'

'You remember me!' His surprise was obvious.

She smiled as his large hand swallowed up hers. 'How could I forget the man who rescued my husband. You were so kind to drop by that evening after the accident.' She thought that sudden smile of his was enough to make her lust after him. 'Perhaps you'd like to come to the house for something to eat after the burial,' she asked.

He was apologetic. 'I've got to go back to work. Sorry.'

Disappointed, she responded lightly, 'Another time perhaps. I know you understand what I'm feeling right now. You know what it's like to lose someone you love.' A muscle tightened his cheek and she wondered for a moment whether she had gone too far. He hesitated and she thought he was going to agree but, instead, he just nodded and walked away.

On the way to the cemetery Edith found herself wondering what line of work Mr Peters was in. He had looked smart in a dark suit but it hadn't been fashioned with the best of fabrics and the style was dated. Even so, she was in no position to sniff at a working man's wages and besides, she reckoned he would be good in bed. It was years since Rodney had tried to please her. Their sex life had consisted of a quick coupling on a Saturday night and that was it for the rest of the week. She could only hope that Harry Peters would not forget her and consoled herself with the thought that at least he knew where she lived.

Greta paused in her task of polishing the brass threshold and sat back on her heels and looked up at her father, shading her eyes from the sun with her hand. 'How did the funeral go, Dad?'

Harry paused on the grid to the coal cellar. 'She gave him the works. Fancy carriage drawn by black horses with plumes and a full service with four hymns!' He removed his cap and wiped the sweat from his brow. 'The church was crowded and one of the daughters cried throughout the service. Poor kid! But Mrs Cox took the time to thank everyone on the way out.' His dark brows knitted in thought.

'What is it? You're not wondering whether you can do something to help them, are you?' asked Greta alarmed, remembering her mother saying on more than one occasion that Harry was far too soft-hearted for their good. He made no answer. She wiped her dirty hands on her apron and scrambled to her feet. Stepping down from the lobby, she clutched his arm. 'Dad! I know you feel sorry for them but if Mrs Cox can afford a fancy carriage and black horses, then she can't be hard up.'

He removed his cap and cleared his throat. 'It's not always money a person needs at these times, luv. It's someone who understands what you're going through, who's been there before you.'

She had a sudden sense of foreboding and that made her voice sharp when she spoke. 'Then you and Mam should have talked more after Alf and Amy died, not only to each other but to me! And when Mam died, we should have said how we were feeling! But no, we had to keep it buttoned up!'

Anger burst from Harry. 'Your mam did talk to me just before she died! She'd been keeping things from me! Now I wish she'd kept her mouth shut. Talk won't change things so what's the point, girl, of raking up the past?'

She opened her mouth to say that she would like to know what her mother had said, that she'd like to talk about the things they'd done as a family, the happy times, that it might make her feel better, but he brushed her hand from his arm and stepping over the threshold went inside. She stood as still a statue. His outburst had brought her near to tears and she wanted to run after him and ask what sort of things Sally had kept from him.

'Something wrong, Greta?'

The girl lifted her head and stared at Rene. 'Dad! He's been to the funeral of one of those men killed on the ship.' Her voice trembled. 'I don't think it did him any good. He's just shouted at me. He was really angry.' Tears shone in her eyes.

'There now, luv,' said Rene, her rosy face concerned as she came over to the girl. She placed an arm about her shoulders. 'That doesn't surprise me. It probably brought back memories. But he shouldn't have shouted at you.'

'No, he shouldn't have!' Greta wiped her eyes with the back of her hand and sniffed back her tears. 'I'd best get on with finishing the brass.'

Rene removed her arm but did not instantly go into next door.

'Alex Armstrong ... how is he getting on with his search? He still hasn't gone back to sea, I take it?'

Greta's expression froze. 'No. It's a bit difficult him not having the name of the man his mother was supposed to have married,' she said lightly. 'He's convinced that the bicycle shop is most likely in Bootle, because that's where his mother was living. So he was going to wander round the area and ask questions. He, also, planned on going to Crosby to look up where he lived before he was put in the orphanage. He's checking to see if any of the people who lived there then still live there now. And if they do ... hopefully they might remember his uncle's surname and address.'

Rene's eyes danced. 'A young man of no small brain!'

'I'd agree with that.' Greta began to feel better.

'Has he thought of visiting the records office and seeing if he can find the record of his parents' marriage? His mother's maiden name would be on the certificate. Then he'd have the uncle's surname and could look that up in the telephone directory.'

'There's a thought,' said Greta. 'I'll suggest it to him. Although,' she shrugged, 'perhaps he doesn't know where his parents were married. He might have to leave doing that if he has no luck in Crosby until the next time he's home. He's talking of going down to the Pool tomorrow to see about a ship. I don't think he gets paid much and all this travelling about costs money.'

Rene nodded. 'He probably wants to get some money put by in case he does find his family. If his idea is for him and his sisters to live together, then not having more than a couple of pennies to his name isn't going to say much for his ability to support them.'

That was true, thought Greta glumly. Money could, be very important to his sisters, if they'd been brought up by an uncle who must have been rich if he could afford to support his own children and his nieces. It was possible his uncle and aunt mightn't want to know Alex. They certainly wouldn't want to know her!

Half an hour later Alex returned to the house. He was looking tired but his face was flushed by the sun and Greta surmised, from the light in his eyes, that he'd had some success in his search. She was darning one of her father's socks and glanced over at Alex as he ate the bowl of scouse. He always ate as if he did not know where the next meal was coming from. She wondered why that was, because surely they must have fed him regularly at the orphanage and at sea. 'So what did you find out, Alex?' she asked.

He looked across at her. 'There was a woman and her daughter who remembered our family. Her husband is a ship's captain, and part owner in a ship, so she was interested in my having been to sea.' Alex reached for a slice of bread. 'She remembers my mother talking about my uncle, and saying that he was a very clever man. She knew more about my father, though, said he was a man of adventure and vision.' There was a note of pride in his voice.

'Why was that?' asked Greta, leaning forward and almost stabbing herself with the darning needle.

'Apparently my father owned a rubber plantation and lived in Malaya. Then he caught some sort of fever and came back to Blighty.' Alex cleaned his plate with the bread. 'He met my mother on the ship.'

Greta's eyes shone. 'A shipboard romance,' she said softly.

'You can make lots of things with rubber,' said Harry, lowering the newspaper. 'Tyres, Wellington boots.'

'School rubbers … there must have been plenty of money in it,' said Greta, relieved that her father had recovered from his burst of temper and was showing an interest. Until Alex had turned up, he had not spoken that evening.

Alex swallowed a mouthful of bread. 'I don't know if he had anything to do with the manufacturing side of it when he came home. In fact, if he sold the plantation he must have put the money in some other business to have lost it all. I mean there was a big market for rubber with the automobile industry taking off.' He frowned.

Greta leaned forward. 'Rene suggested you visit the registry, or was it the records office … to try and find your mother's maiden name. Which means you'd have your uncle's surname.'

Alex shook his head. 'I'm afraid that's out of the question. Apparently it was a whirlwind romance and Mum and Dad were married aboard ship.'

'How romantic!' breathed Greta.

'But a definite setback. You're going to be with us a bit longer, lad,' said Harry with a sort of grim satisfaction, and continued reading the newspaper.

There was a silence and the two young people looked at each

other. Alex grinned and Greta smiled faintly and whispered, 'I don't think he wants to get rid of you. So what'll you do next?'

'It's frustrating but if I still draw a blank tomorrow the search will have to wait until I get back from my next trip.'

She nodded. 'Your mother could be living in Liverpool itself!'

Alex groaned. 'Why couldn't she have said where my uncle lived? I can see me spending years between trips searching for her and the girls. It's bloody maddening! If you'll excuse my language,' he added hastily.

'Will you be away as long this time?' asked Greta, knowing she was going to miss him.

Alex said carefully, 'I suppose that depends on if there's a war.'

From behind the newspaper Harry said, 'If there is, lad, I'd head east if I was you … stay out of the Atlantic.'

Greta was often to recall her father's words in the months to come when Alex signed on a ship going to the Far East.

Harry glanced up at the lowering sky and felt several drops of rain on his face. It was a week since the funeral and he had thought several times about Mrs Cox's invitation. So far, he hadn't acted on it and this weekend was definitely out because it was taken up with ARP training.

From midnight that evening there was to be another four hour blackout as far as Chester. Simulating wartime conditions, there would be mock gas attacks, more explosions, fires and rescue drills from collapsed buildings. The latter was where he came in, because of his experience in the building trade. Never before had he thought he'd be taking a real interest in how a damaged building could collapse in three different ways. Either it completely disintegrated into a pile of rubble or the roof and floors fell in a curve, so that one side held up while the other swung down. Or the floors broke in the middle while the sides of the building held so a kind of V shape, with space in the storey below, was formed. People could survive in that space but no matter which way a building collapsed, more often than not, digging and tunnelling would be involved to get them out.

He hoped with all his heart that he would never have to do it for real because, without doubt, there would be fatalities and women and children were bound to be amongst them. Yet it looked more and more like war with Germany was on the cards. Only last week a proposal had been made in Paris between France, Britain and Poland to issue a direct warning to the Nazi-dominated Danzig Senate against any move to transfer the area to Germany. England and France were ready to help Poland if the Reich forced its hand.

'So what d'you think? Is it a good night for the blackout?' called Rene. 'When the leaflet came through the door the other week the weather was marvellous ... now!'

Harry turned at the sound of her voice and saw that she was putting the cat out. Instantly the hairs rose on the back of his neck and he imagined that tightness in his chest and a sneeze forming. He put a bit more distance between it and himself. He hadn't seen Rene to speak to since the day of the accident the day when his daughter had called Mrs Miller an old crow, the day when he had discovered that Rene's mother had insinuated things about himself and her daughter that had made him so aware of an overwhelming physical desire to take her to bed, that he had consciously avoided Rene. He could hardly do that now. 'Guess they were hoping for clear skies when they made the arrangements,' he replied.

'The British weather – it can always be depended on to do what you don't want it to do.' She came down the step towards him, hugging herself.

'You look cold.'

'It's chillier now than when I went to work in this frock.'

He noticed she was wearing that floral print made of some clingy material that revealed her voluptuous curves. For a moment he could not take his eyes from her breasts, then suddenly aware she was watching him, hoped that she had not noticed the direction of his gaze. Hurriedly he glanced up at the sky and sought frantically for something to say. 'So how are things at work? Are they prepared?'

'One of the wine cellars has been turned into an air raid shelter. It's all reinforced with steel and concrete.' Her voice sounded strained.

'What about furnishings and supplies?'

'Several bunks, bedding, tables, chairs ... plenty of tinned food and containers for water. There's even the means to pass the time while an air raid's on. Toilet facilities, too, and a phone line.'

'Sounds like they know what they're doing.'

Rene wondered what on earth they were doing talking about such things when he could have been kissing her. She knew that he wasn't made of stone where she was concerned. She had seen the expression in his eyes when he looked at her. But perhaps she should keep her mind on the conversation. There was no future in letting her thoughts run on romantic lines. 'Plans have already been made,' she said brightly, 'for rationing our customers. Vintage wines from previous years and certain spirits are being imported at a quickened rate of knots. The same with dried fruit that comes from Europe and California. If war comes ... once the German U boats are in action ...' She left the rest to his imagination.

'I wish young Alex hadn't opted to go to sea,' said Harry.

'What age is he? Sixteen, seventeen? Much too young to die for your country,' she said, her voice almost fierce.

He nodded, thinking again of those children who could die when the bombers came over.

'So what will you be doing tonight, Harry?' She leaned against the garden fence.

He lowered his gaze and caught the gleam of her eyes in the lamplight. For a moment he hesitated before saying, 'I'm a rescue man but don't go telling that to Greta.'

She straightened quickly. 'Dangerous?'

'No more dangerous than men training in the forces.'

'Is that supposed to be reassuring?'

'I'm only telling you the truth, luv.' He gazed into her eyes that he remembered were green with tiny blue flecks round the iris. Aware of that strong tug of attraction between them, he looked away and cleared his throat. 'What are your plans if war comes? It's going to be just as dangerous for women on the home front. Has your mother made any suggestions about leaving Liverpool for the country?'

Rene murmured, 'She hates the country. In some ways she's a bit like Mrs Hardcastle ... this is her home and she's not leaving it for Hitler or anyone. I have to admire their generation. They've been through so much.'

'Don't you think we have, too?' he said passionately. 'During the Great War we mightn't have had the responsibility of family and I was too young to go and fight, but I lost brothers and my parents. It changed your father out of all recognition. We've been through the Depression, done without and suffered the loss of loved ones. It's time we gave thought to ourselves and had some bloody fun before it's too late.' Harry amazed and thrilled Rene by seizing her by the waist and bringing her against him. He kissed her long and hard before releasing her just as abruptly. 'Goodnight!' He walked away down the road, hands in his pockets.

Rene stared after him, a hand to lips that felt swollen. Her insides were trembling. For a moment, she thought of running after him, but remembering where he was going, she turned and went indoors.

'What's up with your face?' asked Vera.

'Nothing!' Rene switched off the wireless. 'Do you want me to help you down to the lav now?'

Vera's eyes narrowed. 'What were you doing out there? You were a long time letting out the cat.'

'I was checking the blackout.'

'I thought I heard voices!'

Rene glanced at the kitchen door. It had been closed. Surely her mother couldn't possibly have heard her and Harry talking from in here when they had been standing at the bottom of the step? 'It'd be the wireless. Now you be careful once we get to the yard.' She helped her mother up from the chair.

'I don't need telling,' snapped Vera, clinging on to her. 'You just make sure you don't let go of me. I wouldn't put it past you wanting to get rid of me.'

Like you longed to be rid of my dad, thought Rene grimly, remembering the day she had realised her mother had stopped loving her father. She had thrown pepper in his face and stormed out of the house. Rene had been shaken, never having believed her mother could act in such a way. Vera had not returned for hours and when she did, she didn't apologise, only said, 'War's a terrible thing. It changes people, just you remember that, madam.'

They reached the lavatory and Rene tugged at the baggy knickers to reveal Vera's bony hips. Her resentment towards her mother overwhelmed her. She wanted to believe that Harry would kiss her again and there could be a future for them together but knew that while Vera was alive it was impossible.

'Next week's National Fitness Week,' said Vera, and sniffed. 'The government wants to make sure we're all healthy when we die. War's coming! I can feel it in my bones.'

Rene made no answer. She could feel it, too.

The following evening she hoped to see Harry but, although she went out onto the step a number of times, there was no sign of him. Several days passed without sight of him and Rene felt depressed, wondering whether he was deliberately avoiding her, having regretted kissing her. She knew, because she had asked Cissie, that he was still working on constructing air raid shelters and was often out evenings. Were more and more ARP practices taking up his time? She wished she had some answers.

One Sunday in August, she saw Greta coming out of the newsagent's. It was the day military action had been reported along the Polish border. Greta's eyes brightened when she saw her.

'I've had a letter from Alex.'

'How is he?'

'Fed up because it definitely looks like war and he doesn't know when he'll be able to get home and on with his search. They're expecting to stay in dock at their next port of call and paint the ship in camouflage colours. He's been told that when war's declared, portholes and windows are to be covered and smoking's not allowed on deck after sunset because the U boats'll be looking for them.' Greta frowned. 'That's worrying, isn't it? Did you know that the glow from a cigarette can be seen miles away? It's to do with the angle of the earth as it turns, apparently. I hope he stays sensible and doesn't smoke at all. My dad never took to smoking, so I hope Alex doesn't either.'

Rene seized her opportunity. 'How is your dad?'

'He's gone off to see some woman.'

Rene froze with shock and several seconds passed before she could get out the words. 'I didn't know he knew any women.' Her voice sounded strangled in her ears.

Greta pulled a face. 'Her name is Mrs Cox. She's the widow of one of those men who were killed in that accident on the ship.'

'You mean the one whose funeral he went to?' Rene did not want to believe that there was any more to it than a sympathy visit.

'You've got it in one! The trouble is, he's been in a peculiar mood lately. I can guess why but ... ' Her voice broke off and then she continued. 'Anyway, I've been left to make the Sunday dinner. Gran's out, too. She's gone gallivanting with her old flame and won't be back until late as she has the evening off. I feel fed up with both of them. I just hope Dad's soft heart doesn't land him in trouble.'

Rene could only hope the same.

Edith cocked her little finger as she lifted the teacup to her lips. She had almost given up on Harry Peters. It was more than a month since the accident and money was getting a little tight. She had begun to look seriously for a job. Munitions would pay well but she hadn't forgotten what the chemicals had done to the complexion of the girls she had known during the Great War. *Canaries* they'd been nicknamed. She didn't really want to work or even get married again, would prefer to be free, with enough money to go to the theatre, cinema, dancing, shopping for clothes, take a cruise. She had enjoyed the one cruise she'd been on. It was just after the end of the Great War and her mistress, who had lost her husband in the last week of the hostilities and was suffering from nervous debility, had been persuaded by Lawrence to take a cruise to Egypt. He had suggested Edith went along, too, to help his sister. The work had not been the slightest bit arduous because May Dunn had wanted to be alone most of the time. Edith and Lawrence had danced on deck under the moon; it wouldn't have done for them to do so in the ballroom. They had been wonderful days. She had sailed along the Nile, seen the Pyramids and the Suez Canal.

'My daughter's younger than your girls.' Harry's statement jerked Edith into the present.

'I beg your pardon?' She stared at him.

'My Greta. She'll be fourteen in October.' His smile was strained. 'The last year hasn't been easy for her, either. First we lost her younger brother and sister and then my wife.'

Edith placed her cup in its saucer with a shaking hand, amazed at the extent of the rage she felt because he hadn't told her that he had a daughter. In fact she felt quite faint.

Harry leaned towards her, his expression concerned. 'Are you all right, Mrs Cox? You've gone pale.' He reached out a hand to her.

She clutched it and whispered, 'Memories! I, too, lost a son and daughter in infancy,' she lied. 'Forgive me. I don't usually lose control.' She reached for the handkerchief tucked up her sleeve.

'Perhaps you'd like me to go,' he said, freeing his hand.

'No, no! It helps having you here.' She stared at him, wide-eyed.

'I get lonely when the girls are out. You know what it's like when they're that age … always gadding about. Not that they're not good girls,' she added, hastily, at the expression on his face.

'They shouldn't be leaving you alone evenings,' he said sternly.

'You don't understand. There are times when I want to be alone,' she babbled. That was true. She had chased Winnie out the back as soon as she'd seen him through the window coming up the street. 'Besides I want them to get on with their lives. They're only young and, with all this talk of war, they'll have to grow up quickly if it comes. I'm sure you haven't forgotten the last war, either.'

'Who could? I lost three brothers. By the end of it my mother had died of a broken heart, and then my father died in the flu epidemic of 1919.'

'How terrible for you! I, too, lost my parents young.' Her mouth trembled, then she forced a smile. 'Enough of far off sad things!' She decided to take a risk. 'Tell me, Mr Peters, do you like the cinema?'

He forced a smile. 'Aye! I like a good film. Not these singing and dancing ones but a comedy or a good thriller.'

Her eyes lit up. 'I'm just the same,' she lied. 'Those musicals, where people burst out into song on trolley cars or in the street and start dancing, are so unrealistic. Of course, at the moment, I'm too sad to enjoy a good film but maybe with time I'll be able to get pleasure from life again. We parents have to go on for our children's sake. I'm sure you know exactly how I feel?' She could tell from his face that he thought he did because he was grieving still for his beloved wife and children. 'Perhaps when I feel I can face going out again we might see a film?' she suggested.

He hesitated, then shrugged. 'Why not.'

That was good enough for her. She reached for the teapot. 'More tea?'

7

Greta looked up as her father came into the kitchen, hating the fact that he had visited that widow again last night. He had been quite brazen about it, saying that he was taking Mrs Cox to an Oyster Bar for supper. Last time he had taken her to the pictures. Her chest swelled with indignation, remembering how he'd polished his shoes until they shone, before putting on a clean shirt, collar and tie and his best suit. He had gone out, smelling of Brylcreem and shaving soap, humming a dance tune beneath his breath. She had wanted to hit him.

How could he behave in such a way when her mother hadn't even been in her grave a year? As for Mrs Cox, whose husband had died only two months ago. What were they to make of her? Yesterday was the fifth time Harry had seen her and obviously he was trying to create a good impression. But for what purpose? Greta worried that Mrs Cox might have marriage on her mind and the existence of the two daughters, also, made her uneasy. Maybe it was because she was reminded of the ugly sisters and the stepmother out of *Cinderella*.

Harry dropped a newspaper on the table and took off his jacket. 'The King has signed the order for full mobilisation of British forces! Emergency Control is in force in Liverpool.' Despite the grimness of his words there was a sparkle in his eyes. Although he had an overriding horror of war, he felt a peculiar sense of relief. At least the waiting was over and they knew what they were up against. It also meant he was going to have his evenings taken up with ARP work.

Since he had kissed Rene he had known he needed a good reason to prevent them being tempted into a clandestine affair. Surely he wasn't mistaken about her wanting him or that she would suffer the same guilt if they fell into bed together? Besides, he could imagine what Mrs Miller would say to her daughter if she ever got wind of a real affair between them. That was why he had deliberately set out to place a barrier between himself and Rene by letting it be known that he was taking Edith Cox out on a regular basis.

This wasn't true. All he had done so far was to visit her. But he'd decided if his relation with the widow was to be taken seriously by

Rene, then it had to appear that they were going out together. Now he wondered if he'd been a little crazy to have thought up such a plan. From the expression on Greta's face, his daughter obviously disapproved strongly of the association. Cissie probably felt the same. His other problem was that he could be heading for trouble with the widow. He wasn't a vain man but he'd have to be blind not to have noticed Edith fancied him. It was probably the loneliness that was making her come on to him so soon. Fortunately, so far, he had managed to keep her at arms' length.

'Wake up, Dad! You seem to have gone into a trance,' snapped Greta. 'What happens next?'

Harry roused himself from his reverie. 'Five mobile control bases are in place in our area, the nearest First Aid post is in Belmont Road Institution.' He placed his hands on the table and stared at his daughter. 'It's come, girl, and you and your gran are out of here. I'll take no more shilly-shallying from either of you. For your own safety, you're going!'

Greta was determined he was not going to get rid of her or her gran, especially with that widow on the scene. More than once she had recalled his words about her mother telling him something before she died and wished for the courage to ask him what it was that had made him so angry. She sighed, and reined in her thoughts. Now was not the right time to be thinking about it, she ought to concentrate on the matter in hand. She knew whole schools were being evacuated three million children was the number bandied about so she definitely had a fight on her hands to stay at home. She glanced at her gran sitting bolt upright on her chair in front of the fire, before turning her attention back to her father. 'I'm not a child, Dad! I'll be leaving school next month and will be able to get a job here.'

The old woman said, 'You tell him, queen!'

Harry's frown deepened. 'That's beside the point! You can get war work in the country … work on a farm.'

'I don't want to work on a farm,' she said indignantly, springing from her chair. 'I want to work in an office and Miss Birkett's promised me that I can work part time in her house and the shop until my birthday! She'll help me learn to type. She has a typewriter since she took over as church magazine editor when the last one joined the army. Working on a farm won't be of any use to me at all once the war's over, so it's a waste of time me doing it.'

'And I'm definitely not going,' said Cissie, folding her arms across her bosom. 'My fella's in the ARP and he said with the young ones joining the forces there's plenty of war work even for a woman of my age.'

Harry swore under his breath. Cissie and Greta looked at each other and winked. 'Wash your mouth out with soap!' they chorused.

'You're both enough to make a saint swear,' muttered Harry, but a reluctant smile was tugging at his mouth.

'And you're no saint,' said Cissie, her eyes challenging him.

She didn't have to put into words what she was insinuating and, for a moment, Harry was tempted to tell her what was behind his visits to Edith. Then he remembered her behaviour over the past years and his expression hardened. 'You dare to judge me?' he rasped.

Cissie's face turned puce and she dropped her gaze. Harry looked at his daughter. 'You've still got to go.'

Greta shook her head, her mouth set in a stubborn line. 'You'll have to carry me out kicking and screaming, Dad, if you want to get rid of me,' she warned. 'I won't go willingly.'

'I could do that, my girl!' he retorted.

Her face fell. 'But-but you wouldn't, would you, Dad? Please don't make me go. I promise I'll be off at the first sign of an enemy aircraft but until then let me stay!' she pleaded.

Silence.

She did not take her eyes from his face and knew the moment he had decided to relent. 'I have your promise, luv, that you'll go when I say?'

'Definitely, Dad!' She crossed her fingers behind her back.

'OK, then. We'll see how things go,' said Harry.

'D'you want me to fill that in for you, Mother?' asked Rene, noticing the sour expression on Vera's face as she read the application form for an identity card.

Britain had been at war with Germany almost two months now and, so far, there had been no Jerry planes over Liverpool, but the U-boats had been in action from the day war was declared. The liner *Athenia* had been torpedoed a few hours out of Liverpool with the loss of one hundred and thirty one lives. Shortly after that terrible loss, a Fleetwood fishing boat had been sunk. Fortunately for the crew, the commander had a conscience and had ferried them to within five miles of the Lancashire coast and left them in a lifeboat where they had been picked up by a naval vessel.

'You should have done it for me in the first place!' Vera hit the arm of her chair with the fountain pen. 'Identity cards, ration books, sticky tape on windows, buckets of water and stirrup pumps, gas masks, ugly blackout curtains! I don't want to be arsed with them! I'm more bloody concerned with how I'm going to get to the shelter if there's an air raid! That's what really bloody concerns me.'

'We'll get you there, Mother, don't you worry,' soothed Rene, trying to hang on to her patience. Something she did not have much of since Greta had told her of Harry's outings with the widow. She had told herself she had to accept that Harry's kiss had been a spur of the moment thing, unlikely to be repeated. Yet the thought of him with another woman made her feel miserable as sin.

'How are yer going to get me there?' demanded Vera. 'Push me in a wheelbarrow?'

Rene looked at Wilf. 'There's an idea,' he said, and chuckled.

Vera called him a very rude name.

His expression changed and he got to his feet. 'I'll go and see if the hens have settled,' he said gruffly.

Rene rested her hand a moment on his shoulder as he brushed past her. 'Don't mind her,' she whispered.

'What was that?' demanded Vera.

'Not for your ears, Mother,' said Rene, closing the back kitchen door on Wilf before turning to her.

Vera dropped the form on the floor. 'People whispering behind my back all the time! It's not right!' she grumbled.

Rene left the form where it lay. She could have hit her mother but, instead, spooned cocoa into a plain white jug and sang loudly so she could not hear Vera's mutterings.

When Wilf came back into the kitchen, he picked up the form and placed it on the table. 'I'm sorry!' mumbled Vera.

They both ignored her.

'The hens are fattening up nicely,' said Wilf. 'I reckon we could have one for our Christmas dinner.'

'I'm sorry!' shouted Vera.

Rene turned and looked at her. 'Did you say something, Mother?'

'I said I was sorry,' she said sullenly.

'I accept your apology,' said Rene, smiling, and poured cocoa into a cup for Vera. 'And I've been thinking that perhaps we could convert one of the chairs into a wheelchair ... put castors on the feet.'

'They wouldn't last five minutes getting on and off the pavement,' said Wilf. 'You let me think about it a mo'!'

Rene was glad to hand the problem over to him.

Soon after, an homemade wheelchair made its appearance. Rene and Wilf had several dummy runs with it, and then used it for the occasional visit to the cinema. These pleasure palaces had been closed briefly in the aftermath of the declaration of war but the government, realising that people needed escapism, soon re-opened them. So, for a while, the wheeled chair was kept in the lobby ready for use, despite Rene banging her shins on it several times. Then as the weeks slipped by towards the first Christmas of the war and still there were no air raids, it was moved into the parlour out of the way.

At the end of October, Harry heard about a vacancy for a junior clerk for a building material suppliers company and so Greta applied for the job and got it. Just before Christmas, she was working in their office in School Lane, to the rear of Church Street, the main shopping centre in the city. That day she had received a letter from Alex but there were bits cut out of it, so she could only hazard a guess at where he was and what he was up to. One thing was certain though, to her delight, he was hoping to be back in Britain for Christmas. She had mixed feelings about his determination to carry on with his search to find his mother and sisters; a part of her wanted him to be happily reunited with his family, whilst the other part worried that if he was, she would see little of him after that, if at all.

In the meantime, Greta was enjoying the company of the older girls and women in the office, feeling almost grown up as she listened to their conversations about films, the shortage of men, dancing, the possibility of being called up and which arm of the forces to join. They also talked about the rationing that was to come into force in January.

Already there were shortages of stockings, as factories were turned over to the war effort, and there was also a shortage of bricks. Thousands of surface shelters were being built as the U-boats got into their stride and Nazi warships roamed the North Atlantic. In

France the expeditionary army was still fighting spasmodic long range artillery duels with the enemy.

'I can't see it being over by Christmas,' said one of the women.

'My younger brothers and sisters are coming home for Christmas,' said a girl.

They weren't the only evacuees to be fetched home by their mothers. Children were arriving in their hundreds in Liverpool and lots of them flocked to see Father Christmas in Toy Town at T.J. Hughes departmental store in London Road.

Greta was glad to hear the noise of children playing in the street, only wishing that Alf and Amy could have been amongst them. She still missed them but was starting to come to terms with her loss.

Harry was not looking forward to Christmas at all. The last one had been bad enough. His grief had been so fresh, as was the wound caused by Sally's deception; both had been physically painful. If it had not been for Greta, he would not have got out of bed. He knew, though, that this year he was going to have to put a better face on things for hers, and Cissie's, sake.

He had been put on the spot by Edith who asked what was he doing on Boxing Day. He had told the truth catching up on odd jobs and maybe going to the park to see some of the local lads playing football. She had suggested that he brought Greta to tea so that she and her girls could meet one another. He had greeted the idea with a blank stare, while inside he was frantically seeking to come up with the perfect excuse. Taking the step of bringing Edith, her girls and Greta together, hinted at the possibility of a future closeness between them which was far from his thoughts.

Yet, Harry did not want to stop visiting her altogether. She helped keep his mind off Rene. Anyway, he did not want to hurt Edith's feeling, so he had told her that Greta was expecting a friend to stay over Christmas, but had accepted her invitation to tea for himself.

'Deck the halls with boughs of holly, fal-la-lah-la-lah-la-lah-la-lah!' sang Greta, determined to be happy as she linked a green strip of paper through a yellow one and pasted it into a loop. After all, even the Government was allowing blackout restrictions to be lifted slightly because it was Christmas.

'Someone's cheerful!'

Her smile vanished and she looked up at Harry. 'Being miserable won't bring them back, Dad. If they could see *me* being sad it would upset them. So I'm pretending.'

He ignored the dig and, despite his hurt, nodded. 'You're right, luv!' He placed his knapsack on the floor by the door. 'Any news from Alex?'

'A telegram!' She read his expression and reassured him quickly. 'It was to say that he hopes to be here sometime this evening. He was paid off in Southampton and was catching the train up.'

She marvelled that they could have got so fond of their *burglar* in such a short time. She couldn't say that he was the elder brother that she had never had because she had feelings for him that weren't a bit sisterly and could not wait to see him. It was also good for Harry to have another male in the house and might take his mind off the widow.

Harry looked relieved and glanced at the clock. 'Five hours to go. Where's your gran?'

'In the kitchen plucking a chicken.'

'Chicken! I thought we were having rabbit.' His face brightened. 'I haven't had chicken for … I don't know how long! Bit late to be plucking it, though, isn't she?'

Greta chuckled. 'We only got it an hour ago! Wilf sneaked in the back way and gave it to Gran. He said that he had a perfect right to give it to us because he had paid for the chicks and bought most of the feed … but just to save any trouble it's best done this way.'

Harry grinned. 'Good ol' Wilf! I don't suppose Rene would mind but …'

'You don't have to say anymore, Dad. Your tea's in the oven, by the way. D'you mind getting it out yourself while I get on with this?'

'Of course, I don't mind. It's Christmas, isn't it? I'll just wash my hands.' He left her alone to carry on with her task.

It was a quarter to midnight when a hammering was heard at the door. By then paper chains were strewn across the ceiling and a pan of giblet soup was simmering on the fire. Greta ran to answer the door.

Alex stood before her with a haversack on his back and a seaman's cap in his hand. Immediately he burst into *Away in a Manger*. He held out the cap with a grin. 'Couple of coppers for the carol singer, missus!'

'Do I know you?' she asked, looking down her dainty nose at him.

His smile hovered uncertainly. 'Don't mess about, Greta! It's me, Alex!'

'Alex! Do I know an Alex?' His jaw dropped, then she smiled and seized his arm. 'Of course I do! Come on in! Welcome home!'

'You little tease,' he said, grinning as his fingers caught hold of hers and squeezed them tightly. 'I never thought I'd get here on time! It's taken me all day.'

'Poor you. I bet you're hungry!' She drew him indoors.

'Starving! And bloo-blinking cold.'

'Then come and get a warm by the fire and some soup.'

'Perfect,' he said, allowing himself to be dragged up the lobby.

'Hello, lad!' said Harry, smiling as he advanced on Alex, hand outstretched. 'You're back at last! It's been a long time.'

'Over five months this time. I never thought I'd be away that long,' said Alex, obviously relieved by Harry's welcome. They shook hands heartily. 'I've been all over the place. India! I never thought I'd get to see India, but it's great to be back. Are you sure you want me here? I don't want to intrude, Mr Peters.'

'We're happy to have him here, aren't we, Mrs Hardcastle?' said Harry, looking in Cissie's direction.

'Of course we are! The more the merrier,' said Cissie, heaving herself up out of her chair. 'Help him off with that bleedin' big weight on his back, Harry! It's a wonder the lad's not on his knees.'

Harry did as ordered. Then while Cissie fussed over Alex, and Harry asked him what he had been doing in India, Greta ladled soup, thick with barley and vegetables, into a bowl and cut several slices of crusty bread.

She called him over to the table. Alex sat down, but before he picked up his spoon, he stared about the decorated, homely room with its shabby furniture. Then his gaze came to rest on the three people watching him, smiles on their faces. 'Thanks!' he said, his eyes bright and sparkly. 'I've got a feeling this is going to be my best Christmas ever!'

It was still gloomy in her room when Greta woke and, for a while, she lay remembering other Christmas mornings full of excitement. At fourteen and a bit, she did not expect to find a stocking filled with goodies at the bottom of her bed but, to her delight, when she pulled back the curtains to let in the wintery light, she noticed a bulging stocking on the floor.

She snatched it up, her heart racing. For a moment she stood, struggling with her emotions, wanting to howl for her lost brother and sister, then she swallowed and took several deep breaths. There! She had herself under control, and brushed back a strand of dark hair with the back of her hand and wiped her damp eyes.

She sat on the bed and began to remove the contents from the sock. A pair of lisle stockings, *Where had her father got them from? Hopefully from Miss Birkett! She was not going to think of the widow today.* A tiny bottle of *Californian Poppy*. She took out the little rubber stopper and sniffed the perfume with her eyes closed, thought of a flower decked meadow, then opened them again and placed it next to the stockings. Next out came a kaleidoscope! *She loved it. Had been hopping mad when Amy had broken the one she had been given when she was eight. Her father must have remembered.* She put it to her eye and turned the rim, watching the coloured shapes form a pattern and then dissolve before forming another pattern. She sighed with pleasure and then put it aside next to the other things on the bedcover before dragging out a small writing pad and pencil. After that there remained just a bar of Cadbury's milk chocolate, an apple, and several hazel nuts, walnuts and a silver three penny bit.

It was a good start to the day.

She went downstairs and found that Harry was there before her and had somehow managed to pull back the curtains and light the fire without disturbing Alex, asleep on the kitchen sofa. Cissie had decided after such a long cold journey that the young man would be better off in the warmth of the kitchen than in the parlour where the Christmas tree had been set up. Later, part of the kitchen fire would be shovelled up and hurriedly carried into the grate in the front room where those not involved in preparing the Christmas meal would sit out of the way of the workers.

She went over to Harry and whispered, 'Thanks, Dad!' She stood on tiptoe and kissed his cheek.

He did not speak but his arm went round her, hugging her against him, and he rested his cheek against her hair a moment. Then he released her and she hurried out of the house and down the yard to the lavatory. When she returned, her father was in the back kitchen, having a shave. She washed her hands and face in the sink and then made the porridge.

She went over to the sofa. Alex's trousers hung over its arm near his stocking feet. His shoulders and his bare upper arms were out of the blanket and she noticed that they were more muscular than last time. His skin was also more tanned than she had realised last night, showing dark against the white of his vest. She inspected his face, thinking that the length of his eyelashes made her envious. Suddenly his mouth, which had been relaxed, tightened and he jerked up. His nose bumped into hers.

'Ouch!' she cried, pulling her head back and rubbing her nose.

He felt his nose, blinking at her, bleary-eyed. 'It's you, Greta!'

'Who did you think it was?' she asked, feeling a pang of unexpected jealousy.

'The mate! I was dreaming I was at sea and they'd given the order to abandon ship, that we'd been torpedoed. Instead, I'm here!' Such relief showed on his face that it made her realise the dangers of war were more real to him than to her, and she experienced a quiver of fear for him. Even so she smiled, relieved that he hadn't expected to see another girl.

'You're here and safe. It's Christmas morning and you're going to have to move yourself because it's later than I thought and I'll have to wake Gran so we can get breakfast over and then get started on the Christmas dinner.'

'Right!' he said, and yawned, stretching his arms. 'If you get out of the room then I'll get up.'

She left him and went upstairs to wake her gran.

They breakfasted to the sound of carols on the wireless. As soon as the meal was over, Cissie suggested that Harry get a fire going in the parlour and then he and Alex might like to go for a walk to work up an appetite for dinner. When they returned, the chicken was done almost to perfection; it was not easy judging the temperature of the oven in the black leaded range, but Harry and Alex fell on the food as if it was a feast set for the King and Queen and said all the right things.

Afterwards they listened to the King's Christmas message, and then, full of food, they moved to the parlour where the fragrant smell of pine overcame the faint smell of gas, and the glow of the fire caused the tinsel on the Christmas tree to glitter.

'I've got presents for you,' said Alex, looking slightly awkward, as he reached for the rucksack in the corner over by the sideboard. 'I wasn't sure when to give them out.'

'You've picked the right time, lad,' said Cissie, opening the sideboard cupboard and taking out several tissue wrapped parcels.

'Mine are upstairs,' said Greta with a smile, and left the room.

Harry pulled out one of the armchairs and, from behind it, lifted a small cardboard box. 'One of these I kept back for an extra surprise for Greta. She's been through a lot but never a moan out of her.'

When Greta entered the room with her presents it was to find the other three seated in front of the fire, waiting for her. 'Eldest first!' said Harry, smiling at his mother-in-law.

'Right,' said Cissie, with a giggle, and handed out her three packages.

'You bought me a present!' said Alex, taken aback. 'I didn't expect anything, Mrs Hardcastle.'

'It gave me pleasure buying it, lad. Me and Greta picked it together.' There was a flush on her cheeks. 'I tell yer now it's second-hand.'

Greta looked at Alex and could tell that it not being new did not matter. It truly was the thought that counted with him. She watched as he unwrapped the parcel. Would her choice match his taste? The paper fell apart to reveal a book, *The Time Machine* by H.G. Wells. His face lit up and she relaxed. 'I thought you'd like science fiction,' she said.

He nodded. 'I'll have to sign on a new ship but I'm sure there'll be other blokes I'll get to know, who'll want to read this after me.' His gaze shifted from Greta's face to Cissie. 'Thanks very much, Mrs Hardcastle.' And he kissed her plump cheek.

'Gerraway with yer!' Her tone was gruff but she patted his shoulder. 'Now you, Greta,' she said. 'Open yours!'

Greta thought she could guess from its shape what her present was but when she opened it, there were two presents. One was a box of chocolates, the other was a lipstick. 'Gran! How could you afford these both? Oh, you are a luv!' She got up and rained kisses on Cissie's face. Then she went over to the sideboard mirror and outlined her lips, before whirling round and facing Harry. 'You don't mind me wearing lipstick, do you, Dad? I won't wear it a lot. But to have my very own lipstick! A Max Factor one, too!' Her eyes shone. 'It makes me feel really grown up.'

'You're not, though, luv,' warned Harry. 'But I guess lipsticks are a commodity that'll probably be in short supply soon, so you're best making it last.' He hesitated. 'You mightn't have noticed that your gran's cut down on the ciggies ... but I have.'

'We all have to make sacrifices,' said Cissie with a shrug. 'There's a war on. Now open your present and shut yer gob.'

'You're incorrigible, Gran,' said Greta, her expression warm.

'I won't ask what that means,' said Cissie with a little giggle, and placing her hands on her thighs. 'Let's just get on with opening the pressies.'

They did just that. Harry's present from Cissie was a pair of gloves. His extra present to Greta was Sally's brooch which he had redeemed from the pawnbroker. 'I remember this, Dad!' Her eyes shone with tears, and even as she was speaking she was trying to open the catch to put it on but was all fingers and thumbs.

'Here, let me do it,' said Harry.

As he fastened it to her dress, she whispered, 'How could you afford to redeem it, Dad?'

'I've built a lot of shelters, luv. We've been making some big enough to take whole schools. There's quite a lot of mothers who couldn't bear to be parted from their children. I think your mam would have been the same if she'd lived,' he said unsteadily. 'I still miss her, you know!'

Greta wanted to ask, *Then why are you taking that widow out?* but couldn't. Instead she asked brightly, 'Does that mean if the Luftwaffe come then I won't have to go away? Will there be enough shelters for all?' she asked.

'Let's hope so, luv. Although ...' He fell silent and moved away to watch Alex as he unwrapped his present. It was a shaving kit. The man's eyes were quizzical. 'Are you thinking what I think you're thinking, lad? That you haven't got much in the way of whiskers right now? But I tell you shaving gear might be in short supply, just when you're ready for it.'

Alex nodded. A muscle moved in his throat and when he spoke, his voice was husky. 'I appreciate that, Mr Peters, and thanks! I didn't expect anything. You've been so kind to me I can't get over it.'

Harry grinned. 'Well, let's be having your presents then and maybe you'll feel better.'

'I wasn't sure what to buy,' said Alex, handing out his parcels. A small one for Greta, a larger, softer-looking present for Cissie, and a square, medium sized one for Harry.

Greta tore at the wrapping to reveal several thin metallic bangles and was delighted with the gift. 'Lovely! Two lots of jewellery!' She slipped the bangles on her arm and waved so that they jingled musically. 'Thanks, Alex!' She wanted to give him a thank you kiss, but felt shy and was unsure whether he would feel embarrassed. 'Now open yours from me.'

She watched him intently. It was another book and perhaps he might not have wanted two books, but she had thought with him being at sea he would need lots of books to fill in the hours when he wasn't on duty.

'*Tarzan of the Apes!*' read Alex, and laughed.

'You think Tarzan is funny?' she said, her face falling.

'No! I just feel so pleased I want to laugh,' he assured her hastily. 'I can't wait to read it. Thanks!'

Cissie was unwrapping the length of scarlet and gold material that Alex had given her. 'That's lovely, lad,' she said, her eyes shining, as she threw it over her hair and crossing it over her bosom and then round her waist.

'One of the married blokes said that his wife loves gifts of material,' said Alex hesitantly. 'It's real silk from India.'

She reached out and drew him to her bosom and hugged and kissed him. His face was scarlet by the time he escaped her embrace.

Harry had opened his gift. It was a wooden box carved with flowers and small birds and the inside smelled of sandalwood. 'This is ... really nice,' he said.

Alex's expression was anxious. 'I thought you might have important things that you didn't want mice or moths to get at.'

Harry nodded. 'You're right, lad. I know just what to put in it.' He placed it on the shelf above the gas cupboard. 'Now how about a glass of sherry for you, ladies? I think we can bend the rules about you being too young to drink, Greta, as it's Christmas. A beer for you, Alex? I'm not sure how old you are but the same goes for you as for Greta.'

'I'll be seventeen on April the first.'

'But you're no fool, lad,' said Cissie, smiling.

Two and a half years older than me, thought Greta. I'll remember that date ... and she wished that she could grow up faster.

Later Cissie fell asleep and the other three played cards for halfpennies. Greta was convinced her father and Alex worked it between them so that she ended up with a pile of coins. They finished the day in the kitchen eating mince pies and Dundee cake, listening to a ghost story on the wireless. Greta was filled with such contentment as she climbed the stairs to bed that she wanted to cry. It had been a happy day and not the lonely, sad Christmas she had dreaded.

8

'So what are you going to do next about finding your mother and sisters, Alex?' asked Greta, swallowing a yawn. It was a topic she didn't really want to talk about and yet couldn't leave alone. In her imagination his family hovered on the edge of her little world as if about to gatecrash.

It was eleven thirty on Boxing Day and they were having a late breakfast. He gazed across the table at her. 'I had hoped that maybe Mum might have written to your mam this Christmas at your old address but I'm sure you'd have mentioned it if a letter had been passed in here.'

Greta looked across at her grandmother, who was getting ready to go out with her old flame. 'Gran?'

'Nothing, luv!' Cissie tilted her hat at a rakish angle so that its peak tipped one eyebrow. 'Perhaps your mother was too busy to write now she's married again, lad.'

'That's what I thought,' said Harry, taking a slice of toast from the toasting fork. 'Fancy coming the park with me to watch the football, Alex? You might be lucky enough to get a kick around.'

Alex hesitated and then smiled. 'I wouldn't mind. I had a few games with the local lads when we were stuck in Argentina. They're really keen.'

'Have you a pair of boots?' asked Harry.

'No, but I've a pair of deck shoes, which I've played in before.'

Harry glanced at his daughter. 'You'll be OK on your own, won't you, luv?'

Greta would have liked to have spent more time in Alex's company but guessed she would spend most of it on her own if she accompanied them, so pretended to be delighted at the thought of having the place to herself. 'Of course, I will! I'll make a rabbit stew. We can have it about three.'

'I've got to be out by then, luv,' said Harry hastily. 'I'm going to Mrs Cox's.'

She scowled, as did Cissie. 'Yer're not visiting that widow on Boxing Day!' said the old woman.

Harry did not respond immediately, his strong teeth crunching into his slice of buttered toast. 'What's wrong with that?

You're visiting your old flame,' he said gruffly, wondering what his mother-in-law would do if her husband turned up on her doorstep one day. Perhaps he should tell her that Sally's father had got in touch with her a couple of years ago. It only took him a moment to decide to stick to what he had decided when his wife had died and keep mum. 'Mrs Cox gets lonely,' he murmured.

'Lots of women know the pain of being left alone,' said Cissie, her colour high, 'but yer want to be careful, she could be getting ideas in her head.'

Harry's expression tightened. 'I'm a grown man, Mrs Hardcastle! I still miss Sally but my moping about won't bring her back. Besides …this old flame of yours … what do you have in mind with him? We don't even know his name or where he lives.'

'It's Mick Donnelly and he lives down by the docks in Toxteth. He has five grown up children and knows I'm still married to that swine that left me. Although, it's that long ago now I could get a divorce for his desertion. Any road, neither of us is in a rush to make changes in our lives just yet.'

The annoyance in Harry's face died, and he said softly, 'Neither am I. So don't be worrying … and that goes for you, too, Greta,' he added.

Greta shrugged. 'Who said I am!'

Yet she was still worrying, and after waving the three of them off and putting the rabbit on to stew, she lay on the sofa for at least ten minutes, thinking about the widow, wondering what she looked like and, also, about her daughters. What if her dad did decide to marry Mrs Cox? There was a war on and couples were rushing in to marriage. Would he move in with her, leaving Greta to stay with her gran? Or would she and her daughters move in with them? It wouldn't half be a squash and maybe the widow would somehow work it so her grandmother would want to leave. Despite what she had said … perhaps she would go and live with that old flame of hers! Frowning, Greta's hand reached for a chocolate, and as she nibbled it, she opened her gran's Mills & Boon library book and began to read, but even as she did so, part of her mind was toying with a couple of ideas.

'How d'you fancy a tram ride to Bootle?' asked Greta.

'What?' Alex's hand holding the comb paused, in the tangle of damp nut brown hair, and his eyes met hers reflected in the mirror above the sofa.

Greta's heart performed a peculiar little dance. 'I've been stuck in all day and I'll be back at work tomorrow so I'd like to go out.'

He glanced towards the window. 'It's going to be dark in half an hour.'

'So-oo! The blackout isn't strict at the moment. Pl-eeease let's go!' She fluttered her eyelashes at him.

'Why Bootle?' Alex stared at her from narrowed eyes. 'You've got something on your mind. I'm not going with you unless you tell me what it is.'

She pulled a face and sighed. 'You probably won't come with me but I was thinking of sort of checking up on this widow Dad's seeing. She lives in Great Mersey Street. I don't know the number but ...'

'No!' said Alex firmly. 'Your dad's been good to me and I'm sure he wouldn't like us spying on him.'

The emotions Greta had been experiencing towards him were set aside and she scowled. 'I don't like it that he's seeing another woman when my mother's only been in her grave for a year.'

'He said you had nothing to worry about. You should trust him!' Alex moved towards the fireplace, flopped into a chair and stretched his legs out towards the fire.

'It's her I don't trust,' retorted Greta with a toss of the head. She began pacing the floor. 'I might feel different if I saw her. If I did that then I'd get her measure and know if I had anything to worry about.' She threw a glance at Alex, who had his eyes closed.

'I don't see the logic of that,' he murmured. 'You can't always tell what people are like by their appearance. Anyway, what are you going to do? You can't knock on the door if you don't know the number. What excuse would you give if she answered? What if your dad came to the door?'

Greta screwed up her face in frustration. 'We'll find someone to point out the house to us! At least we know the name of the widow. You can knock and I can stand in a doorway or something and get a peek at her that way.'

Alex laughed. 'You really are mad. What excuse do I give when I knock?'

Greta smiled and, going over to him, impulsively ruffled his hair. 'You've got brains. I'm sure you'll think of something.'

He groaned. 'I didn't say I would go.'

'Please, Alex!'

He looked into her pleading face and sighed.

Great Mersey Street was one of those long thoroughfares divided by a main road. Immediately this caused Alex and Greta a problem. She knew from living in a street that was divided by another road that the inhabitants of one end, more often than not, did not know those living at the other end. Not knowing the number of Mrs Cox's house, meant that they had to make a choice and it could be the wrong one. Alex suggested they toss a coin. Heads the bottom, tales the top. Heads won and so they strolled down the street in the direction of the Mersey.

Fortunately there were children playing out despite it being dark and one of them directed them to Mrs Cox's house.

'Are you sure you want to do this?' asked Alex, as they stood gazing at the terraced parlour house.

'It-It seems a bit of a waste of time coming here if-if we don't,' said Greta, feeling nervous now they were about to put her plan into action.

But, before either of them could make a move, the door opened and a girl came out. She stood in the doorway, pulling on a glove. Greta could see her face clearly in the light of a street lamp and she caught her breath. She was lovely! A real blonde bombshell. The girl suddenly caught sight of them. 'You looking for someone?'

Greta surprised herself by saying, 'Armstrong! We're looking for a Mr Armstrong.'

Alex's head slewed round and he stared at her. She ignored him. All her attention was on the girl, whom she reckoned was several years older than herself.

The girl smiled at Alex. 'Nobody of that name lives here but haven't I seen you before?'

He stammered, 'I-I would have re-remembered if we'd met.'

Her smile deepened. 'What a nice thing to say. What's your name?'

'Alex! Alex Armstrong! We're-We're looking for my … uncle. My … family moved and we lost touch.' Now it was Greta's turn to stare at him.

The girl held out a hand to him. 'Joyce Cox! Sorry I can't help you.' Her eyes went from Alex to Greta. 'Are you brother and sister?'

'No!' said Greta without hesitation and slipped her hand possessively through Alex's arm. 'Do you have a brother or sister?'

'I'd prefer a brother instead of my sister,' said Joyce with a sigh. 'She drives me mad. So what are you two to each other?'

'We won't keep you, Miss Cox,' said Greta with an edge to her voice. 'It looks like you're going somewhere.' And with that, she dragged Alex away.

'What did you do that for?' Alex was astonished. 'I thought you wanted to see the mother. Although, if she looks anything like the daughter, I can see why your dad keeps on calling.'

'Shut up!' hissed Greta, removing her hand from his arm and glaring at him. 'Just because Joyce Cox looks like a young Jean Harlow and was all sweet to you, it doesn't say my dad can be led astray by a pretty face.'

He protested. 'But that's what you must think to do such a crazy thing as coming here!'

She scowled. 'I don't want to think it but I can't help it. If it's just her S.A. that draws him to Mrs Cox then I'll move heaven and earth to put a stop to it.'

He looked amused. 'Do you think you can do that? Do you think you have that right? As your dad said to your gran, he's a grown man!'

She stared at him in disbelief. 'Of course, I do! I'm his daughter. I bet if you'd been on the scene when your mother met her bicycle shop owner you mightn't have wanted him replacing your father in her affections.'

Alex stared at her as if the idea had never occurred to him. 'I hope I'd have been pleased that she had found someone to take care of her,' he said slowly. 'That's how I felt when I read the letter Mum sent to Sally.' He squared his shoulders. 'Anyway, the situation is different. It's more than eight years since Dad died.'

She smiled in triumph. 'So you admit your mother's situation and my dad's are not the same. Have you thought what your stepfather's feelings will be when faced with your sudden reappearance?'

Alex frowned. 'He's got flesh and blood of his own, so I don't see how, in all honesty, he can resent me.'

122

Greta looked at him in disbelief and said sweetly, 'Love can make people very jealous.'

'Like you're jealous of Mrs Cox and her blonde bombshell daughter,' retorted Alex, and smiled.

Greta knew he was right and she wanted to swipe his smile off with a well aimed slap. She hated him. How could he possible fall for a girl at first sight, who was so obviously a tart? *Haven't I seen you before? I would have remembered if we'd met. Ha!* Greta was so hurt and angry that she did not respond to Alex's attempts to draw her into conversation on the way home.

Neither did she make the effort to speak to him the following evening when she arrived home from work. She had done much soul searching during the day and had come to the conclusion that it would be a mistake to get too fond of him. At the tea table, as she listened to him talking to Harry about his lack of luck in his search of bicycle shops in Litherland, an area to the north of Bootle, she knew that she would have trouble sticking to her decision to keep him at a distance. Finding his presence in the house unsettling, she wished he would go back to sea. As soon as Greta had finished her meal, she washed the dishes and then went out to the pictures on her own.

During the next few days Greta showed no interest in what Alex had to say about his search for his family. She got on with her mending or read a library book. Yet she was conscious of him, glancing in her direction once or twice, but most of the time he ignored her, and one evening he went out without saying where he was going.

The day before New Year's Eve, Greta's hurt had abated somewhat and she felt ashamed of her behaviour, knowing she could not carry on being so rude to Alex, especially when he would probably be leaving soon. 'When d'you have to return to your ship?' she asked as they sat down for tea that evening.

Alex looked across the table at her with such a cool expression in his eyes that she blushed, wondering whether he thought she was asking because she wanted to be rid of him. 'I'm not! I was paid off in Southampton, remember? The ship needed some repairs. I'll go down to the Pool tomorrow and see what's going.' He glanced across the table at Harry. 'That's if it's OK with you, Mr Peters, my still staying on tonight?'

Harry lowered the newspaper. 'Of course you can stay. No skin off my nose as long as you're giving Mrs Hardcastle something for your keep.'

'Of course he is,' said Cissie, taking a cigarette packet from the pocket in her pinnie and smiling. 'He's a good lad and I enjoy his company.'

'Thanks for that, Mrs Hardcastle,' said Alex warmly. 'I just wanted to make sure I'm not wearing my welcome out with anyone.'

Greta felt that remark was aimed at her, and the colour in her cheeks deepened, but the words, *Sorry, I don't want you to go!* stuck in her throat. How was she to know that he hadn't called on Joyce Cox when he went out the other night?

Greta arrived home on New Year's Eve to be greeted with the news that Alex had gone. Having signed on a ship going to the Far East, he'd had to leave immediately. She was furious with herself and felt sick with dismay. What if something terrible happened to him now they had parted, not the best of friends? She was reminded of an argument she'd had with her mother a few days before she had died and knew that she was going to worry about Alex until she saw him again.

The new year of 1940 began with the declaration that the war was costing the country six million pounds a day. 'I know what's coming next,' said Harry heavily. 'Income tax will go up.'

'Rationing of sugar, bacon and butter starts on the 8th, Harry,' said Cissie. 'I don't know why we're being rationed so early in the war. It didn't happen until a couple of years in during the last one.'

'They've learnt their lesson,' said Harry, rustling the newspaper. 'It says here that cauliflowers ended up costing a shilling each, eggs sixpence apiece and tea went up to half a crown a pound. A lot of the poor were literally starving!'

'I've read that article,' said Greta, feeling down in the dumps. 'Further on it tells you how people were urged to try the unusual … such as the caterpillars of the white butterfly. Apparently they're delicious fried in butter.' She spread jam on a slice of bread and bit into it.

'Bleedin' hell, girl! D'yer have to talk about such things while we're eating?' cried Cissie, her eyes almost popping out of her head. 'I could do with cheering up now young Alex's gone … and so could you.'

124

Harry smiled at them both. 'How about the pantomime? I won't be going but if I give you the money, Greta, you could get tickets in town for you and your gran. Ask Rene if she'd like to go. Wilf said that she's in most nights because Vera's at her all the time not to leave her alone.'

Greta did just that.

Rene's face lit up. 'I'd love to go. I've been feeling a bit fed up lately.'

Greta knew just how she felt and managed to get three tickets for *Aladdin*. It was quite an adventure going out in the blackout, armed with a gas mask and a torch, and would be something to write about if Alex got in touch with the name of his ship.

Just as they were ready to go, Cissie stuck a hatpin in the lapel of her coat. 'Yer never know who yer going to bump into in the dark,' she said. Greta took in her words and reached out for the pepper pot and rammed it into her coat pocket.

They met Rene at the bottom of the step. 'Your mam OK?' asked Greta.

'She told me to enjoy myself,' said Rene, unable to keep the amazement out of her voice. 'I think something's pleased her since New Year. She's had this smirk on her face every time I've asked if she's OK and she told me that she couldn't feel better.'

'Maybe she's caught religion,' said Cissie.

Greta and Rene exchanged looks but said nothing.

They caught a tram, lit only by tiny blue lights, and soon were relaxing in the Shakespeare Theatre watching the familiar tale of *Aladdin* unfold. The performance was colourful and cheerful.

'I feel so much better after that,' said Rene, as they came out into the darkness, immediately switching on her torch and focusing its beam on the pavement. The other two followed her example.

The three of them turned the corner into London Road, their heels tip-tapping on the pavement. Suddenly a light flashed in Cissie's face, blinding her. She felt a tug on her handbag. 'Hey! Stop that!' she yelled, dropping her torch and struggling with her unseen attacker.

Greta and Rene shone their torches in the face of a masked man. 'You wicked sod!' cried Rene, and hit him with the box holding her gasmask. The man swore and caught her a blow with his torch. Greta took the pot from her pocket and shook the pepper in his direction.

There was more swearing and the sound of voices. 'What's going on?' shouted a man. The next moment Cissie's attacker had fled and they were surrounded by people.

'What happened?' asked a woman excitedly.

'Lower yer torches!' ordered Cissie. 'Me eyeballs are already burning in their sockets! It was a bleedin' masked man out to steal me handbag but we foiled him,' she added triumphantly.

'It'll need reporting to the bobby!' said a middle aged man.

'It's a disgrace when you can't walk your own streets in safety,' babbled a woman. 'A perfect disgrace! It's Hitler we're fighting!'

Rene reached out and clutched Greta's hand. 'Let's get away from here,' she whispered. 'I'm feeling a bit peculiar and I think I'm bleeding where he hit me.'

'Perhaps you should go the hospital,' suggested Greta anxiously.

'No! I'd rather go home. Don't trust hospitals! It's only a knock on the head,' murmured Rene.

Greta tugged on Cissie's sleeve. 'Rene's not feeling too good. We're going! You coming, Gran?'

Cissie hesitated, enjoying the fuss, but Greta and Rene were already making their way to the tram stop, so she hurried after them.

As they walked up their street, they were spotted by Harry and Wilf, who were talking on the step. 'Hello, you three? Enjoy the pantomime?' called Wilf.

'Guess what!' cried Cissie, bustling up to the two men. 'I was attacked and the swine nearly got away with me handbag.'

'Rene hit him with her gasmask box and I threw pepper in his face,' blurted out Greta. 'Only trouble is he clouted Rene on the head and cut it open.'

'The bloody swine!' Harry gazed at Rene. 'How are you feeling, luv?' His voice was filled with concern.

She nearly burst into tears and wanted to place her head on his shoulder and howl. Instead she remembered his outings with the widow and replied stiffly, 'I'm OK!'

Greta slid a hand through her father's arm, gripping it tightly. 'She went all peculiar but didn't want to go to the hospital.'

'She's a heroine,' said Cissie warmly.

'I always knew Rene had courage,' was Harry's quiet response.

Touched by his words, Rene's insides melted and she said lightly, 'Oh, shut up and save my blushes! Cissie and Greta didn't exactly sit back and let him get away with it. Anyway, I'm knackered and ready for my bed. Goodnight!'

'You take care of yourself, luv,' said Harry. 'Perhaps you should see the doctor in the morning.'

Near to tears again, Rene said brusquely, 'If I survive to the morning I won't need a doctor. Goodnight, all!'

'Sleep tight,' chorused Cissie and Greta.

Rene went indoors, followed by Wilf, and was relieved to see that her mother had gone to bed. 'Don't tell her what happened, Wilf! You know what she's like,' she whispered.

He put a finger to his lips. 'They're zipped, luv. But are you sure yer OK, girl?'

'Positive,' she replied, despite her aching head.

The following evening there was a report in the *Echo* about several attacks on women during the blackout. Some had not been as fortunate as Cissie and their handbags had been stolen.

Vera read the piece out to Rene and then glared at her. 'Why didn't you tell me what happened last night? I felt a right fool when Cissie knocked to ask how you were. She told me what happened and said you were a heroine. I had to pretend I knew what she was talking about. Anyhow, I said that it's me that's the heroine in this house the way I suffer in silence.' She sniffed.

Rene rolled her eyes.

'That's impudent, that is!' snapped Vera. 'And I know where you get it from. I don't like it that you're so friendly with them next door. Cissie wasn't the only one to come round here. Harry arrived at lunch time, asking how you were. He's got a bloody nerve! I'll not have that starting up again.'

Rene's hands curled into fists, 'There's nothing to start up again, Mother! It's all in your imagination.'

'You would say that.' Vera's small dark eyes glittered as she stared at her daughter. 'Immoral lot them next door! What about this widow he's seeing and that lad who was staying there over Christmas … a strange howdy-do if you ask me. Taking in a stranger, who tried to burgle your house. I bet that cheeky little madam has her eye on him.'

'Sally used to work for his mother. They used to keep in touch. He's trying to trace his mother and sisters,' said Rene, struggling to retain her patience.

'I know that,' said Vera, with a smirk. 'There's nothing much I don't know about what goes on in this neighbourhood.'

'Mrs Waters been gossiping again, has she?' said Rene dryly.

Vera smiled sweetly. 'It keeps me in touch with things, Rene dear. Now pour me a cup of tea, I'm dead parched.'

Rene bit hard on her lip to prevent herself from saying something she might regret and poured the tea.

A few days later the capture of the masked man was reported in the local press. Even so, her mother grumbled so much when Rene said that she was going to the Paramount with Cissie and Greta, to see Bob Hope and Paula Goddard in the black comedy *The Cat and the Canary*, that she almost changed her mind. It was Wilf who insisted that she go. 'I'll look after her, luv, don't you worry.' So she allowed herself to be persuaded.

She had mixed feelings about it, though, when she discovered Harry was joining them. He smiled down at her as the four of them gathered on the pavement outside the houses. 'I know he's been caught,' said Harry, 'but I thought I'd come along anyway. The *Echo* gave the film a good review.'

'So I noticed,' said Rene, as the two of them fell behind as Greta linked her arm through her grandmother's and led the way, torches blazing a trail on the pavement.

'How's your head after that blow? I haven't seen you to ask,' said Harry. 'I did ask your mother and could tell she wished me anywhere but on her doorstep.'

Rene said impatiently, 'You shouldn't let Mother put you off. She didn't want me to come out tonight but I have to get out now and again or I'd go mad. I do feel sorry for her but sometimes I-I ... '

Harry took her hand in his and squeezed it. 'You need to get things off your chest sometimes, luv.'

She swallowed and her fingers quivered against his. 'I know but I hate feeling I'm being disloyal. She's my mother. Forget what I said. Tell me instead, how are things going with the ARP?'

'We've more volunteers. Although some of them look on what we're doing as a game. How about you?'

She shrugged. 'I can't see me being able to do much. If the air raid sirens ever go Mother will expect me to help her to the shelter ... which is only right.'

They both fell silent. He was still holding her hand. Despite the guilt she felt when thoughts of Sally came into her mind, how she wished he would kiss her again. Could imagine the feel of his lips on hers and his hands caressing her body. She longed to be loved by him. Had even read Marie Stopes on married love. How she yearned to put what she had read into practice. Rene wanted to ask whether he was still seeing the widow but told herself that it was really none of her business. She must have misread that expression in his eyes in the past. He was just being kind, listening to her concerns, and right now he had probably forgotten that he was holding her hand.

The film was good, witty, humorous and slightly spine chilling at the same time. They all agreed that they should go out like this again.

Despite the daily photographs of British and German aircraft appearing in the *Echo* and news of tensions on the Dutch and Belgian borders, of British and neutral ships being sunk in the North Sea, of Russia bombing Finland, and Norway feeling threatened by Germany, the war seemed unreal to Greta. It was as if it scarcely involved those on the home front. A lot of the children had not returned to the countryside after Christmas, and towards the end of January they could be seen having fun building snowmen and igloos, having snowball fights and making slides. While the grown-ups worried about the pipes being frozen, which meant carrying buckets of water down the yard to flush the lavatory. By the time the thaw came, the Government was speeding up armaments and insisting on the need for even more shelters. They had heard nothing from Alex and Greta was worried.

Spring arrived and so did meat rationing, and on the continent, Hitler and Mussolini talked on a train while the French government resigned and Germany poured more troops into their lines. There was talk of more city schools reopening as there were now air raid shelters for schools in place. But everyone knew the Germans were on the move.

In May, while a Merseyside council debated whether the jitterbug should be banned from their dance halls and Liverpudlians were warned that they still needed to take their torches with them and heed the blackout despite the daylight evenings and moonlit nights, the Prime Minister, Neville Chamberlain, resigned and Winston Churchill took his place.

During the days that followed the Germans swept through Holland, Belgium and Luxembourg and by the 24th May, they had taken Amiens and Arras in France and the British army was in retreat. A few days later Alex arrived in Liverpool but had only time to tell Cissie that he was sailing immediately on the *Lancastria*, a ship of the Cunard White Star line. It was off to France to help rescue British and French troops.

Greta was upset to have missed him but a few days later, she arrived home from work to find Alex sitting at the table in full battledress. He had a bandage about his head and a bruise on his cheek, but that didn't seem to be affecting his appetite as he was digging in to a plate of sausages, liver and eggs.

'What happened to you?' she asked, delighted to see him.

He returned her smile. 'The *Lancastria's* at the bottom of a bay off St Nazaire.'

She gasped. 'You were bombed.'

He nodded. 'We were in the thick of it straight away, taking on troops. There were thousands of them on the beaches and in the water. It was bedlam but bloody marvellous, if you'll excuse my language,' he added hastily, glancing across at Cissie. 'There were craft of all shapes and sizes that had crossed the Channel. The smaller ones were ferrying the soldiers out to us bigger ships and all the time the Luftwaffe were overhead strafing those on the beaches, in the water, and climbing into the boats and ships.'

'That's terrible,' said Greta. 'You could have been killed.'

He nodded, and suddenly his expression sobered and he pushed his plate away. When he spoke, his voice shook. 'We had thousands of soldiers aboard when a couple of Jerries decided to concentrate on us and dropped several bombs. The boat began to list and the master told us to abandon ship.'

Greta gulped and gripped her hands tightly together. 'Can you swim?'

'Fortunately.' He rubbed the back of his neck as if it hurt. 'I was on deck, too, which was handy. I went straight into the water, me and this young kid. We were picked up by a destroyer and brought back to Portsmouth. That's where we were given the battledress and told to go home.'

'So you came here,' she said, her voice quivering.

He said awkwardly, 'It's the nearest place I've got to a home. You don't mind, do you?' He sounded unsure of himself.

'Of course I don't! I'm glad to see you safe! I'm sorry I was so horrible to you before you left. I don't know what got into me!'

He grinned. 'We all get peculiar moods on us, sometimes.'

She was happy that he could think like that and she wanted to hug him but was too shy. 'Are you going to stay on land now? You don't have to go back to sea, do you? It's not as if you were eighteen and had to go,' she babbled.

'I'm due some shore leave, so I'm taking that and it'll give me some time to think.' He drew his plate towards him again and picked up his knife and fork.

'If I was you, I'd stay home until you have to go. It's much safer!' Relieved to have him in the house, she left him eating his meal and went to wash her face and hands.

Part Two

9

The battle for Britain in the air began almost immediately. Some in Liverpool believed that the Luftwaffe would never get over the Pennines but the bombers arrived over Merseyside towards the end of July and began perfecting their targeting; the dockyards, shipping, oil depots and timber yards were hit. The Customs House was set ablaze and even the unfinished Anglican cathedral was damaged.

Alex had decided to stay in Liverpool and join the ARP, so Greta gave up her back bedroom and moved into the front double bedroom with her grandmother. Harry found him a job as a brickie's labourer. Both were kept very busy so had little free time.

Harry still wanted Greta to leave Liverpool, but while her grandmother was refusing to go and she considered her father and Alex in danger, Greta dug in her heels. 'I'd only worry about you both.'

At first she had gone alone to the surface shelter in their street but as the raids continued and the nights drew in she did what the Millers and Wilf did next door after one of the wheels came off Vera's wheeled chair, and went down into the cellar.

Harry had not been pleased but even so he had reinforced the roof and walls and helped Wilf do similar work next door. Rene had been grateful and had kissed him on the cheek, saying how much she appreciated having him as a neighbour. He would have seized her and returned her kiss if Wilf had not been there. The bombing had somehow heightened his senses and he was overwhelmingly aware that death could come suddenly to any of them, and that moments of happiness should be grasped and life lived to its limits.

Edith had said a similar kind of thing after a bomb destroyed a church and couple of houses on Great Mersey Street. Harry had not visited her for some time but had felt compelled to call on Edith when he heard about the bombing. The blast from the explosion had caused cracks to appear in the walls of the Coxes' house. Living so close to the docks they were at much more risk than either his family or Rene's. He felt sorry for Edith and her girls but could imagine Rene's reaction if she set eyes on the widow. On his last visit, Edith had told him that she had managed to find a part time job working in a canteen but said it didn't pay very well and that she felt tired all the time. Didn't they all! he had felt like saying.

Just over a week ago he had helped dig out the bodies of four young children and their grandmother. He had been torn between weeping and wanting to get a gun to shoot every German plane out of the sky. Instead, he'd had to ram down the lid on his feelings. Alex had been with him and, even through the filth on his face, Harry could see how sick the young man felt. Ranting and raving would not have done either of them any good. There were times when he wanted Alex out of it. He was seeing sights that no one of his age should see, but he was young, fit and wiry, and could get into places that Harry and the other men couldn't. But if anything happened to Alex he knew just how upset his daughter would be. The two youngsters squabbled, laughed and made up, just like many a brother and sister would. He still thought of his daughter as a child although she was now fifteen, holding down a job, helping run the household and coping with the blitz.

So far their street had escaped bomb damage, but how long could that last? Harry frowned, thinking of the numbers of people who were homeless or making do in houses that they really should have moved out of. Again he was reminded of Edith and decided that he must visit and see if she and her girls were OK. He hurried downstairs, hoping to get there and back quickly, so he could catch some shut-eye later as he was on duty that night.

'Where are you going?' asked Cissie, looking at him as he adjusted the brim of his trilby in front of the mirror. She was sitting near the fire, warming her feet on the fender. Greta had gone with Alex to the park that Sunday morning to watch him play football. 'I'll be going to Mick's later on so I'd like yer in handy for yer dinner.'

Harry turned on his heel. 'I don't know why you don't ask him to come here. It's much safer than down by the docks.'

'We're attending his church this evening,' she said, with an air of satisfaction. 'Besides, when yer number's up, yer number's up!'

'There's no point in going looking for trouble,' he said exasperated. 'What would happen to Greta if both of us were killed?'

'The lad would look after her,' said Cissie confidently.

'She needs a woman to give her advice,' snapped Harry. 'Besides, Alex works alongside me and it's dangerous.'

Cissie's mouth worked and she pushed herself up out of her

chair. 'Would she listen to me if I did give her advice? She's more likely to take notice of Rene.'

Harry guessed that was true, knowing how fond the two were of each other. If only things could be different. He sighed. 'Rene has enough on her plate with her mother. You heard Greta say that Mrs Miller's turned even nastier since the wheel buckled on that chair Wilf rigged up and she can't get to the shelter. Anyhow, I've got to go out.' He headed for the door.

'Are you going to that widow's again?' shouted Cissie.

He did not answer but slammed the door.

Edith stood in the doorway, one hand resting on the doorjamb and the other holding a cigarette. 'Hello, stranger! I thought you'd given up on us.' She took Harry in from the jauntily angled trilby, white shirt, tie and brown suit, to his highly polished brown shoes.

Harry said calmly, 'You know how I'm fixed. I've a daughter, mother-in-law, young lodger, my job and my duties with the ARP.'

Immediately she was contrite and stretched out a hand to him. 'I'm a selfish cow! You must hardly have a minute to yourself. Do come in.'

'Thanks.' He wiped his feet on the coconut mat and followed her indoors. Once in the kitchen, he immediately went over to the wall to check the props were still doing their job. 'Any trouble?' He turned to face her and only then did he notice that she had discarded her widow's weeds and was wearing a plum skirt and twin set. The colour made her skin look creamy.

She smiled. 'A bit of dust! Nothing worth mentioning.' She waved him to the sofa in front of the fire and sat down herself. 'Cup of tea?'

'Thanks! How have things been?'

She pulled a face and then called out, 'Winnie, put the kettle on! Mr Peters is here.'

The girl popped her head round the door. Fizzy brown hair framed her plump face. 'Oh, it's you,' she muttered, and withdrew her head.

'What would you do with her?' Edith's laugh had an edge to it. 'Her manners have got worse since her father died ... and what with the bombing all our nerves are in shreds.' She took a drag on the cigarette and then flicked ash into the fire. 'I've changed my job. Gone into munitions. It pays better, only thing is it's shift work. Still,

137

we're managing. Winnie is working shifts, too, so between us we cope with the housework and shopping. Joyce has made up her mind that she's going in one of the Forces as soon as she turns eighteen. That's if we haven't joined the angels by then,' she said brightly, drawing comfort from her cigarette again. She paused and called, 'Is that tea ready yet? How about a couple of those scones you made for Mr Peters?'

'Which service is Joyce thinking about?' asked Harry.

'The most glamorous she says.' Edith smiled. 'I don't doubt she'll soon find herself a husband.'

'I suppose he'll be a fighter pilot then. The air force is the one that seems to have the glamour attached to it. Greta vows she'll join the Wrens if the war hasn't ended by the time she's eighteen.'

Edith's brow puckered. 'She and Winnie are about the same age, so if my arithmetic's right, I make it 1943 when it'll be their turn to go. What do you think, Harry, will it be over by then?'

He hesitated. 'I don't think that far ahead.'

Her bottom lip trembled and then she said brightly, 'How wise! That's how I think. Eat, drink and be merry because, who knows, we mightn't be here tomorrow.'

'I didn't mean to sound depressing,' he said hastily, reaching out a hand to her.

She took it and held it tightly and he noticed her eyes were luminous with tears. 'I do try to be brave for my girls, Harry, but it isn't easy being a parent on one's own when such dreadful things are happening.'

'I know, luv. I do understand.'

'I know you do,' she whispered, and leaned closer to him.

She looked so sad and beautiful that Harry found the temptation to kiss her was overwhelming. He was about to give in to the impulse when the door to the back kitchen crashed against the wall, startling them apart.

'Your tea and scones,' said Winnie, carrying in a loaded tray. She placed it on the gate-legged table with a bang that caused the cups on the saucers to rattle. She scowled at her mother. 'I'd best pour for you.'

'There's no need for that,' said Edith sounding cross. 'Get on with cooking the dinner.' Winnie hesitated but when her mother picked up the teapot, she stomped out of the room.

'I can guess what you're thinking,' said Edith wryly, handing a steaming cup to Harry. 'She's put on weight, stuffing her face with bread and the like when I'm not around. She misses her father terribly.'

Harry said, 'Poor kid!'

'Don't stick up for her,' chided Edith. 'She's just plain greedy! Although, I suppose it could have something to do with her glands.' Putting a couple of scones on a plate Edith placed it handy for him on the arm of the sofa before pouring her own tea. She sat down next to him. 'So where were we, Harry?' she said softly.

Harry had control of himself now. 'You were being brave. Keeping your chin up like so many women on the home front. I admire you women.' He bit into a scone and a surprised expression came over his face. 'Hey, these are good.'

'One of Winnie's few talents,' muttered her mother.

Several minutes passed without a word being exchanged. Then, Edith dusted crumbs from her fingers and began telling him about the dangers she thought rife in the munitions factory. She offered him another cup of tea but he glanced at the clock and said, 'Sorry, but I'll have to go.'

'Really, Harry,' she said in a mocking voice. 'I think I'll have to make a date if I'm to spend more than half an hour in your company.'

He couldn't help feeling guilty. 'Sorry,' he repeated. 'But I'm expected home for lunch and I'm on duty tonight.'

She smiled and shrugged her shoulders. 'It's OK. I understand. But perhaps we could go to the pictures one evening next week. I'm on early shift.'

'I'm not sure when I'm free.' He caught the flicker of disappointment in her eyes and experienced that guilt again. 'OK! I can't say what evening but I'll call on spec and see if you're in.'

'That'll be lovely. I'll be waiting,' she murmured. 'But you know, Harry, I've just realised I don't even have your address. If I needed to get in touch with you … say, I had to move suddenly for instance … how would I let you know?'

He hesitated, then taking a scrap of paper and pencil from his pocket, he wrote his address down and handed it to her. 'I'll be in touch.'

She thanked him, pocketed the slip of paper and saw him to the door. She watched him walk away and then went into the back kitchen and slapped Winnie on the arm.

'What's that for?' cried the girl.

'You know what for,' said Edith, exasperated. 'He was just making a move and you burst in.'

'But I don't want you to marry him! He's not my dad,' wailed her daughter.

'Your dad is dead and I need a man in my life!' yelled Edith, and stormed out of the room, leaving Winnie weeping over the pan of vegetables on the gas cooker.

Greta was thinking of the Coxes as she and Alex walked back from Newsham Park. 'Do you think Mrs Cox and her daughters are still living in their house? I mean, they're so close to the docks.'

Alex slanted a sidelong glance at her and looked amused. 'Are you thinking that's where he's gone today?'

She smiled and slipped her hand through his arm. 'How well you know me. Generally, he comes and watches you play.'

'Maybe you should ask him if you're so worried,' suggested Alex, as they walked along a tree lined drive.

'Perhaps I will.' She toyed with the brooch on her lapel. It was two years since Alf and Amy had died. Two years her dad had been without a wife. If only he and Rene could get together, but that awful mother of hers just made it impossible.

'So what d'you think?'

Alex's voice roused Greta from her reverie. 'What?'

A smile lurked in his slate grey eyes. 'Forgotten your own question? The Coxes! They could have moved out. A bomb destroyed a couple of houses and a church in Great Mersey Street a short while ago.'

She stilled. 'How d'you know that? Have you been round there with Dad so you could get a glimpse of the blonde bombshell?'

He fixed her with a stare. 'I think she'd have better fish to fry than the likes of me. Besides when do I get the time? I haven't even begun the search again for Mum and the girls,' he rasped. 'I shouldn't have let your dad persuade me into joining the Sunday football team.'

'But the team needs you. It's short of good players with so many men in the forces ... besides, it's good for you to get the fresh air.'

He looked exasperated. 'But you don't understand how frustrating it is not knowing where they are! I feel like I'm just marking time until I'm called up for the forces.'

Greta did not want to think about Alex going away. She was glad of his company and squeezed his arm affectionately. 'Don't let's think about that ... and we've got off the subject of Dad and the widow. I bet Dad's been there if he knows about the bomb damage in her street. He wouldn't have been able to stop himself.' She chewed on her lower lip.

Alex creased his brow and a lock of nut brown hair flopped onto his forehead. He brushed it back with fingers roughened by handling bricks and rubble and sighed. 'What have you got against her? She might be a really nice woman.'

Greta crinkled her nose. 'I have this picture in my mind of the wicked stepmother and her daughters in *Cinderella*.'

'With you in the role of Cinders, I suppose. There's several things wrong with that picture, kid,' he said dryly.

She gave him a honeyed smile. 'I know! Miss Joyce Cox isn't ugly.'

'I wasn't going to mention her.' His tone was mild. 'What I was going to say was your gran doesn't actually fit the role of the fairy godmother no wand or wings but even so I couldn't see her allowing Mrs Cox to take over the household and turn you into a drudge.'

'No, but-but what if she-she was to die?' Greta forced down the sudden lump in her throat. 'I mean ... you know how she visits Mick some evenings and his place is right by the docks. She's been caught out in a raid before today.'

'You know her philosophy.' Alex rubbed his chin where Greta now noticed there was a smear of mud.

'Pardon?' She took out a handkerchief and dampened it with spit.

Alex mimicked to perfection Cissie' voice. 'When yer number's up, yer number's up!'

'Oh that!' Greta drew him to a halt and reaching up with the handkerchief she rubbed his cheek. 'You're a mucky so and so. There! All gone!' She could not resist kissing the spot.

There was speculative look in his eyes as he gazed down at her. 'She's got a point. Nowhere's safe! That's why you should do what your dad says and leave Liverpool.'

She returned his stare. 'Well, I'm not going. I'll take my chances with the rest of you. I go down to the cellar, so I'm OK. Unless you'd argue with that and say Dad hasn't made a good job of making it safe?'

'I'd trust your dad more than any other man I know. He's the right bloke to have in a tight spot.' He took her arm and hurried her across the road and paused briefly outside St Margaret's Church. 'Shall we get back to *Cinderella?* Who are we casting me as … Buttons or Prince Charming?'

A reluctant smile tugged at her mouth. 'Well, you've no fortune or palace so …'

He groaned. 'Is that all a girl wants a bloke for … to provide for her?'

'What else?' Her eyes danced. 'Although, it could be different after the war if the Labour Party gets in and they start doing things for us women.'

'Us women?' he teased. 'How old were you last month?'

Greta flushed. 'I'm an old soul! I've had to grow up fast,' she said seriously.

Alex stared at her thoughtfully and then nodded. 'I think most our age are doing that with this war. That's what makes it so frustrating and worrying, not knowing where my mum and sisters are. I try not to think of the worst that could happen to them but sometimes …'

She put her hand through his arm once more and squeezed it. 'I know how you must feel. I've been there.' There was a tremor in her voice.

'I know.' He lowered his head and his lips brushed hers as lightly as thistledown. 'Let's drop the subject until I can do something about finding them.'

Greta agreed, thinking she would never forget the feel of his lips on hers even as she told herself it was just a brotherly kiss. They were silent as they walked the rest of the way home.

The sirens sounded that evening just after seven o'clock. As they reached the command post Harry and Alex were informed that this was no ordinary raid. A purple warning had been received from Defence Headquarters, wave after wave of bombers were heading up the Mersey. Within the hour, information was being received of the destruction of property by incendiary and high-explosive bombs and, for the first time since the raids began, parachute mines were spotted drifting silently to earth with devastating effect.

Greta and Rene emerged from their cellars and stood on their respective steps, hugging themselves with nervous excitement and relief that they were still alive. The raid had carried on well into Monday morning. 'Dear God!' said Greta, her voice shaking. 'I never thought it was going to end. I hope Dad, Alex and Gran are OK!'

Rene nodded, trying not to breathe in too deeply. The acrid smell of explosives, smoke and dust was greasy and overpowering. She pointed to the sky beyond the roofs of the houses on the opposite side of the street. Clouds of smoke billowed high into the air and the glow of fires made it appear like day. They could hear the crackle of flames and the shouts of men in the distance.

'It's terrifying,' gulped Greta, an icy coldness gripping her. 'I don't want to look. I think I'll go in.'

'I'd come and keep you company,' said Rene, concerned, 'only Mother will be shouting for me any minute.'

'It's OK!' said Greta, attempting to ease the tightness in her throat. 'I'm OK on my own.'

Rene kissed her cheek. 'See you in the morning.'

Greta went inside and made herself a cup of tea and then fetched a blanket and curled up on the sofa, convinced she would not sleep until Harry, Alex and Cissie arrived home. She was tense with anxiety but due to nervous exhaustion she dozed off eventually.

When she woke, it was to find that she was still alone in the house. Uncertain what to do, she decided to stick to the general motto of those involved in this war and carry on as normal. She told herself that if anything had happened to Harry or Alex then she would have learnt about it by now. She was not so sure about her gran and was bracing herself for bad news as she left the house.

'You OK?' said Rene, hunching her shoulders inside her coat.

'None of them came home,' said Greta, trying not to sound worried as she closed the door behind her. It was a cold, bleak morning and the smell of smoke and explosives still hung in the air.

'I stayed awake for a while but I didn't hear them come in,' said Rene. 'They're probably OK, though. It was such a bad raid that Harry and Alex would be kept busy still, I should imagine.'

Greta nodded and dug her hands into her coat pockets. 'I'm seriously worried about Gran.'

Rene put an arm about Greta's shoulders and hugged her. 'She's a survivor! She'll be home, just you wait and see.'

Greta nodded, unable to speak.

Later, as Greta took the cover off her typewriter, one of the girls said, 'Have you heard that there's fires a mile long down at the docks. The Jerries certainly know what to aim for, don't they?'

'What about the streets down by the docks?' asked Greta anxiously.

The girl sighed. 'Some are bound to have been hit. Why? Do you know someone living down there?'

'My gran went to visit a-a friend and she hadn't come home when I left this morning.' Tears shone in Greta's eyes. 'We don't even know the name of the street where he lives.'

The girl said quickly, 'She could still be OK. There's still plenty of streets standing. Besides, she could have got to a shelter.'

Greta hoped so but she was starting to think like her grandmother. *When your number was up, then it was up*. She wiped her eyes with her sleeve. She mustn't think the worst. She sat down at her desk and got on with her work, praying that she would find her grandmother, Alex and Harry waiting for her when she got home.

The house was in darkness when Greta arrived there. She pulled a chair from the table and fumbled for the matches on the sideboard and lit the gas. Only then did she see Cissie sitting in the chair in front of the empty fireplace, still wearing her coat and hat.

Greta felt a surge of joy. 'Gran, you're OK! What are you doing sitting in the dark without the fire on? What happened to you?' Greta darted over to her, put an arm round her shoulders and kissed her cold cheek. 'You're freezing.' There was no response. 'What's the matter? Are you hurt?' The girl gazed into the old woman's face and was shocked. The light had gone out of her eyes and there was no hint of recognition in them. 'Gran!' Greta shook her. 'Gran, it's me, Greta! Say something!'

Cissie blinked. 'He's dead! My Mick's dead.' The words were only a thread of sound. Greta could not think of anything to say, could only wish that her mother was there. 'I thought things were going to go right for me at last,' whispered Cissie. 'We went to church. The service was over when the raid started and I stayed on me knees, praying that God would forgive me my sinful life and that me marriage could be annulled. Mick had gone into the vestry to talk to the priest, and …' She stopped.

Greta waited for her to continue. Several minutes ticked by and still her grandmother was silent. Greta decided they could not carry on sitting in the cold and slowly released her hold on her grandmother. Hurriedly she cleared out the ashes and scrunched newspaper. She fetched wood and coal and got the fire going. She had just put on the kettle when she heard the sound of a key in the lock.

She left her grandmother and rushed to the front door. As soon as she saw her father she threw herself at him. 'Thank God, you're here! Gran's in a state! Mick's dead!'

Harry swore softly, and setting her aside, stumbled up the lobby. Greta looked at Alex, who stood swaying on the step. 'You OK?' she asked, knowing he wasn't.

He moistened his lips with his tongue but made no answer. She put her arm through his and drew him into the house. Only when they entered the kitchen was she able to see just how filthy he was and that his eyes were not only bloodshot but dazed. He made no move to sit on a chair but stood, swaying in the middle of the room. She took a newspaper and placed it on a chair and then, putting her arm through his, led him over to it, and pushed him gently down. 'You'll feel more yourself when you've had a cup of tea,' she said.

Alex nodded, his shoulders drooped and he stared into the fire with his hands held loosely in his lap. Greta willed the fire to burn redder so she could put the kettle on. She put out a hand and stroked his hair back from his forehead and planted a kiss there, wondering what sights he had seen to cause him to be like this.

'Has she said what happened?' asked Harry, who was on his knees beside Cissie's chair.

'They were in church. She was praying and Mick had gone into the vestry with the priest.' With a pain in her heart, Greta glanced at her grandmother. 'That's all she told me.'

Harry nodded slowly. 'It can happen like that. Some are taken and some are left behind.' He sighed deeply, then forced his shoulders back and said, 'I could do with a bloody bath.'

'Let the fire burn up a bit, Dad, and then we'll warm up the kettles and bring in the tin bath,' she said.

He stared at her and then began to laugh. He went on laughing until she thought he would choke. She went over and shook him. 'Stop it! Stop it, Dad! She'll be OK. She's got us.'

'Us!' he spluttered, and carried on laughing.

She shook him again. 'Stop it! Stop it!' She felt desperate and slapped his face. His laughter came to an abrupt halt. Tears had formed rivulets in the dirt on his unshaven face, and like Alex's, his eyes were bloodshot. Now they were ... oh, so sad!

'A bath,' she said. 'You can both have a bath. It'll make you feel better.' She sat him down and when the fire was red she made tea and soup. Then she boiled more water and brought in the tin bath while her three casualties sat, grieving. It took a lot of kettles to fill the bath six inches and then she did not even have the pleasure of seeing the men sink themselves into the water. She would have scrubbed them clean if they'd allowed it. Instead she saw her gran upstairs to bed, undressing her and providing her later with a hot water bottle. Then she went next door and told Rene that her family were home but that Mick was dead.

'Poor Mrs Hardcastle,' said Rene with heartfelt sympathy. 'She was so happy to have found him.'

'There's no fool like an old fool,' muttered Vera. 'She should have known better at her age.'

Greta shot her a look of disgust and left the house before she said something that would make Rene's life more difficult.

Harry and Alex were out of the bath and with towels wrapped about their waists. At least they looked clean, even though the sadness and shock were still there in their eyes. She wanted to run her hands over Alex's shoulders and chest and kiss his pain better but instead she made cocoa and ordered them to bed.

Harry and Alex never spoke of the bodies they had dug out that day. Neither did Cissie tell of how Mick had died. The old woman would weep in her sleep and Greta would put her arm round her and make soothing noises, just as her mother had done when she was upset as a child. Eventually the sobs would die down and all went silent. In the weeks that followed Cissie was a shadow of the woman she had been. She gave up her job at the pub, and seemed to grow old before their eyes. But Greta was thankful that, at least, during that time the bombers stayed away and Alex and Harry were able to get some rest.

10

They were just over a week into 1941 when the sirens went. Greta was on her way home from work on the tram and almost immediately it stopped to let people off and they scattered down Breck Road. She flicked the switch on her torch but it gave off only a faint light and she remembered that she had meant to buy a new battery. Damn! She could hear the engine of an aeroplane and recognised it as a German Junker, so regardless of the uselessness of her torch she put on a spurt, determined not to stop until she arrived home. Then she heard footsteps behind her and a familiar voice called, 'Is that you, Greta?'

The girl whirled round and peered at the shadowy figure behind the wavering beam of the torch. 'Rene?'

'Yes!' She grabbed Greta's hand and pulled it through her arm. 'Let's go!' she said.

They ran for their lives to the accompaniment of the *boom boom* of explosives and the *ack ack* of the defence artillery. They had just passed the De la Salle school on Breckfield Road South when a man spoke behind them. 'Am I near Barnes Street?' he said.

'This should be it coming up,' gasped Rene.

'Thanks!' He passed them and they dogged his footsteps, even following him as he took a short cut through an entry. They were halfway along it when there was a terrific bang somewhere to the rear of them and they were sent flying.

Greta landed flat on the pavement at the other end of the entry with her ears ringing, feeling completely disoriented. For a moment she had trouble breathing and thought she was going to die, but she managed to catch her breath and lift her head and gaze about for Rene, but she could not see properly and panicked, thinking she would go blind. Suddenly her vision cleared and she saw Rene lying a few feet away. Greta tried to call her but only a faint thread of sound came from her mouth. So she began to drag herself towards Rene, aware of pain in her hands and face.

She seized Rene's shoulder. 'Rene! Wake up, Rene!' she croaked, her voice sounding peculiar inside her head, but there was no response.

Then Greta heard a groan, and then a laugh and she looked up and saw the dark shape of a man pushing himself from the ground. 'I've survived the bloody U-boats, only to be almost blown to Kingdom Come setting foot in the old home town!' Greta only just caught the words because they seemed to be coming from a long way off. She put her fingers in her ears and waggled them about.

He staggered towards them and almost fell on his knees beside Rene's prone body. Greta could see his face clearly in the reflection of the flames lighting up the roofs of the houses on the other side of the street. Taking hold of Rene's wrist he felt for a pulse. 'Not dead,' he mouthed, dropping her hand and facing Greta. 'Want some help with her?'

'Thanks!'

He slid his hands beneath Rene and lifted her into a sitting position. 'If you could give us a hand getting her up, I'll carry her,' he shouted.

Greta hurried to help him, aware of distant voices and the whoosh of flames but both sounded muffled as if she was wearing her hat over her ears. 'Big woman, isn't she?' he gasped, heaving her over his shoulder.

Greta agreed and picked up Rene's handbag with a trembling hand. She did not bother searching for the torches, convinced they would both be broken. She wanted to get home, go down into the cellar and hide beneath the stairs.

'Where are we going?' he asked.

Greta told him and they set off, not bothering to glance skywards, because the aeroplane that had dropped its cluster of bombs had gone. She jogged at the man's side. 'I wonder if she was hit by a chunk of brick or whether her head caught the wall as we were blown out,' said Greta.

'Could be,' he yelled. 'What's her name?'

'Rene. Rene Miller.'

A ragged laugh broke from him. 'Bloody hell! I remember her as a girl. I've come to call on her mother.'

Greta stared at him in astonishment. 'That's some coincidence. Who are you?'

'You won't know me. Far too young. Name's Hardcastle! Jeff Hardcastle. My mother used to live next door to the Millers.'

Greta stopped dead. Had she misheard him? 'Did you say Jeff Hardcastle?' she shouted.

'That's right. Jeff Hardcastle.'

'But you can't be!' Her mind was in a whirl.

He halted and peered at her. The light was poorer now they were further away from the fire. 'I know who I am, girl. Who are you?'

'My mam was your sister. I'm your niece, Greta Peters! As for Gran … she's still living next door to the Millers.'

'But Ma's dead! We were told she was dead.' He sounded completely baffled. 'Our Fred wrote years ago and never got a reply. He kept on writing every Christmas until he got a letter from Mrs Miller saying Ma was dead.'

Greta could not believe it. 'Mrs Miller wrote that?'

Before he could answer, Rene suddenly jerked upright, resting both hands on his shoulder. Her hat was over one eye and she fixed the other on Greta. 'What happened? Where am I?' She turned her head slowly and jumped visibly when she caught a sideward view of Jeff's head.

Greta said joyfully, 'Thank God, you're OK! But perhaps you should see a doctor!'

Rene ignored her, continuing to stare at Jeff's profile. 'Who's this? What's he doing carrying me? Let me down!' She struggled in his hold.

He released her abruptly and she would have fallen if Greta had not grabbed hold of her arm and steadied her. 'Careful, Rene. You were knocked unconscious. You could have a concussion.'

'I can't hear you properly,' said Rene, shaking her head.

Jeff was frowning. 'Is this girl telling me the truth, Rene? Is me mam alive?' he yelled.

'What?' Rene pulled her arm out of Greta's hold and took a step away from him but then her legs buckled beneath her and the girl had to grab hold of her again. Rene clung to her. 'What's he saying? I can't hear properly. I want to go home.'

'I'll take you home,' said Greta, managing to keep Rene upright by forcing her shoulder beneath her armpit. 'He says he's my Uncle Jeff.'

'Still can't hear. Something's wrong with my ears.'

Greta could not be bothered explaining and, ignoring the man who claimed to be her uncle, concentrated on getting Rene home.

149

She wondered how she would manage to open the front door but Wilf was standing in the doorway as she approached.

'Thank God, luv! Yer mam's having hysterics!'

'We got caught in the blast from an explosion,' shouted Greta. 'Rene lost consciousness. Help her in, Wilf.'

'No need to shout, luv. I'm not deaf.' Wilf took Rene from her and managed to lift her into the house.

'Look after her,' said Greta, her voice trembling.

'Of course, I will, girl,' assured Wilf.

The door closed.

Greta turned and bumped into the man standing behind her.

'That wasn't Mr Miller, was it?' he asked.

'No, he's Wilf the lodger, an ex-sailor. Surely you'd know Mr Miller if you were my Uncle Jeff.' She gazed at him suspiciously. 'Mr Miller is dead.'

'I'm Jeff Hardcastle and I grew up in this street,' he said angrily. 'Now let's go and see Ma.' Greta almost demanded to know where the hell he had been since. She crossed over to her own front door. 'Ma won't be in the shelter?' he said.

Greta shook her head. 'She'll be sitting in front of the fire if I'm not mistaken.' She led the way up the darkened lobby and pushed open the kitchen door and blinked in the gaslight. Cissie was sitting in front of the fire just as Greta had said. She wondered if her grandmother would recognise her eldest son. She wondered what had brought him back if he had believed his mother was dead. Just as puzzling was how Mrs Miller had known where to write to her Uncle Fred. 'Hello, Ma! How are yer doin'?' Jeff smiled as he walked over to his mother, but she looked at him like something the cat had brought in and made no move to greet him.

'He says he's your son Jeff, Gran,' said Greta, able to have a proper look at him now. He was a good looking man with a thick crop of tawny hair, a strong nose and a smile that carved dimples in his cheeks. She estimated that he was a few years older than her father.

'I was told you were dead,' said Jeff loudly, removing a dining chair from underneath the table and setting it down next to Cissie's armchair.

'Might as well be dead. My Mick's dead,' muttered Cissie, looking away from him and into the fire.

'What was that she said?' asked Jeff, frowning as he looked up at Greta.

'Her old flame was killed in the blitz and since then it's as if she doesn't want to live anymore.' Greta gazed at her grandmother with sadness in her eyes.

'Can't be bloody having her willing herself to die,' he said impatiently. 'Not when I haven't seen her for donkey's years. It's that bitch next door's fault. She told our Fred Ma was dead and our Sal had been taken away to a lunatic asylum and didn't know anyone.'

Greta gasped with horror. 'Mrs Miller said that about my mam!'

'Yeah!' His eyes were hard. 'I take it that's not true, either?'

'Mam was as sane as I am when she died. I don't think she ever got over her brothers not getting in touch. But if Mrs Miller told you those things then … ' Greta paused. She felt dizzy and sat down on the sofa hastily. She was silent a few moments, aware of her uncle's eyes on her. Then she cried, 'I don't understand! How did she get hold of Uncle Fred's letters? And why the hell didn't you visit Mam years ago if you thought she was in a loony bin? It's a bit late you having a conscience about her now!'

He reddened. 'I've had to make a living, haven't I? Besides, I thought she wouldn't know me. I'm here now because me ship was hit by a torpedo and so we were towed into Liverpool for repairs. That's when I decided to visit Mrs Miller and see if she could give me a berth for the night. See if there was any chance of seeing our Sal, of course. But if she's dead I'm sorry about that.'

Greta wondered just how sincere was his regret. Despite his excuses, surely he could have made an effort to see her mother before now if he had really cared about her.

Unexpectedly, Cissie reached out a hand and placed it on Jeff's arm. 'You say there were letters from our Fred?'

'That's right, Ma.' Jeff squeezed her hand and smiled. 'Found your tongue, have yer?'

Cissie gazed into his face. 'The prodigal has returned, has he? My son, Jeff. What the hell do yer want after all this time?'

'A flying visit, Ma. If yer remember I'm a seaman. That's why I'm away a lot. I sail the seven seas just like one of your heroes, Admiral Horatio Nelson.'

Cissie's mouth hardened. 'The only similarity between you and Nelson is that you carried on with another man's wife. You were only eighteen when I was told you'd been seen with an older woman in a pub,' she snapped. 'You're just like yer father!'

'Hold on, Ma!' he protested. 'That wasn't my fault! She led me astray.'

'Don't give me that! I spoke to her and she told me …'

He interrupted her swiftly, 'You shouldn't be talking like that with the girl here, Ma.'

'Don't mind me!' muttered Greta. 'A brother, who didn't have the decency to come and see how his mother and sister were after the worst war in history, isn't much cop in my opinion.'

Jeff scowled. 'You shut your mouth, girl! I had a pregnant wife to worry about. She needed me.'

'So I've another grandchild,' said Cissie. 'You could have written and told me.'

Jeff hesitated. 'The child died! You can imagine how that made us feel … an-and I lost me missus recently in the blitz on Southampton. Life hasn't been easy for me, Ma.'

'You could have still written,' said Greta.

Her uncle glared at her. 'You have too much to say for yourself. Get the kettle on and make a cup of tea for me and your gran and leave the talking to us.'

Greta was about to say he had no right to give her orders when her grandmother said, 'I could do with a cup of tea, luv.'

Greta nodded and put the kettle on to boil. Her head still felt muggy so she sat on the sofa, intending to listen to their conversation. Instead she fell fast asleep.

She woke with a start and gazed about the kitchen as if in a dream. Daylight was filtering through the curtains and then she remembered not only the explosion but its aftermath. She guessed that her father and Alex had not arrived home because surely they would have roused her. She could only pray that they were OK. She scowled, wondering where her uncle was and presumed he was upstairs in one of the beds. Why hadn't her gran woken her? She felt stiff and sore and looking in the mirror saw that she had a scrape on her cheek, as well as cuts on her hands, and that she had torn her stockings. Damn! She pulled back the curtains in order to see the clock clearly. The time gave her another start. If she didn't get a move on, she would be late for work.

She was on her way out of the house just as Alex and Harry

walked up the street. 'I won't hug the pair of you because you'll make me filthy but you're a sight for sore eyes,' she said and sniffed back tears.

'No need to get yourself upset, luv,' said Harry, putting an arm round her. 'How are things here? Your gran OK?'

She decided not to say anything about the explosion. After all, her hearing had improved and it would only worry them unnecessarily. 'Gran's fine. We had a visitor last night so he could be in either of your beds.' Her mouth set in a disapproving line.

Harry looked surprised and rasped his unshaven chin with a fingernail. 'Who?'

'Mam's brother!' She saw his expression change and added hastily, 'I know what you're thinking because that's how I felt and still do, but one of his excuses is going to amaze you. Anyway, I'm off!'

She rammed her hat on her head and would have hurried past them but Alex caught hold of her arm and gazed into her face. 'You've hurt your cheek. How did you do that?' She was about to make light of it when the neighbouring front door opened and Rene appeared. She looked pale and drawn but was dressed for outdoors. She started when she saw the three of them on the step.

'Hello, Harry, Alex! I'm coming, Greta,' she said.

Gently Greta freed herself from Alex's hold and went over to her. 'Are you sure?' she whispered. 'You were out for the count, you know!'

'I can't remember all that happened but I can't afford to stay off work,' said Rene.

'What's this?' asked Harry, catching her words. 'You don't look too good, Rene.' He looked concerned.

'It's OK. Dad, I'll see she's all right!' Greta said quickly, and grabbing Rene's arm, hurried her away. The girl prayed her father would not follow them. She was in a quandary just what should she say to Rene about what Jeff had told her about Fred's letters? They walked up the street, greeting neighbours on their way to work. Rene was quiet and Greta did not feel up to making conversation either. They'd had a close shave and could so easily have not been there that morning. The weather was cold but Greta was so grateful to feel the wind's chill on her face. Shrapnel, chunks of brick and charred wood littered the ground as they approached the opening to the entry. There was a strong smell of dampened down fire and explosive.

'What actually happened?' said Rene, putting a hand to her head. 'I remember coming to and I was being carried. There was a man, who looked vaguely familiar but I couldn't hear what he was saying. I still can't hear properly.'

Greta hesitated. 'It was my Uncle Jeff. He'd come looking for Mam.'

Rene's eyes flew wide. 'You're joking!'

Greta shook her head.

'He's got a nerve after all this time,' said Rene angrily.

'That's what I thought but,' said Greta hesitantly, 'things aren't as straightforward as that.'

Rene stared at her. 'What d'you mean?'

It was on the tip of Greta's tongue to tell her what her uncle had said but she managed to restrain herself just in time, reminding herself that Rene had to get through a day's work and was already shaken up after their near death experience. She did not need the extra worry of wondering why and how her mother had been able to write to Fred and tell him not only that his mother was dead but that his sister was in a lunatic asylum.

'I think you should talk to him,' she said.

Rene shook her head, then winced. 'Do you have to be so mysterious?'

Greta shrugged and said no more. She could not wait to get home that evening to find out how the news had affected her grandmother. She could not see her taking it lightly and was bound to want to take it up with Rene's mother.

'Ma! I know how yer feel! I'd like to bloody tear the woman apart but according to Harry and that lad Alex she's a cripple,' said Jeff, laying a restraining hand on his mother's arm. She had been chafing at the bit ever since she had got up, just after one o'clock that afternoon. He had been out and bought her flowers and she had accused him of trying to soft-soap her. He had told her that she had the wrong word and that he intended to spoil her. She had grunted and gone out shopping, now the evening meal was in the oven and she was sitting, twiddling her thumbs.

Cissie shook his hand off. 'I can bleedin' well do what I like,' she said, the light of battle in her eyes. 'How did she get her hands on our Fred's letters, that's what I want to know! They were addressed to me and he couldn't have put the wrong number on … couldn't have forgotten the home where he'd grown up.' She choked on the words and Jeff watched her struggle to gain control of herself. He patted her shoulder. She took a deep breath, wiped her eyes with the back of her hand, got to her feet and stormed out of the house.

Jeff swore. He had made up his mind to get his revenge in his own way but he could not tell his mother that. Despite the things she'd done wrong in her life, it was obvious from the way she'd spoken that Cissie wouldn't approve of his idea of revenge. He was going to go after her but he had removed his shoes and had to put them on before hurrying out. Cissie had already disappeared next door but coming towards him were Greta and Rene.

Rene stared at him. 'Greta said it was you. So what made you come back home after all this time? Expected your mother to kill the fatted calf?'

Jeff glanced at his niece. 'Greta hasn't told you?'

'She's been very mysterious, would only say that I should speak to you.'

'Did she now? Well, I'll tell yer, girl. Somehow your mother got hold of our Fred's letters to Ma and she never passed them on. Then your mother wrote and told him that Ma was dead and that Sal was in a lunatic asylum and didn't recognise anyone so it was a waste of time either of us making the effort to come and see her.'

Rene staggered back as if she had been hit. 'I don't believe it,' she gasped, leaning against the fence. 'Why should she do that? How could she do it?'

'I think she's bloody evil, that's why,' snapped Jeff, hands on hips. 'Ma's in with her now, trying to get to the bottom of it.'

'Oh hell!' murmured Greta.

Rene blinked at him, moistened her lips and then blundered towards her front door which was ajar. Greta hastened in her wake but called over her shoulder, 'Uncle Jeff, you'd best stay here. The sight of you might give the old cow a heart attack.'

Jeff hesitated, unsure what to do. He soon decided to go off to the pub and leave it to the women.

It was as silent as the grave as they went up the lobby. Greta wondered if Cissie had slain her long time neighbour with the kitchen knife in her fury and fled out the back way.

Rene pushed open the kitchen door and stopped abruptly. Greta

155

peered over her shoulder to see Wilf with his arm around Cissie. They could not see her face because she had a cloth to it. Vera sat in her chair, facing away from them towards the fire, which crackled and sent out sparks.

'What's happened?' Rene took a couple of paces into the room and Greta closed the door behind them.

Vera turned her head and her bony face held an expression of anger and spite. 'It's only what she deserves! Sweet talking to your father, trying to take him away from me. I was determined I'd get back at her.'

'I was being neighbourly, that's all, girl,' said Cissie, looking at Rene and lowering the cloth to reveal a gash on her cheek. 'He got little love and affection from yer mam. Cruel, she was! The things she'd say to him and in company, too! I wouldn't have spoken to a dog like that. What your father and I said to each other was harmless. You could have listened without being offended. Although, to be honest, he would just sit in silence sometimes, having said it was nice to have some peace and quiet.'

'You're a bloody liar!' said Vera, and she hunched a shoulder and turned her back on them again.

'Has she said how she got the letters?' gasped Rene, her chest felt tight and her head ached.

'Went into me house when I was out cleaning,' said Cissie, anger kindling in her eyes. 'Yer might have forgot, girl, but I used to have a couple of jobs when you and our Sal were young.' She dabbed at the cut on her cheek. 'Seldom received a letter in me life but she knew I was waiting to hear from my lads. So she watched for the postman and then got into the house using the key on the string and pinched my letters,' screeched Cissie in indignation and fury.

Rene was horrified. 'How could you, Mother?'

'It wasn't easy,' said Vera, and sniffed. 'I had to make sure no one was spying on me.' Her eyes held a strange glint. 'I enjoyed reading them letters. Fred wrote a good letter, poetic. It was easier, though, when I told him she was dead and Sally was in the loony bin but asked him to keep in touch as I was interested in knowing how he was going on. After that he wrote to me directly with all the family news twice a year. I would have liked a son. He thought I was a nice person going in to visit Sally and reading his letters to her, hoping it might help her to come to her senses. I never did, though. Not that I told him that.'

'That's because she wasn't there, Mother!' cried Rene, sick to her soul. 'It was all a lie! How could you behave in such a way?'

Vera looked away from her into the fire. 'Wilf's going to have to go,' she muttered. 'He burnt my stick just because I defended myself with it.'

Rene turned to Cissie. 'I'm really sorry, Mrs Hardcastle. All those years when you thought your sons didn't care. And poor Sally! She never got over her brothers not getting in touch.'

Cissie's chin quivered and for a moment she could not speak. Then she rasped, 'I know you're not to blame, Rene. But I'll never speak to your mother again. Our Lord said we should forgive our enemies but I'd find it easier to forgive the Jerries than your mother.' She turned to Wilf and squeezed his hand. 'Yer came up trumps, lad! Thanks!' Then she looked at her granddaughter. 'Come on, girl! Time to go home. I'm in need of something stronger than tea.'

Greta gazed at Rene with compassion in her face. 'Bye, Rene. See you soon.' She took her grandmother's arm and led her out of the house.

There was a silence after they had gone and then Wilf patted Rene's shoulder. 'I'll make you a cuppa, girl.'

'You can get out of my house,' snapped Vera.

'Ignore her,' said Rene, her head in her hands. 'It's not her that pays the rent.'

'You've got a point there, girl,' said Wilf, spooning tea leaves into the teapot. 'Maybe we should send her to Coventry until she learns how to behave herself.' He left the room but was back in a few minutes with a small bottle of rum with which he laced the tea.

Rene lifted her head. She felt icy cold inside. 'Maybe we should leave her to fend for herself,' she said harshly. 'Think of the peace and quiet we'd have! It'd make a nice change from the nastiness and bitterness we have to put up with. But can you imagine my mother trying to be polite or nice? Might as well expect a leopard to change its spots. Remember saying that about Cissie Hardcastle, Mother?' Rene could not bring herself to look at her.

Vera stammered, 'I've-I've-I've … still g-got the l-letters!'

Wilf handed a steaming cup to Rene. 'I've put two sugars in and something stronger. I think you need it, luv.'

157

'L-Listen to me! I said I've still g-got the letters!' cried Vera.

Rene gulped the rum laced tea and looked at her. 'What?'

'Upstairs under the mattress. They're in a big brown envelope with a bit of tape round it,' babbled Vera. 'I hide it somewhere else whenever you do the bed.'

Rene's heart began to beat rapidly. She did not ask why her mother had kept the letters. It only mattered that she had because maybe, even at this late date, being able to read Fred's letters might ease some of Cissie's pain.

Rene left the room with her cup still in her hand and went upstairs. She entered her mother's bedroom and had several sips of the hot beverage before placing it on the chest of drawers. She went over to the bed and lifting the covers, slipped her hands beneath the mattress and searched about for the envelope. It did not take long to find. She drew it out and opened the flap and emptied the letters on to the bed. Sifting through them, she noticed that most bore a Caernarfon postmark. Then she came across an envelope that felt different, was made of better quality paper. She held it close to her face and saw that it was postmarked 12th *May 1939, Keswick.* It was addressed to Mrs H. Peters at the house in the next street.

Rene's heart appeared to do a somersault and she fetched the cup and drained it to the dregs, feeling it doing her good as it went down. Then, putting aside the letter addressed to Sally, she put the rest back inside the large brown envelope and went downstairs.

She loomed over her mother and Vera shrunk away from her. 'How is it you had this?' Rene thrust Sally's letter under her mother's nose.

Vera blinked down at the envelope. Then she smiled. 'It was put through the letterbox. I didn't have to steal it. Plop! Just dropped through. I managed to pick it up and when I saw who it was addressed to, I thought, serve the little bitch right for calling me names.'

Suddenly, Rene's anger was tempered by a deep sadness. 'I never thought you could be so vindictive, Mother.'

Vera made to speak but Rene held up a hand as if to ward her off and left the room.

11

Despite not wanting to lose Alex to his real family, Greta could not wait to see his face when she handed his mother's letter to him as it contained information that could only please him. She decided to leave her grandmother reading the letters from Fred and hurried out of the house with the envelope in her coat pocket. She stood at the bottom of the street, hoping to see Alex and her father come into view but there was no sign of them. So she walked to the sweet shop opposite the church and bought a stick of liquorice. Sucking it, she meandered along the pavement breathing in the clean smell of washing from the Wong Hing laundry before retracing her steps. She gazed up the street on the opposite side of the road but there was still no sign of Alex and Harry. So she continued her stroll, wondering if they could possibly have gone to check up on whether the Coxes were OK.

Suddenly she heard her name being called and whirled round to see Harry and Alex crossing the cobbled road towards her. 'What are you doing here?' asked her father. 'Is Rene OK? Your gran? Why didn't you tell me about …'

She interrupted him. 'Poor Rene! She's really upset about what her mother did! I presume Uncle Jeff told you about the letters.'

Grim-faced, Harry nodded. 'Terrible. But what about …?'

She did not let him finish. 'Good news, Dad! Mrs Miller kept Uncle Fred's letters and among them was this!' She produced the envelope postmarked Keswick and waved it in front of Alex's face. 'It's from your mother! It went to our old address and the new tenant put it through the Millers' letterbox by mistake and the old hag kept it. Your mother's address is on it and so is her married name!'

Never would Greta forget the expression on Alex's face as he snatched the letter from her fingers. 'She tried to find you. Even going to Keswick for a holiday with her husband and visiting the orphanage,' Greta said rapidly, 'then they went to the farm but, of course, the farmer didn't know where you'd gone. She finishes by asking why hadn't Mam written last Christmas and was she well.'

Emotion seized Alex by the throat and he could not speak. He blinked back tears of joy. Then he leapt into the air and ran in the direction of the house.

'Wait!' she called. 'I haven't finished ...' Her voice trailed off.

'He'll read it himself, luv,' said Harry. 'I'm glad the lad's had some good news at last. We're not on duty tonight, either, and that's good news, too. But what's this about you getting caught in a blast?'

'It was nothing, Dad,' said Greta hurriedly. 'I survived and if nothing else it proves Gran's maxim. If it's got your number on it then you don't stand a chance. I think someone up there's looking out for me.' She began to walk towards the house. 'Apparently, Uncle Jeff's gone to pick up his kit from the Seamen's Home.' Greta hesitated. 'How d'you feel about him, Dad?'

Harry glanced down at his daughter, barely able to make out her features in the twilight. 'Believing that Sally was in an asylum, I feel, girl, that he could have come to visit her, even though Mrs Miller told Fred it was pointless.'

She nodded, soberly, 'He never bothered to write to Mam or Gran in the early days, did he?'

Harry shook his head. 'I bet he'd say that he's just not one for writing letters. That's a lot of people's excuse for not keeping in touch.'

Greta smiled. 'Uncle Fred's got a wife and three kids. She's a farmer's daughter. They have a smallholding with chickens, a cow and a pig, they even grow vegetables. It's in one of the letters. Gran read it out to me.'

'Sounds ideal,' said Harry in a thoughtful voice as they reached the house.

They found Alex resting on his elbows at the table with the open letter in front of him. He glanced up and smiled. 'Mum's husband's sold the shop! No wonder I couldn't find him. Her married name is Mawdsley and they're sharing a house with one of his daughters in Bootle. The other interesting thing is,' he paused for effect, 'I've been barking up the wrong tree, thinking it was Mum's brother, who took my sisters. Apparently, it was Dad's! And Mum's brother has emigrated to Canada ... went in the spring of 1939 with his family.'

'I suppose you don't remember where your dad's brother lives?' said Greta.

Alex's brow furrowed. 'I've got a feeling … ' He paused. 'It doesn't matter anyhow. Mum'll know. I can ask her.' His face lit up.

'All these goings and comings,' said Cissie, ladling out the stew. 'I've made up me mind to visit our Fred.'

Her words took the others by surprise. 'I thought Jeff said that he lives in Llanberis, Mrs Hardcastle,' said Harry. 'It's a slate mining town at the foot of Snowdon, smack bang in the middle of the mountains. I thought you hated the country.'

'I'm allowed to change me mind, aren't I?' said Cissie. 'His letters are real poetic.' Her voice was filled with pride. 'You can tell he loves the countryside. He was never out of Liverpool until he was called up so he must get it from my granddaddy. He came from County Wexford and worked on the land.'

'So when are you planning on visiting your mother, Alex?' asked Greta.

'This weekend. I'm not so sure I want to go on my own,' said Alex with a wry smile. 'The idea of seeing her after all this time, meeting her husband and stepchildren, is something I find daunting. Beside's she'll probably be interested to meet Sally's daughter.'

Greta was pleased with his words. 'Shall I come with you then?' He nodded.

'That's settled then,' said Cissie. 'So come and get your tea.'

During the meal, Cissie interspersed mouthfuls of food with extracts from Fred's letters. 'I've two other granddaughters and a grandson … younger than you, Greta. It looks like our Fred and his Megan were late getting started.'

'I think Greta should go to Wales with you,' said Harry, glancing across the table at his daughter.

Immediately she protested, 'But you need someone to cook for you, Dad, if Gran's not here.'

'It would be less worry for me if you were out of Liverpool,' said Harry firmly. 'I'll muddle through.'

'Let's see what Fred and his wife have to say before you two start arguing,' said Cissie. 'What if Megan doesn't want her mother-in-law staying with her? She might think I'd poke me nose in everything.'

'OK! We'll leave it for now,' said Harry, glancing at his daughter. 'But this subject is not going to go away.'

Alex whispered to Greta, 'You and Mrs Hardcastle will be better off in the country. You'll be safe there.'

Grumpily, she thought that she could do without him agreeing with her father. Who was to say, with her and Cissie out of the way, that Alex wouldn't take the opportunity to leave this house to live with his mother, whilst her father would go looking for female company in the shape of Mrs Cox. She muttered, 'There's no guarantee! The Jerries have jettisoned bombs on Wales to lighten their load on their return flights before today. Anyhow, you don't like the country … left that farm as soon as you could.'

Alex shook his head. 'That had nothing to do with the country. I enjoyed roaming the fells. Streams gushing down the mountain side and air so fresh and sweet smelling that, when it blew, you felt clean through and through. It was different on the farm. Wherever there's animals there's always a stink.'

'You've never said anything nice about being up north before,' said Greta.

'That's because I wanted to forget about it but that doesn't mean to say I don't have good memories of the place. And whatever you say about the Jerries jettisoning their load, it will still be safer in Wales.'

She sighed. 'They'll speak Welsh.'

'Why shouldn't they?' said Alex peaceably. 'But they must speak some English, otherwise they couldn't make themselves understood in the shops in town. Your uncle Fred will speak English anyway.'

Mention of Fred reminded her of her other uncle. 'I wonder where Uncle Jeff is! If he's stayed at the Seamen's Home he's really in the firing line down by the docks.'

'Is he staying there?' asked Harry, glancing across at Cissie. 'I would have thought he'd expect to stay here?'

'He didn't say,' replied Cissie, and was suddenly tight-lipped. 'Our Jeff was always a law unto himself, too much like his father. But best make sure there's a key on the string so he can let himself in if he does come back and we've gone to bed. He is me own flesh and blood after all!'

So that was what Harry did. He had his own ideas about where Jeff might be spending the night but kept it to himself. He was glad to have him out of the way. Nothing was said when Jeff turned up the next day and it was accepted by Greta that he had spent the night at the Seamen's Home.

Come Saturday afternoon Jeff arrived at the house, bearing more flowers for Cissie. Rene was washing the Millers' step. 'You're busy,' he commented.

'I have to catch up on jobs when I can with Mother the way she is,' she said, squeezing out the floor cloth. 'Besides it keeps me from brooding. I couldn't sleep last night… had too much on my mind. I feel terrible about what she did but all I can do is to say how sorry I am.'

'You're not to blame, luv.' He rocked on his heels, looking debonair in his navy blue seaman's coat, with his peaked cap set back on his mop of tawny hair.

'Even so, I feel bad about the years Cissie and Sally believed you and Fred wanted to have nothing to do with them. I wish there was some way I could make amends.' She wiped the tiles and shifted down the step to do the next patch.

Instantly Jeff smiled and said, 'How about you giving me the pleasure of your company tonight? Come to the flicks!'

He took Rene by surprise. 'I don't see how I can leave Mother. What if there's another raid?'

'I tell you, they're probably satisfied with the devastation they caused the night I arrived. They made a helluva mess of the South Docks and the Dingle Oil Depot.'

She laughed mirthlessly. 'You know nothing about it. We have these lulls and then over they come again. Just before Christmas there was a real bad raid, worse than the one you're talking about. St George's Hall was set alight, the Royal Infirmary damaged, a block of houses right next to the hospital completely destroyed, and Goodlass's paintworks went up like a rocket. The North Docks really got it, too.' She gave attention to her task, scrubbing energetically at the tiles.

Silence.

Then Jeff said, 'I reckon you're too good to her. Don't be so nice and she might appreciate you better.'

'That'll be the day,' she said bitterly.

'You're probably right, girl. Anyway, couldn't the lodger keep his eye on her?'

'They're not speaking right now. Anyway what about your wife? You are married if I remember.'

There was a pause before he said, 'Dead, girl! She was killed last time the Jerries blitzed Southampton.' His eyes wore a sad expression and his mouth drooped at the corners.

She could have kicked herself. 'I am sorry.'

He shrugged. 'These things happen. The sea's my mistress now. That's not to say I don't enjoy a woman's company. So how about asking your lodger to keep his eye on the old biddy? I think we both could do with cheering up.'

Rene had no particular desire to go out with Jeff, although if Harry had asked she'd have accepted his invitation like a shot. However, after the way her mother had behaved, she felt she owed him something and, in order to keep things friendly said, 'OK. You're on!'

His smile dimpled. 'Good! I'll give you a knock about five,' he drawled.

'If you've a torch, bring it. I lost mine … and don't forget your gasmask, either,' she said.

'Yes, Miss! See you later.' He went in next door.

Rene gave the rest of the step a perfunctory wipe. Then she emptied the dirty water down the grid and thought of the evening ahead. Going out with a man as handsome as Jeff Hardcastle should have made her feel as excited as a young girl on a first date but all she felt was that it was something to get over with. She'd had little to do with him when she was younger because he had been seven or eight years older. For ages she had accepted Sally's opinion of her eldest brother as the generous, caring, protective brother, that was until he had vanished down south after the war. She knew the reason for that now, although, like Greta, Cissie and Harry, she questioned why he had never made any effort to see his sister during the intervening years, even though he had believed her out of her mind. She did not want to go out with him but knew she ought to make an effort to look her best.

So she washed her hair and, as she did so, wondered what to wear. This time of year meant wrapping up. The tip of her nose always went red with the cold. She would look like a clown and he would skit her. Face powder! She still had some somewhere but would have to use it sparingly. Compared to this time two years ago there was so little in the shops.

'What have you washed your hair for?' asked Vera a few minutes later.

'None of your business,' said Rene, glancing in the mirror. To her horror she noticed a silver hair among the red-gold and swiftly pinched it beneath finger and thumb and pulled it out. Ouch!

'You'll be thirty-six in August … that's if you're still alive.'

Rene ignored her, rolling a strand of hair round a pipe cleaner and bending the ends into place.

'What are you putting them in for? You going out? Is it someone from work?' Rene continued to ignore her. 'Is it a serviceman you've met in town? You can't trust men in the armed forces, they're only out for what they can get. He probably thinks you're easy meat, single at your age,' sneered her mother. Rene felt like rapping her over the head with the hairbrush. 'Desperate, that's what you are,' muttered Vera.

Rene turned on her. 'You're right, Mother! That's why I'm going to start making the best of my chances before I'm too old and crabby, like you. And if you don't shut up, and leave me in peace, I'll go to the nearest enrolment centre and join the forces if they'll have me. I'm sure you'll love the Home for the Sick and Elderly on Belmont Road.'

Vera gasped, 'You wouldn't do that to your poor old mother!'

'Wouldn't I? You just push me too far and I'll be off!' snapped Rene.

Vera called her a nasty name and then subsided in her chair, muttering to herself.

A few hours later there was a knock on the door and Rene went to answer it. 'You ready?' asked Jeff.

'Yes! And you're late.' She was unable to see his features clearly because it had been a dull day and so there were no stars or a moon.

'Sorry! I've never known a woman to be on time.' He flashed his torch over her. 'You're the exception and you look very nice, too.' She was wearing a rust jumper beneath a pin-striped brown worsted suit. On her curling hair she wore a hat with a spotted bow on the brim. Her feet were clad in low heeled court shoes. Even so she was taller than him by two inches. 'Who'd have ever thought that you'd have turned out such an Amazon,' he said.

Immediately she felt like a giantess. 'I can't help my height,' she replied.

'I wasn't complaining,' said Jeff, offering his arm.

After the barest of hesitations she moved her handbag to the shoulder that held her gasmask and slipped her hand through his arm.

'So where are we going?' he asked, playing the torch over the pavement as they walked down the street.

'I thought you must have had somewhere in mind. If you haven't I suppose we could go and see Charlie Chaplin in *The Great Dictator*.'

'That'll do me,' said Jeff. 'So why's a girl like you, Rene, still living with that cow of a mam of yours?'

His words irritated her and she withdrew her hand. 'There's no need for that. I know she behaved abominably but that's enough bad news for me, without you adding to it. If you want to talk, then tell me about your travels instead.'

'Sure, if you want to hear.' And he launched into a description of the places he had been. He was a good raconteur and momentarily she forgave him for his thoughtless remark about her mother. Still feeling some ill effect from having been injured in the blast, it was pleasant not to have to make the effort to rattle on herself. So she let him do all the talking.

They reached the cinema and he bought tickets for the back stalls. It was not long before he placed his arm round her shoulders and whispered against her ear, 'Who'd have ever thought that little Rene would grow into a big girl and we'd be sitting together like this?'

She felt like hitting him but instead removed his arm and shushed him. 'I want to watch this film.'

'You mean you're really interested in the little tramp turning into a Adenoid Hynkel? A Hitler imitation if ever I saw one.'

'It's an American propaganda film so that's what he's supposed to be. We could do with the Yanks in the war,' she said, trying not to lose her temper.

'You mean the big *I ams*?' he sneered. 'If they join us we'll never hear the end of it. They'll be saying that they won the war.'

She turned to him. 'Do you know many Yanks?'

'Sister, I've been sailing the briny for years,' he drawled. 'Of course, I know the Yanks … been in a few punch ups with them, too.'

Rene was about to open her mouth, and ask who'd won, when a voice from the row in front, said, 'D'yer think the two of yer could bloody shut up? We're trying to watch the film.'

Instantly Jeff stood up. 'Nobody tells me to shut up,' he said.

'That's it!' said Rene, dragged him down into his seat. 'Another word from you and I'm going.'

Jeff darted her a surprised look and then grinned. 'Keep yer hair on, bossy! Oohh! I love a strong woman.' He settled in his seat, put an arm about her shoulders again and with his free hand forced her head round and kissed her.

She pushed him away. 'Don't! I'm not here for that.'

'Come off it, Rene. You've been missing out … besides, don't you think you owe me something for what your mam did to my family?'

She could not believe what she was hearing. Hadn't she been through enough the last few days without having to put up with this kind of thing from Jeff? Who the hell did he think he was? She had to get away from him. She wrenched herself out of his hold and got up. Excusing herself, she made her way along the row of people, ignoring Jeff's sounds of annoyance.

Outside it was pitch black except for the odd flash of a torch but she could hear footfalls and people's voices coming from the direction of the Grafton dance hall to her left. For a moment her brain seemed incapable of deciding which way was home and then she pulled herself together as her eyes became accustomed to the dark. She heard a shout behind her and that egged her on to make a move. She almost ran across the road. Ahead, a little to her left she could see the shadowy shapes of people outside St Michael's church and she headed towards them, knowing she was going in the right direction. Soon she had left them behind and had passed the red brick office building of Ogden's tobacco company. The noise from the main road gradually faded away.

She felt jumpy being on her own in the pitch black without a torch, but told herself to keep on going and realised suddenly that she had stepped off the pavement and had wandered onto the cobbled road. Then she heard running footsteps, caught the light of a wavering beam and her heart leapt into her throat. She was grabbed from behind. 'What the hell d'you think you're playing at? Nobody walks out on Jeff Hardcastle and gets away with it,' he snarled.

'Let me go!'

'Like hell I will,' Jeff said, clamping Rene's arms against her sides and, despite her size, almost frogmarching her across the road.

Although shorter, he was undoubtedly stronger and forced her past a corner shop and into an entry, whirling her round to face him as he shoved her against the wall. Shock took over, this could not be happening. This was Jeff, Sally's brother! He wouldn't hurt her! Jeff dropped his gasmask and, wrenching her handbag and gasmask from her shoulder, he pitched them into the darkness, before hitting her across the face. She was stunned. His fingers tore at the buttons of her jacket, hands grabbing at her breasts as he brought his head down and bit her neck. The pain jerked her out of her frozen state and she reacted by grabbing his hair and pulling it hard.

'You bitch! Your mam owes me this,' he said, and kneed her in the groin. She gasped and released her hold on his hair, doubled up with pain. For a moment she was utterly defenceless and he pushed her back against the wall and forced up her skirts. No! She wasn't going to let that happen. She ignored the pain in her groin and clawed at his hand and bit whatever part of his flesh she could reach. He grunted and gasped and cursed her, and still she struggled but his strength was beginning to defeat her.

Suddenly a gleam of light shone on them. 'Disgustin'!' said a woman's voice and the next moment a wave of cold water caught Rene and Jeff forcing them apart. 'Get away from my door, the pair of yer! Like animals yer are!'

Jeff spluttered. 'Mind your own business, yer nosy old cow!'

A door slammed and they were in darkness. To Rene's amazement, Jeff began to laugh. 'What d'you think of that, Rene? Saved in the nick of time.'

'I can't believe you,' she said through chattering teeth. Most of her clothing was soaked through and she was freezing.

'You shouldn't have got my temper up. Here!' He flicked on his torch. 'Let's find yer handbag and gasmask.'

She made no move to help him. 'You find them, you filthy sod! How dare you treat me like that.'

'Sorry, Rene! Since the first war I've had trouble controlling myself when people go against me. If you're nice to me it won't happen again.'

It definitely wouldn't happen because she wouldn't be seen dead in his company! He must be mad! It could be the only sensible reason for his behaviour.

'Here they are, luv.' He shone the torch on her and dropped her gasmask on her shoulder. She wrenched her handbag from his hand, not wanting him to touch her. 'Don't get stroppy, Rene. I've said sorry, haven't I?'

'Saying sorry isn't enough,' she said in a seething voice.

'That's how I feel about you apologising for your mam. Just you think on that before criticising me, girl.'

Rene did not say a word but limped away. The other end of the entry came out on the street opposite theirs. She did not look back to see if Jeff was following her. She never wanted to see him again.

12

Greta gazed out of the tram window as it rattled along Stanley Road. Almost there! She turned to Alex, who was looking smart in a navy blue pinstriped suit. 'What'll you do if your mother's not in? It's possible she and her husband could be spending the day with one of his other married children. Perhaps you should have written.'

He nodded. 'I thought about it and made a start on a letter but I ended up tearing it up. What I wanted to say just wouldn't come right. Then Jeff disturbed me coming in.' Alex rolled the tram tickets round his little finger. 'What d'you think of him going out with Rene?'

Greta brushed back a strand of dark hair that had fallen into her eyes. 'I'm not happy about it.'

Alex looked at her with interest. 'Why? Don't you think Rene fancies him the way he was making out to your dad?'

Greta shifted in her seat. 'She was pretty cagey when I met her coming out the paper shop and asked how they'd got on. Besides, what chance has she of any kind of love life with her mother around?'

'Rene and your dad would make a good match.'

Greta said softly, 'I've thought that sometimes ... but what's the use when there's her mother and Mrs Cox? I wish I knew what Dad was up to with that woman.'

Alex took Greta's hand and squeezed it. 'I'm sure he wouldn't do anything, like asking her to marry him, without talking to you first. Anyway, we're here now, kid! So forget them.' The tram rattled to a halt and he dragged her to her feet.

As they crossed Stanley Road, Greta said, 'You look smart. How do I look?'

He paused on the pavement and inspected her appearance. She was wearing a fir green coat, a Christmas gift from her father, and a bronze-coloured hat crocheted by Miss Birkett. Her dark hair was flicked up at the ends and framed her slender face. 'Terrible!' he said.

Her face fell. 'What!'

Alex smiled and his slate grey eyes contained an expression that made her feel breathless. 'There's no need to fish for compliments. Those colours suit you. Don't be worrying!'

'I'm not,' she lied, but for some reason could not forget that her mother had been his mother's maid.

He drew her hand through his arm and headed for one of the wide thoroughfares, named after Oxford colleges: Trinity, Balliol, Merton. The houses were big, built of red brick, and most had three storeys and were fronted by large gardens.

Greta imagined how much space there must be inside just one of the houses, plenty of room for a big family. She drifted into a day dream and was furnishing one such house to her own taste, with items of class and distinction from Waring & Gillows. She jumped when Alex swore and her eyes followed his gaze. 'Oh no!' she whispered.

The roof and the top floor had completely gone, and only smoke blackened walls, like jagged teeth, remained standing. She looked at Alex's pale, tense face, and her eyes met his bleak ones. 'I could strangle Mrs Miller,' he said in a choking voice.

She swallowed the lump in her throat. 'I know how you feel, but this can't have happened recently. There'd be a stronger smell of dampened down fire.'

He took a deep breath. 'You're right! Even so it doesn't change things.' He clenched his fists. 'I've come too late.'

'Perhaps you shouldn't be thinking the worst. Maybe they weren't at home when the house was hit. We'll ask one of the neighbours. They should be able to tell us what happened,' she said.

Without a word, Alex crossed the road to the house directly opposite. She followed him, standing close to him as he banged on the door. From inside the house came the sound of choral music. 'You're going to have to knock louder,' said Greta. He hammered again, and kept on until, eventually, footsteps were heard inside coming towards them.

The door opened and an elderly man stood in the vestibule, his back, ramrod straight. 'Who are you? Do you know what day it is?' he barked.

'Yes, sir,' said Alex, almost snapping to attention. 'Sunday. But this is an emergency! Can you tell me what happened to the people who lived in the bombed house opposite?'

'Dead!'

The colour drained from Alex's face and Greta slipped her hand through his arm. 'All of them?' she blurted out.

'Father, mother and two little girls. Little darlings! Blonde beauties! Bomb came through the roof. All in bed! Heartbreaking!' His rheumy brown eyes were suddenly moist.

Alex cleared his throat. 'What about the older couple?' he croaked. 'The ... grandfather an-and grandmother who were staying there?'

'Nobody else in the house.'

'But they were living there,' insisted Alex.

The man snorted. 'If you mean Mr and Mrs Mawdsley, they sailed for Canada just before war broke out. Went to join her brother.'

Stupefied, Alex stared at him and then he sagged against the door jamb. 'Thank God for that,' he whispered.

'Pull yourself together, lad.' The man looked at him severely. 'Now if you don't mind I'm missing part of a Bach Oratorio.' He made to shut the door and Alex stepped back.

Swiftly Greta placed her foot in the gap between the door and the door jamb. 'Mrs Mawdsley is his mother,' she said. 'You wouldn't happen to know, sir, where they've gone to in Canada?'

The man shook his head.

'The addresses of Mr Mawdsley's other children?' she asked.

'Sorry, young woman! I doubt any of the neighbours would know ... not a thing you go asking,' he said gruffly.

She thanked him and slipping her hand in Alex's arm she hurried him away. 'Canada!' she exclaimed. 'What are you going to do?'

'I'm thinking.'

'Maybe your sisters will have his address,' said Greta.

Alex sighed heavily. 'Let's hope so but that means finding my Uncle George, who must be the one who put me in the Home.'

'Do you think it was his house Mam pointed out to Rene?'

His shoulders drooped. 'Probably! Right now I feel I'm never going to see Mum again.'

'Don't let yourself get downhearted!' Greta squeezed his arm.

Anger flashed across his face and he wrenched his arm out of her grasp. 'It's all right for you to say that! How would you feel if you'd been taken away from your family when you were only a kid and put in a strange place? I know your mother and sister and brother are dead but at least you had their company for years and you still have your father and gran. Not only that, you'll get to see your Uncle Fred, your aunt and cousins! They'll probably welcome you with open arms just because you're family. You'll belong without even having to try! I feel like I don't bloody belong anywhere.'

Greta was shocked by the savagery in his tone. She had hoped because he had been taken into their family and had lived with them for months now that he would begin to feel part of it, but obviously that wasn't true. And she had to admit that if her mother, Amy and Alf were not dead but, instead, alive somewhere, then she'd want to move heaven and earth to be with them again.

'I'm sorry.' Her voice was barely above a whisper. 'I suppose your sisters looked up to you? You being their big brother. I suppose, too, that after your father died you wanted to help take care of them. I bet you've often wondered what your uncle told them after you'd gone?'

He nodded, conflicting emotions flitting across his face. 'I loved my sisters. They used to trail after me like a pair of puppies following their master. I suppose I bossed them about but they didn't seem to mind. Of course it worries me what my uncle might have told them. They could believe I no longer care about them, they might have put me out of their minds.'

'Surely, your mother would have tried to keep your memory alive?'

'I'm sure she would have if she'd had the opportunity.' He clenched his fists. 'I have to find them. I know my uncle's name is Armstrong and he's a solicitor. We could look in a telephone book and find his address. Remember you saying to Mrs Cox's daughter that we were looking for my uncle, Mr Armstrong? I don't know why I didn't consider then that he might have known where they were.'

Greta smiled. 'It sounds easy when you say it like that.'

He grinned and pecked her cheek. 'Sorry about the outburst! I'm an ungrateful sod! You and your dad and gran have done so much for me. Now, let's find a telephone box and look through all the Armstrongs.' He seized her hand and ran with her.

* * *

Greta settled herself next to the window in the railway carriage, which they had to themselves. They had caught a tram to Waterloo station, which was the next one after Seaforth on the Liverpool Southport line. There they had found a telephone box, riffled through the directory and discovered a George Armstrong, who was in partnership with another solicitor called Simmons. They had chambers in Crosby, as well as Liverpool. Alex's uncle also had a house, which Alex had suddenly remembered was somewhere near Hall Road station. It was three stops after Seaforth.

'So tell me what you remember about your father's brother?' said Greta, gazing across at Alex.

'Not much! I don't remember his being part of our lives,' said Alex, knitting his brow. 'I think he was older than Dad, married with no children. Maybe that's why we didn't see much of him.'

'What was his wife like?'

Alex shrugged. 'I don't remember much about her. Perhaps she didn't feel comfortable around children.'

'She took on your sisters.'

'That's true.'

They were quiet a moment, each wondering what kind of reaction their arrival would provoke. 'You've never mentioned the girls by name,' said Greta, leaning towards him.

He smiled. 'That's because Mum and Dad always referred to them as *the girls*. They were called Lydia and Barbara.'

'Have you thought you might have trouble recognising them … and they, you?'

Alex said hesitantly, 'I'm sure I'll know them when I see them.'

'What d'you think your uncle will say?'

'Probably, what the hell are you doing here?' murmured Alex, resting his head against the back of the seat and closing his eyes.

Greta studied his features, wondering what his sisters would make of him. How could they not like what they saw? Lovely grey eyes, a nose that was almost perfectly straight and a mouth that had a deeply curving lower lip. She had an urge to kiss him. *And she woke him with a kiss;* Sleeping Beauty *in reverse*. She smiled mischievously, wondering how he would react if she did such a thing. At that moment, Alex's eyelids lifted and their eyes met.

'What are you smiling about?' he said drowsily.

'Nothing!' She closed her eyes, her emotions confused. She wanted him to be happy. Yet, if he did find his mother and sisters where would that leave her? His family might put pressure on him to have nothing more to do with her. She might end up never seeing him again and that didn't bear thinking about.

They left the train at Hall Road station. On either side of the road were large detached houses of pebbledash and red brick, some had black and white gabling. All had enormous gardens. 'It's real posh, isn't it?' whispered Greta.

Alex did not answer because he was too busy gazing about him. He pointed to a double gateway and, behind a fence, a notice that said *WEST LANCASHIRE GOLF CLUB*. 'I have been here. I remember that sign. I think if we carry on in this direction, we'll come to the sea and that'll clinch it. We are in the right place.'

He headed off down the road so fast that Greta had to run to catch up with him. He took her down to the front where, if they gazed towards the right across the water, they could see part of the Wirral coastline and the Welsh hills beyond. 'I remember my dad saying, *You can see Snowdon on a clear day.* Think about that, Greta, if you go and stay with your uncle Fred. You're not so far away from Liverpool.'

She made no answer but followed him as he retraced his steps. They went up one tree-lined road and then down another. There were few people about because it was a cold day. Suddenly he stopped in front of a driveway, devoid of gates. There was a name on the gatepost. *Hawkshead!* He slapped his hand against it. 'This is it! I remember being here with Dad. There was only Uncle George in the house. Dad sent me out into the garden and told me to play.' Alex spoke rapidly. 'There was a little summer house ... and a shed which was locked. On the grass was a golf club and some balls. I think I picked up the club and had a swipe at them.'

'Are you going to knock?' Greta's heart was beating rapidly as she gazed up the gravelled drive that curved between patches of ground containing frost-blighted plants. Several large trees, devoid of leaves, shielded the house from those on either side.

'That's what we're here for!' He led the way.

There was an open porch and Alex stepped inside. He rattled the letter box and when nobody came he rapped his knuckles on the panel of the door. Are we going to be out of luck again? thought Greta.

Alex peered through the letterbox.

'See anything?' she asked.

Alex shook his head. 'Let's go round the back.' He led the way, squeezing past overgrown holly and laurel bushes. There was a door set in the side of the house but, when he tried the handle, it was locked. So he carried on round to the rear.

The garden was enclosed by trees and at the bottom there was a summer house and a shed. With a triumphant expression, Alex said, 'I was right. This is it! Although there used to be a lawn and flowerbeds.'

'Dig for Victory,' murmured Greta, eyeing the ploughed over space where the lawn must have been.

Alex went over to the rear of the house and peered through the French windows. 'It's really tidy in here! No newspapers, cups or books lying around.' He frowned.

'Perhaps your uncle's away,' suggested Greta.

Alex made no comment but, from his pocket, took out a Swiss Army knife.

'You're not going to break in?' Her voice was startled, and she glanced nervously in the direction of the neighbouring houses, although she could see little of them.

Alex pulled out one of the blades and began to work it between the door and the rotting woodwork. There was a click. He opened the door and stood listening a moment before stepping over the threshold. Greta hesitated but he beckoned her in and closed the door behind them.

She watched Alex as his eyes roamed about the room. 'I'm sure there was some kind of argument going on in here when I came with Dad,' he said, his expression strained. 'Raised voices, anyway, coming from the French windows. Dad came storming out, yanked me by the arm and told me we were going home.'

'He didn't say why?'

'No!' Alex looked rueful. 'And I didn't dare ask. He strode along, pulling me by the hand. I fell over a couple of times but he told me to stop messing about and dragged me to my feet. It wasn't like Dad to be so brusque, but I guess he was upset by whatever his brother had said. It was shortly after that he died.'

'Rene said the coroner's verdict was accidental death,' said Greta.

Alex nodded and made his way across the room with Greta trailing after him, ears alert for any sound that might warn them to get out. 'Dad wouldn't have killed himself!' he said suddenly. 'He wasn't the sort.'

Greta accepted his word for it. 'Did you ever see your uncle again?'

'Must have if he took charge of things after Dad's death,' muttered Alex, 'but those days are a bit of a blank. I was only eight.'

They both fell silent: the joy had gone out of the day.

Alex hurried across the hall and pushed open a door into what was a large kitchen. He quit that and went into another room at the front of the house, which contained a table, chairs and a sideboard. Alex flicked open a cupboard but there was only crockery inside, so he made his way across the hall into another room with a cabinet, shelves of books, a piano and a violin, as well as a couple of armchairs.

'I bet the girls had music lessons,' he murmured. 'I wonder where the hell they are.'

Greta wondered, too. She made a suggestion. 'Let's see if there are any photographs about. I'd love to see what your sisters look like.'

His expression lightened. 'Perhaps there are some upstairs.'

Alex led the way and Greta followed him into one bedroom, and then another. Neither of the single beds looked as if they had been slept in, which, perhaps, suggested the girls weren't living here. Still, they carried on with the search. There was a bathroom and a separate toilet. They didn't go inside the box room, which had a load of junk in it, but entered the master bedroom.

Almost immediately, Greta had the weirdest feeling. The hairs on the back of her neck seemed to stand up and she felt icy cold. 'I don't like this room.' Her voice was barely audible.

'Why? What's wrong?' said Alex, glancing at her with a frown.

She shrugged, feeling stupid, but did not go further into the room. She watched him go over to a chest of drawers and pick up a framed photograph. 'Look at this! It must be my uncle with Lydia and Babs!'

Greta forced herself to cross the room towards him. She took hold of the frame and gazed down at the picture of the man and two girls.

One of them was fair and the other was dark. Neither was what one would call exactly pretty and their smiles appeared fixed, yet there was something about the line of the jaw and their eyes that made her say, 'They do have a look of you.'

His face lit up. 'You really think so?' She nodded. 'What d'you think of him?' asked Alex.

She gazed at the man, who had a hand on each of the girls' shoulders. He was wearing a blazer with some kind of badge on the pocket and what appeared to be a white shirt and flannels. His nose was hooked and beneath it was a toothbrush moustache. His eyes seemed to be fixed intently onto the photographer. 'You'll think I'm daft but he reminds me of a villain in a black and white movie. I don't like the look of him one little bit.' She handed the framed photograph back to Alex.

'I agree with you!' said Alex, his brows lowering. He placed it on the chest of drawers. He took out his Swiss knife and began to undo the screws at the back. He removed the photograph and as he did so a folded sheet of newspaper fell to the floor. Greta picked it up. 'What's this?' she said.

Alex looked at the newspaper. 'Probably just padding. Get rid of it.'

She pocketed it, thinking to throw it away later. Alex replaced the glass and fastened the screws with the tip of the blade. He then returned the frame to the chest of drawers. 'He mightn't notice the photo's gone immediately.'

'And when he does what's he going to think?'

Alex closed his knife. 'I don't particularly care what he thinks. But I've a feeling there's nobody living here. The place is cold and the grates have all been cleared out.' His expression was grim. 'For the moment it looks like we've reached a dead end again.'

'Poor Alex! It could be that the girls have been evacuated.' Greta squeezed his arm. 'This place is starting to gives me the creeps. Let's get out!'

They left by the front door and had just reached the gateway when a voice said, 'I hope you two can explain yourselves.' They both jumped and then stared at the white haired old lady standing on the pavement. She was peering at them through horn rimmed spectacles and, in one hand, she held a stick.

Alex said, 'Mr Armstrong isn't at home?'

'I'm sure, young ruffian, you know the answer to that,' she said, waving the stick about.

Alex stood his ground. 'Yes, but where is he? And where are the girls and my aunt?'

'Aunt!' she exclaimed, startled. 'You're claiming to be Jane Armstrong's nephew? If that was true, young man, you would know that she is dead!'

'Dead!' exclaimed Alex.

'She went to Liverpool to do some shopping for Christmas and had arranged to meet George at his office so they could come home together. A bomb went off just outside the office and she was killed. Poor woman!'

'And my uncle and my sisters? They weren't with her when it went off?' Alex's face had paled.

The woman's eyes almost popped out of her head. 'Your sisters? I-I never knew the girls had a brother?'

'I'm the skeleton in the family cupboard,' said Alex, smiling grimly, and repeated his question.

'Evacuated, young man! Your aunt took them to Wales shortly before the blitz started. As for your uncle he's gone away. No one knows where exactly. His wife's death affected him dreadfully.'

'Thank you,' said Alex, and seizing Greta's hand, dragged her away.

He was silent on the journey back to Liverpool and Greta did not disturb him with idle chatter. To her shame, relief was her uppermost feeling. How could Alex trace any of his family now? But she was soon to be dissuaded from that conclusion.

Over the evening meal he spoke to Harry about going down to the shipping offices of Canadian Pacific. 'If I can get them to search through their records for August of last year and see if they can trace a Mr and Mrs Mawdsley they just might have a destination address in Canada! I could sign on a ship and go out there,' said Alex, his eyes alight with determination.

'Are you sure about going back to sea?' Harry looked concerned. 'What about the U-boats?'

'What about what we've been putting up with here for the last few months?' said Alex.

Jeff, who was eating with them, put down his knife and fork. 'If he takes a ship from Greenock, say, most sail through the North

179

Atlantic. Not that it's much fun up there at this time of year but there's a better chance of avoiding the U-boats.'

'What about icebergs?' said Greta. 'And doesn't one of the Canadian rivers freeze at this time of year so that ships can't get up it?'

Alex nodded. 'She's right! I think it's the St Lawrence. But if I caught a ship heading for Nova Scotia that should be OK.'

'A lot of ships sailing there,' said Jeff. 'Not too difficult to get to the mainland of Canada from there.'

Alex agreed. 'I'll go down the shipping office and see what I come up with and then go down the Pool and see what's going.'

Greta was horrified. 'Wouldn't it be easier to try and trace your sisters in Wales than go all that way to find your mother?'

Alex said quietly, 'I thought that was a job you might be able to do. You can have the photograph and see how you go.'

Thanks a lot! Greta thought wryly. She got up and began to gather the dirty dishes together.

That night she prayed fervently that Alex would meet with no success at the shipping offices. She didn't want him to go, knowing she would worry about him even more than she did at the moment. If only a bomb had destroyed all their files. No such luck! Within the fortnight Alex had left Liverpool for Greenock and a ship going to Nova Scotia. The Mawdsleys had put their destination down as St John in New Brunswick.

13

Greta emerged from the house, muffled to the eyeballs in scarf, hat and with her coat collar turned up, her eyes scanning a sheet of newspaper before she placed it in her pocket. She walked down the front step to where Rene was waiting at the bottom. 'Cold day,' said Rene. 'Heard anything from Alex yet?'

The girl shook her head. 'Uncle Jeff reckons it takes eight to nine days to cross the Atlantic if weather conditions are favourable but it can be rough at this time of year, and what with trying to steer clear of the U-boats it'll be a miracle if he makes it in a fortnight. Uncle Jeff knows just how to cheer you up! Hopefully Alex'll write as soon as he's got news … and that the letter gets to me.' She crossed her fingers and touched the wooden fence.

'Your Uncle Jeff … has he said anything to you about when he's going back to sea?' asked Rene as they walked up the street.

Greta glanced sidelong at her. 'I thought you'd know that better than me.'

Rene shook her head. 'I went out with him only the once.'

Greta looked surprised. 'I thought it was more than that the way he goes on about you.'

'No!'

Greta frowned. 'I wonder why he lied. I can't say I like him myself. I think he's two-faced. He sucks up to Gran by bringing her flowers and when she said she'd rather have a drink or sweets, he used some of his sweet ration to buy her favourite humbugs *and* took her to an oyster bar in town. I don't know what he's up to, it's not as if she's got any money to give him.'

'Perhaps he needs your grandmother's love. After all, who else has he got when it comes to family? I take it he doesn't try to get round you?'

Greta pulled a face. 'He makes an effort to talk to me about Mam sometimes … says how fond they were of each other and how she was her dad's favourite. A lot of good that did her!' She changed the subject. 'By the way, Gran and I did get a letter from Uncle Fred in Wales.'

'What did he have to say?'

'Flabbergasted and thrilled that Gran was alive but sad to hear about Mum and the kids.'

'I bet he had a lot to say about Mother,' said Rene, grim faced.

Greta said smoothly, 'I'm saying nothing about that but you can be sure he doesn't blame you. He sent you his regards and said that he has fond memories of when you were a kid walking to school with Mam.'

Rene's expression softened. 'Did he mention about you and your gran going to stay in Wales?'

'He says we're very welcome but that the weather at this time of year can be filthy and treacherous and Spring's a busy time. He suggests that we wait until the end of April, the beginning of May, says it's lovely then. Which suits me down to the ground.' Greta smiled. 'He seems to have got the impression probably from the newspapers that everything is OK here now, that the worst of the bombing is over.'

There had been no raids worth mentioning since Rene and Greta had been caught in the blast. Who could say, though, how long that would last?

'What was so interesting in that newspaper you were reading?' asked Rene, as they walked up the street.

'I was thinking of showing it to you.' Greta took the newspaper from her pocket and handed it to Rene. 'I didn't mention this before but Alex and I got into his uncle's house and ...'

'How did you manage that?' asked Rene, taken aback.

Greta looked shame faced. 'He didn't do any damage ... just got a door open with his Swiss Army knife. All he took was a photograph of his uncle and sisters.' She hurried on before Rene could ask any more questions. 'In the back of the frame was that page of the *Crosby Herald*. It's dated 1936 when the Abdication was big news. I'd forgotten I had it until the other day. Alex said it was just backing at the time but I think it could be significant.'

Rene raised her eyebrows and said dryly, 'Where am I supposed to read?'

Greta pointed at a heading. 'It's a book review.'

Rene began to read and soon realised the article was about a local crime writer, who'd had the idea of turning a so called suicide, following the Wall Street Crash, into a murder. In his research, he had turned up information about several similar cases and questioned just how much the Great War had affected the mental health of the suicide victims. A number of them had invested their money in land and the newly developing industries of film, gramophone records and the wireless, tying up the income in trusts to provide for their children until they came of age.

Rene lifted her head and stared at Greta. 'Are you saying such a thing could have happened in Alex's father's case? That the coroner's verdict was wrong and his death was really murder? I've always been of the opinion that Sal and Mrs Armstrong believed he took his own life! But are you thinking that there could be money tied up in a trust for Alex and his sisters? Because I don't see how that could be true. Mr Armstrong moved his family to a smaller house. Would he have done that if he had money?'

'I don't know! I didn't know the man. Alex is convinced his father wouldn't have committed suicide. What if his brother, the solicitor, somehow managed to make use of the money and lost it? Say Alex's father got into difficulties and wanted to get to the money but his brother refused to help him out. Alex said there was a big argument between the pair of them and his father stormed out of the house.'

Rene smiled and handed the page of newspaper to Greta. 'You and that writer have some imagination.'

Greta's face fell. 'You don't believe it could have happened like that?'

'Why should the brother murder Alex's father? If he was already in control of the money there wouldn't be any need. This is real life, luv, not a Whodunnit. Besides, didn't he and his wife take Alex's sisters into their home? Would he have done that if he was a murderer?'

Greta scowled. 'You're forgetting he was also responsible for putting Alex in an orphanage! Not so Mr Nice Uncle to him!'

Rene said, 'Sorry! You are right there. But what you've just had me read is about a work of fiction. Enough said?'

Greta nodded but felt completely deflated and could only speak in monosyllables during the rest of the journey into town.

That evening Rene almost collided with Jeff in the blackout as she walked down the street, having missed seeing Greta on the tram on the way home. 'Sorry!' she said tersely, the beam of her torch shooting in several directions. She would have carried on walking if he hadn't seized hold of her arm.

'Is that all you've got to say?' said Jeff, clicking off his torch.

'I don't think we've got anything to say to each other,' she retorted.

'Why not?' His fingers bit into her arm. 'We could have had a good night out if only you'd been prepared to let yourself go. I'm surprised you're so prudish. Although, maybe that bitch of a mother of yours kept you under her thumb, determined not to have you take risks and have fun the way she did during the last war.'

'Let me go! I don't want to hear it.' She struggled but he was not about to release her.

'She liked coons, the Yankee kind. How do I know? I had a navy mate who lived close by a school which had been turned into a hospital, where some were billeted. I saw her with my own eyes when I was home on leave. She was arm in arm, slobbering over one of them. But then I can understand your mam's taste for coons. Had a darkie girl myself once. She was really something, double-jointed, could move her body in some interesting positions. Could teach you a trick or two!'

Rene's cheeks were aflame. 'What's Mother's business is her business and what's yours is yours. I have no part in your life so let me go.'

'Not until you give me a kiss.'

'No!' She struggled to free herself but was hampered by her torch, handbag and gasmask. He fastened his mouth over hers, crushing her lips against her teeth. She attempted to hit him with her handbag but he imprisoned her arms. Then she heard footsteps and the beam of a torch caught them in its light.

A voice came out of the darkness. 'Sorry!'

She recognised Harry's voice and managed to pull her head away but, before she could speak, Jeff put a hand over her mouth and twisted her arm up her back. She struggled to free herself, despairing as she listened to Harry's footsteps fade into the distance. Jeff released her abruptly. 'That was a close call! I don't think ol' Harry likes me.'

'I'm going home,' she said, almost choking on tears.

He made no move to prevent her but called, 'That was an *I'll be seeing you* kiss! I'm sailing in the morning. Save yerself for me, girl! You haven't seen the last of me.'

Rene shuddered and fled.

Greta sat the breakfast table with an open letter in front of her on the tablecloth.

Dear Greta,

You're not going to believe this but I got an address and went to it, only to find that Uncle David, his family, Mum and my stepfather have moved out. The landlord said that they complained of the cold and so have gone to the States. You can imagine how bloody fed up I felt. I went out and got drunk! Back to square one again. I don't know what to do next about carrying on the search for Mum, but I'm hoping you might have had some luck in finding the girls. With this b....... war there's no chance of my getting home just yet. We've picked up some ....and ... to ....

'Damn censors!' muttered Greta under her breath, wondering what the missing words were.

Hope you are well and will go to Wales. I know getting there won't be easy, travel being what it is at the moment, but I'm sure you'll try. I want you there, not just to look for the girls, but because, like your dad, I'd feel happier knowing you were away from the bombing. I miss your funny little ways. Take care of yourself. Love to you all Alex. X

Greta's eyes were damp by the time she came to the end of the letter. She brushed the tears away with the back of her hand.

'Well?' said Cissie, staring at her. 'Tears could mean one of two things.'

'He found his uncle's house but the whole family, including his mother and stepfather had left and gone to America.' Greta's voice quivered. 'He's really fed up. I just wish I'd been there with him.'

'There's a war on, luv. We can't always be where we want,' said Cissie. 'What do you say, Harry?' She had to repeat herself.

'What?' said Greta's father, appearing to pull himself back from somewhere.

'You're in another world, Harry! It's a letter from Alex,' said Cissie, jerking her head in Greta's direction. 'I don't know what's up with you lately. You don't appear to hear half of what I say.'

'I know what you mean, Gran,' said Greta.

Harry stared unblinking at the pair of them. 'It's you two. I worry about you. I've kept quiet about you going to Wales, so far, and I know Fred and his wife don't seem to want you there until the end of April, but I'd really like you out of Liverpool before then. I'm sure the Luftwaffe haven't finished with us yet.'

Cissie and Greta exchanged looks. 'Sorry, Harry! But we're not leaving until our Fred and his missus are ready for us,' declared the old woman. 'I don't want to go to strangers uninvited.'

'Me neither,' said Greta, tilting her chin. 'If the country in winter is as bad as Uncle Fred says it is, then it's the last place I want to be. Besides it won't be easy getting there at this time of year. We can probably only get there by train. The carriages will be unheated, I bet, and we'd have to change trains, there could be all kinds of delays. Besides everything's been quiet here for weeks. They've given up and gone home.'

Harry said angrily, 'You're a stubborn pair. But on your head be it,' and he stood up and walked out. For a moment he considered visiting Edith. It was some time since he'd seen her and he felt guilty about that. He sighed and came to the decision it was best to let things stay as they were. It would be wrong to use her to work out his frustrations. Having caught sight of Rene in Jeff's arms he had wanted both to knock Jeff's block off and ravish Rene.

'Temper, temper,' murmured Cissie.

'I don't know what's got into him. He didn't seem to listen to the news about Alex,' said Greta. 'I'm really disappointed in him. I bet Rene will be interested, though.'

'Rene!' yelled Vera. 'Where are you?'

Rene entered the kitchen, wiping her hands on her apron. 'What is it, Mother!' She gazed down at the hunched figure in the chair.

'I'm uncomfortable. I need the lav! Then I'll go to bed. Perhaps you could light a fire in the bedroom for me … and give me a piggy-back up them stairs. I'm finding them real difficult these days.'

Rene fought down her despair. 'Don't be daft, Mother! I couldn't carry you upstairs. Who do you think I am? Samson! As for having a fire up there … we have to watch the coal.'

Vera's mouth quivered and then she snarled, 'You don't know what it's like being me. Stuck here day in, day out! I ask for one little thing from you but all you can think of is saving money.'

Rene sighed. 'It's not only to do with money, Mother. You know there are all kinds of shortages now. I can make a suggestion, though. Why don't you consider having my single bed brought downstairs and put in the parlour and I'll use your bed. That will save you the stairs and you could have a fire in there during the day instead of in here. We could try and buy a second hand gas stove to cook on instead of using the fire. That would save us money in summer when it's warm enough to do without a fire.'

Vera frowned and made no comment. Rene was just about to return to washing the dishes when her mother said, 'I've always slept in a double bed and at night I really need turning because I get that stiff and sore.'

Rene spoke in a conciliatory tone. 'It would be easier to turn you on a single bed and you'd be able to watch people through the window. You'd feel more in touch. You wouldn't have to wait for the neighbours to come in and tell you everything that's going on.'

Vera's eyes brightened. 'You've a point there. I'll do it as long as I can have the wireless in there, too.'

Anything for a bit of peace, thought Rene, who was still upset by the episode with Jeff. At least he had left Liverpool but she dreaded his return. She thought of Harry, whom she had seen going in and out of next door a couple of times in the last week. She was convinced his manner had been cool towards her. He must have recognised them and drawn his own conclusions. She sighed, telling herself she had to stop thinking about Harry or she would go mad. After all she had plenty of other things on her mind.

The next day Rene and Wilf brought down the single bed and installed Vera in the parlour. Rene hoped that life for the three of them would be easier now and if there should be a raid, it would be less difficult getting her mother into the cellar.

At the end of the first week in March the British army marched into Ethiopia and, during the following week, word got out that the American Congress had agreed to a Lease and Lend Bill to help Britain replace her losses and win the war. It was on the Wednesday evening of that week that the Luftwaffe returned. They arrived at a quarter past seven dropping flares on the docks, the commercial heart of the city, and the factories on its outer rim. Rene was on fire watch duty and frantically threw sand on the fires caused by the flares as they landed on the roof of the company building. She was assisted by a couple of older men and another woman but there were so many flares that it was terrifying. Gradually the sound of aeroplane engines died away to give them some blessed respite but from where they were they could see over the rooftops, towards the docks, that other buildings were still burning.

Rene gazed in a strange kind of fascination as the roof of the main post office, just across the way, went up with a whoosh. The heat was terrific and made her gasp and she took several paces back, glad she was not alone. She turned to one of the men. 'Hadn't we better do something?'

Before he could answer the warning siren went again. 'I'm sure their own people have already phoned the fire brigade, but you can put a call through, just in case,' he rasped. 'Then, you women, get down to the shelter!' The familiar drone of the engines of the German Junker 88s and Heinkel's engines could be heard in the distance. Then came the boom boom of explosives from the direction of the docks.

Rene and the other woman hurried downstairs and phoned as he had suggested, only to be informed that the telephone exchange at South John Street had their own fire. There were so many fires that calls had been put through to fire brigades in other districts to ask for help.

Rene replaced the telephone and retreated to the shelter in the cellar, hoping and praying that, if the building above was hit, the reinforced ceiling could take the weight of the debris and that the rescue workers would be able to dig them out. She thought of Harry, Cissie, Greta, her mother and Wilf with a sinking heart and knew it was going to be a long night.

'Bleedin' hell! There must be some fires burning in town,' said Cissie, gazing out of the front bedroom window. 'Look at that glow in the sky.'

'I know! And Rene's caught up in that! Come away from there, Gran! We should be down in the cellar. Dad would have a fit if he knew we were still up here. If a bomb was to drop in the street it would shatter the windows.' Greta took hold of Cissie's arm and dragged her away. She closed the bedroom door and hurried her grandmother along the landing. They had just reached the top of the stairs when there was an almighty bang. She clutched the banister and saw the front bedroom door blast off its hinges and skid along the landing. It crashed against the wall next to Harry's bedroom door, narrowly missing them.

'Oh Mary, Joseph and our Lord!' cried Cissie, clinging to Greta's arm and crossing herself with her free hand. 'That was bleedin' close! Someone up there's keeping their eye on us, luv.' Greta's throat was so clogged up with shock that she could not speak. Cissie babbled on, 'It's as if yer had a premonition! But it's no use standing here at the top of the stairs, luv. We've got to get down!' She nudged her granddaughter with her elbow.

Greta pulled herself together and gingerly felt her way downstairs. She could hear the tinkling of glass and the sound of raised voices. She thought of Miss Birkett and some of the other neighbours who were still using the surface shelter down the street and hoped they were safe. Her heart was pounding and she felt sick. The front door hung drunkenly to one side but she managed to slip through the gap, only to teeter on the threshold, as she caught the glow of a chunk of smouldering metal on the front step. The glow in the sky from the burning fires enabled her to see that the path was covered in shrapnel and debris. Further up the street in the middle of the road was a smoking crater. People had come out of their houses and the shelter and were heading for the crater but Greta crossed to the Millers' step. She was about to walk over the door that lay flat in the lobby when she was caught in the beam of a torch.

'Who-Who's that?' stammered Wilf.

'It's Greta! Thank God, you're OK, Wilf.'

He lowered the torch. 'Where's your gran?' His voice was hoarse.

'I'm here,' panted Cissie, who would have had a worse struggle squeezing her ample figure through the gap between the door and the jamb. She stood on the step and gazed at the shattered front windows of both houses.

'How are yer feeling, Mrs Hardcastle? Yer ticker OK?' asked Wilf, shambling towards her.

She smiled. 'All things considered! That's not to say it wasn't a shock to me system.'

'Can it take another?' he said in a low voice.

She stared at him and he brought his head close to hers so that they were almost eyeball to eyeball. 'Herself is it?' she whispered.

'Dead as a doornail! Must have been the shock. She's covered in broken glass and soot. The blast must have shaken it loose from the chimney. The place is in a helluva mess. I was seeing where the cat was because I'd already asked her did she want to go down in the cellar and she'd refused.'

'Well, God forgive me, but all I can say is … good riddance!' said Cissie.

They jumped as a hand clapped them on the shoulder. 'What are you two whispering about?' demanded Greta.

'Vera's dead!' Cissie cleared her throat. 'I think that news deserves a drink, don't you?'

Greta knew it was wrong but she began to laugh. Several of the neighbours looked her way and she stopped abruptly, struggling to swallow the hysteria that had her in its grip. Her whole body shook and she thought she might explode. Cissie took a firm hold on her and shook her. Greta gasped. 'Sorry!'

The old woman put an arm round her. 'There now, my luv'ly girl! Take a grip on yourself. Yer're only young to be havin' to cope with all this but the ol' cow has lived her life and now Rene can live hers. Who's to say that I mightn't have a new daughter-in-law before this war's over if what our Jeff's said is anything to go by.'

Greta wondered if she should disillusion her gran and tell her that Jeff was a liar and Rene wasn't interested in him. Then she decided that her gran'd had enough shocks for one night. She wished her dad would open his eyes and see what a wife he could have if only he'd make a move in the right direction. But she was jumping her fences. Rene did not even know yet that her mother was dead and she was free to do what she wanted at last. That was only if fate had been kind and Rene had survived the bombing in the city centre.

Rene stepped out of the office building, avoiding the pools of water left by the firemen's hoses. She walked round the corner and gazed up at the main post office, amazed to see that it was still standing, although all that remained of its top floor and roof were charred timbers and debris. She did not linger for long and was soon heading for Dale Street, trying not to breathe in the stench of destruction. She had told her boss that she needed to go home before starting work. She had to see that her mother was OK, but had promised to return before lunchtime. It seemed miraculous that despite the fires last night there was so little damage to be seen, although, as she came to Dale Street, she noticed that part of the Municipal Buildings had been hit and she knew the docks would have suffered badly. Rene caught a 15d tram near the tunnel and headed for home, looking forward to having a good wash down and changing her clothes.

Rene gazed down at the still figure in the bed. Wilf had told her how he had found her mother covered in soot but that Cissie had washed the dead woman's face. There was not a mark on her and Rene found it difficult to comprehend that she was dead. Vera's wrinkled, parchment textured features were fixed in a snarl, the lips drawn back, revealing her gums and teeth. Rene felt a deep sadness that even in death her mother did not look at peace.

'Forasmuch as it hath pleased Almighty God of his great mercy to take unto himself the soul of our dear sister here departed, we therefore commit her body to the ground,' intoned the vicar. 'Earth to earth, ashes to ashes, dust to dust; in sure and certain hope of the Resurrection to eternal life, through our Lord Jesus Christ; who shall change our vile body, that it may be like unto his glorious body ... '

The rest of the words seemed to fade away as Rene gazed down at the coffin as it was lowered into the grave to join her father's remains. Would her mother have been nicer if she had been given a different body? Rene could only hope God would forgive her mother's sins and that Vera would find some spiritual joy now that she was rid of this mortal coil.

Rene shook hands with the vicar and then, accompanied by Wilf, Cissie, Harry and Greta, she made her way towards the waiting car. The sun shone, daffodils bloomed and there were buds on the trees in Stanley Park opposite the cemetery.

'Yer couldn't have had a nicer day for it, luv,' said Cissie, linking her arm through Rene's.

'I think Spring's on its way,' said Greta.

A sigh escaped Harry as he looked at the three females he most cared about and wished that he had never caught the glimpse of Rene and Jeff in the light of his torch. What would happen now with Rene free to marry if she wanted? He didn't want to contemplate it. He'd taken an instant dislike to Jeff, convinced that he cared for no one but himself. He also suspected that Jeff visited prostitutes, because he had turned down all offers of a bed, obviously preferring to spend his nights in town. Harry could not deny that women might find him attractive, but he kept asking himself how Rene could be taken in by a handsome face. He had credited her with more sense than that. He could only hope with Jeff at sea that absence wouldn't make the heart grow fonder.

14

Greta sent a card to Alex, hoping he would get it in time for his eighteenth birthday on the 1st of April, promising to treat him to a trip to the cinema on his return and also suggesting that they go dancing, as she had been taking lessons. She told him of the death of Rene's mother, adding that she thought her older friend needed taking out of herself. *She says she's OK, but, to me, she appears tired and jumpy, as if her nerves are in a bad state. Dad's all for us looking after Rene because she was such a good friend to Mam, and us, but he makes no move towards her so I suppose he's still visiting that woman! Gran told Rene to see the doctor and he's given her a tonic, but said that what she really needs is a holiday. So Gran's bullied her into taking a week off and she's coming away with us to Uncle Fred's at the end of April using the insurance money left over after paying for her mother's funeral. I wrote to Uncle Fred and he says it's fine as long as she pays her way and brings her ration book. I'll make enquiries for you about evacuees when I'm there, although, to be honest, I don't know where to start. I'll do my best, though. Have you bumped into Uncle Jeff at any of the ports you've visited wherever they are? Gran thinks he might marry Rene!!! She's got very fond of her since she went for that thief in the blackout. Let us know your news and I look forward to seeing you. Gran sends her love and Dad his regards. Take care of yourself, love, Greta.*

She licked the envelope and posted it, wishing that she could have told him all her news face to face.

Rene dragged a nightgown from the clothes rack that was suspended from the ceiling and spread the garment on the folded towels on the table. She stood, barefoot, and reached for the flat iron on the fire, and spat on its bottom. The spit sizzled and she wiped the iron on a rag. It was six weeks since her mother's death and she was getting rid of Vera's clothes, giving them to those who had lost everything in the bombing. Tomorrow, she was leaving for Wales and so the task had to be finished today. Once she had finished ironing, she would hand them over to Miss Birkett, who would take them to the used clothing depot at the church hall.

Rene sighed and decided on some music to cheer herself up. She switched on the wireless but it gave out only the faintest of sound. She made a mental note to remind Wilf to take the accumulator to be changed at the wireless shop.

At that moment the letterbox rattled. Damn! She'd never get the ironing finished at this rate. She placed the iron on the hearth and then glanced in the mirror. She pulled a face at her reflection. Her cheeks were flushed, her nose shiny with the heat and her hair stood up on end. She pushed back the mop of red gold hair from her damp forehead and, noticing several more silver threads, groaned. But this was no time to pull them out and she hurried to the door, to find a postcard on the doormat. She picked it up, looked at the photograph of camels and palm trees and turned it over to read the message on the back.

Dear Rene, I hope this postcard will do the job of keeping me fresh in your memory. The camels reminded me of your mother. I'm getting it hot out here in more ways than one. I really can't wait to take you in my arms and teach you a few tricks, Jeff.

Rage surged up inside her. Why did he persist in persecuting her? She found it almost unbelievable that the brother Sally had adored could behave in such a way. It just proved that someone could never know another person through and through. Jeff was definitely sick in the head. At that moment there was a knock on the door. With the postcard still in her hand, she went to answer it.

Harry stood on the step. 'Hi, Rene! I see the postman called at your house.' He glanced at the postcard and rasped, 'From Jeff, is it?'

'Yes!' Her colour was already high but now it deepened as Harry's intense blue eyes took her in from head to toe. Immediately, she was conscious of her dishevelled, barefoot appearance and wished that she had not changed after work into the faded print frock. Her mother had once likened Rene's bare feet to canoes, saying that Cinderella's slipper would never have fitted her. Rene had been terribly hurt. Now here was Harry on her doorstep when they hadn't even exchanged the time of day for what seemed ages. What a time for him to call. 'What can I do for you, Harry?'

'Not disturbing you, am I?'

'No! Just ironing.' She pinned on a smile.

'Getting ready for tomorrow? The holiday will do you good.'

'I'm sure it will.' She rested a hand on the doorjamb and tried to conceal one foot behind the other, only to trip over in the attempt. The postcard fluttered from her fingers. She would have fallen if he had not put out both arms and caught her. Her breasts were squashed against his chest and she found herself gulping in air as if she had been running. 'Sorry!' she gasped. 'That was stupid of me.' But being held in his arms roused all kinds of sensations inside her. It would be lovely if, for once, he would say something romantic to her.

'Not a problem,' he said unevenly, his breath warming her cheek. 'Can I come in? Is it safe?'

'Safe?' She swallowed.

He said tersely, 'The cat! Is it in or out?'

'Oh! It disappeared when the bomb went off.'

He looked relieved and slowly released her. She bent to retrieve the postcard but he got there first and picked it up, glancing at the writing on the back. She snatched it from his fingers and shoved it in the pocket of her frock. 'Come on in!'

She led the way into the kitchen, hoping he had not managed to read any of the words, at the same time trying to remember the last time he had set foot in this house. She couldn't. He hadn't even come in after the funeral and it had been Wilf who had repaired her front wall, re-hung the door, and replaced the glass in the windows.

'So what can I do for you?' she repeated, waving him to a chair. 'Sit down, Harry.' Her voice was strained.

He made no move to do so but instead, rested an elbow on the mantelshelf. 'Jeff gets around. I've been no further than Wales and Blackpool,' he murmured.

'You're not alone in that. Sit down!' she insisted.

He lowered himself into an easy chair. 'So how do you find him?'

She stiffened. 'Who?'

'Jeff!' he said, sounding vexed.

She stared at him and blushed. 'He tells a good story,' she mumbled, lowering herself into a chair and gazing down at her fingernails. 'What can I do for you, Harry?'

He ignored the question. 'He can do that OK! You just make sure that you don't believe everything he says ... that he doesn't let you down.'

'I'm not a fool, Harry.' She raised her eyes. 'You still haven't answered my question. What can I do for you?' He did not answer her right away. 'Harry!' she cried, at the end of her tether. 'Will you get to the point!'

He rested his hands on his knees. 'I want you to try and persuade Greta and her gran to stay on in Wales after the week's up. I'd feel happier with them out of the way. It's just a pity you can't stay on as well. I suppose you could if you could find some work there.'

Instantly she thought, is it only my safety he's concerned about as a friend or does he have an ulterior motive for wanting the three of us to stay on in Wales? A picture of the widow Cox popped into her head and she felt hurt and angry. 'Nice of you to worry about me, Harry. But my staying in Wales is out of the question. I have a job I like,' she said, struggling to keep her voice calm. 'And there's Wilf. But I'll do my best to persuade Greta and Mrs Hardcastle.'

He said simply, 'That's all I ask.'

They stared at one another and there was an expression in his eyes that caused her heartbeat to quicken and made her question whether she had misjudged him. Perhaps the widow meant as little to him as Jeff did to her. But before she could say anything there was a sound at the front door and Wilf called up the lobby, 'Are yer there, Rene?' She could have hit him.

'Are yer ready, girl? Are yer ready?' sang out Cissie through Rene's open front door.

'Ready as I'll ever be,' said Rene with a sigh, picking up the carpetbag containing her clothes, a towel, toiletries and a library book. She felt even more exhausted than ever, having not slept a wink, wondering what would have happened if Wilf had not come in on her and Harry.

'I could carry that for you, Rene,' said Wilf, following her out.

'No need for that. I can manage,' said Rene, forcing a smile. He wasn't to know he had interrupted what might have been the defining moment in her life. Earlier that morning, she had stood at the bedroom window, watching Harry leave for work. She had been in her nightgown and had lacked the courage to run downstairs and speak to him. Now she regretted her cowardice, knowing she would not have the opportunity to speak to him again until she returned from Wales.

Her thoughts were interrupted by Cissie saying, 'I'd appreciate you giving me a hand with my baggage, Wilf. I'm not a tall, strapping girl like Rene, but just a slip of a thing.'

'You are joking, Gran!' said Greta, her eyes twinkling as she checked the front door was closed.

Wilf winked at the girl. 'I don't mind carrying her baggage. If your gran likes to pretend she's twenty-one, again, that's fine by me. Neither of us might look the people we once were but, inside, we still feel young and want to kick up our heels. I'll troddle along with yer to the station and wave yer off.'

Cissie beamed at him. 'That's the gear, Wilf,' she said.

His ears turned pink and he said gruffly, 'Anything to help a lady.'

'I only wish …' said Greta.

'Don't start wishing,' interrupted Cissie firmly. 'Alex's not here so it's no use dreaming. As for yer dad, maybe he'll be able to make it another time. Having us three staying with them will be enough for Fred and Megan for the moment. Agreed?'

Greta said, 'Agreed.'

As they set off down the street several of the neighbours waved and called, 'Have a good time, girls!'

'You betcha!' called Cissie, and linking arms with Wilf, danced him down the street. Rene and Greta raised their eyebrows and followed more sedately.

An hour later they waved goodbye to Wilf as the train clattered its way out of the station. The carriage was crowded and Greta and Rene had to stand all the way to Chester. There they were to change onto the London Holyhead train but it had not arrived when they reached the platform. They were told it was expected three hours later than planned, due to delays in the Midlands caused by bombing. Impatiently they waited and when it did arrive there was a concerted rush to get aboard. Only Cissie was able to find a seat in a carriage. Greta and Rene had to stand again, jammed in the corridor between a couple of gossiping Welsh women and a burly soldier, who smoked incessantly whilst staring out of the window.

Their route lay along the North Welsh coast and Greta, Rene and Cissie would leave the train at Bangor, where hopefully they would change to another that would deliver them to Carnarfon and on to a little train that would take them to Llanberis. At least the weather was fine, thought Greta, delighted when she caught sight of what she called *the real sea*. It helped her put aside her apprehension about meeting her new relatives, her worry about leaving her father and her concern for Alex, wherever he might be right now.

Rene was also nervous about meeting her host and hostess, wondering what Fred's wife made of her spending a week's holiday with them. Had he told her that she was the daughter of the woman who had deceived him for years? She was also concerned about whether Jeff had written lying letters about her to Fred, and was in two minds whether to say anything about him.

Only Cissie had no qualms about the journey she was making, convinced that a warm welcome awaited her at its end. Her heart still ached for Mick and what might have been, but she'd had to cope with so many hurts and setbacks in her life that she did not doubt that *a change was as good as a rest,* as the saying went, and she would return home in a better frame of mind and bodily health after being reunited with her younger son and his family.

Having left a city scarred by explosion and fire, the journey was to leave an indelible impression on them all. Greta kept repeating, as if she could not believe it, 'Everything is so green, so fresh, so beautiful and undamaged!'

'And the houses look different from those in Liverpool,' said Rene, forgetting her sore heart, and pointing to one built of the slate from which many a quarry owner had made his fortune in North Wales. 'Do you think we'll get to visit any castles?' asked Greta wistfully, knowing there were several along the coast. She imagined Alex, clad in shining armour rescuing her from a tower and carrying her off on a white charger.

'We'll see them. I don't know about getting to visit them,' said Rene.

The journey took much longer than any of them had imagined and it was with a great deal of relief that they eventually descended onto the platform at Llanberis, exhausted. They looked around for Fred and saw a man striding towards them. Instantly, Greta knew it was her uncle because he had a look of her mother about his face.

He smiled down at Cissie. 'I'd know you anywhere, Ma. You've hardly changed a bit!' His Liverpudlian accent was tempered by a Welsh lilt.

'Flattery'll get yer anywhere, lad!' she said, beaming up at him as he grasped both her hands. 'Let's have a proper look at yer!'

While Cissie checked over her younger son, Greta and Rene were also scrutinising him. He was almost as tall as Rene but painfully thin. The wrists that protruded from the too short sleeves of the well worn tweed jacket were knobbly. His neck was scrawny and his Adam's apple was prominent, as were the bones in his face. Grey mingled with the gold in hair that lay lank on his forehead and covered his ears. As they stared at him they noticed a nerve twitching his left eyelid and Greta recalled that he had been shell-shocked in the Great War.

'I thought yer'd have put weight on, lad,' said Cissie, sounding distressed. 'I imagined yer eating fresh home baked bread spread thick with Welsh butter.'

'I eat plenty, Ma,' he hastened to reassure her. 'Megan reckons because I'm a worrier that I use too much nervous energy.'

'I'm looking forward to meeting your Megan,' said Cissie, patting his arm. 'I hope she's got the kettle on. I'm dying for a cuppa.'

'Not her, Ma,' he said with a hint of embarrassment. 'It's me that looks after that side of things. Since the factory opened for making aeroplane wings, she's been working there. I look after the land and the livestock, write my poetry and information books and do the cooking.'

Cissie said, 'Bleedin' hell, lad, you do surprise me. There was nothing about this in your letter!'

'I didn't want people thinking I was a cissy or henpecked, Ma. It's just that with my nervous debility I couldn't settle in a proper job outside the home.'

She nodded and said kindly, 'Well, lad, if that way suits the pair of you, who am I to argue?'

He smiled. 'It also means that I can spend more time with you and …' He paused to look at Greta and Rene. 'Sorry! I haven't said hello yet. Hi, Rene! You've shot up since last I saw you.' He shook her hand before turning to his niece. 'You must be Greta. Welcome to Wales!'

'Thanks,' said Greta. 'You remind me of Mam.' And standing on tiptoe she kissed his cheek.

A flush ran along his cheekbones and tears welled in his eyes. Hastily, he brushed them away and, taking Cissie's baggage, he led the way out of the station and along a main street to the edge of the town. There, he paused in front of a detached house, constructed of the now familiar slate. He opened the gate and led them up a crazy pavement path and round the side of the house to a door at the back. Several hens cluck-clucked and fluttered out of the way as he opened the door and ushered them inside. He directed them to the scullery to wash their hands and then showed them to a well-scrubbed table in the enormous kitchen.

The table was situated in front of a window, overlooking a cultivated plot of land. Through an opening at the top of the window came the bleating of sheep and the lowing of a cow. The room was lovely and warm, heated by an enormous black leaded range.

'I'll show you the bedrooms after you've eaten,' said Fred, placing plates of fruit cake and floury scones, as well as a pat of butter, on the table. 'We have a cooked meal when the kids come home from school. Megan eats depending on her shift. Help yourself. I'm sure you don't get food like this in Liverpool.' They all agreed and fell on the scones and cakes as he continued to talk. 'Llanberis is a quiet place if you compare it to the resorts along the coast. I'm hoping you won't find it dull after Liverpool.'

'Stop worrying, lad,' Cissie said firmly. 'We can cope with a bit of quiet. We're not the first to head for the hills in times of trouble. While we're not exactly evacuees, yer must have seen plenty out this way.'

Greta's ears pricked up as she was reminded that Alex expected her to try and discover his sisters' whereabouts while she was here. 'Are there any evacuees in the village, Uncle Fred?' she asked, reaching for another scone.

He glanced at her. 'There's folk who have family from the cities staying and there's the odd couple of kids, unrelated, but if you're talking about whole schools being billeted here, you won't find them. Plenty in the coastal towns, though, I should imagine.' He turned to Rene. 'So how is Liverpool? News does get to us when the bombers are heading that way. The enemy comes in from the Irish Sea and zooms along the coast towards Merseyside. We heard it's been pretty quiet lately.'

'Let's not talk about the bombing,' said Cissie gruffly, shifting her bulk on the sofa. 'We came here to get away from the war. To relax and enjoy the peace and quiet.'

'Sorry, Ma,' said Fred hastily. 'I know you'll get plenty of that here.'

He was to be proved right. On the Sunday after they arrived, they all attended chapel led by Fred's wife like a mother hen with her brood of chicks. She was a buxom, rosy cheeked, warm-hearted woman who alternately chided and cosseted her husband. She made them feel welcome in her home. The children, who had been shy of them at first, were soon climbing on their grandmother's knee and demanding that she tell them what their dadda was like when he was a little boy. Cissie was delighted, but remembered to speak slowly, having discovered that, although her three grandchildren were bilingual, Welsh was their first language.

Come Monday, Fred took them up the foothills of Snowdon along an old slate quarry road to Gladstone Rock, named after the Victorian prime minister. His mother begged him for an easier day on Tuesday. So he borrowed a friend's pony and trap and took them to Betws-coed to see the Swallow Falls. The weather was perfect. On Wednesday afternoon, he made a picnic lunch and they walked to Llyn Padarn.

'It's beautiful! Really beautiful!' Rene sat on the grass, gazing at the stretch of water. It was so still and clear that the mountains were reflected in its shining surface. How she wished Harry was here.

'Would you like to stretch your legs further, Rene?' asked Fred.

She looked at him and demanded with a hint of laughter in her voice, 'Depends on how far you expect me to walk. I'm not used to country walks, remember.' He had been kind to her, not once had his attitude shown any resentment towards her for her mother's actions. So different from his brother. She liked him a lot. More often than not in the last few days it was he and she who walked ahead, leaving Greta and Cissie trailing behind. They talked about the old days, about Sally and Cissie, and the years between the wars and she asked him about his writing. His company was undemanding and restful.

'I promise we'll just walk along the lakeside,' said Fred, holding down a hand to her.

Rene allowed herself to be dragged to her feet. 'What about you two?' she asked, gazing down at Greta and Cissie, who were lying on rugs on the grass, heads resting on their folded coats.

'You can go without me,' murmured Greta, without opening her eyes. Cissie's only response was a snore.

Rene and Fred smiled at each other and set off. They had not gone

201

far when he said, 'I'm glad we're alone because there's a couple of things I want to ask you about.' He looked anxious as he gazed into her face. 'I'm not sure how to start …'

'Start at the beginning,' she prompted.

'It's about our Jeff.'

Immediately her smile vanished. 'What about him?' she said warily.

From his pocket Fred produced a letter. 'I know you haven't mentioned him but Ma has and, although I've not disillusioned her, I know he's deceived you both.' He thrust the letter at Rene. 'You can read it if you like. It's from his wife.'

'Wife!' She was stunned. 'But-but he told me she was killed in the blitz on Southampton.'

'He's a b-bloody l-liar!' stuttered Fred. 'In that l-letter she asks me wh-whether I've heard from him. Ap-parently she hasn't done so for ages and has no-no idea where he is. I'm-I'm sorry, Rene.' He took her hand and gripped it tightly.

Rene was glad that she could reassure him. 'That's OK! Thanks for telling me. Whatever Mrs Hardcastle has said she's mistaken. I detest Jeff, he was horrible to me, thinking that I should pay, in the worst of ways, for what my mother did. You must know how sorry I am about it all but I had no idea what was going on.'

He looked relieved. 'He-He was always was a bit of a swine. I could never understand why our Sal thought the sun shone out of him.'

'I'm sure he can charm the birds out of the trees if he wants to,' said Rene.

Fred nodded. 'Just like me dad. Sal thought him the bees' knees when he turned up … always with a present for her. He used to call her his little doll. I don't know if you remember him, Rene?'

'Hardly at all.'

He grimaced. 'Not surprising. I saw little enough of him he was a travelling salesman but what I did see of him I could have done without. That's all I'm saying.'

They walked on in silence for a while, breathing in the sweet air and listening to birdsong. Then Rene said abruptly, 'What was the other thing you wanted to talk about?'

Fred's face, which had worn a brooding expression, lightened. 'Oh, I wanted to ask you to back me up and try and persuade Mam to stay on here for a while. She respects your opinion. The kids love her and we've got a lot of years to make up and she's getting on. And to be honest,' he said ruefully, 'since she's been here, I can see she'd be an asset to the place. It would give me more time for my writing.'

Rene smiled. 'I've been wondering how to broach the question of her staying here. Harry asked me to try and persuade her and Greta to stay.'

He looked pleased and then his brow knitted. 'Do you think Greta would want to stay? I know that Carnarfon and Bangor aren't that far away but in winter when the snows come travel isn't easy. She's young and could soon miss the bright lights of Liverpool.'

'The lights are a bit dimmed in Liverpool at the moment,' said Rene softly. 'But we could ask and see what she says. My conscience will be clear then.'

So the matter of Cissie and Greta staying on in Llanberis was raised as the four of them walked back to the house. 'I'd really like you to stay, Ma,' said Fred earnestly. 'Greta, too! I've been thinking that she could probably get a job at the factory where Megan works. She'd be contributing to the war effort then.'

Greta was not so sure about staying. What if Alex came home? She might not get to see him and besides she would miss her father … and what about the widow? She made her decision. 'Thanks for the offer, Uncle Fred. I've loved being here but I'd rather not leave Dad on his own.'

Fred touched her shoulder. 'You think about it, lovey.' He glanced at Cissie. 'You're quiet, Ma.'

'I'm thinking, lad, that I'll miss Harry and Wilf.'

Greta and Rene exchanged a wink. 'Who's Wilf?' asked Fred, looking surprised.

'Just a friend,' said Cissie casually. 'But I'd be willing to give it a try here. You could do with a hand in the house with Megan out at work … and what with summer coming you'll need to be out on your plot more, looking after your veggies and the like.' She nodded thoughtfully. 'Besides, I don't know how many more years I've got left and I want to spend some of them with you and the kids. I'm not saying I'll stay forever, mind. Don't want to wear me welcome out with Megan. But we'll see how it goes for a while.'

Fred looked delighted and placed his arm round his mother's shoulders and hugged her. 'That's great news, Ma.'

Rene and Greta watched mother and son as they walked ahead of them back to the house. Rene smiled as she linked her arm through that of Greta. 'I wonder how Wilf feels about your gran these days?'

'I wonder,' said Greta, and chuckled. 'Perhaps absence will make his heart grow fonder.'

Rene's expression sobered. 'About your staying here. Your dad wanted you to stay. Think about that before you make your final decision.'

Greta promised she would, thinking that if she did stay on she could enquire about Alex's sisters at the coastal resorts, showing the photograph of the girls in shops, etc. The trouble was she didn't really want them to be found. What was she to do?

Two days later Megan arrived home from the night shift with news that shocked them all. 'Waves and waves of Jerry aeroplanes were seen coming in from the Irish Sea last night! I heard it from one of the women this morning. She had an aunt living in Rhyl on the coast and they were on the phone to each other.' Megan's eyes were like saucers. 'They could see the glow from the fires lighting up the sky! Some reckon the fires were still burning this morning and that people are deserting Liverpool in droves! That there's thousands of homes destroyed.'

Greta looked at Rene in horror. 'What are we going to do?' she whispered.

Rene did not know what to say. The truth was that she did not know what to do. She felt sick at heart, terrified that luck might have deserted Harry and he was dead.

15

Harry removed his cap and wiped the sweat from his brow that threatened to trickle into his eyes and blur his vision. His mouth was raw and dry with dust. He reached for the tin mug standing on a convenient brick and gulped down some of the hot, sweet tea. A cry came again from the rubble and Harry put the mug down remembering how, back in March, another rescue worker had found a baby still alive after three days of being buried beside her dead parents.

He looked up at the men, who took orders from him. Just like him they were exhausted, having gone without sleep for two nights. He had returned home yesterday for a brief rest and to check whether Greta and Cissie had returned home but the house had been empty and, according to Wilf, Rene had not come back home, either. So he had returned to Mill Road Infirmary where a parachute mine had caused devastation. They had dug people out alive, but there had also been more than fifty dead. A sigh escaped him. He was near the end of his tether, but if there was a baby trapped under the debris, he wanted to be the one to get it out. Such moments of lifesaving were sweet and made the danger worthwhile. He imagined taking the baby in his arms.

He pocketed his trowel and his eyes narrowed as he gazed into the tunnel entrance, angled to a degree by a kitchen table and a chair, which had become locked together beneath tons of bricks and charred wood. He reached for the piece of wood used to protect his head and crawled into the hole, inching his way along, careful not to disturb the wall of rubble held up with props of wood. The cry came again and it was close. With a delicate touch he withdrew a chunk of brick and mortar without disturbing the broken timber beside it that might bring down a ton of debris.

Something shot out of the hole and straight into his face. He felt claws dig into his skin and his chest began to heave. He couldn't breathe! Panicking, he struggled to get a hold on the ball of fur with his free hand. He managed to get a grip and threw the kitten over his shoulder; he heard it scampering along the tunnel. He sucked in air, heavy with dust. His face stung where the cat's claws had dug in. He felt a sneeze coming on and struggled to back out of the tunnel, the wood that he held over his head wobbling. A sneeze exploded from him and the force caused him to bang his head against the wood, which hit the roof. His chest was wheezing and dust and tiny bits of brick and plaster fell about him. Another sneeze and everything started to slide. He put up an arm to protect himself as that part of the tunnel caved in.

'You're staying here,' said Fred in a voice that brooked no argument. 'It's what your father wanted. There's no point going back to Liverpool; even if you could get back, you could be killed before you made it to your front door if things are as bad as they sound.'

They had been discussing the matter for several hours.

'But what about Dad?' cried Greta, her voice catching on a sob. 'He could be … he could be … '

'Now don't let's think the worst,' said Rene, sounding calmer than she felt. 'It was bad just before Christmas and we all survived. Perhaps we could phone the dairy and see what they have to say.'

'That's a great idea,' said Fred, looking relieved.

'Let's go then,' decided Rene, unable to remain still any longer, and she hustled Greta and Fred out of the house.

'Come on, Harry! Open yer eyes!'

Harry felt a slap on his face and moved his head, wincing.

'That's it, mate! Yer gonna be alright!' said the voice.

Harry groaned, coughed, and tried to open eyes that were heavy. His throat and chest felt raw and breathing was difficult. Water splashed on to his face and he gasped and attempted to wipe it away but his arm hurt like hell.

'It's broken, mate!' said the voice.

Harry opened his eyes and focused his gaze on the first aid man kneeling at his side. 'Bloody hell!' he gasped.

The man smiled. 'That's the ticket! I don't think you've got any serious head injury and I'm pretty sure the arm's a clean break but we'll have you X-rayed and sort that out for you in no time.'

One of the rescue team, who had Harry's head cradled in his lap, said, 'Yer were lucky that you'd managed to get near the opening of the tunnel so we got yer out dead quick.'

'Thanks!' said Harry in heartfelt tones.

'D'you have someone at home to look after you?' asked the first aid man. Harry had no wish to stay in hospital and so nodded. 'Right, we'll get you out of here and have that arm seen to.'

Harry was taken home in style; a car dropping him off in front of the house. The street was Sunday quiet and he reckoned everyone was indoors having their tea. He walked slowly up the step, his jacket slung over his shoulders, one button fastened at his chest, keeping it in place. They had slit up his shirt sleeve, straightened the bone and put his arm in plaster. In a jacket pocket were some pills to help him sleep. He banged on the door but no one came. Which in a way was a relief; it meant Greta and her grandmother were probably still in Wales. So he reached through the letterbox with his left hand, grabbed the string and dragged the key out. He managed to open the door and step inside.

He shut it behind him and walked like a zombie along the lobby and into the kitchen. He removed his cap and dropped it in a corner and then unbuttoned his jacket and allowed that to fall onto the floor, as well. He stood a moment, swaying with weariness before dragging out a dining chair from the table and sinking on to it. They had provided him with some hot soup, bread, and a cup of strong sweet tea at the first aid post, and also washed his hands and face and dealt with the scratches inflicted by the kitten. He longed for a bath but knew it was out of the question with his arm he couldn't boil the water himself.

It was at that moment that someone knocked on the door and then called through the letterbox. 'Mr Peters, are you in?'

He recognised the voice of the woman from the dairy and shouted, 'Hang on!' He hurried to open the front door. 'What is it, luv?'

The woman gazed up at him with concern. 'There was a phone call earlier from Rene in Wales but of course you weren't in.'

Relief made him light-headed. 'What did you tell her?'

'That I'd seen you earlier in the day. So she said she'd phone back and she's on the line now.'

Harry's face lit up. 'Thanks, luv! You don't mind my shirt sleeves, do you? But my jacket's filthy and ...'

'There's no need to say anything about that. We know the kind of work you've being doing.' She patted his injured arm in a kindly manner. 'But hurry up in case we lose the connection.'

He wasted no time following her and was led into a sitting room behind the shop. He picked up the telephone. 'Hello! Is that you, Rene?' he shouted.

There was a crackling down the line and then he heard Rene say, 'Is that you, Harry? Are you OK?'

He felt a sweetness inside him at the sound of her voice, could hear the concern for him. 'Yes, it's me! How are you? Where are you exactly?'

'We're still at Llanberis. We heard about the raids and so Fred said we were to stay here. We've been sick with worry. Are you and Wilf OK?'

He hastened to reassure her. 'We're fine. No need for you to worry at all. Stay where you are! We don't know if the raiders will be back and I can cope better knowing the three of you are safe.' He hesitated only a moment, wanting to say more but not knowing how to put into words the way he felt. 'Rene, I just want to say how much I …' He did not get a chance to finish because a terrible crackling noise drowned out his words. Then it cleared and his daughter's voice came on the line. It sounded unnaturally high-pitched. 'Dad, is that really you?'

'Yes, luv! It's me and I'm fine. You're to stay where you are and not to worry. Now put Rene back on the phone, please? I've something to say to her.'

'In a minute, Dad. We were told that Liverpool was in flames and that people were leaving. Is it true?'

Harry struggled for patience. 'It was a bad raid but we're fighting back.' He changed the subject quickly. 'Have you been having a good time?'

'Yes! It's lovely here but I've missed you. Are you sure you're OK, Dad? Is our house still there?'

Harry laughed wearily. 'The whole bloody street is still here.'

'We heard there'd been a huge explosion in one of the docks.'

'An ammunition ship! Now could you put Rene back on?' There came the murmur of voices and then suddenly the line went dead. He shook the receiver but there was no response. 'They've gone,' he said, feeling bereft.

'Perhaps they'll ring again tomorrow,' said the shopkeeper, taking the receiver from him and placing it on its cradle. 'You told a whopper, though … you said you were OK.' She gazed at him with understanding eyes.

'So I am,' said Harry, conscious of his aches and pains. 'I don't want them worrying about me and rushing back here until I'm sure it's safe. Thanks, missus, for the use of your phone. Can I pay you for the ...'

'No, no, no ... they've paid,' she said hastily. 'Besides, what are neighbours for if it isn't to help each other.'

Harry thanked her again and made his way back to the house. He closed the door behind him and walked up the lobby. His legs felt heavy and he wanted nothing more than to get to bed. For a moment he leaned against the wall at the foot of the stairs, overcome with weakness and frustration. Then he told himself that he'd get the chance to speak to Rene tomorrow. Gathering his strength, he climbed the stairs. He felt as if he was wading through cotton wool. The telephone conversation played over in his head and he thought about what Greta had said about the huge explosion down at the docks. One of the rescuers had mentioned the Huskisson, not far from where Edith Cox and her daughters lived. He frowned, hoping they were OK, and pushed open the bedroom door. He staggered over to the bed, crashed on to it and went out like a light.

Edith's hand shook as she lit yet another cigarette. Winnie wiped dust from the table and slammed a plate of sandwiches in front of her mother. 'You shouldn't be smoking.'

Edith ignored her and drew in a lungful of smoke. 'I thought he would have been to see us. He must know how close that bloody *Malakand* was to us.'

The ammunition on the ship had taken hours to tear the vessel apart. Minor explosions had carried on throughout the day before the major one that had shattered it and sent metal plates flying through the air. The blast had been so powerful that new cracks had appeared in the walls of the house, making it a dangerous place to be. The neighbours had already left.

'There could be fractured gas mains and we could blow up,' muttered Winnie, pouring tea into the only two undamaged cups in the house.

'You do go on!' snapped Edith, glanced about nervously. 'I don't need you telling me that we've got to get out.'

'Our Joyce is the lucky one down in Leicester. I wish I was in her place,' said Winnie.

'She wouldn't whine the way you do. She'd make me feel better,' said Edith, placing the cigarette on the edge of her saucer and picking up her teacup.

'That's not fair!' Winnie scowled. 'I tell you something, Mum! She wouldn't slave for you the way I do. Not Lady Muck who thinks herself somebody! She wouldn't clean and sweep and cook meals.' Winnie picked up two sandwiches and, putting them together, bit into them.

Edith looked at her in disgust. 'Don't eat two like that. It's pure greed.'

Winnie flushed and swallowed. 'I'm hungry!' she cried. 'And you've forgotten I could have been killed if I'd been on my normal tram last night … but-but maybe you'd have liked me to have been blown up.'

'Don't be silly,' said Edith with asperity. 'You're my daughter! I do have some feelings for you. Anyway, we will leave here. I'm just concerned that Harry Peters won't know where to find me once I've gone.'

Not taking her eyes from her mother's face, and speaking with her mouth full, Winnie said, 'I thought he gave you his address.'

Edith's eyes widened and then she laughed. 'Of course, he bloody did! Where have my wits gone? It must be the bloody bombing that's affected my brain.' She smiled and reached for a sandwich. 'The piece of paper is under the runner on the sideboard.'

'So what are we going to do?' asked Winnie.

Edith swallowed. 'We'll go and visit him, of course.'

Winnie wasn't convinced. 'What if he doesn't want us?'

Edith's face was determined as she picked up her smouldering cigarette. 'We're homeless, girl. He won't turn us away. When we've finished eating, we'll grab a few essentials and then be off!'

'Good God! Would you believe this?' said Edith, her head turning from side to side as they walked down the street where Harry lived. It was gone nine o'clock and would be dark within the hour. 'Every house is still standing and scarcely any damage.'

'Not bad houses either, Mum,' said Winnie, staggering under the weight of a couple of holdalls, stuffed with clothes and linen.

Edith nodded, noticed a curtain twitch in one of the parlours and knew they were being watched. Nosey neighbours! But you got them everywhere. If only she could persuade Harry into marriage then this street could suit her. She had taken to dreaming in the last few months of her lost love, her Mr Lawrence, Joyce's father, but she decided that such dreaming wouldn't lead her anywhere. Although, the other week, overcome by frustration and nostalgia, she had given in to impulse and taken Winnie to see the house where she had once been in service. An elderly man had been working in the garden and Edith had plucked up her courage and asked if Lawrence Macauley and his sister still lived there. He had told her that Mr Macauley was away at an army camp, training recruits, and that his sister had remarried but that the happy couple had chosen to live in this house, as Mr Chisholm's in Bootle had been damaged in the bombing … but, no, the marriage hadn't been blessed with children.

Edith sighed, glanced at the piece of paper in her hand to check the number of Harry's house and realised they had arrived at their destination. She gazed at the green and cream painted house. The front door was closed but the curtains were still open. She hesitated, teetering on her high heels, before making up her mind and click clacking up to the front door. She rapped her knuckles on the door panel and listened for the sound of footsteps inside. Nothing! She knocked again, but still there was no response.

Winnie moaned, 'I knew it was too good to be true. He isn't in! Nobody's in and it'll be dark soon. What if there's a raid? We'll have to go in a shelter. I hate shelters.'

'Be quiet!' muttered Edith, putting her hand through the letterbox and scrabbling around in the hope of finding a key. Her face lit up as her fingers fastened on a string and she dragged it out. Her gaze darted from side to side and across the road but she could see no sign of being watched. She inserted the key in the lock and opened the door. Swiftly, she stepped over the threshold and beckoned her daughter inside.

Edith glanced inside the darkened parlour and found it empty as she expected. The kitchen was the same but here she discovered the remains of a fire and on the floor a cap and a filthy jacket. Gingerly, Edith picked the latter up and felt in the pockets, finding some small change and a bottle of pills. She peered at the label but could not make out the instructions in the poor light.

'We need a light and then you can get a fire going, Win, while I look around,' said Edith, dragging out a dining chair. She took matches from her handbag and lit the gaslight. Shadows danced around the room until she stepped down. 'That's better,' she murmured, gazing about her.

The furniture was well worn but good stuff. On the mantelshelf was a pottery dog, similar to one of a set she remembered dusting when in service. There was also a rather nice vase. She picked it up and looked at the base and was impressed. Lawrence had taught her a bit about pottery and she hadn't forgotten it.

Winnie hurried to close the blackout curtains while Edith went into the back kitchen. By the remaining daylight she lit the gaslight in there and noticed that this room was clean and tidy. It was bare except for a kitchen cabinet and small drop-leaved table. On the draining board stood a clean mug, plate, knife and fork. This was promising, she thought, her spirits lifting. She drew the blackout curtains and unlocked the door and went down the yard.

When she returned to the house, she found Winnie emptying ash and cinders on to a sheet of newspaper. Leaving her daughter to her task, Edith searched in her handbag for a torch and took it out. Carefully, she climbed the stairs, its beam showing up the wooden treads. Believing that Harry's bedroom would be the front one, she made her way along the landing to the front of the house. The room was empty and keeping the beam of her torch on the floor she went over to the window and pulled the blackout curtains across.

She retraced her steps along the landing as far as the middle bedroom and would have only glanced inside if she had not heard the sound of laboured breathing. With her heart beating jerkily, she stepped inside the room and shone her torch on the bed and caught Harry in its beam. He was lying flat on his back with his arm in a sling and scratches on his face, as well as several days' growth of beard. He was partially covered by a bedspread but was fully dressed, even down to his boots.

What had happened to him? Poor Harry! He had been in the wars. Should she wake him or let him sleep? First things first! She closed the blackout curtains and then placed her torch on the chest of drawers, its beam directed on the bed, before sitting next to Harry.

212

She shook him by the shoulder. 'Harry! Harry! Wake up, Harry!' There was no response. She tried again. 'Harry! Wake up, Harry!'

The rhythm of his breathing altered and he made to turn over but she was sitting in the way. She reached out a hand and pushed back the curly hair from his face. Her fingers found a swelling and he winced as she pressed it. 'Rene?' he muttered.

Edith was taken aback. Rene! Who the hell was Rene? Why was there another woman's name on his lips when he was coming round from a stupor? Had he been keeping secrets from her? She didn't want some other bloody woman spoiling her plans.

Then Winnie called up upstairs, 'Mum, I've got the fire going. There doesn't seem to be a stove in the kitchen, so will I heat water on the fire?'

Edith swore. What was the girl thinking of, shouting loud enough to disturb the neighbours! Harry opened his eyes and looked up at her. 'What the hell are you doing here?'

She was annoyed. Not a friendly welcome! Even so Edith pinned a smile on her face and snatched up his right hand and cradled it against her bosom. 'Never mind that for now, Harry! There doesn't appear to be anyone else in the house and you've broken your arm! It looks like I've arrived in the nick of time.'

Harry attempted to free his hand but she clung to it and he had to wrench it out of her grasp. 'Could you get off the bed and out of the room. I need to get out of these clothes,' he said firmly.

She bit back an angry retort and stood up. 'I'd like to see how you're going to do it, Harry.' She folded her arms and tapped her foot on the linoleum, watching him get to his feet, only to fall back on the bed.

'Damn and bloody hell!' he muttered.

Immediately she bent over him. 'You're not fit, Harry! You need help! Let me help you. You've been so good to me in the past that it would be my way of returning a great, big favour.'

He groaned. 'Will you bloody get out of here, Edith! I can't have you helping me undress.'

Her eyes flashed but, with a great deal of effort, she was able to hang on to her temper. 'Don't be silly! You can't manage on your own.' She reached out and attempted to unbutton the neck of his shirt but his hand fastened over her wrist.

'Edith, I'm sure you mean well but I'll do it myself. As you say, there doesn't appear to be anyone else in the house. That's because my daughter and mother-in-law are in Wales. They've gone to my brother-in-law's place along with Rene next door.'

So Rene lived next door! Edith gazed at him with a doe-like expression. 'Poor you, Harry. You are in trouble. I had no idea I'd find you all alone.'

'It doesn't matter,' he said wearily. 'How did you get in?'

'Key on the string.'

'Shades of Alex,' he said, cradling his broken arm in his undamaged arm.

'Pardon?'

'I'm sure I mentioned him to you.'

'If you did I don't remember. Who is he?'

'It doesn't matter. What are you doing here?'

'Winnie and I came looking for help.'

He looked relieved. 'So Winnie is with you.'

'You didn't think I was suggesting that we stayed in the house all alone, Harry?' she said in a teasing voice, reaching for her cigarettes and matches. Her fingers touched the pill bottle which she had dropped into her pocket and she wondered if they were sleeping pills and that was why he'd been so dead to the world when she came in. 'It was Winnie shouting that woke you up. Our house isn't safe anymore. The explosion from the *Malakand* finished it off ... cracks in the wall wide enough to put your hand through and shake with the neighbours.'

'I'm sorry about that.'

He sounded genuine, so she decided to play it for all it was worth. 'Terrible shock! We were really happy in that house before Rodney died. Since then it's been one thing on top of another.' She picked a fleck of tobacco from her tongue. 'I didn't know what to do, Harry, then I remembered you'd given me your address. So here I am.' Her voice came to a quivering halt.

Then Harry rasped, 'I'm sorry. But you must see that the neighbours would have a field day if they knew you were here.'

'But we're not alone, Harry. Winnie can be our chaperone.'

'No! But let's go downstairs. She'll be wondering what's keeping you.' This time Harry managed to stand up without falling and made it out of the room.

214

Edith hurried after him. 'Please, Harry! We've got nowhere else to go!'

'The authorities will help you.'

She was so annoyed with him that, just for a second, she was tempted to put a hand against his back and push him downstairs. Fortunately the moment passed and she regretted having had such thoughts because he really had been good visiting her in the past.

Winnie was spooning tea into a teapot and looked up quickly when Harry entered the kitchen. She put down the spoon and smiled tentatively. 'Mr Peters! I thought I heard voices. But what have you done to yourself? You look like you've broken your arm.'

'That's because I have broken my arm,' he said with a faint smile. 'How are you, Winnie? Your mother tells me your house is unsafe.'

'That's right, Mr Peters. Huge cracks in the walls. Shall I pour you a cup of tea? And I see you've some bacon and potatoes. I could slice the potatoes and fry them with the bacon for you if you like?'

He hesitated and then smiled. 'I'd appreciate that, Winnie. I know you're a good cook.'

She flushed and said, 'Thank you! I'll get cracking as soon as I've poured you a cup of tea.'

Edith said swiftly, 'I'll see to that, Win. You get on with the cooking.'

Harry excused himself and went to the lavatory. Winnie hurried into the back kitchen to peel the potatoes. Quickly, Edith poured out the tea and then took the bottle of pills from her pocket and read the label. She dropped one in the cup she had delegated for Harry, put a spoonful of sugar in and stirred vigorously. She put a couple more in her handbag and returned the bottle to his jacket.

A couple of minutes later Harry entered the room and sat down. Immediately she handed the cup of tea to him. 'Get that down you, Harry. You'll feel a lot better after it.'

'Thanks!' He took a gulp before smiling up at her. 'Sorry if I sounded hard hearted but people love a bit of scandal and I've got to think of Greta. She wouldn't like it at all if the neighbours had a juicy gossip about me.'

She pressed a hand down on his good shoulder. 'Perish the thought, Harry. I have my reputation to think of, too, you know.'

'I'm positive the authorities will find you somewhere. It could be that you'd be better out of Liverpool.'

'You're right,' said Edith with a sigh. 'It just bothers me that we'll end up living with strangers who might not want us there … and there mightn't be room for Joyce to stay when she can get away from the camp. But that's not your problem.' She smiled. 'Drink up your tea.'

Obediently, Harry drank his tea.

Winnie entered the room, carrying a colander of peeled and sliced potatoes. 'These won't take long.' She smiled down at Harry. 'You look tired, Mr Peters, and you've scratches on your face.'

'It was a kitten,' he said grimly. 'But don't ask me to explain.'

They didn't and Winnie got on with the cooking while Edith talked of this and that, her eyes on Harry's face.

The warning siren went off just as Harry was finishing the fried potatoes and bacon. It had been real tasty but now he could hardly keep his eyes open. Mother and daughter started up from their chairs. 'What are we going to do, Harry?' said Edith.

'What?' Harry attempted to lift his head which seemed to weigh a ton.

'It's a raid!' said Winnie, her hands trembling as she collected the dirty plates. She had to lift Harry's head to remove his from beneath his cheek. He said something but the words were slurred.

'What's up with him?' asked Winnie, glancing at her mother.

Edith moved round the table and stood behind Harry. 'His injuries must be catching up on him. I think we'd best get him to bed.'

'You mean one of the camp beds I saw down in the cellar?' said Winnie.

Edith smiled sweetly at her daughter. 'No! But you can go down there if you're worried about sleeping upstairs … but not until you help me with Harry. He's in no condition to sleep in a cellar.'

'Couldn't we put him on the sofa?' said Winnie. 'What if a bomb was to come through the roof? He… could be killed.'

'Oh, Winnie!' Edith slapped her daughter lightly on the cheek. 'You've seen this street. Not a house down. The Jerries'll be aiming for the docks again. Now give me a hand with him.'

Reluctantly, Winnie did as she was told and, as she was a strong girl, it was she who bore most of Harry's weight as they dragged him upstairs. Pausing to have a rest on the landing, Edith gasped, 'The front bedroom, girl. Then you can take your pick of the other two rooms if you change your mind about going down to the cellar.'

Winnie shook her head and, taking a deep breath, pushed her arms beneath Harry's armpits and dragged him along the floor to the front bedroom. By the time they had managed to hoist him onto the bed, the warning siren had tailed off and the distant sound of aircraft engines could be heard.

'Take off his boots!' ordered Edith. 'And then you can leave us alone.'

Winnie peered across the darkened bedroom at her mother. 'You don't think you should get a doctor for him?'

A sharp laugh escaped Edith. 'You are a bloody idiot! Where will I find a doctor during a raid in an area I don't know? Just do what I tell you and keep quiet about this! I don't want you telling anyone.'

Winnie had a struggle on her hands to remove Harry's boots but managed it at last and then, before Edith could ask her to do anything more, she hurried out of the bedroom and down to the cellar.

Edith hummed beneath her breath as she removed Harry's trousers and underpants. She covered his whatnots with the bottom of his shirt before drawing the bedcovers over him. Then she sat on the side of the bed and took out her cigarettes and lit up with a trembling hand. Bloody hell! Was she mad or what? But she did not want to go and stay with strangers and this way Harry might be persuaded into letting them stay. For a moment she took comfort in nicotine, listening to the boom boom of explosives, thinking how far away they sounded. The docks and city centre were really getting it again, no doubt about that.

She finished her cigarette and then undressed and slid beneath the bedcovers alongside Harry. She ran a hand over his body, thinking what a shame it was that he cared so much for his reputation and wasn't in love with her. They could have had fun. He was going to get a big surprise when he woke up in the morning and found her in his bed, wondering how the hell he had got there and whether they had done anything. Although, commonsense would tell him that he couldn't have done much with a broken arm. She rested her head on his shoulder and felt safer than she had for a long time. Eventually she fell asleep.

16

Harry could hear banging and a voice calling his name. He did not immediately realise that he was not in his own bed, that his arm was broken and he was not alone. Until he was shocked into opening his eyes by a woman's voice in his ear. 'I think you'd better get up, Harry, and deal with whoever that is. Unless you want me to go down?'

Harry received one of those shocks in life that one never forgets. Broken arm! No trousers or underpants! Edith in his bed, in a frilly nightgown and her blonde hair all wispy about her lovely, golden face. 'How the hell did we get here?'

She smiled. 'Don't tell me you don't remember, Harry? I never thought you'd manage it but you were so determined.'

He was speechless, couldn't remember a thing. At that moment his name was called again and he recognised Wilf's voice coming from inside the house! Harry shoved down the bedcovers with his feet, only to stop abruptly as he remembered he was naked down below. 'Get my trousers, Edith!' he hissed.

'Say please?' she teased.

He swore and got out of bed. After all she was a bloody widow and must have seen it all before. He tugged on his vest and shirt to cover himself, groaning inwardly, thinking of what Rene might say if she got to know about this.

'You OK, Harry? I heard you've broken your arm.' Wilf's voice sounded as if he was on the landing.

'I'm OK, Wilf,' shouted Harry. 'Could you do us a favour and light the fire? I'm bloody desperate for a wash and a cup of tea. I'll be down as soon as I'm dressed.'

'The fire's lit, mate. Kettle's hot! You sure you didn't get a bang on the head?'

'Winnie must have lit it,' whispered Edith. 'She's on early shift so will have left for work.'

Harry cleared his throat. 'You're right, Wilf. I did bang my head. Tunnel caved in. I'll be down in a minute.' Adding in a mutter, 'As soon as I get my bloody trousers on.'

'Want a hand?' Edith smirked as she slid off the bed.

Harry was grateful to hear Wilf descending the stairs and glowered at her. 'You surprise me, Edith! You've bloody set me up, haven't you?'

Her eyes widened. 'As if I would! But I'd like to know what Rene would think if she knew that we'd slept together.'

'You bitch!' he said grimly. 'How d'you know about Rene?'

Edith smiled. She was enjoying herself. 'Her name was on your lips when you woke. I'll keep my mouth shut if you'll let me and Winnie stay just for a while.'

'And how do I explain the pair of you being here without incriminating myself?' said Harry, dragging the bedspread from the bed and wrapping it round him. He needed clean clothes and they were in his own bedroom.

'You can keep us quiet. We'll come and go by the back door and no one need know we're here,' said Edith with a giggle and reached for her cigarettes on the mantelshelf.

'That's a daft thing to say if ever I heard one. Some of them could spy for Hitler in this street,' he said grimly.

'You need someone to look after you, Harry! You could tell them I'm your private nurse.' She regarded him provocatively.

Harry darted her an exasperated look and left the room. His mouth felt terrible, his head was muggy and his body was stiff and sore. But most of all, he was furious with himself for getting in this mess. He closed his bedroom door firmly, hoping Edith would have the decency to respect his privacy and prayed for a bloody miracle.

By the time Harry arrived downstairs Wilf had made a pile of toast and a pot of tea. 'Bad raid last night,' he said, filling a mug with steaming amber liquid.

'Was it?' Harry had noticed the two holdalls on the floor next to the sofa and his heart plummeted like a stone dropped in a well. 'Heard of any damage?'

Wilf's gaze followed Harry. 'You weren't taking much notice then? Whitefield Road church was hit!'

'Shame! Bloody close!' Harry sat down, wondering why, if he'd slept for several hours earlier in the day, he'd been so deep in slumber that a full blown raid hadn't disturbed him. Then a thought struck him. Would she? Could she have?' He reached over for his working jacket which someone had hung on the back of a chair and searched inside the pockets and found what he was looking for. He didn't remember taking any of the sleeping pills and yet he would have sworn the bottle had been full. A relieved smile eased his mouth. For a moment in the bedroom he had wondered whether he could have possibly done what Edith had hinted at. He dropped the bottle back in one of the pockets and hung the jacket back on the chair before turning to Wilf.

'I'd best explain,' said Harry gruffly.

The old man listened and would have looked suitably horrified if it wasn't for the twinkle in his eye. 'So what's she like this widow?'

'A real eyeful and that only makes it worse,' said Harry, grimacing. 'You've got to help me out of this, Wilf! I have an idea but you'd have to say yes.'

'And what's that?' asked Wilf.

Harry told him.

Greta slammed down the telephone and marched out of Llanberis post office as if to the beat of a military drum. Rene hurried after her. 'What did you do that for? I didn't get a chance to speak to Harry.' They had been trying for days to get through to him, only to be told that the lines were down.

'I didn't get to speak to him myself. I was cut off but not before I was told something that made up my mind for me. I'm going home!'

'Why? What's wrong?' Rene was alarmed by the expression on Greta's face. 'Has something happened to Harry?'

'Yes!' Her eyes glinted. 'A woman and her daughter are living in our house. A Mrs Cox! I knew it! I just knew that woman wanted to get her hooks into Dad,' said Greta in a seething voice.

Rene felt dizzy and had to stop and rest against a garden wall. 'There must be some mistake! Harry wouldn't do such a thing.'

'I found it hard to believe, too! But-But she said "a Mrs Cox" as clear as day!'

'But how? Why?' Rene felt as if her world had collapsed around her.

Greta swiped the head of a weed with the shopping bag. 'He's been lying to us about how well he is, too! He's got a broken arm. I bet that's how she got in. Saw he needed a woman to look after him and so she came as soon as she knew.'

'How did he break his arm?'

'I don't know! Mrs Ridgeway never got round to telling me that. What she did say was that there hasn't been a raid since Wednesday night so it could be that it's safe to go home, anyway.'

Instantly Rene said, 'I'm going with you!'

'I knew you'd say that!' Greta's face crumpled and tears filled her eyes. 'I don't know what's got into him! What's he thinking of, having that woman and her daughter in our house? What if Alex was to come home and that blonde bombshell Joyce was there? She fancied him I could tell!'

'You mean … you and Alex have met Mrs Cox's daughter?'

Greta nodded. 'Joyce! She's got *It*, Rene. And Alex had the cheek to say that if the mother was anything like the daughter then he could understand why Dad kept on visiting her.' A sob broke from her.

'Oh, heaven help us!' Rene placed an arm round Greta's shoulders. 'It'll be alright,' she said unsteadily. 'If he marries that woman you can always come and live with me.'

Greta stared at her, tears rolling down her cheeks. 'What do I tell Gran? I mean this woman's not only moved into her house … although Dad pays the rent … but has replaced her daughter! My mam! I wouldn't have minded if it was you he was marrying. But her! How could he?'

'We know how!' blurted out Rene. 'She's got *It!* Something I haven't! And yet …' She stopped abruptly.

'What?' Greta brushed away her tears. 'He likes you a lot. He does, Rene. I know that for a fact. But I think you going out with Uncle Jeff threw him off balance. Probably he'd taken it for granted that you'd always be there for us.'

'But I don't like your uncle Jeff,' said Rene slowly. 'In fact I positively dislike him. Anyway, we don't have to tell your gran anything about Mrs Cox and her daughter at the moment. We just tell her that Harry's broken his arm and that's why we're going home. Hopefully, we've still got jobs waiting for us there.'

Greta's and Rene's heads were so full of Harry, Mrs Cox and her daughter that it wasn't until they came out of the railway station in Lime Street and saw the utter devastation the Luftwaffe had inflicted that they realised that some of the rumours had been true, for all Harry's reassurances to the contrary. Greta clung tightly to Rene's arm as she gazed at the fire ravaged walls of the gutted Lewis's departmental store. 'It's terrible! I can scarcely believe it!'

Rene could only nod because words were beyond her.

Slowly, they wandered along Great Charlotte Street where the ruined Blackler's emporium displayed blackened walls. Then they went on as if in a trance towards Greta's workplace, but when they arrived at the spot it was to find it too was just an empty burnt out shell.

'Looks like I'm out of a job,' said Greta, trying to hold back tears. 'I feel so lucky to be alive.'

'That's the spirit!' said Rene huskily. 'Shall we go and get the tram home or do you want to see what else has gone?'

'Let's head for the Pierhead. I want to see if the Liver birds are still there.'

So they walked in the direction of the Mersey, their shock increasing by what they saw as they drew nearer to the river. Civilians and soldiers were working to clear great acres of land where, once, there had been a thriving business and shopping centre. Amidst what now looked like brickfields was the Victoria monument. They gazed up at the bronze face of the queen, who had once ruled over a mighty empire. Her proud expression seemed to say, *Do your worst, but this city, this country, this British empire will not give in! We shall not be defeated!*

Then they turned and looked down towards the river and caught a glimpse of the Liver birds, still poised as if about to take flight. Greta smiled. 'I've seen enough. Let's go home.'

They went via Victoria Street, so they could check whether Rene's firm was still in business, and thankfully, the building was still standing. So they caught a tram in Dale Street and were soon walking along Whitefield Road.

'Perhaps Miss Birkett'll be able to tell us something about Mrs Cox and her daughter,' said Greta, as they came to the draper's shop.

'You can ask her if you like,' said Rene with a sigh. 'But I'd rather go straight home.'

Greta said, 'No! We'll go together.' After all, what could her old friend tell her that she wasn't going to find out for herself? As they approached their street they saw that the church opposite the sweet shop was just a ruin. Greta gasped. 'So close!'

Rene was silent, her mouth taut. She felt so angry. That church had been part of her childhood. She had gone to Sunday School there. They were aware of being watched as they walked up the street. A couple of women waved and they waved back but made no effort to go over and talk to them.

At their houses, both front doors were closed. 'I suppose Wilf's down at the Pierhead talking to his cronies,' said Rene, opening her door.

Greta pulled the key out on the string and put it in the lock. She stood listening as she stepped into the lobby. 'Can't hear a thing,' she whispered.

'Perhaps they've left,' said Rene.

'Or they could be at work or have gone shopping. I wonder where Dad is? Surely he can't be working with a broken arm?'

'You wouldn't think so.' Rene wished she didn't care so much about Harry. That she could switch off her feelings. 'See you later,' she said wearily, closing her door behind her.

Greta took a deep breath and strode up the lobby and into the kitchen. She had never seen it so clean and tidy. The back kitchen was the same, not a dirty dish in sight. Damn the woman and her daughter! Why couldn't they have given her something to criticise? She went down the yard to the lavatory but even here everything was tidy; the wooden seat scrubbed and neatly cut squares of newspaper on a string.

She used the toilet then returned to the house. From her holdall, she took the eggs and bara brith Fred had given her. Then picking up her bag, she climbed the stairs, only to hesitate outside her own bedroom door. She decided not to go in there but instead went along to the front bedroom. Surely if her father was sleeping with that woman she would find signs of it there. She turned the handle and pushed open the door.

A dusting of face powder clouded the shiny wooden surface of the dressing table and on top of it was a hairbrush with blonde hairs clinging to its bristles. On the floor was a pair of flesh coloured satin knickers and a crumpled white blouse. A peach cotton nightgown trimmed with lace was flung on the bed. The words, *Who's been sleeping in my bed?* came into her head. Damn! Damn! And bloody damn! How could her dad do this to her? Bring that woman to this house and sleep with her in Gran's bed!

She left the room and hurried downstairs and out of the house and banged on Rene's door. It was opened within minutes. 'What is it?' asked Rene.

'It's true! There's a woman's clothes flung around Gran's bedroom and there's blonde hairs in her hairbrush. Her and Dad must be sleeping in the double bed,' said Greta in a trembling voice.

Rene said nothing and closed the door.

Greta was about to ask her to open up again when she realised that Rene was really upset and wanted to be alone. The girl went back into her own home and upstairs to her bedroom and pushed open the door. She froze. There was someone sleeping in her bed! Greta was so angry that she slammed the door. The humped up shape in the bed shifted. Greta opened the door and banged it shut again. This time an aggrieved sleepy voice, muttered, 'I'm awake, Mum! I'm awake!'

'I'm not your mother,' said Greta loudly, moving to the bottom of the bed and gripping the footboard with both hands.

The bedcovers were pushed back and the flushed, chubby face of a girl showed above them. Greta gasped. 'You're not Joyce!'

'No! I'm the ugly one. Winnie,' said the girl sullenly.

'I wouldn't say you're exactly ugly. Where's my dad?'

'Work!' Winnie clutched the bedcovers, holding them high so they covered her shoulders. 'You-You must be Greta! He said you wouldn't be coming home just yet.'

'He did, did he?' snapped Greta, drumming her fingers on the wooden board. 'Guilty conscience, I suppose! Get out of my bed, you lazy cow! D'you know what time it is?'

'I work shifts. I didn't get to bed until this morning.'

'So my dad and your mother were all alone in this house sleeping together!' snapped Greta.

'No!'

Greta stared at her, taken aback. 'Did you say no?'

'Yes! He's been sleeping next door,' said Winnie.

Her words so amazed Greta that she sat down on the bed. Then she thought quickly. 'How can you be so sure if you were out all night?'

'Mum's face! But not just that,' she said hastily, hoisting herself up and bouncing back against the pillows. She was wearing a voluminous nightgown that served only to make her look even larger. 'I overheard them talking. It was one in the eye for Mum when he said he was going to sleep there. You wouldn't believe the way I laughed. She clouted me for it, mind, but it was worth it, just to see her not get her way for once.'

Greta's interest in the girl was aroused and, now she knew that Harry and that woman weren't sleeping together, she was able to relax. 'Don't you like your mother?'

'She prefers our Joyce.' Winnie sighed. 'I do love Mum but she never appreciates all I do for her. It's always been "our Joyce this, our Joyce that". Our Joyce is a conceited, selfish cow. They think I'm a fat stupid lump.'

'And what do you think?'

'I think the same.'

'Then you'll always be that way. Where is Joyce?'

'In the WAAF!'

Greta smiled. 'Well, thank God for that! I was worried about the blonde bombshell being here.'

Winnie looked puzzled. 'I didn't know you'd met her.'

'Well, I have,' said Greta, kicking off her shoes and sprawling on the bed. 'When Alex and I were searching for his mother.'

'Who's Alex?'

'The fella I'd like to marry one day. But when he saw your sister, he couldn't take his eyes off her. I reckon she could be a heartbreaker.'

Winnie nodded, wrapping arms, which were the sizes of hams, around her hunched up knees. 'I know what you mean. I'm really glad she's out the way.'

'So does your sister know you and your mother are here?' said Greta.

Winnie shrugged. 'I won't tell her but you can bet anything that Mum already has. She's been here less than a week and she already thinks she's dug in and your dad can be persuaded to let us stay.'

Greta frowned. 'How? I don't want your mum marrying my dad. I've got someone else in mind for him.'

Winnie smiled. 'I'm sure he doesn't want to marry Mum.'

Greta stared at her and said abruptly, 'You want to smile more. It makes a difference. How do you know Dad doesn't want to marry your Mum?'

'Because I heard him say so,' informed Winnie, continuing to smile.

Greta got up. 'You can stay in my bed for now, seeing as how you've been on nights and you've given me news that's made me happy. I'm going out for a few minutes. I'll see you later.'

Greta almost flew down the stairs and out of the front door but, when she knocked at Rene's, there was no answer.

Rene was so upset by what Greta had said that she had to get out. She checked the larder and the meat safe and left by the back door, so she wouldn't have to talk to the neighbours, setting off for Breck Road to do some shopping.

She went through the motions as if she was standing outside herself watching someone else perform the acts. It took her longer to get all she needed than she had reckoned on and by the time she emerged from Hughes the butcher's shop, her feet were killing her. She waited to cross the road whilst a tram disgorged its passengers. The last person she expected to see was Harry with his arm in a sling and scratches on his face.

Her first instinct was to run away. He had slept with *That woman!* giving the neighbours plenty to talk about, and still she found it difficult to believe that he could do such a thing. Yet Greta had said it was true. Deep disappointment and anger surged through her and, before she realised her intent, she was calling his name and walking towards him.

'Rene! You're home!' The pleasure in his eyes caught her off guard.

But she rallied swiftly. 'Yes, I'm home. And what a homecoming! You really lay on the surprises, don't you?' Her voice shook. 'A broken arm! Mrs Cox! You lied to me, Harry!'

Consternation showed in his face. 'I suppose I can understand you feeling like that but what else could I do in the circumstances? I'm sorry if Edith and her daughter staying at our house has upset you but I'll try and explain.'

'You don't have to explain anything to me, Harry,' she said stiffly. 'I'm not your keeper. Although, I'd never have believed it of you but, obviously, I don't know you as well as I thought I did. Goodbye, Harry!' She glanced both ways and was across the road before he could stop her. She heard him shout something but did not catch the words. Instead she was thinking that love was for fools! Perhaps her mother had been right on a few counts after all.

Maybe Vera had seen something in Harry that Rene had been blind to. Rene wanted to cry but told herself she didn't need to be in love to be happy with someone. Look at the walks she'd had with Fred in Wales. She had enjoyed his company without love getting in the way. Perhaps she could find someone else with whom she could share such companionship. She would leave Liverpool! She was a free agent with no one to answer to. Wilf would manage without her. Yes, she would look for work elsewhere. She walked swiftly, hoping Harry would not catch up with her.

As Rene approached the house, she saw a woman standing at the foot of Harry's step, smoking a cigarette. She was blonde with a lovely face but her skin was a little yellow and with tiny lines about her mouth and eyes. Of medium height, with an hourglass figure, Rene knew this must be Edith and hated her on the spot. She would have ignored her and swept into her own house if the woman had not put out a hand and said, 'You must be Rene Miller! Harry's daughter told me you were home.'

Rene was barely able to control her temper. 'I presume you're Mrs Cox?'

Edith held out a hand. 'Please call me Edith! After all we're neighbours.'

Rene looked down at it with disdain. 'Maybe at the moment we are but it doesn't mean that we will be tomorrow. Good afternoon!' She walked up to her front door and drew out the key.

'I didn't expect you to be rude!' called Edith. 'Although, I suppose you believe you've got cause.'

Rene dumped her shopping bags on the step and turned slowly. 'I don't know you. I don't want to know you. Good day!'

Edith raised her pencilled eyebrows. 'I see you're a fool, too.'

Rene was furious and turned to tell Edith just what she thought of her when the other woman said, 'Ah, here's Harry!'

Harry ignored Edith and looked at Rene. 'You'll want me to move my things out right away, I suppose?'

'Pardon!'

She was about to ask what he meant when Greta emerged from next door and flew down the step. 'Dad! I've been watching for you.' She planted a smacking kiss on his cheek. 'You're naughty deceiving us the way you did but you're a sight for sore eyes and I forgive you. How's the broken arm?'

'A pain in the neck!' he said, reluctantly giving her all his attention.

'So when are you moving back home and Mrs Cox moving out?'

'That's not very friendly, Greta,' said Edith, frowning.

'But you and Dad can't stay in the same house.'

'Shut up, Greta!' said Harry in a voice that boded ill if she said anymore. He turned to Rene. 'Do I have your permission to pack my things? I thought you wouldn't mind me staying at yours while you were away.'

Rene's cheeks burned as she met his gaze. Her mouth felt dry and it was an effort to speak, aware that they were the focus of at least a dozen pair of eyes in the street. 'Why didn't you say?' she whispered.

'You didn't give me a chance to explain. Edith and her daughter's house was declared unsafe, so they came looking for me to help. They needed somewhere to stay and didn't realise I'd broken my arm and was on my own. I didn't tell you and Greta because I didn't want you worrying and rushing back to Liverpool because the raids were really bad.'

Rene did not know what to say. Any thought of leaving Liverpool and never seeing him again, evaporated. How could she have thought the worst of him? If only Greta had not thought the worst and Mrs Cox wasn't so attractive and Rene, herself, wasn't such a large lump of a woman. If only she did not love him so much. A thought occurred to her, and although she didn't really want to make such a suggestion, she cleared her throat and said, 'Perhaps I can make amends. Maybe you and Mrs Cox can swop places. I have a spare room.'

'Edith lodge with you!' He stared at her as if unable to believe his ears.

Edith wafted cigarette smoke out of her vision and smiled. 'I accept.'

'What about Winnie?' said Greta, surprised by the way things had turned out.

Edith rolled her eyes. 'I doubt there'll be room for her as well.'

Greta glanced at Harry. 'Perhaps she can stay on with us while Gran's still living in Wales. I'd enjoy having another girl of my own age in the house. What do you think?'

Harry nodded. 'Whatever you say! Perhaps you can see to

moving my things from Rene's.' Without another word he left the three of them standing there and went indoors.

The move was achieved with the minimum of fuss. Wilf and the two girls did most of the carrying back and forth between the two houses. Greta viewed Edith with suspicion, not only because of what Winnie had said about her but because Edith had been extremely sweet to Greta when she had arrived home from work and shopping and found her there, which must have been a shock.

Harry suggested that Greta use the front bedroom, whilst Winnie stayed in her smaller one. 'If your gran decides to come home then the pair of you can share.'

'That suits me but at the moment she seems happy in Wales.'

'No unhappy memories there, that's why,' murmured Harry.

'You mean memories of Mick, Mam and the kids,' said Greta softly. 'Is that the answer, Dad, to escape?'

He made no reply but asked if there was anything for tea. 'Mrs Cox brought something in and Winnie said she'll do the cooking tonight. We'll take turn and turn about, depending on her shift. We'll have to work out how we're going to do the shopping and housework between us. I'll need to look for another job because our place has gone up in smoke. I suppose I could go and ask at their other office but they mightn't need me.' Greta sighed. 'It's not going to be easy getting the shopping in and doing the housework with Gran gone and Winnie and I both working full time.'

'Then stay at home, luv,' said Harry. 'We can cope without your wages.'

She did not fancy that idea and would much rather be earning money and having the company of the girls and women in the office. 'I'm not so sure about that, Dad. I like having a bit of money of my own. I'm sure Winnie and I'll be able to work it between us.'

'You'll wear yourself out. I'll see you don't go without money, luv,' he said, patting her shoulder.

She had no choice but to agree. It was then she thought to ask how he'd broken his arm and how was he managing to work. So he told her about the accident and how his boss at the Corpy had given him a desk job, ordering supplies and seeing that they get to where they should. What he didn't tell her was that it was not what he wanted, that he missed the sheer physical work and being with his mates. Nor did he tell her that he wished Edith was out of his life but at the moment there was no way he could see that happening. As for his feelings for Rene, and hers for him, he was confused. She was obviously angry and upset about Edith staying at his house but he could not understand why she cared so much if Jeff was the man in her life. Harry wished he could get away from everything for a while but, for the foreseeable future, it would not be possible.

17

Rene knocked on the parlour door and entered with a pile of clean washing balanced against her bosom. The autumn sun streamed into the room. Edith was sitting in an armchair in front of the bay window, cigarette in one hand, reading the *Echo*.

'It says here that 1000 Morrison shelters are being delivered to Liverpool every week,' she said, glancing up from the newspaper. 'What do you think of that, Rene? It's months since there were any air raids worth mentioning, Germany's declared war on Russia and we're getting air raid shelters! Harry says it's obvious Hitler's going to need the Luftwaffe over there, so what's the point?'

'Too little when needed, too much too late,' murmured Rene, who still asked herself daily why she had been so daft as to offer Edith a home. She saw her as a Delilah, a Jezebel, a thorn in her side and a pain in her backside; the woman with *It*, who saw more of Harry than she did because she had the excuse of needing to see her daughter, whenever she felt like nipping next door. 'At least the Yanks are doing something now Roosevelt and Churchill have signed the Atlantic Charter. We need all the help we can get to beat the U-boats. I'm glad they've moved the Centre for Counter Measures to Liverpool. We've got a better chance of beating them, especially with Captain Johnny Walker at the centre of things. Did you know he was responsible for organising part of the Dunkirk evacuation?'

'I know,' murmured Edith, flicking over a page to the *Births, Marriages, Deaths*. 'Greta thinks he's the tops. Says she's going to join the Wrens, if the war's still on when she's eighteen, and hopes to stick around Liverpool.'

'What does Harry say about that?' asked Rene, a tartness in her voice.

Edith lowered the *Echo* and said with a honeyed smile, 'You hate me going next door, don't you?'

Rene held on to her temper. 'Why should I? As you're forever telling me, you have to check up on Winnie and see she's behaving herself. From what Greta's said to me about your daughter she's a model guest. Hands over her keep and is prepared to muck in.'

Edith raised her shoulders and then let them drop. 'Is that my washing?'

'You know it's yours and it's the last time I do it unless you give me an extra five bob.' Rene dumped the clothes on a chair. 'It's a mystery to me how it finds its way into mine.'

Edith's lovely eyes widened. 'I'm sorry, Rene. I thought the washing was included in the rent I pay.'

'Rubbish!' Rene's eyes glinted. 'I've mentioned about your washing getting mixed up with mine dozens of times. You need to do your arithmetic and think again, Edith … and don't pretend to me that you're hard up. Munitions workers get well paid.'

'It's bloody dangerous work, too!' snapped Edith, her rouged mouth twisting so that for a moment she looked ugly. 'The cordite can make you sleepy. I know a woman who dozed off and lost a finger in the machinery.'

'You don't have to snap,' said Rene, taken aback by the other woman's reaction.

Edith swallowed and quickly gained control of herself and forced a smile. 'No, I'm sorry. It's just that I hate the job!' She reached down the side of the chair for her handbag and took out her purse. She placed two half crowns on the arm of the chair. 'That do you?'

'Thanks!' Rene picked up the money and walked out of the parlour, wondering if she had got Edith wrong. Yet since she had moved in, Rene had seen next to nothing of Harry and not much of Greta either. If only she knew what Edith really was up to with Harry she might feel better. Yet she could hardly ask the pair of them. If only she could get rid of Edith. Yet how could Rene tell her to go when there were thousands of people who had lost their homes on Merseyside, who were living in a couple of rooms in a stranger's house? Rene had tried volunteering for the forces but had been told that unless she had special skills, such as nursing, then she was too old at thirty-seven and could have spit! So Rene was stuck with her for now, at least.

At that moment, the parlour door opened and Edith came out. 'I'm just nipping next door to have a word with my daughter. See you later!' She winked and twiddled her fingers in Rene's direction and left the house.

Damn her! Rene dreaded Edith arriving back one evening and

telling her that Harry had asked her to marry him. Rene knew then that she would have to move.

'So what d'you think, Harry?' Edith did a twirl. She was wearing a frock she had bought from a modiste's on Breck Road before clothing had gone on ration in June. The dress was tangerine with black spots and had a skirt just on the knee and a pinched in waist and short sleeves.

'You look very nice,' he said, without looking up from the envelope he was addressing.

Her lips tightened. 'Is that the best you can do?'

'I'm not one for fancy words.'

With a provocative smile she sashayed up to him and pressed herself against him. 'The girls have gone to the first house at the pictures so we're all alone. Any suggestions how we can spend the time?'

He stamped the envelope. 'Perhaps you'd like to go dancing?'

Edith stared at him in astonishment. 'Good God, at last I've got a reaction after weeks of trying. I didn't know you could dance.'

'I wasn't asking you, Edith. I was making a suggestion,' said Harry, looking her straight in the eye. 'I'm sure you'll find someone who'll ask you onto the floor if you went along to the Grafton.'

She laughed lightly. 'How ungallant of you, Harry. And there's me being nice to you. I've even kept my mouth shut so far about that night we slept together.'

'I question that,' he said harshly. 'Otherwise, I'm sure Rene would have popped in. I know she's got Jeff but ...'

'Jeff! Who's Jeff?' Edith's eyes were alight with interest. 'She's never mentioned a Jeff to me! But then we're not bosom buddies. She'd have me out if she could.' Harry understood why. How he regretted ever going along to see Edith. He had been a fool and felt certain his love life would have been different if he had not taken pity on her. 'Well?' said Edith.

'He's my wife's brother. A merchant seaman. We haven't seen him since the beginning of the year.'

Edith was taken aback. 'You do surprise me. Well, if she's got someone why are you worried about me having told her our secret. Why don't you be nice to me because, honestly, I have kept my mouth shut ... cross my heart! Take me dancing, please?' she cajoled.

Harry gazed at her for a long moment, then said, 'OK! But you've to behave yourself.'

She ignored those words and said with a catch in her throat, 'It's a long time since I've danced.'

'Me too, but if it's like riding a bike it'll come back to us as soon as we get on the dance floor. Ever been to the Grafton? The floor bounces.'

She stared at him in silence and then moved to kiss him lightly on the lips. 'You romantic ol' thing. Let's bounce together.'

He gazed down at her, his craggy face expressionless. 'I said behave yourself. I'll go and get changed. I won't be long.'

Two hours later Harry was asking Edith where she had learnt to dance after a charming, middle-aged gentleman, dressed in full evening gear, had complimented her on her style.

'I thought I told you I'd been on a cruise ship,' she said, fluttering her eyelashes at Harry. She had imbibed three port and lemons in the pub opposite the Grafton and was feeling good.

'Can't remember. How did that come about?'

She tapped him on the arm playfully. 'You men! Do you ever listen to us women?'

He smiled. 'Sometimes. So tell me more?'

'I was in service and I accompanied Mr Lawrence and his sister, who was a war widow, to Egypt. It gave me a taste for the good life.'

Harry steered Edith round the dance floor. 'Sally was in service. The family name was Armstrong. She helped look after the children and kept in touch even after we were married. After she died, one of the children came looking for her. Alex ended up staying with us. I think I've mentioned him to you.'

She laughed. 'I don't remember but the name sounds familiar. But honestly, Harry, when we get to repeating ourselves as we seem to be doing it makes me feel like a half of an old married couple.'

Harry muffed his step, recovered himself and said, 'I don't think I repeat myself that many times.'

'No?' She shrugged and said in vague tones, 'So tell me more about this family? Where did they live?'

'Out Crosby way.'

'Oh!' Her expression altered. 'I was in service not far from Crosby. Perhaps that's why the name's familiar. Do you know any more about the family?'

'The father lost his money and Alex ended up in an orphanage. There's an uncle but he didn't treat the lad well. His mother's in America and his sisters are in Wales somewhere.'

'My Mr Lawrence is training recruits.' She sighed, hiccupped and put a hand to her mouth. 'Beg pardon! I didn't have a proper meal before I came out.'

'Why not?'

'I couldn't be bothered. Our Win's the cook in the family and with working on shifts I don't expect Rene to do it for me.' She sighed and her eyes took on a faraway look. 'Happy days when I danced aboard ship in frocks better than this one. At least my Mr Lawrence was generous where money for clothes was concerned. An extra bonus he called it. Although, the money probably came from his sister.' She yawned. 'God, I'm hungry and sleepy.'

'I'll buy you some chips on the way home. Want to go now?'

'Anything you say, Harry!' She slipped a hand through his arm.

He escorted her from the dance floor to the cloakroom, removed her ticket from her handbag and handed it to the attendant, in exchange for her jacket. He took her outside. It was just getting dark. He bought chips from a shop on West Derby Road before turning the corner on which Ogden's tobacco factory was situated.

Edith tore open the newspaper and began to eat the chips. Harry watched her, wondering what she would make of his news. She'd probably explode because she had come to him expecting more than he was prepared to give her. 'I've had my call up papers,' he said abruptly. *It was a lie; he had volunteered.* 'I'll be leaving Liverpool soon for a training camp in Wales.' He expected an immediate reaction but there was nothing, so he repeated his words.

'I heard you the first time, Harry,' she said, scrunching the newspaper between her hands. 'Is that why you took me dancing and poured drink down me? Expecting a farewell bit of loving?' she said sarcastically.

He said grimly, 'I thought you deserved an outing.'

'What!' She stared at him in surprise.

'You heard me. I'm sorry that I couldn't give you what you wanted.'

A mirthless laugh escaped Edith. 'The conceit of you men! You were just a consolation prize, Harry. I've never stopping wanting my Mr Lawrence. My husband couldn't match up to him. I'll admit

I was attracted to you but that's all.' There was a silence. Then she said, 'Have you told Greta?'

'Not yet! I'll tell her tonight.'

'What about Rene?'

He did not answer. If it had not been for Jeff, he might have chanced his arm.

'Where've you been, Dad?' asked Greta, looking up from darning a stocking as he entered the kitchen. Winnie, who was spooning cocoa into a jug glanced his way and then at Greta, who added, 'You're looking serious. Something gone wrong at work?'

He hesitated, 'No, luv! But you're not going to like what I'mgoing to say.'

She dropped her mending in the basket and moistened her lips. 'I know what it is! It's Alex! He's been killed!' Her face was white.

'No, luv!'

'It's Gran then, isn't it? She's had a heart attack climbing Snowdon and is dead.'

Harry shook his head, knowing he should not smile, but the image of his mother-in-law climbing a mountain was a funny one. 'No, luv! It's me. I've had my call up papers and I'm going in the army.'

Greta's reaction was what he had expected. 'So that's what that letter was that came for you. I thought you were too old for them to take you!' she said rapidly. 'It's not fair! I don't want you to go.'

'I've got no choice, luv.' He felt terrible for lying to her but felt he had to get away and do his bit.

Her bottom lip quivered and she swallowed. 'I'm going to miss you, Dad. I'll not stop worrying.'

'I'll miss you, as well, luv.' He put an arm round her shoulders and squeezed her. 'You mustn't worry, though. They're hardly going to put me on the front line, not when they've got trained younger men. Besides, I survived the blitz, didn't I?'

She nodded and sighed deeply. 'When are you going? And where?'

'A training camp in Pembrokeshire ... and within a fortnight.'

Greta's eyes filled with tears and there was an emotionally charged moment, which was broken by Winnie. 'What about me, Mr Peters? Will I have to leave this house now?' Her dark eyes were anxious and wisps of soft brown hair clung to her flushed cheeks as she handed a cup of cocoa to him.

He reassured her swiftly, 'I wouldn't see you homeless, Winnie. You must know that. Besides Greta will want company. We don't know when her grandmother's coming home. She's never said that she wanted to live in Wales for the rest of her life but at the moment it looks like she's going to stay there. I'll write to her and explain things.'

'What about Alex, Dad?' said Greta softly.

Harry looked across at her. 'Write to him by all means, luv. '

'I will but … what if he comes home? Will he still be able to stay here?' Her expression was anxious.

Harry hesitated. 'I want to say this is his home as long as he needs it but with you two young girls on your own in the house people will talk. Although, I suppose …' He paused, undecided.

'What is it, Dad? You got an idea?' said Greta eagerly.

He nodded. 'Winnie's mother! If your gran doesn't want to come home then I suppose Edith might be prepared to move back in here when I'm gone.'

Winnie made a noise in her throat but no words came out.

Harry sat down and downed half the cup of cocoa and then said, 'Sorry, Winnie! I know you and your mother … have a few problems.'

'I'm not her favourite,' mumbled Winnie. 'She doesn't appreciate me the way you do, Mr Peters. She'll criticise me and I'll start eating too much all over again.'

'You mustn't let her get you down,' said Greta firmly, adding hastily, 'Not that I want her living here.'

'I think you've got no choice in the matter,' said Harry seriously. 'I think you'll find her contribution to the housekeeping will be essential. Although, I'll send you some money to help you out but soldiers don't earn that much.'

The two girls looked gloomy.

Harry sighed. 'She is your mother, Winnie, and Greta, you still need an older woman around. There's a war on so we all have to make sacrifices. Besides, from what she said to me, she and Rene haven't been getting on. Probably it'll be better all round if she moves in here. I'll ask her tomorrow.' He did not doubt Edith would jump at the opportunity. He was right.

When Rene was told the news that Harry had been called up and that Edith was moving in next door to keep her eye on the two girls, she did not know what to say. Her emotions were all mixed up and she wanted to burst into tears. It seemed so unfair that, at his age, he should be acceptable to the forces just because he was a man. Surely she would hear any day now that Edith and Harry were getting married and half expected them to tie the knot before he left for the training camp in Pembrokeshire but it did not happen.

Rene was at work when Harry said his goodbyes so she never did get to wish him all the best. She thought of all the soldiers, airmen and sailors' girlfriends and wives in Liverpool who waved off their men folk on a regular basis, never knowing if they would return. She thought of young Greta in love with Alex, remembering that last time she and Harry's daughter had spoken she had said that it was a while since she had heard from him but was trying not to worry.

15th November 1941

Dear Greta,

Thank you for your letters. Plenty of surprises there! Glad you enjoyed the Welsh hills. I'm disappointed you had no time to look up my sisters but I understand. I feel real fed up about the whole thing. Still, while there's life there's hope of my finding them. Pity about your dad breaking his arm but relieved it wasn't worse. Amazed to hear that Mrs Cox and her daughter are now living with you and that your dad is in the army. He'll be a great asset I'm sure. I see it's the other daughter who's staying with you. The Blonde Bombshell as you call her having joined the WAAF. I bet she's breaking hearts there.

Now for my apologies. Sorry I have not written for ages. You must have been wondering what has happened to me but I'm glad you never gave up on me. Our ship was hit by a torpedo but managed to stay afloat. We were lucky that a fog came down which meant the U-boats could not see us. We drifted for a while. Not the best fun I've ever had. Fortunately we were spotted and towed to .... some of the crew and I were taken off and assigned to .... heading for .... to pick up .... and go to .... Then I caught malaria and was out of my head for a while and afterwards was sent to convalesce. I'm feeling much better now but have no idea when I'll get home leave so I can get on with trying to find the girls. This war's a real pain! We're doing a lot of ferrying about.

*How's Rene taking it all? Any news of your Uncle Jeff? Give my best wishes
to Rene, Wilf, and your dad and gran when you write to them. I hope you
had a happy sixteenth birthday in October. I enclose a photograph taken
somewhere hot.*

Love Alex. X

Greta placed the letter back under her pillow and sighed, wishing
the paper kiss could have been a real one. She closed her eyes and
dozed off, dreaming of Alex.

'Right, madam, stir yourself and get up!' The bedcovers were
whipped off Greta and flung over the board at the foot of the bed.

The girl groaned and ignored the words, crawling down the bed
and seizing the covers. She dragged them over her and curled up
at the bottom of the bed. She wanted to get back to her dream
about Alex. Now she was sixteen she felt certain he would see her
as more of a *femme fatale,* the way she imagined herself in her
dream. She should get her photograph taken and send it to him.
She loved the one of him in shorts and singlet; otherwise she could
so easily have forgotten what he looked like. She had managed to
get together a box of goodies: hand knitted socks, chocolate, fruit
cake and a couple of second-hand H Rider Haggard adventure
books and had sent it to his shipping company, keeping her fingers
crossed that it would get to him and not be sent to the bottom of
the ocean.

'Are you deaf?' said Edith, gripping the covers and attempting to
remove them again. 'There's the ironing waiting to be done.'

'I'll do it! Just let me have a few more minutes in bed,' murmured
Greta, hanging on to the bedclothes for dear life. Every weekday she
got up at half six, lit the fire and prepared breakfast. Then came the
housework and the shopping, the washing and the cleaning.
Saturday and Sunday she liked a little lie-in.

Exasperated, Edith thumped the humped figure in the bed.
Fortunately the bedcovers cushioned the blow but Greta still felt it.
She wondered what was getting to Edith. Whatever the reason for
her being in a mood, it wasn't right for her to lash out. For months
they had managed to rub along OK but yesterday a slap had left the
imprint of her fingers on Greta's arm when she had given Edith
backchat.

'Get up!' Another thump.

'I'll get up when you get out of the room,' said Greta, her voice muffled by the bedcovers. 'I like a bit of privacy.'

Edith drew in her breath. 'There's nothing you've got, girl, that I want to see.'

'Good! Then you'll get out!'

'You really have got a cheek!'

'Got three,' said Greta cheerfully.

'That is rude. I don't know what your father would think.'

'I'll write to him and ask him. I'll tell him that you've started lashing out at me, too.'

'You do, girl! A lot of good it'll do you. Think he'll rush home because you go whinging to him?'

Greta knew she was right but longed for the days when her grandmother, Dad and Alex had been home and they had been happy together. Cissie had written saying that she couldn't come home just yet as Megan was having another baby and would need her help.

Edith interrupted her reverie. 'I'll expect you downstairs in ten minutes. I've got to go out and I want to make sure you're up before I leave.'

Greta poked her head out of the covers. 'Going anywhere nice?'

For a moment Edith's eyes warmed and then she said sharply, 'Mind your own business.'

'In that case, why have I got to get up? Winnie's at work. You're going out. I've got plenty of time to do the ironing and the shopping.'

Edith hesitated. 'Joyce has got a pass and is hoping to get here from Leicester.'

Greta raised her eyebrows. 'You surprise me. I thought you'd be staying around with her coming to visit.'

'Well, something has turned up.'

'Must be important.'

Edith made no answer but left the bedroom.

The girl wriggled back up the bed and lay on her back, gazing up at the ceiling, irritated because she was going to have to stick around and be nice to the blonde bombshell. She had visited once before and that had been enough for Greta, because Joyce was as beautiful as she remembered but as selfish as Winnie had said.

Greta sighed and, wide-awake now, decided to get up. She found

240

Edith dusting her face with the dregs of the face powder in her compact. The girl had to admit she looked smart in a black suit with a white jumper. On her newly dyed hair was perched a black hat with a white flower and a tiny veil. 'You look nice.'

'Thanks!' Edith applied lipstick with a trembling hand. 'There's no milk by the way.'

'OK. I'll nip out and get a bottle.'

Edith glanced at her. 'If I've gone by the time you come back, remember what I said about making Joyce welcome. If she wants to stay put clean sheets on the bed.'

'Of course! I don't need telling.' Greta picked up the empty bottle, took some money out of a jar in the sideboard cupboard and left the house.

She paused on the step to look up at the sky. It was a clear blue streaked with peach and silver edged mackerel clouds. There was a definite wintery feel to the day as she walked to the dairy. Rene was coming out of the shop as Greta approached. 'How are you?' said the girl solicitously. 'I don't see much of you these days. I hope Mrs Cox living at ours doesn't put you off dropping by.'

Rene smiled wryly. 'She does actually.'

'But she's not always at home,' said Greta swiftly. 'You could drop by when there's just me or me and Winnie. I miss our talks on the way to work.'

'I miss them, too.' Rene hesitated. 'How's Harry?'

'Fine. He's in a lovely part of Wales. He's training to be a gunner. You could write to him if you wanted. I'm sure he'd appreciate it. Says he loves getting my letters and Gran writes to him, too.'

Rene said, 'That's nice for him. I'm sure he'll enjoy her letters. I'd best go now. Wilf's waiting for his breakfast.'

At that moment Greta caught a glimpse of Edith as she was leaving the house and seized Rene's arm. 'Have a quick look at Edith dressed up to the nines. Joyce is visiting but Edith is going out and is being very secretive about where she's going. It makes me wonder if she's got another fella.'

Rene could not imagine anyone who could have Harry wanting someone else but she could not help wondering if perhaps Greta was right and Edith was two-timing him. If so, perhaps there was hope for Rene yet.

241

18

GNR. H. PETERS,
367 C.D. BATTERY R.A.
SOLDIERS ROCK,
ST ISHMAELS
NR HAVERFORD WEST,
PEMBROKESHIRE . S. WALES

18th January 1942

Hello Rene,
    I was really pleased to get your letter but I don't agree with you that it was stupid of you to get upset over my offering Edith a place to stay. I should have made the effort to explain how it all came about but I took offence, thought you knew me better than to be carrying on with her "in full view of the neighbours", so to speak. She and Winnie just turned up out of the blue and found me dead to the world upstairs the day of the accident. There was a raid that night, which I don't remember at all as the doctor had given me some sleeping pills. The next morning I realised that I could hardly ask them to leave, them being homeless, so suggested to Wilf that I moved into your place. There's nothing much else to tell about those days before you and Greta came home. I've always appreciated your concern for me and mine and hope you'll keep your eye on Greta for me. Since she's been living with Edith and Winnie and occasional visits from the "blonde bombshell", as she calls Joyce, she seems to be casting herself in the role of Cinderella. Can understand how it must be for a girl of her age staying at home and I know she worries about me and Alex. With Winnie and Edith doing shifts maybe it's time that daughter of mine thought of getting herself a job then maybe she'd have less time to worry. The other two must be around some part of the day to do the shopping so perhaps you can suggest it to her.
    You ask what it's like here. Freezing cold when on guard duty, standing on the seafront on top of cliffs two to three hundred feet high. When off duty we're miles away from a town. I missed an opportunity the other week. We were asked if anybody wanted a transfer. I was interested but the C.O. put a kindly hand on my shoulder and looked sorrowfully into my eyes and said, "Gosh, Harry, you wouldn't leave us, would yer?" Well, you know

how soft-hearted I am. He told me it was only to another boring Royal Artillery camp in the middle of nowhere and he slipped me ten bob when I said I'd stay put. Only later did I discover he'd tricked me when he picked out six other blokes and I found out they were going to Gravesend London! We'd done a forty eight hour manoeuvre exercise, so I can only think I'd played my part too well.

So what d'you make of the Japs bombing Pearl Harbour and Britain joining America in declaring war on them? At least it seems that the Yanks are in this one with us so I agree with Churchill that we'll soon have the Jerries on the run. Not sure when next I'll get some leave. Heard anything from Jeff? Mrs Hardcastle doesn't mention him.

I hope you're keeping well.
Yours affectionately,
Harry.

Rene reread the letter, her heart beating erratically, and took special note of three things in it. First and most importantly was what she saw as his need to reassure her that nothing had happened between him and Edith. Which, in light of what Greta had told her about overhearing Edith telling Joyce that she had a man friend, a Mr Lawrence, was probably true. But what proof did she have, herself? She wondered if Greta had mentioned him to Harry. Somehow, Rene did not think it would be right coming from her.

Secondly was his signature *Yours affectionately*, when what she longed for was *All my love, Harry*. She sighed. Was that just down to his believing there was something between her and Jeff? Or was affection all that he felt for her? Should she risk putting a *love Rene* on her next letter and telling him the truth about Jeff? Or should she keep things light? She was uncertain. Although, what did she have to lose after all? Thank God that she hadn't heard from Jeff since that last postcard!

Thirdly, Harry's mention of Greta needing a job could not have come at a more opportune moment. One of the younger women in the office had joined the forces and there was a vacancy. Rene decided not to waste time and immediately went next door to speak to Greta.

Immediately she was pounced on, not only by Greta but Winnie, also. 'Rene, how would you like to go to a dance at the Grafton?' they both chorused.

'Mum said we couldn't go without someone there to keep their eye on us!' Winnie sounded disgruntled. 'But she wasn't prepared to do it herself, said that she had other fish to fry and went out in her best frock.'

Rene said ruefully, 'It's years since I danced.'

'Then it's time you took it up again,' said Greta, smiling. 'So go and put your glad rags on and let's go before it gets that full we can't get in.' And she pushed Rene towards the door.

'But I came to tell you I've had a letter from Harry,' blurted out Rene.

'Good,' said Greta. 'You can tell us what he had to say on the way. I want to get dancing practice in before Alex comes home.'

With a smile on her face Rene did as she was told. She needed cheering up and it was nice of the two younger girls to want her company. She searched in her wardrobe for a frock and a pair of shoes that she hoped would be suitable, wondering as she did so whether Harry would approve of his daughter going dancing. From what she'd heard the girls discussing in the office there were plenty of servicemen on the make at these dances. Still, she would be there to keep her eye on Greta and besides the girl obviously loved Alex. Anyway, Harry was no spoilsport and the three of them could do with a change from the pictures.

They managed to get to the Grafton by seven o'clock and the talk on the way was of different dance steps, so Rene didn't get a chance to speak about the job at their place. The dance started at seven thirty but the queue outside the dance hall was already past the pub on the corner. 'We'll never get in,' cried Winnie, who was desperate to have a good time. Despite Edith having moved back into the house, Winnie had managed to refrain from stuffing herself thanks, not only to Greta taking her side when Edith got stroppy with her, but also because her mother was less moody than she used to be. Maybe her good mood was due to Edith having a man in her life!

Greta nibbled on her lower lip. 'I just dread the commissioner on the door putting his arm out when he gets to us and saying "No more!"'

But he didn't, and instead said, 'Have a good time, girls!'

They were inside and, as soon as they had left their coats in the cloakroom, they bought themselves soft drinks and made their way to the dance hall. The three of them were instantly mesmerised by the music, the glistening ball overhead and the whirling figures of the dancers. 'Wow!' cried Greta.

'Lively, isn't it?' said Winnie, her eyes sparkling.

'It's jumping, doll,' said a voice behind her.

The three girls turned and gazed at the American sailor. Crew cut, square jaw and bold blue eyes and youthful. 'Wanna cut a rug?' he asked, looking straight at Winnie.

'Pardon?' she said, with an expression of wonder on her face.

'Wanna dance?'

'Yes, please!' She grabbed his hand and dragged him on to the dance floor.

Rene and Greta exchanged a wink and watched Winnie and the sailor as they began to jitterbug; the dance was a quickstep but that didn't appear to bother either of them. 'Let's find somewhere to sit,' said Rene. But that proved difficult and they both ended up standing on the edge of the dance floor. Rene watched the different couples, interested in how they reacted to each other, noticing how close some danced and how others kept several inches between them and their partner. Some chattered away ten to the dozen, others were silent, dancing as if in a dream.

The music came to an end and there were a few minutes respite while the band replaced their sheet music and people left the dance floor. A British sailor came up and asked Greta to dance. The girl looked at Rene, who smiled and nodded. She was content to be left on her own to watch others dance. She noticed Winnie gazing about her and presumed she was looking for them and waved; the girl's eyes lit up and she waved back before the band struck up again with, *Don't Sit Under the Apple Tree with Anyone Else But Me.*

Rene tapped her foot to the music and then suddenly, to her amazement, spotted Edith being twirled around the dance floor by an elderly man dressed in a *penguin* suit; the kind she had seen Fred Astaire wearing when dancing cheek to cheek with Ginger Rogers on the silver screen. She could scarcely believe her eyes.

She was soon to find out who it was because Edith had also seen her and when the dance ended she brought him over. 'What are you doing here? I'm really surprised to see you,' she said.

Only for an instant did Rene consider telling Edith that she was there with Greta and Winnie but instead she kept her mouth shut. Let the girls have their fun for now; Edith might just put an end to it all too swiftly! 'I'm with a woman from work,' said Rene lightly. 'She thought it would do me good.'

Edith raised her sooty eyebrows. 'Well, it's not going to do you any good standing there. You have to get on the dance floor! Here, have my partner. I could do with a smoke! Teddy, show her how to do it!' And she deserted them both.

Rene and Teddy weighed each other up. He had a head of thick salt and pepper hair, faded blue eyes, a distinctive mole on his cheek and a smile that revealed perfect teeth for a man of his age. 'Please, do give me the pleasure?' he said, offering his hand.

Rene said regretfully, 'It's ages since I danced. I'll probably step on your toes.'

'Then I'll stand this one out,' he said with a twinkle in his eyes. 'A pity, though. It's fun. I've never lost my love for it. I could teach you if you could afford me. Right now there's plenty on the floor who could do with a lesson or two.'

She smiled. 'I thought you danced very well.'

'That's because, dear lady, I am a professional dancer. Haven't always been … used to go cruising after the Great War and that was where I took to it like a duck to water. Marvellous! But sad! Lots of pretty girls who'd lost their young men. Dance, dance, dance, little lady, they were frantic, trying to forget, to escape life because they couldn't make sense of their existence anymore.'

She was fascinated. 'It's sad, as you say, but did you go anywhere interesting? Like Egypt?'

He smiled, flashing his white teeth. 'I've danced my way around the world since then. Rich widows, as well as young girls, enjoyed nothing more than a cruise up the Nile to see the pyramids and experience the romance of the desert as depicted in *The Sheik* by Rudolph Valentino.'

Rene was delighted to hear the great Valentino mentioned. 'I was mad about him. Cried my eyes out when he died.'

'My little lady adored him. We met on a cruise before I turned professional. Then we both lost all our money and dancing was the only thing I knew. My parents hadn't had me trained for anything.'

'A wife! You have a wife!' In a way Rene felt she was reliving that moment when Fred had told her Jeff's wife was still alive. She had not considered that Edith would carry on with a married man.

'Had. Sadly Mrs Thomas was killed in the blitz.' His eyes were bleak for a moment and then he squared his shoulders. 'But I come here most nights although, professionally, I only dance twice weekly for exhibition purposes.'

He had silenced her. Even so Rene's head was full of questions. So this man wasn't Edith's Mr Lawrence but a Mr Thomas. Suddenly, Edith reappeared in front of them as the band struck up *I've Got You Under My Skin* and she seized Teddy's hand and drew him on to the dance floor without a word to Rene.

Rene stared after them, annoyed with Edith and almost wishing that she had not come. On the way home she took the opportunity to tell Greta what Harry had said about her getting a job and that there was an invoice clerk's position going in their office. The girl's eyes brightened. 'If Dad's in favour then I'd like to apply for that. Edith mightn't be too keen but I don't take orders from her.'

'Then I'll put a word in for you and you can apply for the job.' Rene turned to Winnie and said, 'Did you spot your mother at the dance?'

'No!' Winnie gasped. 'I didn't know she was going to be there. She never said, the mean thing. Still, if we'd gone with her she'd have had something to say when that Yank asked me to dance. I was perfectly safe with him, although I was a bit sad at having to refuse his offer to see me home. Still, there's plenty more fish in the sea. Did you speak to Mum? Did you tell her we were at the dance?'

Rene shook her head. 'She came over and introduced me to her partner. A professional dancer called Teddy Thomas.'

Both girls raised their eyebrows. 'I wonder what's happened to Mr Lawrence?' said Greta.

Winnie smiled slowly and said tartly, 'Nothing might have happened to him. Our Joyce said he's down at a camp in the South training recruits. Mum skips off to see him once a month when she can work having a few days off with him. Looks to me like Mum wants to have her cake and eat it.'

Rene agreed but considered it wiser not to say anything more. She wrote Harry a friendly letter, telling him about the dance but made no mention of Edith's Mr Lawrence or Teddy and all she said about Jeff was that she had heard nothing from him. Let Harry make of that what he would.

Greta applied for the job with Rene's firm and, due to her

recommendation, was taken on. They both felt it was like old times when they set off for work together.

Harry wrote back thanking her for helping Greta get a job, and suggested that Rene do a refresher course in dancing so that when next they saw each other perhaps they could go dancing, and to keep him posted on Greta's progress at work. Rene liked the idea of dancing with Harry and decided that she would do as he said. There was a dancing school half an hour's walk away. She told him that Greta was very popular in the office. *You know your daughter, warm and friendly and so caring towards people and she wants to do well, too.*

Edith had made no comment about Greta going out to work until she and Rene met one Saturday afternoon in late Spring when they were leaving their respective houses. 'It makes more work for me but as it means more money coming into the house, I suppose I've got no complaints,' she said. 'The cheeky madam had the nerve to tell me that it's only Harry she has to answer to and that as he wrote to you and made the suggestion that it was OK.'

Rene sensed her irritation, and said, 'You don't object to Harry writing to me, do you?'

Edith shrugged, settled a shoulder against the door jamb and took a packet of cigarettes out of her bag, then lit up. 'I've a feeling it wouldn't make any difference to you if it did. Besides you must have realised by now there's nothing serious going on between Harry and me.'

Rene hesitated. 'I hoped not. I take it you've got other fish to fry.'

Edith smiled and blew out a smoke ring. 'I know Teddy's a good few years older than me but he's a smashing dancer and a bit of charmer, takes me out of myself, but Lawrence is my first love.' She added pensively, 'His sister was my employer when I was in service. That woman! She's so unlucky with her husbands. The last one died of a heart attack. I saw it in the *Echo* and went along to the funeral, hoping Lawrence would be there … and he was.' Her voice softened. 'I don't feel for him the same as I did in that first girlish flush of love but I do care about him.' She waved her cigarette about as if to emphasise what she was about to add, 'I know he's middle class but the war's breaking down barriers. If he was to ask me to marry him I'd say yes.'

There was a long silence but it was not the strained silence of the times when they had lived under the same roof. Edith flicked ash from her cigarette and appeared to hesitate a moment before saying, 'What about you and Harry getting together? He did mention you having someone called Jeff but from the way you behaved towards us when you returned from Wales, I thought you must feel something more than sheer neighbourliness. I think Harry's the one for you. Not that I know anything about this Jeff except he's a seaman.'

Rene's eyes glinted. 'Jeff is a married man and I have no time for him. I should have told Harry that but I was too hurt when I came back from Wales and thought you and he ...'

'He loves you,' said Edith abruptly.

Rene's heart seemed to flip over and she could not take her eyes from Edith's face. 'How ... do ... you know?'

Edith laughed. 'Your name was the first on his lips when I woke him! There he was lying on the bed, out for the count with a broken arm and scratches on his face. I thought he'd be glad to see me, but what did he whisper before opening his eyes? *Rene!* I was mad, I can tell you! So you go and write to him and put him straight about that Jeff.'

Rene stared at her, thoughtfully. 'You're nicer than I thought.'

Edith raised her eyebrows. 'Don't you believe it! Things are going my way at the moment. It only needs for something to go wrong and ... ' She shrugged.

The two women parted. Edith to the Grafton, Rene to knock at next door. She and the girls were going to the pictures to see Bob Hope and Bing Crosby in a film called *The Road to* some place or other. She felt on a high, thinking that tomorrow she would write to Harry but exactly how she was to word what she wanted to say she was uncertain.

Dearest Harry, No! She could be presuming too much as she only had Edith's word for it that Harry loved her. Rene tore off the sheet from her writing pad, then realised there was no other way of letting him know how she felt without laying bare her feelings. She just had to take the chance. She picked up the sheet of paper again.

Dearest Harry,
Just thought you might like to know that Edith has told me that you love me and as I love you, too, and Jeff never meant anything to me, I thought I'd

best let you know. After all, there is a war on and who knows what tomorrow might bring? I await a swift answer as I'll be in a right state until you reply to this.

Lots of love, Rene

She hesitated before putting *xxxxx* on the bottom. Then she swiftly placed the letter in an envelope, addressed and stamped it and left the house to post it. She pressed a kiss on it before popping it into the pillar box. Then she went home and could not sleep that night for wondering what his answer would be.

Rene did not expect to receive an answer the next day, but was hopeful that maybe the day after that she might. She was to be disappointed. And continued to be so each day for a week. When ten days passed, Rene had lost all hope and was utterly depressed. She must have looked so miserable that morning because Greta asked her what was wrong.

'Nothing!' sighed Rene. And she turned Greta's attention away from herself by asking if there was any news on the Edith/Lawrence front.

'There's talk that his battalion might be going abroad, according to Joyce.'

Rene glanced sidelong at Greta. 'She's been up here again? It doesn't seem that long since the last time.'

Greta glowered. 'Winnie reckons Joyce comes on the cadge and she might even be at the house more often in the future. The Yanks are at Burtonwood airbase, out Warrington way, and who knows … maybe she'll put in for a transfer.'

Rene said softly, 'Poor Winnie. It must be difficult living under the shadow of an elder, beautiful sister.'

Greta nodded, digging her hands deep into her pockets. 'I'm praying that she won't go back to the way she used to be … although, maybe she's moved on too far for that.' Greta smiled suddenly. 'I'm sure she has because she often gets asked up to dance at the Grafton and even at the dance at the church hall, she's popular. They love her carrot cake she takes along.'

Rene said, 'Thank God, there's a lot of men who like a woman with a bit of meat on them. Any news from Alex?'

Greta sighed. 'Poor luv! He's been suffering from a heat rash.'

'So we can guess where he is,' said Rene, echoing her sigh.

Another day passed with no letter from Harry. The following day, Rene arrived home from work, hoping against hope, yet wondering if her original note had been lost in the post and whether she should write another. Her emotions had veered from hopelessness to anger in the last fortnight, thinking at least he could have had the decency to put her out of her misery if his feelings did not go as deep as hers. She sighed and decided to have a good wash down, do her hair and pamper herself.

It was nine o'clock that evening when someone knocked on the front door. She was reluctant to answer it, thinking if it was Wilf, who had gone to the pub with one of his cronies, then he should use the key. But the knocking continued and so she had no option but to answer the door in her curlers and with blobs of Pond's vanishing cream on her face. 'Alright, alright, I'm coming,' she called and wrenched open the door.

A pulse began to beat at her throat when she saw Harry standing on the doorstep but before she could even open her mouth, he said, 'I had to come! Couldn't write! Had the 'flu! Showed the C.O. your letter and he agreed that I had to come. Only got a forty eight hour pass, though!'

'Oh Harry,' she whispered, her legs turning to jelly.

He stepped into the lobby and closed the door behind him and immediately seemed to fill the space. They were so close together that she couldn't make out his features in the darkened lobby. He reached for her and brought her against him. 'Harry, I've ...' His mouth came down over hers, stifling what she had been about to say.

The kiss seemed to go on forever and when he lifted his head all she could do was to lean weakly against him to get her breath back. He kissed her ear. 'I love you, Rene. I want you to marry me!'

She reached up with a shaking hand to touch his face where cream had been transferred from her nose to his cheek. She smoothed it into his skin. 'You believed what I said about Jeff?' She was trembling from head to toe, scarcely able to believe that he'd finally said the words that she had longed to hear.

'Why should I doubt you? I just wish I'd known earlier.'

'What about your feelings for Sally?'

'I'll never forget Sally ... but what I felt for her was different to what I feel for you. I can say in all sincerity that I love you deeply.

You're kind, you're unselfish, you're honest, you're a worker, you're beautiful, loving and giving!' He kissed her then again and again. She returned his kisses with a passion she had never known herself capable of, wrapping her arms round him and pressing herself against him. 'So will you marry me? You haven't said yes yet!' he said, when at last they drew apart a little.

'You haven't given me a chance. But yes, yes and yes!' she said, feeling as if she was floating.

'Good!' He buried his head against her neck and nuzzled her skin. She felt herself melting inside and wished they were already married.

'I can't arrange it in forty eight hours, Harry,' she said, with a tiny laugh. 'Although, I wish I could.'

'Less than that, luv. It took me nearly a day to get here. I've only tonight and then I'll have to leave in the morning. I don't know when I'll get home again.'

She seized his hand. 'You must stay here. I don't care what the neighbours say anymore,' she said firmly.

'No, luv! I wouldn't ruin your reputation by staying the night,' he said huskily.

Her face fell. 'But you will come in?'

'Of course, I'll come in.' He caressed her cheek with a gentle hand. 'Is Wilf around?'

Mutely, she shook her head.

'Good,' he murmured, reaching for the key on the string and removing it. 'We've got a lot of catching up to do.'

Rene's spirits soared, thinking of what she'd read about married love, hoping that Harry would be willing to jump the gun and have a practice. She did not need to worry. He laughed with joy when she tentatively voiced her thoughts and lifted her off her feet. He gazed up into her flushed face and repeated those magical words, 'Oh, I do love you, Rene!' Then he kissed her and carried her upstairs to bed.

Afterwards, as they lay in each other's arms, Rene whispered shyly that she hoped she had done things right. 'It was marvellous!' His voice was unsteady. 'I'd hate you to think that what me and Sally had was perfect and what we have is second-best. It isn't! It's the best.'

She was deeply touched and buried herself in him. 'I'll arrange the wedding for when you can get some real leave. We can have a proper wedding and a honeymoon!' she said in a muffled voice.

'It mightn't be for a while, luv.' He took her face between his hands with infinite tenderness and gazed into her eyes.

'I've longed for years to be Mrs Harry Peters,' whispered Rene. 'As long as you come back to me I can wait a little longer.'

19

'Right, madam, stir yourself!' The bedcovers were whipped off Greta and flung over the board at the bottom of the bed.

How many times had she heard those words before and done this same thing, thought Greta, crawling down the bed and dragging the covers back over her. She had been dreaming of Alex again. Having written and told him the date, she had prayed that he would manage to get home for Rene and Harry's wedding in a week's time. He had missed her seventeenth birthday. It was twenty-two months since she had last seen him; a year and a half since they had been to Wales. Greta had visited there in the summer and her gran had told her that she'd give Megan and Fred a few more months and then she'd be home. Rene and Harry's getting married had come as a shock; as did the news that Jeff's wife was still alive. So she had promised to be at the wedding and to bring Fred along. Greta was impatient to see them both.

'Are you deaf?' said Edith, gripping the covers and attempting to wrench them out of Greta's hold. 'There's the ironing and the step needs washing, too.'

'I'll do both! Just let me have a few minutes more in bed.'

Edith thumped the humped figure. 'I'll expect you up in ten minutes. I'm hoping Joyce is coming but I have to go out.' Her voice trembled. 'She's got her transfer and I told her I must see her as soon as possible. Change the sheets in case she decides to stay … and don't forget to put the rabbit on for dinner. Winnie's gone to deliver a message for me.'

So what else is new? thought Greta, but she popped her head out of the bedclothes and looked up at Edith, who was wearing her black suit and black and white hat. 'Where are you going? Am I allowed to know?'

Her persecutor's eyes looked bleak as if she'd had a shock and she cleared her throat before saying, 'Winnie'll explain! I'll see you later.'

Greta lay back in bed, wondering if something had happened to Mr Lawrence. His battalion had left England months ago and if he had been killed then she felt really sorry for Edith. Greta decided she might as well get up as she was wide awake and had all the chores to do. She was going to the first house at the pictures with Winnie and Rene later. The front door slammed as she was getting dressed. It seemed that for once she had the house to herself. She had breakfast, then did the ironing and changed the sheets on the spare bed. After that she put the rabbit and vegetables on to stew and then half filled a bucket with hot water and went outside to wash the front step. When she had finished she crossed the street to empty the dirty water down the grid.

She was in the act of straightening up when she happened to glance up the street. What she saw caused her heart to beat erratically. A young man wearing a peaked cap, navy blue jacket and trousers was coming down the street. He had the rolling gait of a seaman and carried a kitbag on his shoulder. She had waited so long to see Alex that she had trouble believing it was really him.

Hastily she crossed the road and placed the empty bucket at the foot of the step. The man came closer and closer. Was it Alex? Yes it was! She could wait no longer but ran to meet him. 'Alex! Alex!' she called. His face lit up and the kitbag slid from his shoulder. He caught Greta up in his arms and swung her off her feet. She gazed down into his tanned face and straight into his shining grey eyes, seeing herself reflected there. 'Alex!' she whispered.

'Greta!' There was a wondering note in his voice.

'Alex! I've been hoping and hoping you'd make it.' She caressed his cheek with the back of her hand.

'We shipped some Italian prisoners-of-war over here. It seems forever since I've seen you!' His voice had deepened with emotion. 'You've grown up.'

'I'm seventeen!' She rubbed her cheek against his rough one.

'Is that a fact,' he teased, and turned his head so his lips met hers. It was an awkward, experimental kiss and Greta thought they could probably do better. She was in the process of proving so when they were interrupted.

'Should you be kissing on the street?' The girl's voice caused Greta's heart to sink. Slowly and reluctantly she turned her head and stared at the blonde, wearing the blue uniform of the WAAF. On her shoulder Joyce carried a bag but otherwise she was empty-handed.

'Is it any of your business?' said Greta, her tone definitely chilly as she felt Alex's hold slacken and her feet touching earth again as he lowered her to the ground.

Joyce raised her eyebrows. 'No need to be touchy. Is Mum in?'

'She's gone out, didn't say where. I think Winnie knows but she's been sent on a message,' said Greta, keeping an arm firmly round Alex's waist, not daring to stare him in the face in case he looked besotted.

'Damn!' cried Joyce, frowning. 'She told me to get here straight-away. I came as soon as I could. Besides I need money from her. I went and parcelled all my spare kit and sent it on by rail. I just couldn't be bothered carrying it because it weighs a ton. Now it's gone missing! I've had a strip torn off me and been told I've got to pay for replacements. Orders are orders they said and I should never have let it out of my sight.' She raised her shoulders. 'How was I to know that someone would go and pinch it?'

Alex said kindly, 'There's a war on, luv. All kinds of things go missing. They won't go demanding the whole lot at once but take the money a bit at a time out of your pay.'

Joyce looked him up and down. 'I know that! But Mum's been saying for ages that one day we'll have plenty of loot.'

'How does she make that out? She's always crying poverty to Winnie and me,' said Greta.

A tinkling laugh issued from between Joyce's rouged mouth. 'Didn't she tell you? She married Mr Lawrence before he went over-seas and his sister, Mrs Chisholm, is a wealthy, childless widow. That's why Mum wanted me to put in for a transfer up here.'

Greta felt really annoyed. The secretive cow! Why couldn't Edith have told her and Winnie. She was about to say as much when Joyce smiled at Alex. 'Who are you?'

'Alex Armstrong. We met once.'

Her smile faded. 'You're the one who was put in the orphanage. Mum told me about it. Your family used to have money.'

'Once upon a time,' he murmured, taking Greta's hand and squeezing it.

'You won't be of much help to me then.' She sighed and tapped her fingernails against her shoulder bag. 'Mum being out is a damn nuisance. I haven't got all day to hang around here waiting for her.'

'Don't then!' said Greta, who couldn't wait to be rid of her.

There was a silence and for a minute Greta thought Joyce was going to leave them in peace but then she made a move towards the house. 'Got anything to eat, Greta? I'm starving!'

Greta remembered the rabbit stewing in the pot on the fire. She cried, 'Excuse me!' and dashed inside the house. It was at that moment Winnie turned up.

Edith was nervous but trying not to show it. She toyed with her wedding ring as she paused half way up the drive and gazed up at the leaden-paned bedroom window in the roof. It was here that Joyce had been conceived and, if everything went according to plan, where they might live together. The next few hours would decide.

She took a deep breath, walked up to the entrance and knocked on the door. It was opened by a fresh-faced young maid with a tear-stained face. 'Sorry! But the-the mistress isn't seeing anyone today.' She made to close the door but Edith wedged it open with her foot.

'I'm Mrs Macauley. I must see Mrs Chisholm.'

The maid stared at her as if she had seen a ghost. 'M-Mrs Macauley! Oh, my goodness!' And she left Edith standing on the doorstep and vanished inside the house.

Edith pushed the door wide and stepped inside. The maid was nowhere in sight but she could hear voices coming from one of the rooms. She decided not to disturb them immediately and glanced about the well-appointed hall. For a moment she forgot her panic and sadness and looked at her surroundings appreciatively. Although the parquet floor didn't appear as well polished as it had in her day and the Axminster rug was definitely worse for wear, this was still an attractive place. The grandfather clock, whose chimes she remembered so well, stood against the stretch of wall between the dining room and drawing room and there was a telephone on a dark oak table attached to a padded seat; this was new.

She sat on the seat, glad to rest her feet and grateful for the sun slanting through the stained glass window on the half landing. How she loved this house.

'You are Mrs Macauley?' The voice was harsh and sounded unfriendly in her ears.

Edith looked up at its owner. His nose was hooked and he had a toothbrush moustache and eyes that reminded her of acid drops. His hair was brown with wings of grey at the temples and he was wearing a plain dark suit. 'Yes. Who are you?' she said coolly.

'I'm George Armstrong. Mrs Chisholm's solicitor and friend. She sent for me when she received the news about Lawrence. I presume that is why you are here.'

'Yes!'

'He never told her that he was married.'

'He was working up to it. Despite his age, she still treated him very much like a younger brother and he knew that she wouldn't be pleased.'

His mouth thinned. 'She is devastated by his death.'

'Naturally.' Edith's mouth quivered but, she told herself, she must not think about how Lawrence met his death. The telegram had come when Greta was out and Edith had blurted out its contents to her younger daughter, who had been surprisingly understanding when asked to go and inform Teddy that Edith would not be able to meet him that Sunday afternoon for the tea dance.

'When were you married? Do you have your marriage lines with you?' asked the solicitor.

Edith pulled herself together. 'I do. We were married before he went overseas.'

'I see.' The breath hissed between his teeth. 'This is most irregular. Marrying so suddenly like that.'

Edith said incredulously, 'Where have you been living, Mr Armstrong? There's a war on. People are rushing into marriage all the time. Although, Lawrence and I have known each other a long time and had a long wait.'

His overgrown eyebrows came together. 'What do you mean by that?'

'Mrs Chisholm will understand when I see her. I'd like to speak to her now. Lawrence would not like it that his wife has been kept waiting in the hall,' she said with a touch of hauteur worthy of her erstwhile mistress.

He looked angry and Edith recognised an enemy when she saw one. 'Come this way then!' he barked.

She followed him, knowing that she would need all her wits about her if she was to get what she wanted for Lawrence's daughter.

'I'm sorry about the rabbit,' said Greta, glancing across the table at Alex.

He grinned. 'You've said that six times.'

Joyce took out a packet of Camel cigarettes and lit up. 'You're not the best of cooks, are you?'

Winnie glared at her. 'You're so ungrateful! It only caught a bit and anyway, the burnt parts of the stew reminded me of potatoes done on a bonfire on Guy Fawkes night. I thought it was tasty.'

Joyce looked at her and smirked. 'But then you'd eat anything and it goes straight to your hips.'

'Leave her alone,' snapped Greta. 'I can tell you there's plenty of fellas who find Winnie attractive. Anyway, we're not here for you to criticise.'

Joyce blew a smoke ring and there was a sulky droop to her mouth. 'I don't want to be here at all. I just wish Mum would get a move on and come home.' She looked at her sister. 'So where've you been this morning?'

'You're going to allow me to get a word in edgeways, are you?' said Winnie, starting to collect the dishes.

'There's no need to be touchy! Tell us!'

Winnie sat down and gazed across the table at Greta. 'Mum sent me to see Teddy. She had a date with him this afternoon for a tea dance.'

'Who's Teddy?' asked Joyce, astonished. 'She's never mentioned a Teddy to me.'

'She probably didn't want you to know about him,' said Winnie, looking pleased for an instant, then her expression changed and was grave. 'But when she got the telegram she knew that it wouldn't be right to go.'

'What telegram?' demanded Joyce, flicking ash on her saucer.

Greta said slowly, 'I know. Mr Lawrence has been killed. Your mum didn't say so in so many words but she was obviously in a mood and looked a bit tragic.'

'Oh hell! Poor Mum,' said Joyce, sounding like she cared. 'I wonder what will happen to Mrs Chisholm's money now.'

'Is that all you think about money?' snapped Alex.

She looked at him in surprise. 'It's alright for you to talk like that. You're a bloke, you'll earn a decent wage after the war. We girls have to look out for ourselves and Mum getting an allowance from Mr Lawrence's sister would have come in handy.'

At that moment there was a knock on the door. Greta glanced at the clock. 'It could be Rene to check whether we're still going to the pictures tonight.'

Alex sprang to his feet. 'I hope it is her. I haven't had a chance to tell you yet but your Uncle Jeff is back in Liverpool. We were on the same ship and I don't think you need me to tell you that your dad's worth at least ten of him.'

Greta nodded as they both went to answer the door. 'He lied to us, you know! Told us his wife was dead and she wasn't! D'you think we should warn Rene?'

'Definitely! I hope that's not him now.'

It was a relief to Greta to find it was Rene standing on the doorstep. 'Come on in. Look who's managed to get home for the wedding!'

Rene's eyes lit up. 'Alex! Oh, luv! That's marvellous!' She put out her hands to both of them. 'Harry's going to be so pleased. And, somehow, I don't think you'll be wanting to go the pictures tonight, Greta.'

Greta glanced up at Alex with a smile. 'I don't know about that. Perhaps Alex would enjoy seeing a good film after being away so long.'

'What about me?' Joyce stood in the kitchen doorway. 'I'd enjoy seeing a good film. We could leave a note for Mum. I'll stay the night so she'll still get to see me.'

'Who said you're staying?' said Greta in unfriendly tones. 'Alex always stays here when he's home from sea.'

Rene knew there was no love lost between the two girls and immediately suggested that Alex sleep next door. 'Wilf will enjoy your company and so will I,' she said to him, adding with a twinkle, 'and it'll stop the neighbours having something else to gossip about, a handsome young man like you sharing a house with four females.'

'Thanks, Rene. I appreciate that.' He congratulated her on her forthcoming marriage with warmth in his eyes and squeezed her hands. 'I couldn't be happier for you both.' He hesitated a moment before adding in a low voice, 'I hate to put a dampener on things but I think you should know Jeff's in town.'

Rene's face froze and then she squared her shoulders and tilted her chin. 'Thanks for telling me. Forewarned is forearmed! If he turns up at my front door I'll know exactly what to say to him.' They moved into the kitchen. 'Where's Edith?' she asked.

Greta told her of the death of Mr Lawrence and how Edith had left the house without saying where she was going. 'I would have thought the most likely place would be to see his sister,' said Rene. 'They share a common grief.'

'Of course!' said Winnie, and smiled with relief.

Rene said, 'In the circumstances it wouldn't be right for us all to go to the pictures. Someone should be here for Edith when she comes home.'

'I suggest Joyce then,' said Greta, trying not to look pleased. 'After all it's her mother she's come to see.'

Winnie agreed, as did Rene, so Joyce had to accept their decision with ill-grace. After Alex had dropped his kitbag off at Rene's house, washed and changed, they set off for the pictures.

Greta could scarcely keep her eyes on the screen and kept glancing at Alex, sitting at her side, his hand clasping hers. She did not know what the future held for the pair of them but knew, more than anything, that she wanted to marry him. He had made no mention of his sisters or mother so far and she wondered if tomorrow he would resume his search for them. She was reluctant to dwell on the difference finding them might make to her dream of the future.

They left the cinema and whilst Rene and Winnie went on ahead, she and Alex strolled together, discussing the film and filling in the spaces of their lives that there hadn't been room for in letters or that the censor had cut out.

When they arrived home they expected to find Edith and Joyce waiting for them but the house was empty. A note was propped up against the clock on the mantelpiece. Winnie picked it up and read it. Then she looked at Greta with a furious expression on her face. 'It says that your Uncle Jeff called and, as she was fed up of waiting for Mum, she accepted his offer of a drink and has gone out with him. Don't wait up! The selfish cow! She used to care about Mum once but since she left home the only person she seems to care about is herself.'

Greta, Rene and Alex exchanged swift glances. 'So what are we going to do about her?' asked Greta, scarcely able to contain her annoyance.

'There's nothing we can do,' said Alex.

'He's right!' said Rene. 'They both might have bitten off more than they can chew in each other. I'm more concerned about Edith. She's been out hours and it's pitch black out there.'

Winnie held out her hands in a helpless gesture. 'What do I do? I can hardly go visiting Mr Lawrence's sister's house at this time of night asking for her.'

'You know where Mr Lawrence's sister lives?' asked Alex.

Winnie nodded. 'Mum showed me the house near Hall Road.' She added in a determined voice, 'If she doesn't turn up by tomorrow lunch time, I'm going there to find out what's happened to her. Knowing our Joyce was supposed to be coming, there's very few things that would have kept her away.'

'I might just go that way with you,' said Alex, his expression thoughtful.

Greta glanced at him and immediately decided that, tomorrow, she was taking the day off. As for her Uncle Jeff, if he thought he'd get a welcome here then he had another think coming.

20

'Good morning, Alex! Have you any idea of the time?' said Rene, feeling slightly jaded, having not slept well. He entered the kitchen, tousled haired and sleepy eyed. He was wearing grey trousers and a fir green sweater and had a towel flung over one shoulder. She presumed he had just washed in the kitchen while she had been out for a loaf and a bottle of milk. She wondered if he would get round to popping the question before going back to sea. Greta might only be seventeen but she was mature for her age, and besides it would make her feel more sure of him, worrying as she did about that mother of his and his sisters. Greta and Alex looked such a nice couple together and they were kind, thoughtful young people, willing to help others; that boded well for their future in her estimation. Although, one couldn't think too far ahead when there was a war on.

Alex smiled ruefully. 'Blame the comfortable bed. After sleeping in a hammock for the best part of a year it was a treat. I did intend getting up early, hoping to see Greta before she went to work and see if Jeff had turned up but ...'

'I met her at the dairy ... she hasn't gone in to work. She's taken time off.' Rene smiled faintly. 'I should imagine it's to accompany you and Winnie to Hall Road. Apparently Edith still hasn't arrived home. So far Jeff and Joyce haven't arrived either.'

'Great!' he said, his expression grim. 'She's a fool! But I'm not going to waste my thoughts on either of them. I want to spend as much time as I can with Greta. Shore leave can go over so fast that, before one knows it, it's back to sea for God only knows how long.' He hesitated, then from his pocket he took a tiny box and thrust it at Rene. 'I thought of ... giving her this! I know we're only young, but do you think Harry would give his permission for us to get engaged?'

Rene opened the box and gazed at the diamond and ruby ring. Her face lit up. 'It's lovely. I hope it fits. I'll refuse to marry Harry if he hums and hahs about her age and there being a war on. I do know he's very fond of you.' She closed the box and handed it back to him. 'But make sure you pick the right moment to ask her. A girl appreciates these things and she's had a tough life so she could do with a bit of fussing over.'

'I'll remember that,' said Alex, and sat at the table.

'What are your plans to trace your sisters?' asked Rene, watching him spread jam on a slice of bread.

'I was rereading some of Mum's letters and it struck me that maybe the headmistress at the girls' school might know where the girls were sent. So I thought I'd pop along to Crosby and see if she'll speak to me. I'm presuming the school won't have been closed for the duration.'

'You haven't thought of trying to see your uncle again?'

'You mean see if he's back from wherever he went?' said Alex dryly. 'I had but I've decided to see how I get on at the school first.' He changed the subject and asked after Harry.

'He's being transferred down to Kent, the Garden of England as he calls it,' Rene replied. 'He says there's plenty of seaside places with boarding houses where I could stay whenever I get the chance to visit. As you know it takes some planning, travelling in wartime.'

At that moment the kitchen door to the lobby opened and Wilf came in. 'I've finished cleaning the parlour windows, Rene, and thought you might like to know that Winnie and Greta have just slammed the front door. They'll be looking for Alex here next.'

Alex got to his feet, reached for his jacket and hurried out.

The three of them caught the tram to Exchange Station and Alex told the girls his plan to visit his sisters' school. 'If I have no luck there I'll see what I can find out about my uncle's whereabouts.'

'You don't want me to come with you?' asked Greta, looking disappointed.

He smiled. 'I'd love your company, luv, but I'm not sure if the headmistress will see me, and then I'm going to call at my uncle's office. If he's there he might be more open if I'm on my own. It's a fair bit of walking and besides I think Winnie needs your moral support.'

Greta could understand what he meant and didn't argue with him. She bought a ticket for Hall Road and continued on the Southport train with Winnie after Alex left it at Crosby and Blundellsands.

'Now you definitely know where you're going?' asked Greta, glancing about her as Winnie led the way up a tree lined road.

'There's nothing wrong with my memory,' said Winnie.

A few minutes later she came to a halt in front of a house with lead paned windows either side of the door. 'This is it.'

'Are you going to knock?' said Greta as they stood in the gateway.

Winnie nodded and slipped her hand through her arm. 'But I'd like you to come with me.' So they walked up to the house and Winnie thumped on the door.

It was opened by a maid, whose face was flushed and who appeared extremely pleased to see them. 'I don't know who you are but come in! I've been trying to get the doctor on the telephone but it doesn't seem to be answering and I don't like leaving my mistress on her own. She's had one of her turns.'

Greta could not resist saying, 'What kind of turn?'

The maid sighed. 'I thought it was just nerves but her solicitor says it's her heart. She had a terrible shock the other day. Her brother was killed.'

Winnie and Greta exchanged significant glances. 'Does she have pills for her heart?' asked Greta.

'Yeah!' The maid's eyes widened. 'But she keeps hiding them. I've asked her where they are but I can't make sense of what she's saying. When I offered to get in touch with Mr Armstrong she … '

'Armstrong!' exclaimed Greta, her heart giving a peculiar jump.

'Yes, Mr George Armstrong! He's her solicitor and a close friend of the family.'

'I thought he'd gone away,' said Greta.

'No!' The maid shook her head. 'Although, yes, you're right. He did go away for a while but he's back now. He's been keeping an eye on her since a bomb dropped on the golf course and her nerves were all shot to pieces. Then her husband died.' The maid twisted her hands agitatedly. 'I feel like my nerves are going the same way.'

'You're best taking deep breaths and trying to keep calm,' said Greta, who was feeling anything but calm.

The maid sighed. 'The doctor could be on his rounds but maybe he isn't. Perhaps I should ring again!'

'You do that,' said Greta, and stepped over the threshold into a pleasant hall, dragging Winnie with her. 'We'll come in and have a look at your mistress.'

'Your mistress didn't have a visitor yesterday, did she?' asked Winnie. 'A blonde woman. A Mrs Macauley?'

The maid stared at her and her mouth trembled. 'You mean Mr Lawrence's widow. Yes, she was here! But I don't know if you should go speaking of her to the mistress,' she said dubiously.

'We won't. If you tell us when she left,' said Greta soothingly.

'About eight o'clock. I heard her say she wanted to be home before dark as she was expecting her daughter. Mr Armstrong had kept her there talking for ages, asking her all sorts of questions.'

'She never got home,' whispered Winnie, gripping Greta's hand.

'Oh dear!' said the maid, looking concerned. 'No one's safe in the blackout these days. But-But maybe she went somewhere else. Perhaps Mr Armstrong could help you. He left a few minutes later.'

'We'd like to see your mistress first,' said Greta. 'She might be able to tell us something more.'

They were shown into the drawing room where a woman lay on a chaise longue. Her hands fluttered in an agitated fashion and when she saw the two young women, she said in a querulous voice, 'Who are these people? I'm not well enough to see visitors.'

'We won't stay long,' said Greta, smiling. 'Your maid was worried about you and thought we might be able to help.'

The two girls moved closer to the chaise longue. Mrs Chisholm's greying fair hair, fashioned in a heavy chignon, looked like a bird's nest. 'Is there anything we can get you?' asked Winnie. 'A drink of water perhaps?'

'Yes! I'll take one of my pills!'

Greta did not show her surprise. 'You've remembered where they are?'

Mrs Chisholm's eyes went from side to side. 'You won't tell him?'

'Tell who?'

'George.'

'He's not here,' said Greta.

Relief flooded Mrs Chisholm's face and she reached up and fumbled with her chignon and drew out a small pill box. Both girls stared at her in astonishment. 'I'll go and find the kitchen and get her some water,' muttered Winnie, and left the room.

'So why don't you want Mr Armstrong knowing where your pills are?' asked Greta.

'He's after my money! That's what dear Edith said.' Mrs Chisholm leaned forward and said in a conspiring manner. 'She's had a little baby, you know. Dear Lawrence's daughter. I said that I must see her and she said she'd bring her and I'd be able to see that she was telling the truth because she's the spitting image of him. George didn't like that. He wants me to change my will. Said the woman's a complete stranger and she and her daughter have no right to my money. That they've done nothing for me. I didn't tell him Edith had once worked for me and that's how she and Lawrence got to know each other. George would have looked down his nose at her. So I just kept on repeating that she was Lawrence's widow and the girl is my niece … that finally shut him up.'

Greta was puzzled and tried to make sense of what the woman had said. Edith didn't have a baby so what did it mean? Then a thought occurred to her and she understood a lot more about Edith and Joyce and Winnie than she had ten minutes ago.

Winnie reappeared with a glass of water and handed it to Mrs Chisholm. The woman washed the pill down with the water and then closed her eyes. For several minutes there was only the sound of the ticking of the grandfather clock in the hall.

Suddenly the silence was disturbed by voices and Mrs Chisholm opened her eyes and smiled at Winnie. 'You've been very kind. But that sounds like the doctor so perhaps you should go. Come again and see me if you like.'

Winnie looked surprised but pleased and said that she'd quite like to do that and left the room with Greta. 'What a nice old lady! I think she liked me.'

'I'm sure she liked you,' said Greta, amused. 'The question is where's your mother?'

Both were silent as they left the house and then Winnie said, 'I don't trust that solicitor and you seemed to know something about him. I also noticed that he has the same surname as Alex.' There was a question in her soft brown eyes as she looked at Greta.

'He's Alex's uncle and I know where he lives,' said Greta, her eyes thoughtful. 'I wonder what his game is?'

'Perhaps we should go and ask him. He could be at home as it's lunch time,' said Winnie.

Greta grabbed her arm and hurried across the road.

All was quiet on that October afternoon as they approached the front door of the house. The wind from the sea blew leaves from the trees and Michaelmass daisies appeared to huddle together in the garden. Greta hesitated only a moment but then, squaring her shoulders, she marched up the path, with Winnie on her heels.

No one came in response to her first knock, so Greta knocked again but when there was still no answer she and Winnie walked round the back. Greta tried the door in the french windows but the lock had been made more secure. 'It looks like we're going to have to come back another time,' she said.

They were about to walk away when Greta thought she heard a noise coming from inside the house. 'What was that?' she said, her dark head tilted to one side.

'What was what?' asked Winnie.

'I thought I heard something. Shush!'

They both listened and the voice came again. 'Perhaps it's a wireless,' said Winnie.

Greta hesitated and then stepped away from the house into the middle of the garden and looked up. It was then she saw the face at the window. 'I don't believe this,' she said. 'Winnie, come and have a look!'

The other girl came and stood beside her and gazed up at the window. She swallowed audibly as the woman's mouth opened and she called for help. 'I think it's Mum! I knew I didn't trust that Mr Armstrong,' said Winnie wrathfully.

'What the hell's he thinking of?' said Greta.

Winnie did not answer but hurried over to the french window. Greta followed her swiftly. They both looked at each other. 'It's my mum in there,' said Winnie, and removing a shoe hit one of the small panes of glass next to the lock sharply. Greta's hands were smaller than Winnie's, so she slipped one inside the hole and turned the key. She led the way through the room into the hall, up the stairs and along the landing. At the sound of their footsteps, Edith called out for help once again in a hoarse voice. The key to the door was on an oak chest on the landing and within seconds they had the door open.

Edith's ankles and arms were tied to a chair, her hair was dishevelled and her face bruised. 'Winnie! Greta! I don't know how you found me but untie me and get me out of here. That solicitor's bloody mad!'

Greta untied her hands while Winnie loosened what appeared to be a length of washing line from about her ankles. 'What happened, Mum?' asked Winnie.

Edith croaked, 'He jumped on me when I was walking to the station, hit me hard enough to knock me out and when I came to, I was trussed up like a Christmas turkey. He said he'd killed before and I was to behave myself or it'd be the worse for me. It was like something from an American gangster film. I need a drink. I've been shouting for hours.'

She tried to stand up, only for her legs to crumple beneath her and would have fallen if Winnie and Greta had not caught her in time. They led her over to the bed and sat her down. 'What did he say to you?' asked Winnie. 'We've seen Mrs Chisholm and she didn't trust him.' She got down on her knees and began to rub her mother's ankles.

Edith licked her dry lips. 'What did she say to you?'

'I don't think that matters right now,' said Greta hastily. 'We want to know what he said. You mightn't have realised it but he's Alex's uncle. The one who put him in the orphanage.'

'I can believe it,' said Edith harshly, rubbing her wrists where the cord had bit in. She groaned. 'I'm desperate for a drink and a ciggie! He's mad, quite mad. From the wild things he was saying I think he got it into his head to marry her to get his hands on her money.' She attempted to stand up again. 'Come on! Let's get out of here. I don't want to be here when he returns. Help me down the stairs.'

They did as she asked and had just reached the front door when it opened from the other side to reveal George Armstrong. He stared at them and then slammed the door.

Greta could not take her eyes off him. Edith was hanging on to her daughter's arm on her other side. 'If you were thinking of killing us, people know we're here,' said the woman in a high-pitched voice.

'Back up!' he rasped, a nerve twitching at the corner of his eye as he gestured with his hands. They did not move.

'There's three of us to one of you,' said Greta.

'We-We could jump him,' cried Winnie, her head going from side to side. 'One, two ...'

Before she could reach three, he shoved her aside and rushed into the music room. They were just in time to see him take something from a drawer. He swung round to face them with an old service revolver in his hand. 'Oh my God! He's going to shoot us,' shrieked Edith, and collapsed in a heap, dragging the girls down with her.

269

On her hands and knees on the carpet, Greta was just about to launch herself at his legs in a rugby tackle when a voice said, 'Put the gun down, Uncle George!'

Greta felt relief and fear in equal measure. 'Alex, be careful! I think he killed your sisters!' she cried.

'I don't think so, luv,' he said, without taking his eyes off the gun in his uncle's hand. 'According to his partner, Uncle George doesn't know where they are and neither does the school.'

'But he told Edith he'd killed before!' said Greta.

Winnie nodded. She was slapping her mother on both cheeks trying to bring her round. Alex made no comment but asked his uncle again to put the gun down. Suddenly Edith gained consciousness and began to weep. Alex said, 'Get her out of here, both of you. Leave this to me.' His face was set.

Greta helped Edith to her feet and she and Winnie half-carried her from the room. Alex's uncle made no effort to stop them. Greta left Winnie tending her mother in the drawing room, having concluded that Alex had got into the house through the french windows. She tiptoed to the music room and was about to enter when she heard his uncle speaking and paused in the doorway.

'I've made a mess of everything,' he said, dropping the gun and sinking into one of the chairs.

'You shouldn't have sent me away! You should have spoken to me,' said Alex angrily.

George reared in his seat. 'For God's sake, boy! You were only eight years old! How could I explain it to a child. Besides, I didn't know what you'd heard and I didn't want you blurting things out to your mother or the police. As long as Abby and that maid of hers believed that your father would never have killed himself and played their part then I was home and dry. Abby would get the insurance money and I'd still be in business.'

Alex cleared his throat. 'You're trying to tell me that you helped Dad kill himself?'

George did not look at him. 'I killed him. I gave him the fatal dose.'

Alex stared at him and then picked up the gun.

Hell! thought Greta. Alex is going to kill him! She burst into the room. 'Don't do it, Alex!' she gasped. 'He's not worth it … but if you do I'll lie for you and say it was self-defence.'

270

Both men stared at her in astonishment. 'I'm not going to kill him,' said Alex.

'Why not? I'd want to kill him if he killed my father.'

George sighed and sat down heavily on a chair. 'Perhaps Alex has guessed. My brother had a terminal disease which he was determined to keep from his wife and children. He was in terrible pain. Having lived out East for years he believed in herbal medicine and thought it would heal him. I told him he was a bloody fool and should see a proper doctor but he refused.'

'That's what you were arguing about that time Dad brought me here,' said Alex.

George nodded. 'He was a stubborn man but he was my brother. I couldn't bear to see him in pain. I had a close friend, who was a doctor. He owed me a favour.'

There was a silence.

Greta was astonished. 'It's still murder. Mrs Chisholm didn't trust you. She hid her pills and said you were after her money … and you hit Edith over the head and tied her up.'

George swayed in the chair and, for a moment, Greta thought he was going to faint. Alex said swiftly, 'Have you any whisky … brandy, Uncle George?'

'Whisky in the drawing room,' said George hoarsely. 'Glasses, too.'

Alex looked at Greta. She hurried out of the room. Edith and Winnie watched her opening cupboards. 'What are you looking for? What's happening?' asked Edith, visibly shaking.

'Nothing for you to worry about,' replied Greta tersely, having found the whisky and a tumbler.

She rushed out the room, not wanting to miss any of the conversation between Alex and his uncle. She watched Alex half-fill the tumbler and hand it to George. He drank and, slowly, the colour returned to his face.

'That Edith woman is out for what she can get. I recognised her sort and it made me angry,' said George. 'I suppose I went a bit mad. I've had a few problems like that since my wife … died.' He hung his head and clasped it in his hands. 'As for what Mrs Chisholm said… she's another like your father, Alex, and needs protecting from herself. Her nerves have been in a delicate state since her first husband was killed in the Great War. Then this war hasn't been kind to her. I feared she'd get muddled and take an overdose of her tranquillisers.'

Greta shot a glance at Alex. It sounded perfectly plausible but was it true? Alex shook his head as if in disbelief. 'It was a crazy thing to do! She's got every reason to have you arrested,' he said.

George moaned. 'Perhaps we could do a deal with her. If you explained to her that I'd get my partner to see Mrs Chisholm, he could deal with the will and have Lawrence's name removed and the daughter's included.'

Alex nodded. 'I'll tell her.'

Silence.

'Is that everything then?' asked Greta, still not convinced of George Armstrong's innocence.

Alex took her hand and squeezed it. 'I don't think we're going to find out where the girls are here.'

George looked up at him piteously. 'My wife took them away from me ... wouldn't tell me their address. It was a cruel thing to do. She said they were in Wales but I can't find any trace of them.' His eyes darkened and when he spoke his voice was harsh. 'She had no right to lie to me! I'm their uncle! They were in my charge. I tried to make her understand that ... that what I felt for them wasn't what she thought ... b-but she turned her back on me and ...' A nerve twitched beneath his left eye and he clenched his fists.

The silence that followed was almost tangible. Neither Alex or Greta could think what to say. Then George cleared his throat. 'They loved me and would do anything to please me. Why couldn't she tell me where they were?' His eyes bored into Alex's. 'Perhaps you really do know where they are, boy. Why don't you tell me?'

Alex felt a cold shiver pass through him. 'Have you forgotten that I came here looking for them? Strange that they've never written to you, Uncle George, if they loved you that much.'

George swallowed convulsively. 'They could be dead for all I know. I can't bear that thought. I feel lonely in this big house all on my own. You...You wouldn't consider making this your home, would you?'

'No thanks!' said Alex, his voice strained. 'Let's go home, Greta.'

21

'So what are you going to do, Alex?' Rene gazed across the breakfast table at her house guest. She had to repeat her question before he lifted his head and looked at her.

'About what?'

'Tracing your sisters and mother, of course! I know you're putting a brave face on things ... especially when Greta's around ... but I hope you're not going to give up. How old are your sisters? Younger than Greta according to her.'

He nodded.

'With your mother in America and their aunt dead and an uncle who they don't appear to want to keep in touch with, I'd say they need to be found.'

'I wouldn't argue with you, Rene, but I'm out of ideas of how to find them, if they don't want to be found.' He pushed back his hair from his forehead with an impatient gesture.

'There must be some way. There's something wrong about this whole thing. I mean why did your aunt not tell him where they were going when she took them to Wales? They were his nieces.'

Alex felt heartsick about the whole thing and there was no way he could voice his suspicions but before he could come up with some kind of response, there was a hammering on the door. Rene frowned, 'I wonder who that is? It can't be Harry. He's not due home for another five days. I hope it's not Jeff! I'm in no mood to see him.'

The noise came again. 'They're impatient, whoever they are,' said Alex, and rose to his feet. 'If it's Jeff I'll tell him to get lost.'

Rene followed him out of the kitchen and was just behind him as he opened the front door. Her heart seemed to turn over in her breast as she saw a policeman. He wasn't alone. Edith stood beside him. 'This is Alex Armstrong,' she said, a suppressed excitement in her voice.

'What's this about?' said Alex.

'You're Mr Alexander Armstrong, nephew of Mr George Alan Armstrong?' asked the policeman.

'Yes!'

'Perhaps I can come in, sir? I have news of a disturbing nature for you,' said the policeman.

Alex glanced at Rene, who nodded, her heartbeat having steadied now she knew the officer's appearance had nothing to do with Harry.

Edith followed them in, plonking herself next to Rene on the sofa and lighting a cigarette. 'I reckon this has something to do with my refusal to be bought off by that swine of an uncle of his,' she whispered, as the policeman seated himself at the table across from Alex. 'Assault and abduction, those are the charges I've brought against him.'

Rene glanced at her sidelong. 'I don't blame you! But if it was then surely he'd be interviewing you and not have asked for Alex?' she said in an undertone. 'How did they know where to find him, anyway? Did you give them his address?'

She shook her head. 'Alex must have given it to his uncle's business partner, Mr Simmons.'

'I see.'

They both fell silent, hoping to overhear the conversation between the two men at the table, but could only catch the odd word.

It was not until the policeman stood up and left the room, that the two women discovered the officer's reason for being there.

'Uncle George is dead,' informed Alex, appearing pale beneath his tan. 'He shot himself.'

Neither women spoke for a moment, then Edith asked, 'Did he leave a note? Was it the shame of it coming out about what he'd done to me that pushed him over the edge?' She drew on her cigarette.

'That might have been the last straw.' Alex's face felt stiff with shock. 'He confessed not only to my father's murder but, also, that of my aunt. I could scarcely believe it when the policeman told me that. She wasn't killed in the blitz after all! My uncle strangled her because she took the girls away and hid them from him. He lost his temper when she wouldn't tell him where they were. He dug up the lawn and buried her in the back garden.'

'Oh my God!' whispered Rene, and getting to her feet she put her arm about Alex's shoulders.

He wondered whether she was thinking the same terrible thing that had tormented him since that final conversation with his uncle. 'Greta said he had the look of a villain out of a gangster film and she was right,' he said huskily.

'What are you going to do?' asked Edith.

Alex squared his shoulders. 'I've got to see his partner. Apparently my uncle left a will.'

The women exchanged glances but did not say a word.

Greta entered the house like a whirlwind, expecting to find Winnie and Edith there but Rene was also sitting at the table, talking and drinking tea. 'Have you seen this?' Greta demanded, placing that evening's *Echo* on the table. 'I can't wait for Alex to see it. I didn't get an answer at yours, Rene. D'you know where he is?'

Rene made no reply but snatched up the newspaper. She read *Crosby Solicitor Confesses To Double Murder!* Beneath the headlines was a photograph of George Armstrong.

'He's dead!' cried Greta to no one in particular. 'He shot himself!'

Rene glanced up. 'We know, luv. A policeman called and spoke to Alex. He's gone to see his uncle's partner.'

Greta stared at her, wide-eyed, and sank on to a chair.

Winnie beamed at her. 'It could be that Alex'll be rich. His uncle left a will, which, in my book, means he must have money to leave.'

With sparkling eyes, Edith said, 'Maybe we'll be rich, too, one day. Lawrence's sister was insistent that I visit her again. I think I'll go tomorrow. It's a pity that Joyce had to go back to camp but maybe she'll drop by soon. The old lady's going to be shocked by what's happened and will need her family round her. I mean, she could have been his next victim.'

Winnie's face stiffened. 'You mean you and our Joyce when you say family, don't you, Mum? I'm not stupid, you know, I have got a brain. Joyce is your Mr Lawrence's daughter, isn't she?'

Edith looked uncomfortable. 'Yes! I was very young and innocent and these things happen.'

Winnie's eyes glinted. 'Well, you should warn our Joyce because she could end up following in your footsteps. She didn't have to go back to camp, she just couldn't be bothered waiting for you. Greta's uncle turned up, while we were out, and she went off with him. He's old enough to be her father.'

Edith paled. 'What's got into her?'

Greta rolled her eyes at Rene and wondered whether to mention that Jeff was also a married man.

Winnie said, 'You spoilt her, Mum. She's always been selfish.'

In the silence that followed there was the sound of the key on the string being pulled through the letterbox. Immediately Greta sprung to her feet. 'Perhaps that's Alex!' She rushed to the front door.

But it wasn't Alex, it was Jeff and he didn't look pleased. 'Where is she? Is she here?' he demanded.

'Who's "she?" The cat's mother?' said Greta tartly, hands on hips. 'You're not welcome here, Uncle Jeff. So why don't you just turn round and leave!'

'She's here, isn't she? The conniving little bitch!' He shoved his niece aside and blundered up the lobby. Greta drew herself upright and hurried after him. He had paused in the doorway and was staring at Rene. 'I should have known you'd be here! I bet you were in on it!'

'I don't know what you're talking about,' said Rene, getting to her feet. 'What is it you want, Jeff?'

'My bloody money! The bloody bitch went through my pockets and took nearly every penny and now she's bloody disappeared.'

'Oh dear!' exclaimed Rene, unable to prevent a smile.

There was a deadly hush and then he launched himself at her. Edith thrust out a foot and he fell over it, landing face down on the rag rug. Having stepped aside just in time, Rene gazed down at him. 'You really should look before you leap, Jeff.'

He uttered a profanity.

'Wash your mouth out with soap!' chorused four female voices.

Jeff staggered to his feet and his gaze whirled round from one to the other. 'You're all in it together. You're hiding her?'

Edith said icily, 'If you're talking about my daughter, she doesn't live here. Now get out, you disgusting man.' She glared at him and then a tiny crease appeared between her eyebrows. 'Have I seen you before? Have you been hanging round here?'

Unexpectedly Jeff smiled. 'I think I'd have remembered if we'd met, darlin'! I can see where your daughter gets her looks from. Are your morals the same, too?'

Edith's lips tightened and she smacked him across the face. 'Get out! And don't let's see you round here again.'

Before he could make a recovery, Rene and Greta seized him by the arms and Winnie placed a hand on his back, helping to propel him towards the door, along the lobby and out of the house. There they released him. 'Never darken our doors again!' said Greta, and wiped a hand against the other. The other two did the same and then the three of them went back inside the house, slamming the door behind them.

They went into the kitchen where Edith was standing, tapping her fingernails on the mantelpiece. She glanced up at them. 'Don't say it!'

'We weren't going to,' said Rene, looking sympathetic. 'Cup of tea?'

'I need something stronger than that.' Edith sighed.

'You're out of luck,' said Greta, and put the kettle on.

Half an hour later there was the sound of the key on the string being pulled through the door. 'This time it has to be Alex,' said Greta, springing to her feet and rushing out of the kitchen.

Alex stood in the doorway, his face serious.

'Are you OK?' she asked tentatively.

He smiled faintly. 'I'm rich, Greta luv!'

To her shame, she found it difficult to be pleased for him. There was a sinking feeling in her stomach and words failed her. Then she found her voice. 'That's ... wonderful!'

He drew her to him and planted a kiss on her lips. 'At least, I feel that I'll find the girls now and be able to help them if they need me to. What really pleases me is that Dad left money in a trust for me and the girls!' He frowned. 'But Uncle George used it to get himself out of a hole ... but in doing so, he eventually got rich all over again.' His expression lightened. 'It was Dad's money so I'm only getting money that I'm entitled to ... that is, me and the girls. Otherwise, I wouldn't want to touch his filthy lucre.' He hugged her. 'I tell you, Greta, this is going to make a difference to us, too. I can't wait to tell your dad!'

22

Rene gazed at her reflection in the mirror. The suit was made of cream linen and there was a snowy white, pleated, lace trimmed blouse to go with it. She'd had real problems finding anything to fit her size and, if it had not been for Miss Birkett, would have had to get married in a frock she had bought before clothing coupons came in. As it was, the older woman had come to her rescue with a suit that was fashionable at the end of the Great War. She recalled Miss Birkett saying that she had bought it, thinking that she would wear it for her own wedding one day. Sadly, that day had never arrived but she hadn't had the heart to wear it or sell it. So she had wrapped it in tissue paper and put it away in a box.

The skirt was unfashionably long for wartime but that had meant Rene only had to take it up a few inches to fit her. As for the jacket, having been endowed with a generous bosom, Miss Birkett had suggested inserting some material of almost the same cream colour down the sides. She had made a good job of the task, so the suit fitted a treat.

'Well, I must say, Rene, it pays you to dress up!' said Edith, her powdered face appearing in the mirror next to Rene's rosy one. The older woman fixed the veiling on the black hat to her liking and met Rene's eyes in the mirror. 'I'm looking forward to this. Who'd have thought I'd be a widow again and attending your wedding. You did say that I could bring a friend?'

'Yes, of course,' said Rene hastily, guessing that the friend might be Teddy. Whoever it was, she had no worries about how Harry would feel about Edith now. She experienced a rush of warmth and excitement thinking about him. He had arrived yesterday and they'd only had time for a few kisses before Alex had demanded to speak to him alone.

Edith interrupted Rene's reverie. 'Right! I'll see you in church.' She picked up her black jacket and slipped it on over the black spotted tangerine frock she had worn to the Grafton with Harry and left.

'You ready, girl?' asked Wilf, who was giving Rene away. He was spruced up in his Sunday best suit and looked slightly uncomfortable in a new starched collar and tie.

'Almost,' she said, picking up the cream felt hat, with a curly wisp of ostrich feather sprouting from its turned up brim. Placing it on her red gold hair, she fiddled with it for a few moments until the angle was just right. Then she picked up the bouquet of white and yellow chrysanthemums and followed Wilf out of the room. She glanced in the parlour to reassure herself that everything was all right with the buffet laid out on the table and to tell Greta that she was ready. In the last few days Rene had sensed that her future step-daughter had something on her mind, and the fact that she had not spoken to her about it worried Rene.

'You look lovely,' said Greta, pinning a determined smile on her face. This was Rene's day and she wasn't going to let her worries, about the moneyed Alex being able to re-enter that middle class world he'd once been part of, spoil it.

'You don't look so bad yourself, luv,' said Rene.

Greta's long black hair was twisted into a knot on the top of her head and the floral silky frock of mainly pinks and lilacs hugged her shapely figure. She looked older than her seventeen years. 'Dad should be proud of us,' said Greta, smiling.

'I should hope so,' laughed Rene. 'We've put in enough effort. Come on! Let's go knock them sideways!'

Outside, the neighbours had gathered and a concerted, *oohh* sounded as Rene came out of the house on Wilf's arm with Greta following in her wake. Cissie emerged from next door almost at the same time. 'I thought you'd be waiting at the church, Gran!' said Greta, pleased to see her.

'I forgot something, didn't I! Yer both look luv'ly!' Cissie's eyes fell on the man at Rene's side. 'Even you look quite tasty, Wilf.' She freed an expressive sigh and winked at Greta.

Wilf blushed and Greta tried to hide her smile. Rene inclined her head graciously, and suggested Cissie ride with them to the church. Wilf led Rene over to the pony and trap standing at the kerb. The vehicle, along with its driver, was on loan to him for a favour done in the woodwork line. The driver opened the small door in the side. Rene told Wilf to help Cissie in first and he did so, having a bit of a struggle in the process as she insisted on putting her arms around his neck as he heaved her up. Both bride and bridesmaid were about to climb into the trap when a voice called, 'Excuse me! But is this the wedding of Rene Miller? We're looking for Alex Armstrong and were told he was staying with her and would be attending the wedding.'

Instantly Greta's head shot round, searching for the owner of that voice. She spotted the girls, recognising them from their photograph. They were dressed, almost identically, in frocks of white spotted with navy blue. Each girl wore navy blue berets and an anxious expression. Her heart began to pound and she felt sick.

Rene's eyes had followed Greta and now she said, 'I'm Rene Miller.'

The dark haired girl dragged her sister forward. 'We don't want to make you late but if you could just tell us where the church is we'll find our own way.'

Rene glanced at Greta's set pale face and said in an undertone, 'I know how you're feeling, luv, but we have to help them.' Greta nodded, and Rene turned to the girls and said, 'Why walk when you can ride? Climb aboard! I'm sure your brother will be delighted to see you.'

'Th-That's very kind of you but-but we don't want to-to intrude to that extent,' stammered the fair-haired sister, glancing at Greta.

Rene smiled and said gently, 'I wouldn't have suggested it if I thought your presence was a intrusion. But hurry, I don't want to keep people waiting.'

She grasped Wilf's hand and climbed into the trap and seated herself next to Cissie. Greta followed her and sat the other side of her grandmother, then watched Alex's sisters seat themselves on the facing wooden seat. She knew that she was behaving badly but could not help herself. Her emotions were in confusion and the fear that she would lose Alex was uppermost. Wilf climbed up beside the driver, who picked up the reins and flicked them over the back of the horse. He clicked his tongue and they were on their way.

Rene placed her bouquet on her lap and then grasped Cissie's arm in one hand and Greta's in the other. 'This is Mrs Hardcastle and this is Greta Peters, her granddaughter, and a great friend of your brother. Alex made his home with them originally.'

The dark-haired girl smiled at Greta. 'You're Sally's daughter! We loved Sally! Missed her terribly when Uncle wouldn't let her visit. I'm Lydia Armstrong and this is my younger sister, Barbara.' She held out her white gloved hand. Without being rude, Greta had no choice but to shake hands.

'Alex has been looking for you. I presume you saw your uncle's death reported in the Welsh edition of the *Echo*?'

The sisters glanced at each other. 'We never went to Wales. We have been living on a farm near Ormskirk,' replied Lydia. 'But we have seen a copy of the *Echo* and called on Mr Simmons, my uncle's partner, as soon as we could.'

'Why didn't you go to Wales?'

Lydia darted a sidelong glance at her sister, who slipped a small hand through her arm. The elder girl took a deep breath and then said gravely, 'We'd rather not talk about it, if you don't mind. I can only say that Aunt Jane thought it wise to mislead Uncle about our whereabouts. She wouldn't even allow us to write to her in case he spotted the postmark on the envelope. Although, she wrote to us and visited when she was able. Then her letters stopped coming and we didn't know what to do at first because she had told us we must never get in touch with her, so I wrote to Mummy.'

Greta started. 'You know where your mother lives!'

'Of course!' Lydia smiled. 'She wrote to my aunt, wanted us to join her in America, but Aunt Jane told her that she wouldn't risk sending us after what happened to the *Athenia*. Mummy advised us to send a friend to one of the neighbours, pretending Babs and I were still in Wales, and ask after Aunt Jane. Of course, we were told she had been killed in the blitz. Now we know that wasn't true.' Her voice trailed away sadly.

'It's horrible!' whispered Barbara. 'Po-Poor Aunt Jane! She was so brave the way she stood up to him when she realised what was going on!'

Greta noticed all the colour had drained out of the younger girl's face and she looked about to faint. Swiftly Greta leaned forward and pushed the younger girl against the back rest before moving to sit the other side of her, propping her upright with her shoulder. 'I'm so sorry! But he can't hurt you anymore so there's no need to be frightened,' assured Greta, her compassion overcoming her fear of losing Alex.

Lydia reached out and took her sister's hand. 'I hope he's burning in hell for not only the terrible thing he did to Aunt Jane, but what he did to us and Alex, as well.' Smiling tentatively at Greta, she added, 'How is Alex and how is it you met?'

Greta began to explain.

Cissie brought her head close to Rene's and whispered, 'That swine interfered with them, I bet. Poor kids! It says something about the aunt that she got them away from him as soon as she could. I still think the mother isn't much cop leaving them, though. It wouldn't have happened if she'd had a bit of guts.'

Rene could only agree. They both fell silent in time to hear Greta say, 'I wouldn't be surprised if he sheds a few tears himself. But, please, save the reunion until after the wedding. Sit at the back of the church so he doesn't see you straightaway. This is Rene's day.' The two girls promised to do what she said.

It was Rene's wish that they married in church and Harry had given in to her wishes, saying her happiness was all he wanted. His head turned as the organ burst into the wedding march from Wagner's *Lohengrin* and he smiled. Rene experienced a soaring happiness and felt as if she floated down the aisle. Cissie slipped into a front pew next to Fred, Alex, Miss Birkett and Winnie, not noticing at first Edith and Teddy sitting in the pew behind them. Rene handed her bouquet to Greta, then placed her hand in Harry's and beamed up at him.

'Dearly beloved, we are gathered here in the sight of God and this congregation,' intoned the vicar. The service had begun.

'So do you still feel like Cinderella?' whispered Alex in Greta's ear as he caught up with her as she followed the newly married couple up the aisle.

'More so since you've become rich,' murmured Greta.

Alex smiled. 'So my role now is?'

'Prince Charming, I suppose.'

'Then stop here a moment and let people leave before us.' He drew her to a halt.

Feeling apprehensive, she looked up at him. 'What's this about? We shouldn't be delaying. The photographer will want me for the photos ... and besides ...'

'He'll be taking your dad and Rene first. This won't take long. I've something important to ask you.'

She thought he looked suddenly nervous and her heart sank. 'I've something important to say, as well.'

He took her hand, ignoring the neighbours and friends pushing past them. 'Whatever it is, it can't be as important as what I have to say, so don't argue with me.'

She caught sight of Lydia and Barbara hovering a few feet away and interrupted him. 'But, Alex, it's your …'

'Say you'll marry me,' said Alex, ploughing on determinedly. 'I meant to go down on one knee and speak all those romantic words such as …'

'I'd like nothing more than to hear them,' interrupted Greta huskily. 'But there's two important people waiting to speak to you.' Gently she withdrew her hand from his and left him with his sisters.

The noise in Rene's parlour was deafening. Some of the neighbours had joined the wedding celebrations and Greta could feel a headache coming on. Her father and Rene had already left for their honeymoon and Cissie and Wilf had taken charge of the proceedings indoors. Greta wandered outside and stood on the step, gazing up at the starlit sky, wondering where Alex and his sisters were. He had missed the wedding breakfast and she was trying not to worry, longing for him to return and say all those romantic words he hadn't got round to.

'Don't you think it's a bit cold out here?'

Greta lowered her gaze swiftly and stared at Alex. There were so many things she wanted to say but she could only look at him.

He covered the distance between them in two strides and pulled her into his arms. 'I asked your dad's permission and, sensible, understanding bloke that he is, he said yes. He wants you to be secure and seems to think you would be with me. I've already bought a special licence so we could do the deed as soon as he and Rene come back from their honeymoon.'

Greta was overwhelmed. 'Are you sure? What about you having all that money?'

'It's great for both of us! Besides, you're not as poor as you think! That vase on the mantelpiece Mum gave your mother. It's Royal Doulton and worth a few bob, so you won't be coming empty-handed.'

That was good news. 'What about your sisters? What about your mother?' she babbled.

'Of course I'm looking forward to seeing Mum again … and it's great meeting up with my sisters … they're my family so I'll want to spend time with them when possible.' He shook her gently. 'But you come first! You're the love of my life.'

Warmed through and through by his words, she said, 'It goes without saying, that I love you, too.' There was a catch in her voice.

He smiled and took a tiny box from his pocket and told her to hold out her left hand. Obediently, she did as she was told and he slipped the ring on her third finger. By some miracle it fitted perfectly, just as Cinderella's slipper had fitted her tiny foot. They were about to kiss when they heard familiar voices just behind them.

'Joyce doesn't know that she's Lawrence's daughter and there's no need to tell her,' said Edith. 'I'm not the least bit pleased with her at the moment. In my hour of need, where was she? But you came to my rescue when Mr Armstrong could so easily have killed me.'

'You mean that?' asked Winnie, sounding thrilled.

'Of course, I mean it. I've decided I don't want her muscling in, thinking she has a right to everything. You're my daughter, too, and from what you've said Lawrence's sister took a liking to you. We don't have to tell her any lies. When I say you're my daughter she'll presume the rest.'

Greta and Alex heard Winnie gasp and both turned and gazed at mother and daughter, just in time to see Winnie fling her arms around her mother. 'Thanks, Mum!'

'OK! OK! Don't get carried away,' said Edith, patting her shoulder and rolling her eyes at Greta and Alex. 'We've been a burden on those that live in these two houses long enough. It's time we found another place we can call home.' She drew her daughter back inside the house, leaving the young lovers to seal their betrothal in the time honoured fashion.